Death
at

THORBURN
HALL

Books by Julianna Deering

From Bethany House Publishers

THE DREW FARTHERING MYSTERIES

Rules of Murder
Death by the Book
Murder at the Mikado
Dressed for Death
Murder on the Moor
Death at Thorburn Hall

A DREW
FARTHERING
MYSTERY

Death
- at -
THORBURN
HALL

JULIANNA
DEERING

BETHANYHOUSE
a division of Baker Publishing Group
Minneapolis, Minnesota

Published by Bethany House Publishers
11400 Hampshire Avenue South
Bloomington, Minnesota 55438
www.bethanyhouse.com

Bethany House Publishers is a division of
Baker Publishing Group, Grand Rapids, Michigan

Printed in the United States of America

Library of Congress Control Number: 2017945290

ISBN 978-0-7642-1829-3 (trade paper)
ISBN 978-0-7642-3116-2 (cloth)

Scripture quotations are from the King James Version of the Bible.

This is a work of fiction. Names, characters, incidents, and dialogues are products of the author's imagination and are not to be construed as real. Any resemblance to actual events or persons, living or dead, is entirely coincidental.

Cover design by Faceout Studio
Cover illustration by John Mattos

Author is represented by Books & Such Literary Agency.

17 18 19 20 21 22 23   7 6 5 4 3 2 1

To the One who is loving
toward all He has made

— One —

Madeline Farthering gripped her husband's arm a little more tightly as they made their way through the mass of people crowding Waverley Station, certain that if they were separated in this chaos she'd never be able to find him again. Drew said something to her, but she could only shake her head and shrug.

He repeated whatever it was he had said, but the crackling announcement of a delayed train arrival blaring through the station made it impossible to make out.

She pressed closer to his side. "What did you say?"

By then the announcement had ended, and her shouted question drew the attention of several passersby. A blush heated her cheeks.

Drew's gray eyes were warm and laughing. "Having fun, darling?"

She pursed her lips. "Not yet. Is Edinburgh always like this?"

"It's a fairly busy place most of the time, I expect, but people come from all over for the tournament."

She smiled, enjoying his excitement. "I've always wanted to see the British Open."

"*The* Open, darling," he corrected. "Ever and always, *the* Open."

"Oh, yes, of course." She managed to keep from rolling her eyes. "Anyway, I've been to our Open, the U.S. Open, and I've been to the PGA. They started a new tournament in Georgia, too. Last year."

"Ah, yes, at Augusta. I remember reading about that one. Well, if they're still having it in the next year or two, perhaps we'll toddle on over to the States and have a look. How would that be?"

She beamed at him. As much as she loved her husband and his beautiful country, she sometimes missed the sounds and sights of her native land. "That would be—"

"Monstrous!"

Madeline blinked, and she and Drew both turned toward the heavily accented voice.

"Monstrous," the man repeated, this time on a heavy sigh as an elderly porter, obviously ill at ease, looked at him. "And yet it must be borne, must it not?"

He was somewhere in his late thirties, tall and slender, with a pencil-thin mustache and a look of pale tragedy about him. An actor or artist, Madeline decided. His ivory silk suit was flawless and quite expensive. He must be extremely successful. Either that or he had a wealthy patron. She couldn't decide exactly what sort of accent he had. Perhaps Russian.

"Can you believe, madam," he said, catching her eye, "I come here to this great country to escape oppression and corruption, and what do I find?"

Yes, the accent was definitely Russian. Madeline shook her head. "I'm sure I don't know."

He opened his mouth and then stopped short, a look of pure delight suddenly on his face. "Ah, you are American, no? I am certain such things never happen in your country." He swept the stylish hat from his pomaded head and held it over his heart. "Not to so heavenly a creature as you, madam."

There was only the slightest tension in Drew's smile. "Is there some way we might be of help?"

"You are too kind, sir, but I fear there is no help to be had." Again the foreigner heaved a tragic sigh. "One can only grieve and carry on."

"I'm very sorry, sir," the porter said, a Scottish burr in his voice and his rheumy eyes anxious. "We have looked everywhere. Once the train has emptied, we'll make another search and send it along to you the minute it's found."

The Russian pursed his lips. "And what until then? I present myself for dinner this evening looking as if I have just come from the jungle? From being three weeks lost at sea? It cannot and must not be done."

"But, sir—"

"Misha! Misha!" A portly little woman in her mid-fifties waved from a few feet away and then bustled up to them, puffing with exertion but still triumphant. "Look what I have," she singsonged, and she presented the foreign man with a small leather toiletry case.

The porter heaved a sigh of relief as the Russian clasped the case to his chest with one elegant white hand and used the other to bring the woman's heavily ringed fingers to his lips. "Oh, madam, once again you have saved me from utter ruin."

"Will there be anything else, sir?" the porter asked as the woman stood simpering.

"That will be all, my good man." The Russian gave him what

could only be described as a regal nod of dismissal, and then he faltered when the old man stood looking expectantly at him. "Ah, er . . ." He patted his breast pocket and looked with some distress at the woman. "I hesitate to trouble you, madam, but it seems . . . uh . . ."

She looked at him for a moment, obviously puzzled, and then realization dawned in her eyes. "Oh. Oh, yes. Yes, of course."

She popped open her beaded handbag and rummaged through it, finally coming up with an assortment of small coins that she pressed into the porter's gnarled hand. "There you are. We're so sorry to have caused you any bother. My husband had accidentally put it with our things. Such a silly mistake, isn't it, though it does look rather like his. But no harm done in the least. You've been a great help."

The little man touched his fingers to the brim of his blue cap and then wove his way into the crowd.

Drew gave the woman a polite smile. "If there's nothing else . . . ?"

"Oughtn't you to introduce me to your friends, Misha?" she said, turning appealingly to the Russian.

"Merely passersby, ma'am," Drew said with a tip of his hat. "If you have everything sorted here . . ."

"Oh, yes. Certainly. It's too good of you to try to help. Poor Misha, he can't be troubled with practical matters, you know. The brain of the artist is simply too profound for the trivialities you and I must deal with. I'm sure you understand."

The man was standing now with his hand spread across his shirtfront, his brow furrowed as if his recent near-tragedy had quite overcome him.

"I'm certain he bears it as bravely as he is able," Drew told the woman, somehow managing to look earnestly solicitous.

"I am never one to complain," the Russian said dolefully.

"No, of course not," the woman soothed.

"The past is gone," he sighed, "and we must carry on."

"Good man," Drew said with hearty finality. "Stiff upper lip and that, eh? Well, I'm afraid we have a car waiting for us, so we'd best be off. Good luck to you both."

"Oh, dear," the woman said, standing tiptoe as she attempted to see over the crowd. "Where is Alfred now? I don't want them waiting dinner for us."

"Oh, no you don't," Madeline hissed, tugging her husband's arm.

He followed her toward the station exit, looking baffled.

"You were going to go back and help her. Don't bother denying it."

"Nonsense. I was merely trying to see where Nick had got to." He lifted his head, looking back toward the train. "I thought I saw him just over there."

She pressed her lips together. "And what would he be doing over there? The way he bolted off the train, you'd have thought it was on fire."

It was too loud in the station to hear her husband's low laughter, but she could feel the soft rumble of it in his chest. "He *was* rather worried about not being on the platform when Carrie's train comes in. I don't think he much cared for her coming all this way alone, and I can't blame him."

"Judging by the telegram she sent from the dock, she got along just fine. And she wasn't exactly alone."

But she was alone. Carrie Holland had been her best friend for just ages. Carrie's father had walked Madeline down the aisle at her wedding, taking her own late father's place in the ceremony in giving her to Drew. She had teased and scolded

Carrie's little brother as if he were her own. But now both father and brother were gone. Her mother had passed on years ago. Carrie had no one left.

Drew squeezed her hand. "I know you're worried about her, darling, but I'm hoping this visit is just what she needs to put things right."

"I'm hoping it won't be just a visit."

He gave her a wink. "That, my love, is where Nick steps in."

Madeline nodded. Poor Nick. He had fallen hard for Carrie three years ago when she and Madeline had come to Drew's Hampshire estate, Farthering Place, as part of their European tour. Madeline had stayed and married Drew, while Carrie had gone on with her tour and then returned home. After a year of letters between her and Nick, she had come back to England to visit. Absence had certainly made their hearts grow fonder, but then the loss of her brother made it necessary for her to return home once more to care for her grieving father. Now there was nothing in America to hold her, yet were letters enough? After two more years apart, would things be the same between her and Nick?

"He should have asked her to marry him long before now," Madeline said.

Drew shrugged. "It was a bit awkward when she left the last time, you know. She had her father to deal with along with everything else, and he didn't want to make it any more difficult for her, trying to keep her in Hampshire when she needed to see to things at home. And you wouldn't want him to pop the question via telegram, would you? That would be shockingly vulgar."

She giggled at the look of melodramatic horror on his face. "I suppose there are more romantic methods."

"Mine, for example."

She stopped short, one hand on her hip. "Yours? Your method was to nearly get yourself killed so I was forced to stay and keep you out of trouble."

He looked positively smug. "It worked, didn't it?"

She lifted an eyebrow and then started them walking once more. Feeling him laugh again, she prodded him with her elbow and nodded toward the platform they were approaching.

"You'd better go rescue Nick before he topples off."

Hat in hand and tawny hair ruffled by the wind, Nick was leaning out over the track, obviously looking for any sign of the train.

Drew hurried up beside him and pulled him back a little. "Best look out there, old man. It'd be a bit of a letdown for your Miss Holland if she finds you under the train rather than waiting beside it."

Nick's smile was more nervous than convincing. "Just wondering why the deuced thing isn't here yet. You don't think there was a breakdown or anything, do you?"

"Of course not." Madeline took his arm and gave her husband a look that discouraged a flippant response. "It's not even due yet."

"Isn't it?" Nick looked up at the station clock and then gave Madeline a rather sheepish grin. "I suppose it isn't." Then his expression became urgent. "She *is* coming, isn't she?"

"You have her telegram, don't you?" Drew asked.

Nick beamed and patted his breast pocket, eliciting the crackle of paper. "Shall I quote it for you?"

Drew turned to Madeline, shaking one accusing finger at her. "I hold you responsible for every bit of this, wife. Here I thought I had a fine estate manager and stout fellow for any

13

emergency, and you arrange for him to be turned into some helpless form of jelly."

She looked at him with disdain. "Carrie and I came to Hampshire on vacation. Any jellification on the part of either of you is entirely your own fault."

"I see," Drew said gravely. "When we go home to Hampshire, I will see that inquiries are made."

Knowing her reply would never be heard over the sudden clatter of the approaching train, Madeline merely wrinkled her nose at him. As soon as the train began to slow, Nick loped alongside, looking into the first-class compartments for any sign of a diminutive American girl with a sweet face and strawberry-blond curls.

Madeline tugged Drew along behind him, pausing from time to time to stand tiptoe to peer into the soot-grimed windows. With a squeal of brakes and a hiss of steam, the engine came to a stop, and Drew nodded toward the open door of the compartment they had just passed.

"Carrie!" Madeline slipped her arm out of Drew's and hurried over to her friend. "You're here. You're really here."

"I'm so glad to see you." Carrie hugged Madeline tightly. "I thought the train would never get in." Still with one arm around Madeline, she reached for Drew's hand. "How are you, Drew?"

"Pleased you could join us." Drew gave her slim hand a squeeze, his gray eyes holding just a hint of humor as he glanced toward the front of the train. "Though I daresay not as pleased as someone I could name."

Nick was coming back down the platform, his hat wadded in both hands and an uncertain smile on his pale lips. "Hullo."

A tinge of eager pink came into Carrie's cheeks. "Hello."

Hiding a smile, Madeline moved back to her husband's side, leaving a clear path between Carrie and Nick.

"Shall I . . . ?" Nick cleared his throat. "Shall I see to your luggage?"

Madeline glared at him. *Don't be an idiot. Don't just leave her standing there. Don't—*

An instant later, she knew she needn't have worried.

With a whisper of her name, Nick took Carrie into his arms, and she melted against him, twin tears slipping from under her closed eyelids.

"Come along, darling," Drew murmured, tucking Madeline's arm into his own. "I'm sure they'll join us in a moment. Plumfield will see to the bags."

They walked out into the damp and blustery June afternoon, leaving the long-parted couple still clasped together, oblivious to anyone and anything outside their embrace.

"Mr. Farthering?" A liveried chauffeur stepped away from a sleek black Triumph saloon and touched the brim of his cap. "I'm Phillips, sir. Lord Rainsby sent me for your party."

"Ah, excellent." Drew looked back toward the station. "There are two more of us just coming now."

Madeline turned to see Nick and Carrie walking hand in hand, eyes soft and voices low. Then, realizing they were observed, they both laughed and quickened their pace. In a few minutes more they were all driving along the coast of the Firth of Forth.

"It's nice of your friends to let me come up to Scotland along with you all," Carrie said, looking out over the waving grasses that thinned onto a wide sandy beach, which in turn sank into the blue-green water. "Will it be a large party?"

"I'm not really sure," Drew admitted. "Being the week of the

Open, I'd be surprised if they didn't have more people staying, but the Rainsbys didn't particularly say."

"Still, it's nice." Carrie gave Nick a shy glance and then smiled at Madeline. "It'll give us a chance to catch up." She blushed at Madeline's knowing grin. "Uh . . . have you known the Rainsbys long, Drew?"

"Lady Rainsby, all my life," Drew said, "but I haven't seen her often."

"The last time was at our wedding," Madeline said, "though I don't think she and Lord Rainsby stayed for the reception. I was introduced to her, but there were so many introductions that day, I really don't remember her at all."

"I was twelve the last time I had a chance to talk to her for more than a few minutes," Drew told Carrie. "It was at my father's funeral."

Carrie's expression clouded.

"Sorry." Drew looked at Madeline, eyes anxious. "I didn't mean—"

"It's all right." Carrie took a deep breath and managed a smile. "Really. Daddy wouldn't want me to be sad remembering him, and I'm not going to be. We're going to have fun and not think of anything dreary."

"Of course we are," Nick said with a fierce look at Drew. "Despite certain ham-fisted remarks."

"No, really," Carrie said, her earnest voice softened by her South Carolina drawl. "I don't want you all tiptoeing around me all the time. It's not as if Daddy passed just the day before yesterday. And it's not as if it came as a surprise."

"I just wish I could have been with you all the way over," Nick said.

Madeline huffed. "She didn't come from America all by herself, you know. Just this last part on the train. All the rest of the time she was with Frannie and Amy Haslett and their mother."

"I'd have felt better if their father had come along," Nick muttered.

"You never met their maid, Miss Hannah," Carrie said, giving his hand a squeeze. "She'd intimidate anyone."

"You're safely here at any rate," Drew said. "Even if golf doesn't much interest you, it should be a jolly nice time. Little Gullane ought to be bustling just now."

They drove through the village, which was indeed bustling, and out toward the golf course. They saw a few homes along the way, tiny cottages and farmhouses, a grand old manor house, and one extremely modern one with its back at the very edge of a high, rocky outcropping overlooking the water.

"Look at that one." Carrie pointed to the tall cylinder of a structure, gleaming white with large curved windows that must have stretched from floor to ceiling in the rooms on the top three levels. "I've never seen one like it."

Madeline wrinkled her nose. "It's that terribly modern style I've seen in some of the magazines. All the architects are doing it. Guimard is one of the famous ones, isn't he?"

"Lovely for the Paris Metro or a Radio City Music Hall, but as a home?" Drew shrugged. "Rather cold looking."

"I like the old historic ones," Carrie said, still staring at the house. "Like the one back there at the crossroads. What's Thorburn Hall like?"

"I've never seen it." Drew leaned toward the front seat. "I say, Phillips, how long before we reach the Hall?"

"Just coming to it now, sir."

The chauffeur turned onto a long drive that curved up to the white house perched on the overlook.

Drew winced slightly and cleared his throat. "Ah. Yes. Thank you, Phillips. Grand place, I'm sure."

Madeline covered a giggle with her gloved hand.

"Well handled," Nick said in a snide stage whisper. "Very subtle."

The chauffeur chuckled. "I expect you were thinking you'd see something a bit more traditional, sir."

"Yes," Drew admitted. "I was."

"It used to be, sir. A grand Jacobean manor house. Not so large as some I seen, but very fine. It burnt to the ground a few years ago. Nothing left but the little Grecian-looking folly out beyond the garden. Her ladyship had them build this new house with everything sleek and modern. Said she could never abide the old one. Too dreary and all that."

"My wife says the same thing about our place," Drew told him.

"Not the house, darling," Madeline said sweetly. "Just you."

"Ah. I knew I'd heard it somewhere."

Madeline giggled and kissed his cheek, making him grin.

Carrie pursed her lips, but there was a glint of laughter in her blue eyes, and some of her anxiousness seemed to fade. "It's so good to be with you again." She colored faintly and didn't look at Nick. "All of you, I mean."

"I can't wait till we get settled in," Madeline told her, "and you and I can really catch up."

In just a few minutes, the chauffeur pulled up in front of the house. The butler, a small, rather bent elderly man called Twining was waiting at the door. He led them through the spacious white entry hall and into the equally spacious and equally white drawing room. There on a white velvet chaise longue sat a woman of unmistakable style and breeding. She had to be Lady Louisa Rainsby.

"Mr. and Mrs. Farthering, madam," the butler intoned. "Miss Holland and Mr. Dennison."

Lady Rainsby was immediately on her feet, hurrying to them with both hands outstretched. "Drew, darling, how are you? You look more like your father than ever. Hello, Madeline, dear. With everything that was going on, I'm sure you don't remember me at your wedding. I'm glad we'll have a chance to get acquainted."

"Of course I remember you," Madeline said, and now that she saw the woman again, she did have a vague recollection of her, tall and dark, no longer young but lovely in tasteful orchid silk and a cloche hat with a diamond clasp. "Thank you for having us, Lady Rainsby."

"Oh, Louisa, please," she insisted.

"Lady Louisa," Madeline said, liking her already.

"It's my pleasure, I'm sure. Lord Rainsby insists on going to the Open every year, and it's that much more fun if we make a bit of a party out of the week."

"You remember Nick Dennison," Drew said, pulling Nick up next to him.

"Oh, yes. The best man." Lady Louisa's smile was just the tiniest bit forced, but she gave Nick a gracious nod. "We're happy to have you with us, of course. And you must be Miss Holland, Madeline's friend." She looked at Carrie, friendly but the slightest bit puzzled. "We have met before, haven't we?"

"She was my maid of honor," Madeline explained, and the older woman's face lit.

"Of course. I thought you were the loveliest thing in that pale robin's-egg satin." She squeezed Carrie's hand. "I hope we shall all become the best of friends. You know, Lord Rainsby teases me terribly about it, but I so enjoy having people to stay. We're not having a great many guests this time, but that will give us all a better chance to become acquainted, don't you think?" She turned to the man who had risen from an overstuffed, white velvet chair in the corner. "Do allow me to introduce Gerald's friend and business partner, Mr. Reginald MacArthur."

MacArthur was a solidly built man, fiftyish but active looking, his clothes stylish but not fussy, his skin weathered as if he preferred to be outdoors whenever possible. He shook hands all around.

"It seems we're to have a bit of weather for the tournament," he said, smiling from under his heavy reddish mustache. "I trust you ladies shan't mind too much."

"It should be interesting to see how the players do once they get on the greens," Madeline said. "They'll be soft and hard to read. I just hope they don't suspend play due to the wind."

MacArthur's smile broadened. "You must be a golfer, Mrs. Farthering."

"Oh, not really. I never can hit the ball without taking out a chunk of grass with it. But I've heard my husband complaining enough about his game to know what's what. And I do enjoy the tournaments. My father used to take me to some of them when I lived in America."

"You're a lucky man, Farthering. A golfer whose wife appreciates the sport is to be envied."

Before Drew could reply to that, the bell rang. A moment later the butler returned to the drawing room door. "Mr. and Mrs. Pike, madam, and"—he grimaced almost imperceptibly—"Count Kuznetsov."

"Louisa!"

Drew glanced at Madeline in disbelief as the portly, bright-eyed woman from the train station bustled into the room and straight into their hostess's outstretched arms.

"Elspeth. I thought you'd never arrive." Lady Louisa reached out to the heavyset middle-aged man beside her. "Mr. Pike, so good to see you again."

He bent awkwardly over her hand. "Good afternoon, Lady Rainsby," he said in a gravelly, deep bass voice. "It's good of you to have us." He gave the languid Russian accompanying them a disdainful glance. "All of us."

"Welcome back to Thorburn Hall, Count Kuznetsov." Lady Louisa slipped her hand out of Pike's and extended it to the younger man. "Elspeth has told me so much about you since your last visit. What a tragedy."

The Russian bowed his head, a look of pain shadowing his mobile face. "You are too kind, madam. Such pleasantries as we shall have here are a most welcome distraction."

Seeing Drew and Madeline, Mrs. Pike clasped her plump hands. "Isn't this just the most delicious coincidence, Alfred? This is the very kind couple Misha and I met in the station. I thought at the time that they were just the sort of young people Misha might find amusing. *They* wouldn't sneer at a fine artiste."

"Neither would I," Pike muttered, half under his breath, "if I were ever to meet one."

"You know, we never were introduced," Mrs. Pike chattered on, and Lady Louisa made sure everyone knew who was who.

"Madam Farthering," the count said, bowing over Madeline's hand. "Again I am enchanted. And you, sir." He took Drew's arm. "You absolutely must tell me everything about yourself and your charming wife. I am certain we shall all be the dearest of friends."

"Misha is writing a symphony," Mrs. Pike said, her eyes wide and sparkling as if she was writing it herself. "It's wonderful."

"And maybe one day we'll actually hear a note or two," Pike grumbled.

Madeline gave Drew a subtle elbow to the ribs and a look that warned him not to laugh.

"I'm sure it will be wonderful," Mrs. Pike insisted cheerfully. "We mustn't be impatient, must we, Misha? Art simply cannot be rushed."

The count released Drew's arm so he could press her hand with a fervent kiss. "Ah, my so perceptive muse."

Pike snorted and then shook hands with Drew. "If I'm not mistaken, you're the Farthering who sorted out that nasty business in Yorkshire last year."

Drew shrugged. "Along with my wife and Nick here, we managed to help out a bit." He glanced over at Carrie and, seeing a touch of pensiveness in her polite smile, quickly added, "But that's old news. I'm much more interested in watching Henry Cotton win another Open."

"It should be a fine match. Do you play?"

"Now, now, Alfred," Mrs. Pike scolded playfully, "you boys will have plenty of time to talk about golf the whole week long."

"Why don't we all get acquainted?" Lady Louisa suggested, indicating the sleek-lined sofa and chairs situated in front of the wide, curved window. "And I'll ring for tea."

⬥

"This should be entertaining," Drew said when they were dressing for dinner in their very modern all-white room with its almost-clinical white bathroom en suite. "What did you think of them all?"

Madeline smoothed the aqua lamé silk of her gown, looking

at her reflection with a critical eye. "I like Lady Louisa very much. Tell me again how you're related?"

"Her grandfather and my great-grandfather were brothers. So I suppose that makes us second cousins once removed. I'm still not quite sure why she invited us, though. It's not as if we'd met more than a time or two since I was a boy."

"We wanted to see the Open. She wanted to get better acquainted. There's nothing wrong with that, is there?"

"Of course not." He took out his pocket watch with their wedding sixpence hanging from the chain and checked the time. Just five minutes to the hour. "We ought to go down soon."

Madeline turned her head to one side and picked up two earrings, one pearl and one antique gold, and held them up, one by each ear. "Which one?"

"The pearls," he said without hesitation.

"You always choose the pearls," she huffed, putting them on.

"The pearls suit you," he said, leaning close. "Always lovely, never out of style. Rich but not gaudy."

There was a sudden hint of mischief in her periwinkle eyes. "Unlike Count Kuznetsov, who is gaudy but not rich."

Drew chuckled. "Inquisitive chap, isn't he, deviling all of us for our life stories?"

"And entertaining," she said. "His impersonations of the English, German, and French politicians were too funny."

"Somehow he's clever enough to find himself a soft berth for just the price of a bit of artistic posturing. Though if he's been a guest at the Hall before now, I'm rather surprised Lady Louisa and, indeed, everyone else in the house didn't hear about the count's tragic past, whatever it is, during the first visit."

"Maybe he doesn't have a tragic past." Madeline considered. "Or maybe he just doesn't like to talk about it."

"Oh, he has one," Drew assured her. "And I can promise you he loves to talk about it."

"Well, he seems to make Mrs. Pike very happy without being more than an annoyance to Mr. Pike, so I suppose it works out nicely for everyone."

"One wonders how anyone has the brass to simply expect to be supported in such a way," Drew said. "But if the three of them are happy . . ."

Madeline unstoppered one of her perfume bottles, and the smell of gardenias filled the room. She touched the tiniest bit to her wrists and behind both ears, only enough to intrigue, enough to draw a man closer rather than drive him away. Drew breathed it deeply, smiling at her reflection.

"I, on the other hand, would object most strenuously if you took up with a confidence trickster and brought him to Farthering Place to live."

"Do you think he is?" she asked, eyes bright as she turned to face him. "A fraud, I mean?"

Drew scoffed. "Oh, he plays it well, and I don't suppose there's any real harm in him, but I shouldn't like to hold my breath waiting for his symphony to be finished."

"Now you're sounding like Mr. Pike." Madeline stood up, looking him over. "You'd better go get Nick before we're late. I'll see if Carrie's ready. Beryl is over doing her hair, as if she needed help."

"She's like you, my love," Drew said, dropping a kiss on her delicately powdered cheek. "Whether it takes you five minutes on your own or three hours and a brigade of handmaids to make yourself presentable, you always look as fresh and artless as a newly budded rose."

She only laughed at that, but it did bring the pleased color to her cheeks. "After two and a half years of marriage, you're supposed to have left behind the niceties and become a thoughtless brute."

"I shall put forth a better effort," he promised.

She nestled into his arms for just a moment. "How long have Lord and Lady Louisa been married? And what's he like?"

"He was at our wedding, too, you know. Not that I've had more than a few polite words with him. Nice enough chap as far as I recall. They must have been married well more than twenty years, I'd guess. Perhaps we'd better go downstairs and get better acquainted with them and everyone else."

"You just want to find out more about that so-called count." She slipped her arm into his. "And so do I."

— Two —

They collected Nick and Carrie from their rooms and went down to find the Pikes, Kuznetsov, and Lady Louisa having drinks in the drawing room.

"You must forgive my husband," Lady Louisa said. "He's generally very particular about coming to dinner on time, but there was a car smash in the road from Edinburgh, and it's made him late getting dressed."

"All right, Louisa," said an unfamiliar voice. "I've made it down only three minutes past my time. My apologies, everyone, for not being here when you arrived this afternoon."

Lord Rainsby was not a remarkable-looking man. His face was pleasant enough, the lines in it and the warmth in the faded blue eyes indicative of a tendency to laugh easily. He was tall, a bit stoop-shouldered and balding, a trifle paunchy in the middle, and on the whole someone who looked as if he were a pleasant enough fellow to know.

"It's too good of you and Lady Rainsby to let me come visit along with Drew and Madeline," Carrie told him once everyone had been introduced. "I've never been to Scotland."

"It's a bit dreary at the moment," Rainsby admitted, "but there's hope for a bit of sunshine for the tournament. Joan will be very disappointed if it's delayed."

"Will she be joining us, sir?" Drew asked.

"Oh, you know these modern girls," his lordship said with a bark of a laugh. "She'll be along when she decides to come. In Cannes just now, you know. The old home place a bit too quiet to suit, though I think that's more her friends' idea than her own, but she'll be back for the last day. She always is." He looked out the wide, curved window overlooking the tossing gray sea. "I do hope we get a bit of break in the weather, not just for the tournament. I thought we all might enjoy a bit of riding too, if it's fine enough tomorrow or next day."

"That would be lovely," Madeline said, and he beamed at her.

"Do you ride, Mrs. Farthering? Somehow I knew you would."

"Not as often as I'd like," she admitted, "even at home, but I do enjoy it."

"Oh, then you must come."

"Really, we must make a regular event of it," Lady Louisa said. "And Mac will join us, and the Fartherings and Miss Holland and Mr.—" she looked at Nick, suddenly puzzled—"I'm sorry, dear boy, Mr. . . . ?"

"Dennison," Nick supplied good-naturedly.

"Mr. Dennison, of course. Do forgive me." She waved both hands airily. "I do have such a memory. Still, I remember Dennison from Farthering Place. A good, trusty fellow, I'm sure. Anyhow, Elspeth and her husband don't ride. Or have you decided to take it up in earnest?"

Mrs. Pike's eyes widened in horror. "After last time? Good heavens, no."

"No," Mr. Pike said. "We won't be making that mistake again, thank you."

"Why not, Pike?" Rainsby asked. "You did fine, especially seeing you haven't ridden much."

"It's not myself I'm worried about," Pike grumbled, shooting his oblivious wife a sour look.

"No, I couldn't possibly," Mrs. Pike said, her good humor returning. "I haven't brought a proper riding costume, you know, and I don't think the horses like it when one isn't properly dressed. That must have been the problem the last time."

"I'm sure that must be it," Rainsby said, a twinkle in his eye. "And what about the count? You'll join us, won't you?"

"Ah." Kuznetsov put one white hand up to his temple. "When I think of the fine-blooded horses the tsar used to keep, I cannot bear even to look upon those in your country. I mean no disrespect, of course, but surely you can understand."

"Oh, naturally. Naturally."

"And, as I told madam, I have had the most amazing revelations in the night about my poor little symphony. I must get it all on paper or it will vanish entirely. My muse is uncommonly fickle."

"Well, then," Mrs. Pike said eagerly, "while they're all out riding, Alfred and I can help you jot it down. Won't that be fun?"

Pike and Kuznetsov looked equally dismayed at the prospect, but before either could reply, dinner was announced.

❦

Dinner was splendid: tomato soup, fillet of salmon, and potatoes dauphinoise, followed by crème brûlée and then Scottish woodcock as the savoury. It was clear that Lady Rainsby loved having guests and was an accomplished hostess, putting everyone at ease and having them chatting like old friends by the time the main course was served. Afterwards, when the others retired to the drawing room, Lord Rainsby invited Drew into his private study.

"Sit down, will you, my boy." There was a glint of humor in Rainsby's faded blue eyes as Drew briefly hesitated and then sat in the well-worn Morris chair in front of the equally battered desk. "The ladies of the house insist on redecorating the whole place at what they call 'decent intervals,' and I reckon it's little enough to buy me a deal of peace and quiet. But I won't have them in here."

"Quite right," Drew said. "A man must put his foot down somewhere."

"Precisely. At least in his own study."

"I am blessed to have a wife who likes all the Farthering relics, myself included."

Rainsby chuckled. "Fortunately, our place in Cornwall hasn't been tampered with. Apart from plumbing and electricity, needless to say, though our cook there won't hear of using a gas cooker. She likes 'a real fire, thank you very much.'"

"One thing I've learned," Drew said confidentially, "is that one never, *ever* unsettles one's cook."

"Very true," his lordship said with a bit of a laugh. "Oh, and Louisa has decided we must all go riding Thursday morning. We'll have the first round of the Open tomorrow, of course, and get to see if our Mr. Cotton can hold the lead. But the day after we'll have a ride in our meadow and then take in round two. If it's fine enough, of course. Can't say I'm not always eager to show off my mare Atalanta."

"Splendid."

Rainsby leaned back in his leather chair and began filling

29

his pipe with rather pungent tobacco. "There are cigarettes in the box. Help yourself."

Drew moved the black lacquer container to one side and picked up the photograph it had been in front of. The girl in the picture gazed with a dreamy half smile into the distance, her eyes large and dark, her dark hair pulled back with a velvet bow as pale as her creamy skin.

"This must be your daughter."

"Yes," Rainsby said, brightening. "That's our Joanie."

"You say she never misses the final round. Does she play?"

"Yes. She always enjoyed the Open but never was very interested in playing herself until a year or so ago. Then she insisted upon having lessons and now she's rather good. For a girl, of course." Rainsby put a match to his pipe and puffed it into life. "You play, I believe."

"If you care to call it that," Drew said with a wry grin, "but I do enjoy it."

"Fair enough. Perhaps we could play when Joan gets home. What do you say? You and Dennison and Joan and I could make up a four, eh?"

"I'd like that very much, sir, if we have an opportunity. I suppose we'll have to wait until after the tournament, but—"

"You needn't hurry away after it's over." Rainsby glanced toward the closed door of his study and then leaned forward in his leather chair. "There isn't anything you need to get to, is there?"

Drew knew the look. His lordship had something troubling him. "I suppose not, sir. Why do you ask?"

"Do you know why Lady Rainsby invited you here?"

Drew lifted one eyebrow. "I take it it was not merely to renew our cousinly acquaintance."

"Not entirely. No."

"Then . . . ?"

Rainsby tapped his pipe against the ashtray and puffed on it a moment more. "She invited you," he said finally, "because I asked her to."

"Oh, yes?"

"It's rather a delicate matter, you understand. I thought someone with your experience in helping out in this sort of situation might be able to have a look at what we have up here."

Of course, even so charming an invitation as Lady Rainsby's would come at a price. "You've been taking those old newspaper accounts far too seriously."

"Nonsense," Rainsby blustered. "You're the very man, I should think. If I wanted the police or some private investigation, I would have engaged them already. This requires tact and subtlety."

"So your wife suggested me."

"Don't be daft, man. She knows nothing about any of this. She is one of the reasons I cannot and will not have some oaf from the local police bungling about, asking indelicate questions and stirring up gossip among the staff."

"I see." Drew should have known he wouldn't be allowed to simply enjoy the Open without interruption. "Then it's a domestic matter."

Rainsby took another three puffs on his pipe and blew out the smoke in one choking cloud. "Yes," he admitted at last, drawing out the word reluctantly, "and no."

"Look here, sir. Why don't you just tell me the thing straight out, and then we can see if there's anything I can do about it. What do you say?"

Rainsby looked faintly relieved. "That's the best way, isn't it? Of course it is. Very well, here it is. Reginald MacArthur and I were in the war together. Afterward he was a bit at loose ends. He'd come from money, don't you see, but he'd lost most of his helping where he could in the war effort. Capital of him, though a bit of a problem afterward."

"No doubt," Drew murmured, remembering the huge amounts his own father had poured into the war effort, though he had managed to stay solvent long enough to recover.

"Mac had been a cartographer during the war," Rainsby said, "so he decided he'd give that a go afterward. Maps for schools and city councils and that sort of thing, right? Good, steady work, even if it is somewhat dull."

"Seems a logical step."

"Needless to say," Rainsby continued, drawing audibly on his pipe, "he hadn't the wherewithal to start a business of any sort."

Drew nodded. "And that's where you came in."

"Precisely. I put up the capital, and we went into it as partners. It's made each of us a tidy sum these past fifteen years, and he's given me no reason to regret my decision to come in with him."

"Until now," Drew ventured.

"Until now." Rainsby winced ever so slightly. "In the past year or so the firm has had a difficult time of it. Not surprising, not really, given the state of the world's economies."

"Perhaps rather than a detective, you ought to engage an auditor."

"I have done," Rainsby said, "and he found not even the slightest irregularity. Dash it all, man, I'd seen Mac in the war. Stout fellow. Give his all for king and country. I've been in business with him, mostly a silent partner, I'll grant you, but he discussed matters with me. I knew what was going on."

"And now he's not as forthcoming, is that it?"

Again, Rainsby winced. "I—I don't know if I can even call it that. There's just something different about him. Something furtive. It unsettles me."

Drew smiled. "That's hardly a crime."

"But it might be the sign of one," Rainsby snapped.

"True. Very true."

"I, uh . . ." Rainsby gave his grizzled mustache a sheepish tug. "I just thought you might be able to tell me whether or not I ought to be concerned. I hate to stir up something that's not even there, eh?"

"Perfectly understandable. Tell me more about him. Wife? Children? Unconscionable number of greyhounds?"

Rainsby snorted. "No dogs of any variety to my knowledge. No children. Wife left him a year or more ago."

"Did she now? Do you happen to know why?"

"He never said, naturally." Rainsby's mouth turned down. "Another woman, no doubt, though I wouldn't have thought it of him before the divorce, but that's precisely what I mean. There's something not quite right about it, though I know hundreds of people get divorced these days. Why it should be different just because it's Mac, I can't say. I just wouldn't have thought it of him."

Drew gave a mental shrug. No harm in chatting with this MacArthur fellow. Might even give Nick some investigating to do when he wasn't mooning over Miss Holland. Either way, Rainsby had been kind enough to invite them all up to see the Open. A little snooping on his behalf wouldn't be asking too much, would it? He stood up.

"I'll see what I can find out. Discreetly, of course."

Rainsby fairly leapt out of his chair and seized Drew's hand in one of his own, using the other to clasp his shoulder. "Excellent. Quite, quite excellent. Now, mum's the word, eh? Nothing to the ladies, are we agreed?"

"My Madeline excepted, sir," Drew said. "But you needn't worry about her. She's been in on all the cases I've looked into. I couldn't have managed without her."

Rainsby frowned. "Well, if you're certain it'll be all right. I never will understand these modern girls. Glad I got one of the last of the reliable ones in Lady Rainsby, don't you know."

"Madeline's a brick," Drew said with a wink. "You'll see."

"I'll leave that to you, then." Rainsby ushered him to the door. "You'll get to know Mac a little better when we're out riding, I expect."

"I'll see to it I do."

Muirfield was a longtime venue of the Honorable Company of Edinburgh Golfers. Designed by Old Tom Morris himself, it overlooked the Firth of Forth, though it was hard to distinguish land from sea from sky on that gray and blustery first day of the Open. But that didn't seem to keep the spectators at home.

Everyone from Thorburn Hall agreed to Drew's suggestion that they follow last year's champion Henry Cotton, at least to begin with. But after a few holes, the group began to scatter. Lady Rainsby, Mrs. Pike, and Count Kuznetsov went to take shelter in the clubhouse where it wasn't quite so windy. Lord Rainsby saw that the local MP happened to be in attendance and went to talk to him about an upcoming election, and Mr. Pike went along with him. MacArthur muttered something about an old friend and disappeared. Nick and Carrie drifted to the back of the crowd, chattering away, clearly more interested in each other than the game.

"It looks as though we're on our own again, Mrs. Farthering," Drew observed. "Do you want to keep following Cotton, or shall we find us a nice spot by one of the greens and watch them all play through?"

"Stumbled across any murders yet, Detective Farthering?"

Madeline's eyes widened at the sound of the grumbling voice, and Drew fought a grin as he turned around. "Chief Inspector Birdsong."

Birdsong shook Drew's hand and touched the brim of his hat as he nodded to Madeline. "And I thought I was on holiday."

"On holiday?" Drew asked with exaggerated alarm. "Are we to understand that Hampshire is left unprotected?"

"Even I am allowed a day off now and again," Birdsong said with a sanctimonious sniff.

Madeline looked over the crowd. "Is Mrs. Birdsong with you? We never did get to meet her."

"Mrs. Birdsong and I have an agreement, ma'am. She has my blessing to invite her mother and sisters to visit during the week of the Open. And, while they're nattering away at home all hours, a couple of lads from the department and I come to the tournament."

"That seems an equitable arrangement," Drew said.

"It's served us well these past ten or fifteen years," Birdsong told him. "You'll find, young Farthering, these little accommodations make for a long and happy marriage."

"I'm sure they do."

The chief inspector lowered his voice confidentially. "Makes it much easier to spend the week with her people at Christmastime if I haven't already had enough of them by June."

They were silent as Cotton putted. The ball made a lazy curve toward the hole, looked as if it would stop just on the lip of the cup, then dropped in. The crowd broke into applause.

"The man's a marvel," Drew said. "I wouldn't be at all surprised if he wins it again this year."

Birdsong narrowed his eyes. "So you're here just for the tournament?"

"Guests of Lord Rainsby out at Thorburn Hall."

"Nothing suspicious going on?"

Drew shook his head.

"Your old nanny or the chap who used to trim your lawn or the vicar from the next village but one doesn't need your help?"

Again Drew shook his head. "Just the tournament. Like you, we are on holiday."

Birdsong lifted both heavy eyebrows speculatively. "See you keep it that way." With a tip of his battered hat, he turned and wove his way into the crowd.

Madeline giggled. "Too bad he doesn't know Nick's here, too. He would have been sure we're up to something."

"Nick's got enough to think about just now," Drew said, scanning the crowd, "wherever he's got to."

They finally met up with Nick and Carrie sheltering under a tree near the tee on fifteen. When the girls hurried off to the clubhouse to freshen up, Drew and Nick stood watching the game.

"How are you coming along?" Drew asked once the most recent foursome had teed off.

Nick exhaled heavily, looking as perplexed as he was delighted. "It's awfully good to have her back."

"But?"

"Well, I don't like the idea of her going home again."

"I know that already. What are you going to do about it?"

Nick frowned. "I can't just blunder into a proposal, you know. 'Welcome back to Britain, Miss Holland, would you marry me? Today?'"

Drew chuckled. "You might phrase it just a bit more subtly than that."

"I just don't know if I have any right to say anything."

"No right? The girl's absolutely potty about you. No right, man? Then who does have the right?"

Nick kicked at the spotty turf under the shade of the tree. "Dunno. That Kip Moran fellow."

Drew scoffed. "You're not on about him again, are you? I thought you figured out two years ago that she doesn't care for him in the least."

"But she—"

He broke off, silent while another group of golfers hit their tee shots. One of them ended up hooking his ball into the hazard, eliciting a sympathetic groan from the spectators.

"She's been back in the States two years now," he continued, low-voiced, once play had stopped. "I don't expect she sat home all that while."

"She was looking after her father, you know, and then in mourning after his death. Do you think she was out every night?"

Nick gave a grudging shrug. "Maybe not every night. But there had to be *some* nights."

"Maybe. But even if she let one fellow or another escort her to a party or two, that doesn't mean she was contemplating marriage. Come on, old man, you know the girl. Do you think she's the type to string you along when she doesn't mean it?"

"No," Nick admitted. "I'm not saying she was seeing anyone

else, just that she deserves someone like Moran. He's more her type."

"You mean the type with money."

Again Nick shrugged. "It's not the money. Not *just* the money."

"Then what?"

Nick watched the approach of another foursome, saying nothing.

"What?" Drew urged.

"I can ignore it most of the time," Nick said finally. "But now Carrie's here and I have the chance to propose, I can't help realizing how it would be for her if she married me. I'll always be the working-class bloke who isn't quite fit to appear at society functions. No, don't tell me it doesn't matter. It doesn't matter to you, and don't think I haven't appreciated that every day of my life, and I truly don't believe it matters to Carrie, but it matters to other people. Lady Rainsby is a charming woman, and I don't believe she even realizes herself she's doing it, but it's quite clear she isn't at all comfortable with my rubbing elbows with you and the rest of her guests. The butler's son? Shocking."

"Nick—"

Someone in the crowd shushed them as play resumed.

"Nick," Drew said once the latest group moved onto the fairway, "not everyone thinks that way."

"If this was a hundred years ago, I would certainly be bad ton. Not received."

Drew looked at him for a long moment. Then he crossed his arms over his chest. "And are you going to let silly, outmoded class distinctions keep you from marrying the girl you love? The girl who loves you?"

Nick lifted his chin, defiant. "I might."

Drew snickered. "What a great nitwit you are. Now come on. We'd better go find our ladies fair and then see if we can't catch up to Cotton's group. I still think our best money's on him for a second consecutive title."

"I still think . . ." Nick's eyes widened in horror. "What am I going to do?"

"Try to look as if you've got good sense at any rate," Drew said, realizing he had caught sight of Carrie and Madeline coming through the crowd. "Unless you think looking like some large-mouthed fish of very low intellect will entice Miss Holland to accept your proposal."

Nick snapped his mouth shut, glaring at him.

"There you are," Madeline said, taking Drew's arm. "We thought you might have moved on."

"Waiting for you, darling." Drew smiled at both girls. "So what shall it be? Would you two like to follow Mr. Cotton a while? Or shall we find somewhere to make camp?"

Carrie slipped her arm through Nick's. "I'd like to walk a bit if that's all right."

"Then we'll walk," he said. "I believe that's one of your countrymen coming just now. Picard. Shall we watch him?"

They watched Picard and the rest of his foursome tee off, then followed them down the fairway along with the crowd.

"Oh, look," Carrie said, looking across to the trees on the other side of one of the hazards. "It's Mr. MacArthur. Who is that girl?"

Drew looked over to see MacArthur talking to a young blonde probably no more than half his age. She had her arm through his and was leaning close, a coy little smile on her red lips as he lit her cigarette.

"Hmmm," he said, "perhaps she's the reason things grew

less than blissful between him and Mrs. MacArthur. No, don't look at them."

"Trick is to look just beyond and to one side and pretend you're telling someone about what you're seeing," Nick said, evidently finding this a good excuse to pull Carrie just a bit closer to his side. "Then the observed party doesn't realize he's observed."

"We saw that girl before," Madeline said, not looking toward her. "When we were in the clubhouse. One of the men, I thought he was probably a caddie, came over and said something to her. She answered him, and he said something else, something right in her ear, and then took her hand. She answered that, and they both went in opposite directions. It is the same one, isn't it, Carrie?"

"She didn't look very happy about whatever he said," Carrie added. "Mad enough to have her fist clenched. I don't know why. He's a very nice-looking man."

"She's a very nice-looking girl," Drew said, pretending to watch one of the golfers as he knocked a bit of dirt and grass out of his cleats.

"There's always one sure way of finding out if someone's covering up," Nick said. "We suddenly notice he's over there and say we've been looking for him and ask him to introduce us to his friend. If he's hiding something, it'll probably be noticeable."

"I'm not sure that would get us what we want quite yet," Drew said. He put his arm around Madeline's waist, guiding her a bit more deeply into the crowd. "For now, I'd rather he not suspect we've seen them together. Might be nothing after all, but if it is, I don't want him to get the wind up."

"I can see why the three of you enjoy this so much," Carrie

said, a gleam of intrigue in her eyes. "This part is actually fun. What do you suppose he's up to?"

Nick squeezed her hand. "I'll tell you when you're older."

She wrinkled her nose at him. "If it's just that, you'd think she'd be more interested in the handsome young caddie than the old duffer, wouldn't you?"

"Depends on if she's after looks or money," Drew said, and seeing the crowd was walking on to follow the last foursome to the next tee, he waited for MacArthur and his companion to move on as well and then led everyone after him.

— Three —

Your post, sir."

The butler came into the library that afternoon once everyone had come back from the tournament and handed Drew a large envelope with Farthering Place as the return address.

"If you would care to respond, the necessary supplies are in the desk here as well as up in your room. If you wish, you may leave your letters on the silver tray on the side table in the foyer to be posted."

"Thank you, Twining."

Drew waited until the butler closed the library door silently behind him, leaving him and Madeline alone. He used his pocketknife to slit one end of the envelope. Eight smaller envelopes fell into his lap. Madeline came from where she had been exploring the titles on the bookshelves and stood by his overstuffed chair as he sorted through them, still unopened.

"Party invitation. Party invitation. Engagement announcement. Wedding invitation. Invitation to serve as groomsman—"

"Wait." She put a hand on his arm, stopping him before he could go on. "How do you know what those last three are?"

"My dear girl," he said, holding up the first of them. "That is the Marwood crest. You saw Miss Marwood and Wills Featherstone at the Benningtons' last month. What else could it be? And if I'm right about that, then the wedding invitation will follow, though I'd say the Dowager Duchess has been uncommon quick about it. And who do we know in Kent apart from the Featherstones? And what would Wills be writing me about just now if it weren't to have me take part in this very special event?"

"Smarty," she said. "What's that one?"

Drew squinted at the lazily scrawled characters in the address and then slit open the envelope. "What's he writing me for?"

"Who?" She tried to peek over his shoulder as he unfolded the letter, but he turned to block her view.

"Mind your business, madam," he said as he scanned the contents. "It's very impolite to . . . good heavens. I'm to be a groomsman again."

"What?"

She tried again to see, and he passed the letter to her. A moment later she started to giggle.

"Bunny's engaged to Daphne Pomphrey-Hughes? Not really."

"It would seem so. Heaven help us."

"I suppose Daphne has finally given up on catching you."

"You're a wicked girl, and I shan't dignify that remark with a reply."

"How many does that make now for Bunny?" she asked, still giggling.

"This year or since I've known him?"

"Just the past three months."

43

"Only one," he admitted. "He's slacked off considerably."

She shook her head. "At least Mrs. Pomphrey-Hughes will finally have her daughter married. I suppose it will be the grandest wedding of the year."

"If they both remember to turn up at the church."

Laughing, she handed the letter back to him. "I guess the rest are bills."

"Not if Denny's done his job properly. Those can wait till our estate manager is back in residence."

"I'm sure Nick will be delighted to return to Farthering Place and deal with the bills while Carrie and I go shopping."

Drew chuckled and then frowned abruptly. There was one more party invitation in the group, but the last of the envelopes was from the firm of Whyland, Clifton and Benn, his solicitors in London. Madeline recognized it, too.

"Were you expecting something from them?" she asked.

"Not in particular." He slid the blade of his pocketknife under the flap. "They're supposed to be looking over a contract for mineral rights in some of our Canadian properties, but I'd have thought they'd contact Landis at the office if there were any difficulties about that." He took out the heavy sheet of writing paper and unfolded it. "I don't think there's any—"

He knew what it was the moment he began to read. He had received one like it in June of both 1933 and 1934. Once again he had to make a decision.

Dear Mr. Farthering,

As you have requested, we are contacting you to ascertain your wishes concerning our efforts to locate a Miss Marie Fabron, last known to be employed in a milliner's shop on the Rue de la Paix in Paris, France, in 1908.

It is with regret that we must once again report that, despite their continued efforts, our agents have not made any significant progress in their search. The leads that seemed so promising early on have proved entirely unfruitful, and no new information has come to light that might be of any use. Sadly the passage of so many years since her whereabouts were last known has made our task a challenging one, perhaps an unachievable one.

Needless to say, the decision about whether or not you wish our efforts to continue rests entirely with you, but at this point in time we can offer little hope that we can bring this search to a successful conclusion.

At your earliest convenience, please let us know whether we should proceed with the inquiry.

> *Yours faithfully,*
> *Aubrey C. Whyland*

He handed it to Madeline and was silent as she read it. Three years. He had found out three years ago that his father's wife, the woman he had always believed to be his mother, had claimed him only for his father's sake. For the sake of their marriage.

But Drew's mother, the one who had given birth to him, was this Marie Fabron, French shopgirl, the partner in his father's brief foray into dalliance. Somehow his father and his wife had managed to mend their marriage and brought home his child to raise as their own. And Drew had, in the past three years, come to appreciate that even in their stumbling, they had done their best in a difficult situation. He had been given a life not only of privilege, but of love.

Still, what had happened to the woman who had given him

up? It had gnawed at him in the days when he had first found out about her. He had wanted to know, was desperate to know, so desperate that he had risked losing Madeline over it.

Thank God, Madeline had stood by him, and he had learned in time to push the question of his natural mother to the back of his mind. For days and weeks at a time, he never thought of her, but then June would come round again, bringing with it another letter from Mr. Whyland. Another letter, another decision. Did he want them to continue searching?

Nick had always known Drew's secrets, and this one was no exception. As estate manager for Farthering Place, Nick knew just how much it cost to have one obscure little hatmaker out of all the obscure little hatmakers in Paris tracked down, but Drew had always been reluctant to ask. Was it worth it? And what was the grand total after three years? These investigators couldn't make bricks without straw, and all the information Drew could give them went only up to the time of his birth twenty-seven years ago. The costs must be mounting up. Surely there were better things that might be done with so much money.

Still, he knew so very little about her. Her name was Marie Fabron, and she had been about twenty years old when she and his father first met. She had made hats in a Paris shop. She may have had family in Marseilles. Her eyes were blue. There was no more than that. Even after three years of searching by those who claimed to be the very best at the business of finding obscure information, there was still no more than that.

No, there was one thing more, one thing that made him want to find her more than ever. She had given him up. He had to know why. Was it to give him the privileged life his father could offer him and she could not? Or was it because his father had paid her to give him up? Paid her to keep quiet? Or was it because she wanted to be rid of him? To put even the memory of his existence so far away that it could not taint her future prospects?

His father was dead, had been dead a dozen years before Drew knew about Marie Fabron. If only he could have asked— no, that wouldn't have done. Not at all. His father had put his indiscretion behind him. By all accounts, he had asked forgiveness of God and of his wife and not strayed again. How could Drew have ever asked the man he had thought could do no wrong about his one-time mistress?

His mother, the woman he had always thought of as mother, he hadn't known all she had done to protect him, to shield him from those who would shame him because of his heritage, to preserve the boyish devotion he had had to his father. He hadn't known even a part of it until it was too late and she, too, was gone. He couldn't ask her to forgive him for not understanding either of them. He couldn't ask her what she knew about Marie Fabron. Was all of this a dead end? He had to make a decision.

"What will you do?" Madeline handed the letter back to him, her expression tender. "I thought you'd forgotten all about this."

"No." He read the letter once more before putting it back into the envelope. "I hadn't forgotten. I just . . . I didn't want to trouble you with it, and I didn't know what I ought to do about it."

She sat down on the padded arm of his chair, stroking the hair at the back of his neck. He closed his eyes for a moment and concentrated on nothing but the familiar gentleness of her touch.

"I suppose it's a monumental waste," he said after a while. "Not just the money but the time. The effort. The hope."

"It's not a waste if it's what you need."

He wrapped his arm around her waist, pulling her closer to him, holding her there. And then he let her go, smiling before he made a great fool of himself. Not that she would hold that against him. She hadn't yet.

"I'm not saying they aren't trying, but surely they ought to have found out something after this long. Anything."

"Marie is a very common name, especially in France," she reminded him. "And it's been such a long time. She might have left Paris right after you were born. She might have left France. Perhaps she married and became Marie Dupont or Marie Dumont or Marie Dubois. Maybe she just moved away and started using an entirely different name. It's difficult for a woman who has a child and not a husband."

"True. And she would have had some money then. I know my father gave her some at the time. She might have gone anywhere." He lifted his eyes to hers, searching. "What do you think I ought to do?"

"What do you want to do?"

"I don't know. I just don't know."

She stroked the back of his neck again, playing her fingers through his hair. "Then don't do anything."

"I have to give them some sort of answer, don't I?"

"Not right this minute. Why not enjoy the tournament and the riding and whatever else we get to do up here? I'm sure your lawyers are very well able to carry on as they are until you decide what to do."

He sighed. "Maybe I'm not meant to know. I've asked God to show me how to find her. I've begged Him to help me find out something. Anything. And there's just nothing. Maybe I'd find out things I'd rather not have known and ought to quit before it's too late. Perhaps this is His answer."

"That could be. Or maybe He has something else in mind. Some other way for you to find out what you want to know. A better way." She kissed his forehead. "Or maybe it just isn't time yet and His answer isn't no, but 'not now.'"

He put his hands on both sides of her sweet face and brought her lips down to his. "Whatever would I do without you?"

"Maybe you'd have ended up like Count Kuznetsov, a charming con man, living off his wits and silver tongue."

"Me? A con man? Madam, I protest."

She giggled. "All right, I suppose you'd always be a champion of goodness and decency, no matter what. But reasonably charming all the same."

"Reasonably," he growled. Then he lifted an eyebrow and asked, "Do you think he's charming?"

"In his way," she admitted. "He seems like the type who could talk himself out of anything he got himself into."

"I wouldn't bet against him on that."

"Like you," she added.

Drew huffed. "I want to like the chap, I really do. If nothing else, he's never dull. But I don't trust him. I think I'll write Mr. Whyland and see what he and his people can find out for me. Perhaps the count is merely taking advantage of Mr. Pike's generosity and Mrs. Pike's gullibility, or maybe there's something deeper going on." He gave her a wink. "Either way, it might be fun to find out."

Drew's store of information about Count Kuznetsov was increased that evening after dinner. He wasn't quite sure he'd seen anything at first, but he was certain the count had been given a silver demitasse spoon along with his Turkish coffee. It was not on the table now. Drew kept subtle watch as Kuznetsov attended to Mrs. Pike's dropped napkin a few minutes later and realized that now she, too, had no spoon. Carrie, seated at the count's left, was similarly situated, as was Mr. MacArthur on her other side. This Kuznetsov fellow was nimble-fingered if nothing else.

When the coffee was finished and the others were wandering, talking, into the drawing room, Drew fell a little behind.

"I say, Kuznetsov?"

The so-called count started and set down the little silver tray he had picked up from the long side table in the corridor and then turned, looking rather bored. "Yes?"

"It's rather nice, isn't it?"

"I'm sure everything the Rainsbys have is quality. I was merely admiring it." Kuznetsov sniffed. "It was much grander, of course, but His Imperial Majesty had one much like it."

"And the spoons?" Drew asked with a solicitous smile.

"I beg your pardon?"

"The spoons. The demitasse spoons we had with the coffee after dinner. Did the tsar have something of the sort, as well?"

Kuznetsov drew himself up. "I beg your pardon?"

"The spoons." Drew patted the man's coat pocket and got a satisfying metallic jangle in response. "Did Tsar Nicholas have some? They are extremely attractive, I must admit."

The Russian's eyes widened rather convincingly as he extracted a pair of miniature spoons from his pocket. "How terribly embarrassing. I cannot imagine how they could possibly have ended up there."

Drew merely held out his hand, watching as Kuznetsov laid the spoons in it.

"I'm quite certain there were four," he prompted when Kuznetsov seemed to be waiting for his response.

With an hauteur that the tsar himself might have envied, the Russian fished in his pocket once more, brought out two more of the diminutive spoons, and placed them in Drew's hand.

Drew inclined his head. "Thank you very much."

"What will you do now?"

Drew shrugged. "I think I'll play a rubber or two of bridge before retiring for the night."

"I mean about the spoons. Surely there is no need to disturb Lady Rainsby over so foolish an error. It might have happened to anyone."

"Anyone who meant to walk off with the silver," Drew said pleasantly. "Yes, I know."

Kuznetsov's dark eyes flashed. "I will have you know, sir, that if we were in my country, I would have no choice but to call you out upon such a monstrous accusation."

"Another reason, I am sure, you are grateful not to be in your country."

The Russian pursed his lips and then seemed to suddenly wilt. "Ah, the grand and glorious days are gone. Noblemen are no longer allowed to defend their honor with their lives and must bear whatever insult is cast upon them."

Drew managed to look sympathetic. "It is a trial, no doubt. But better this sort than one that actually involves the criminal courts, eh?"

Kuznetsov merely huffed.

"At any rate," Drew told him, "I will see these are returned to their proper place. In the meantime, you see that nothing else accidentally finds its way into your pockets. Agreed?"

"How one is to predict accidental happenings, I cannot say," Kuznetsov mourned, "but I will do as best I'm able."

"Excellent." There was a muffled rattle as Drew dropped the

spoons into his own coat pocket. "Lady Rainsby is quite fond of Mrs. Pike, and I shouldn't like to have to step in to make sure neither of those ladies is upset."

The count laid a hand over his heart. "I shouldn't like to have you trouble yourself over it." With a slight bow, he made his way up the metal stairway and down the corridor toward his room.

Drew went back to the dining room and found the butler inspecting the table, already set for the next day's breakfast. He tapped on the half-open door. "Pardon me, Twining, might I have a word with you?"

The butler gave a very correct bow. "Certainly, sir. Is there some way I might be of service?"

"Yes, well, it's a bit awkward, but these seem to have wandered out of the dining room unattended." He took the spoons from his pocket and put them on the table. "I thought you might want to escort them home."

One pale eyebrow went up. "Thank you, sir. I will not inquire as to how they came to be in your possession, but I do thank you for sparing me a most unpleasant task."

"I take it, then, that you were already aware they had gone missing."

"I was, sir. I did not like to speak to Lady Rainsby about it, but I have my duty to perform."

"And did you know who had taken them?" Drew asked.

"I had grave misgivings, sir."

"About . . . ?"

Twining gave a discreet cough. "The Russian gentleman seems more than commonly attracted to shiny objects, sir."

"He certainly does, but I'll be keeping my eye on him in the future."

"It's not my place to say, sir," the butler said, "but the gentleman does bear watching."

"At least now he knows he's being watched."

"I suppose that will make him mend his ways," Twining said with a morose nod. "Or improve his craft."

Drew was sure that, one way or another, the man was right.

The riding party was scheduled for early the next day, just a short jaunt in the meadow that ran alongside Thorburn Hall. Nothing that would interfere with all of them going back to Muirfield for the second round of the Open.

There was no rain, so despite the soggy grounds and the brisk wind, they set out in good spirits. The Pikes stayed behind to attend to Count Kuznetsov's fickle muse, and Nick and Carrie decided they would remain at the Hall as well until it was time to go out to Muirfield.

Despite his age and sedentary appearance, Rainsby proved to be a good rider. Certainly an enthusiastic one. He led them all to a low rock wall and took it at a jump.

"Didn't expect that of an old man, eh?" he crowed from the other side.

Lady Louisa frowned. "Gerald, do behave. You're likely to end up on your backside in the mud."

"In his dotage, I tell you," Mac said with a shake of his head. "If you break another leg, Rainsby, don't say you weren't warned."

"Dotage, is it? Did you hear that, young Farthering? Remind me to tell you how I nearly rode for Hurlingham at the London Olympics. The way he talks, you'd think Mac was your age rather than mine."

"I'm beginning to think you're the one who's my age, sir," Drew said. "I suppose there's nothing to do but match you."

Drew took the jump and then looked back at Madeline, beaming.

"I'm sure you two must be the same age," she said, scowling. "About five and a half."

"Come on, darling," Drew coaxed. "It's not much of a jump."

"Not in this mud, thank you very much."

"Not to worry, ma'am," Rainsby said. "I'll see to the gate." He gave Mac a rather smug look. "For all you ladies."

He rode a few yards along the wall until he reached a wooden gate. In another moment, he had it open and held it for the others to pass through.

"Come along now, all of you," he said, closing the gate once more. "At this rate, I'll be in the drawing room with my feet up before any of you make it back to the house."

He dug his heels into his horse's sides, making it spring forward, and soon he disappeared into the thick trees ahead.

With a little glance at Drew, Madeline nudged her mount and pulled up next to Lady Louisa. "Isn't the meadow lovely?"

"Oh, yes," the older woman said. "It's the best time of the year for wildflowers." As they rode along, she began pointing out the cranesbill and campion and the red poppies that stretched as far as one could see.

Drew dropped back beside MacArthur. "I understand you and his lordship have known each other a long while."

Mac nodded. "Since before the war. He always did have a bit of swagger to him, especially on horseback."

"He seems all right enough," Drew said, glancing over to where the ladies were going into the wood.

"Of course he is," Mac blustered. "He's in his fifties, not his eighties. But you know horses. I can tell by the way you ride. You know as well as I do that even the best of us gets tossed off now and again." He put one hand to the small of his back with a rueful smile. "Those falls leave more of an ache than they did twenty years ago."

"No doubt." Drew was silent for a moment, then said, "I understand you're a cartographer. I don't believe I've met one before."

"You haven't missed much."

"I don't know about that," Drew said. "I daresay the army would've been a bit stuck without good maps during the war or even now."

"Oh, to be sure." Mac shrugged, suddenly concerned with watching his horse's hooves. "Most of what I do now goes into atlases and textbooks. Perhaps the odd bit of work for a town council now and again." He glanced up with a nonchalant smile. "Still, better that than war, eh? Those were dark days, young man, and we're well rid of them."

Drew narrowed his eyes, peering into the dense trees. "It's growing rather dark again, wouldn't you say? Italy and Ethiopia. Spain. And that fellow in Berlin . . ."

MacArthur shrugged. "Oh, I don't know. It seems Mr. Hitler has to have done something right, eh? Aren't his people working again? It might be some of our chaps in Parliament could learn a thing or two from him."

Drew managed to look only mildly surprised. "I suppose you're right so far as it goes. But if most of their work is the wholesale manufacture of arms, tanks, and aircraft—"

"Poppycock. I wouldn't have pegged you as one of those nervous Nellies, Farthering. You're sounding like Rainsby now.

He looks at me as if I'd just spat on the Union Jack any time I mention something Hitler's done that seems to be good for his country and for Europe at large."

"Still, if all they're preparing for is peace . . ."

"Of course, it seems a tremendous amount of weapons now, but you must see that they had everything taken from them after the war. Surely a nation ought to be able to defend itself. So long as Germany is held down and made to feel abused, then it is a danger. Like a whipped cur that'll bite the moment it gets the chance, eh? But if we allow the Germans to stand again, heads held high, shoulder to shoulder with the rest of Europe, surely they'll feel no need for war."

"Perhaps so," Drew said, not believing it in the least. "But with the Dollfuss assassination last year and . . ." He broke off, looking toward the commotion coming from the other side of the trees.

"Gerald?" Lady Louisa was calling, her voice high and taut. "Gerald!"

With a glance at MacArthur, Drew urged his horse into a trot and caught up to her. She and Madeline were hurrying their mounts across a low, open space, where Lord Rainsby's gray stood wild-eyed, saddleless and riderless.

"What's happened, Louisa?" Mac asked.

"Oh, Gerald *will* make an utter fool of himself when we have company. If he's broken something again, Dr. Portland will be very cross. Gerald!"

Drew moved closer to the skittish horse and managed to catch its bridle. "Here, darling." He tossed Madeline the gray's reins and then smiled at Lady Louisa. "Not to worry, ma'am. We'll fetch him back, good as new. Mac, you'd better give me a hand hunting him down. Where's he likely to be?"

"This way. There's a path."

Mac led him through the trees and then pulled up short. There in a heap, with his saddle under him, lay Lord Gerald Rainsby. His sightless eyes and the awkward angle of his neck made it clear he was dead.

— Four —

The doctor and the police arrived at nearly the same moment, not very long after Drew and MacArthur had found Lord Rainsby dead there in the meadow with his broken saddle under him. Dr. Portland, the Rainsbys' physician, proved to be a dour but unflappably competent man. He was quick to pronounce the victim dead and then hurried a dazed Lady Rainsby to the house to be looked after.

By then the local police had inspected the site of the accident and questioned the witnesses. Satisfied that there was nothing untoward about the scene or the victim, there seemed little for the inspector and his sergeant to do after that other than allow two sturdy footmen to carry the body back into the Hall and up to the waiting Dr. Portland as decorously as possible.

Half an hour later, with the pall of mourning settled heavily over the house, Dr. Portland came down the stainless-steel stairway, his purposeful steps loud. At Drew's request, he came into the drawing room, sank onto the sofa, removed his spectacles and rubbed the bridge of his nose.

"I wish there were more I could tell you. He'd been warned, time and again, to take it easy."

"Was it his heart?" Drew asked, careful to keep his voice low.

"I thought his neck—"

"Oh, quite right. Quite right. His neck was definitely broken. The girth on the saddle pulled loose and he was thrown."

The doctor glanced at the door that led into the hallway, clearly impatient for his promised cup of tea. He looked weary. Perhaps he was tired of giving medical advice that was seldom followed.

"Then there's no question of its being an accident," Drew said.

"I see no reason to think otherwise. But it was foolish all the same. He was a heavy smoker and a heavy drinker. Diabetic as well. His bones were brittle, and I told him he ought to give up riding if he couldn't give up the whisky and cigarettes. At least the jumping, at any rate. After he broke the same leg twice, I told him a fall could easily kill him. But he knew better. Ah well, I'm just the doctor. What would I know about it?"

The man was well into middle age and must have been in practice thirty years or more. This sort of thing had to have grown tiresome to him years ago.

"How's Lady Rainsby bearing up?"

"As well as might be expected," Dr. Portland answered. "It's all a shock, naturally, but she isn't the hysterical type. Still, I'm glad you and Mrs. Farthering and the others are here. Lady Rainsby oughtn't to be left alone at such a time."

"Not to worry. My wife and I will stay and see if we can be of any assistance. And then there's Mrs. Pike, whom she's known for years. I doubt she'll be much help, but Lady Rainsby might find her a comfort. Or at the very least, a distraction."

"Excellent." The doctor looked to the doorway again, sighed, and pushed himself to his feet. "I won't wait. I've got other patients who'll want to ignore my advice. If you would, when Lady Rainsby is up to it, let her know I will see to the death certificate and send over the undertakers."

"I'm sure she'll be most grateful."

"And Miss Rainsby? I take it she's from home."

Drew nodded. "Coming back today sometime. I believe she's been sent a wire to let her know what's happened."

"Very good. Do let me know if you think Lady Rainsby needs me to return."

Drew stood and shook the doctor's hand, then walked with him to the front door.

Lady Rainsby spent the evening in her room accompanied only by Mrs. Pike. All the others spent an hour or so after dinner playing cards, but eventually the games broke up, and one by one everyone retired for the evening. Everyone but Drew.

"Someone ought to wait up for Miss Rainsby," he'd told them.

Madeline had offered to wait with him, but when she dozed off for the second time, he walked her upstairs and put her to bed. Then he went back into the library, found an unabridged edition of *War and Peace*, and settled himself in an armchair to await the return of the daughter of the house.

Finally, well after midnight, a cab pulled up to the front steps, and a young woman in a plain black frock let herself out through the rear door. Drew recognized the girl from the photograph in Rainsby's study, dark-haired, patrician-looking, though she was a bit older now. Older and in mourning.

She crushed out her cigarette on the drive and came into the house.

"Miss Rainsby?"

She started when he spoke to her. She hadn't noticed him waiting there. "Who are you? Where's my mother?"

"In her room, I believe. I'm Drew Farthering. She and my father were cousins."

Joan blinked and then gave an almost imperceptible shrug. "Oh. I remember now. She said she was going to ask you here. I'm sorry."

"My condolences." Drew made a slight bow. "May I escort you up to her?"

That brought a touch of a wry smile. "I'm not quite the hothouse bloom my father thought I was. I think I can find my own way."

"Just as you say." He stepped back. "If I can be of any help to either of you, do let me know."

She put her black-gloved hand on the gleaming steel stair rail and then stopped, not looking at him. "I hate to make my mother think about all this just now, but, well . . ." She drew a little breath, not quite enough to be a sob. "Were you there? I mean, when he fell?"

"I didn't see the accident, no. But Mr. MacArthur and I found him a few minutes afterward. He'd ridden ahead. My wife, Madeline, and your mother were following him while MacArthur and I were a little behind, talking. Your father's horse came back without him, and without its saddle, so MacArthur and I went out looking."

She turned, her pale forehead puckered. "Atalanta didn't have a saddle?"

"No," Drew replied. "It was a blustery day and there were

several tree branches down. It seems something of that nature must have startled the horse and, while your father was trying to get it under control, the girth must have broken and he was thrown. That saddle seemed awfully worn."

"He liked that one." There was a touch of wistfulness in her expression. "We'd got him several others, very nice, very expensive, but he finally told us not to bother. He said that the one was comfortable and he was too old to adjust to another."

Drew nodded. "It seems rather a shame, doesn't it?"

"I suppose things like this happen. Still, it wasn't like him not to check his tack before he rode. He was very particular about that. From his polo days, I imagine." She rubbed her eyes, looking perplexed and horribly exhausted. "I'd better go up to Mother."

"If there's anything I can do for either of you . . ."

Without offering a response, she trudged up the stairs and disappeared into the white hallway.

⬬

"It's a bit awkward, isn't it?" Drew ate another bite of onion-and-bacon tart, trying to keep the divine combination of flavors from interfering with his ability to think logically. Clearly the staff were well trained, and the excellent service continued even in the face of tragedy. "I don't quite feel right staying on when the ladies of the house are in mourning, but it would seem unfeeling to rabbit off before the funeral, don't you think?"

Lady Rainsby and her daughter had not appeared at breakfast that morning and were absent from the midday meal now.

"Perhaps we ought to find out what Lady Rainsby would prefer," Carrie suggested. "I didn't really want anyone around when my father died. Not in the house anyway. I needed someplace to get away from all of them, no matter how kind they all were."

Madeline nodded. "I felt that way when Uncle Mason died. I didn't want to talk to anyone." A smile touched her lips, and she squeezed Drew's hand. "Hardly anyone."

"I tried to speak to Lady Rainsby this morning," Drew said, "but her maid informed me that she wasn't seeing anyone quite yet. According to Twining, however, she's left word that we're all welcome to stay for as long as we like."

Kuznetsov perked up at that and helped himself to another plateful of rashers.

"Until the funeral," Pike growled at him. "Then we're going."

"But if Louisa needs us . . ." Mrs. Pike began, her bright eyes pleading, and her husband softened.

"We'll see."

She turned to Madeline and Carrie. "I know if either of you had a terrible loss like this, you'd want the other to stand by you."

"Naturally," Carrie said.

"Well, that's how Louisa and I are. We've been friends since well before we were your age, you know. I couldn't leave her on her own at a time like this, now, could I?"

Madeline gave her plump arm a pat. "No, not at all. And if there's anything Drew and I can do to help, we'll stay, too."

"It's awful, that accident," Carrie said, looking down at her half-eaten tart. "I'm glad it was only an accident. I don't know if I could take it if it were more than that."

Nick glanced at Drew. All right, they hadn't discussed it, but clearly Nick was wondering it as much as Drew was—wondering if Lord Rainsby's death had been something more than just an accident. Drew returned him the subtlest shake of the head.

No. There was no evidence of anything extraordinary about the death. Rainsby had taken a silly risk and had paid for it with his life. Sad? Yes. Even tragic. But not sinister.

Following the pork pie, cold pea-and-basil soup, and the goose confit salad, there was a pudding of strawberries, blackberries, blueberries, and raspberries with sponge cake and whipped cream. Afterward, Mrs. Pike went up to see Lady Rainsby while Mr. Pike shut himself in the library to make some business-related telephone calls, and Count Kuznetsov announced that he was going to go write the more tragic parts of his long-awaited symphony. Somehow Drew suspected his efforts would begin and end with his napping on the library sofa.

Pleased to find they would be left on their own for a while, Drew and Nick and the girls settled up on the Hall's flat roof where there was an assortment of chaises and comfortable chairs. The view was magnificent, the lush rose garden and the little ivy-covered folly at one side, the wood with the road that wound down into the village on the other, and at the back of the house, the sheer cliff, the rocks, and the wide expanse of the sea.

Nick looked out toward the water, shading his eyes with one hand. "Last day of the Open and *now* we get the sun. I was listening to the wireless before lunch, and I heard this Alf Perry cove is making a run for the championship, record-breaking third round and all that. You know, Drew, your Mr. Cotton might not be everything advertised."

Drew huffed. "As our dear Chief Inspector Birdsong likes to tell us, it's early days yet. I don't know if they'll have even begun the final round by now, and you saw Cotton on Wednesday. I doubt he has much to worry himself over."

"I don't, uh . . ." Nick glanced guiltily at Carrie and Madeline. "I don't suppose it would be quite the thing for one or two of us to toddle off to see the last round."

They both shot him poisonous glares, and he sank down in his chair.

"No. No, of course it wouldn't. I didn't mean that *I* wanted to—"

Drew leaned closer to him, lowering his voice to a stage whisper. "You ought to just stop talking now, old man, discretion being the better part of valor and all that."

Nick winced and was silent.

Madeline pointedly turned her back on him and smiled at Carrie. "You are still coming back to Hampshire with us for a nice long visit, aren't you? I mean, if you're sure you want to stay in the same country with certain brutes I won't bother to name."

"I guess you're all stuck with me." Carrie gave Nick a mischievous glance. "Even the brute."

Before Nick could throw himself at her feet and pledge to lead a blameless life ever after, there was the sound of a motor car on the gravel drive. A few minutes later, MacArthur came up onto the roof, hat in hand, his clothing not quite mourning but certainly somber enough for a home bereaved.

"Good afternoon, everyone. I didn't want to disturb anyone, but I saw you all up here and thought I'd find out how Lady Louisa and little Joanie are doing."

Drew stood to shake the man's hand. "We haven't seen them today, I'm afraid. Quite understandable."

"Yes, of course," MacArthur said, shaking Nick's hand. "Terrible business, all of this, just terrible. I suppose I'll just leave my card with Twining, and a note to let them know they can call upon me at any time."

"That won't be necessary."

Joan stood before the door that led out onto the roof. She was wearing an old jumper of an indeterminate gray color and a dark skirt, something she must have worn when she was still in school, something that made her look as if she were still in school. Her face was scrubbed clean of makeup, and her bobbed dark hair was held back with a piece of grosgrain ribbon as faded as the jumper.

"Joanie, darling," MacArthur said, going to her. "How are you? I know what happened to your father must be quite a—"

"I am *not* your darling," she said, her eyes as cold as her voice. "And please don't call me Joanie. I've asked you before."

He cleared his throat, twisting up the hat he held. "Terribly sorry. Terribly sorry. Just didn't think."

She took two audible breaths and smiled faintly. "I'm sorry. That was rude of me and I apologize. It's just that Dad always called me . . ." Her face twisted up as if she might burst into tears, but then it smoothed again into impassivity. "I'm sorry."

"Don't mention it," he told her. "Perfectly understandable, and it was rotten of me to be so thoughtless."

Madeline got up and went to Joan. "Why don't you both sit down with us? It's so nice and sunny right now, and there's a delicious breeze off the water."

She sat the younger girl between her and Carrie, and MacArthur sat on the low wall that ran around the top of the house.

"How are you feeling, Joan?" Madeline asked when no one else had anything to say. "Have you had anything for lunch?"

"I don't want anything." Joan bit her lip and once more managed a smile. "Really, I'm all right. It's just odd right now, and it's worse because nobody knows what to say or do around me and I don't know what to say or do. I guess I'm supposed to be hysterical or something, but I'm not. He's dead. It doesn't seem real yet. Maybe I'll be hysterical later." She seized Madeline's wrist. "Do you think I'll be hysterical later?"

Madeline covered Joan's hand with her own. "I don't think so, but you might be. If you are, it's all right. Everyone will understand."

"Strange as it sounds," Drew said gently, "I believe the funeral will help. Makes everything more real, and you have your friends and loved ones close by to let you know you're not mourning alone."

"Yes," she said. There was a sudden softness in her expression. "That will help, I think."

MacArthur cleared his throat. "I won't disturb your mother just now, but if you would, please tell her I'd be honored to escort her to the church tomorrow."

Her gentle expression vanished, and she was once again emotionless. "I don't know what she's going to want to do."

"Please just tell her. It would be very good of you."

"I'll tell her."

With that seen to, MacArthur made a hasty retreat, and with the sputter and roar of his motor car, he was gone.

Drew looked expectantly at Joan, but she looked away from him out over the sea. "He seems to have upset you," he said. "I'm sorry."

She only shrugged.

"Funny how some people just rub us the wrong way." Madeline also looked toward the water. "It's lovely, isn't it? But I guess you get tired of seeing it all the time."

Joan shook her head, her eyes still fixed on the horizon. "Every morning I get up and go out to the little balcony outside my bedroom and watch the sea. It's never the same, and yet it never changes."

Madeline gave her a gentle smile. "I believe it's warm enough to go swimming. I never would have expected that when we first came into Waverley Station. Or would the water still be cold?"

"You don't have to humor me," Joan said. "I shouldn't have snapped at him, but the man just gets on my nerves. Why can't he leave my mother alone?"

"They seem on friendly terms," Drew said. "Has he been annoying her?"

"No. Actually, she enjoys his company. Always has. I suppose it's me he's been annoying."

"What's he done?" Nick asked

"I just don't like how he talks. He always knows everything about everything. Exactly who ought to be doing what and when. It's all very annoying."

"He does have some very strong opinions," Drew agreed. "What does your mother say about that?"

"Oh, Mother doesn't care. She and Mac have always been good friends. If you ask me—" she broke off, smiling a little— "she and my father, of course."

She didn't say more, and the conversation moved on to the usual trivialities. But that evening after dinner, when they were all sitting on the roof, chatting and watching the night, she pulled Drew aside.

"I just can't make myself believe it." She sat beside him on the low wall where MacArthur had sat before, puffing smoke like a train engine, her voice low and urgent. "Dad was an excellent rider. You can ask anyone. And I'm sure he must have told you about the London Olympics."

Drew nodded. "But that's getting on thirty years ago. He wasn't a young man anymore."

"I don't care. That doesn't mean he couldn't stay in the saddle. Also, I can't believe he wouldn't have checked his tack before he rode. It was one thing he always drummed into my head when I was a girl. Never ride without making sure your equipment is sound."

"That may be so. But either way, that girth broke loose and he was thrown, and that's as much as there is to say. I'm sorry. With a saddle that old—"

"Yes, it was old. He was forever having it mended. But that's why it makes me wonder. Spender and Martin's have been our saddlers since before I was born. I'm not prepared to swear to it, but they must have replaced those buckles six or seven times by now. I can't imagine they didn't secure them properly. But even if they hadn't, I tell you my father would have checked. He would have noticed anything coming apart."

"What do you think happened, then?" Drew asked, thinking back to the private conversation he'd had with her father before his accident.

"I don't know. I'm just saying it wasn't like him. Maybe there was something on his mind that day and he was too worried over it to do what he usually did. I know he's been a bit preoccupied lately."

"There's something not quite right," Rainsby had said. But was that something enough to precipitate a murder? Not that Joan had suggested her father was murdered, just that he had been preoccupied enough to make him careless. But still . . .

"Would it help at all if I were to make inquiries?" he asked.

She frowned. "I already asked Mother about it. She said there were some business matters he was worried about, but nothing out of the ordinary. I mean, isn't everyone worried about business matters these days? Losses and unemployment and unrest? It would be strange if he weren't worried over something, wouldn't it?"

"Yes," Drew said, "I suppose it would. But maybe I can ask a question or two here and there and set your mind at ease. Sometimes an accident is just an accident."

"I'd be very grateful."

"All right then." He gave her shoulder a comforting pat. "Leave it to me. If there's anything to be found out, I'll find it. If not, at least we'll know, eh?"

"Right." She closed her eyes and exhaled. "Right."

Then the maid brought up the coffee, and they went to join the others.

— Five —

ord Rainsby's funeral was well attended. Mourners as well as the idly curious filled Gullane's parish church and the churchyard outside. The wind still whipped off the sea, tugging and pulling at hats and coats, but the sun was out, somehow making the whole affair seem like a scene from a play. Lady Rainsby clung to MacArthur's arm throughout the service and at the graveside, yet she never spoke a word. Any emotion that might have shown on her face was hidden by her heavy veil.

Her daughter's veil was not so concealing, just a little black net that curved under at her jawline, adding a bit of softness to her otherwise severe attire. She was also silent, her expression void of any emotion save self-control.

When they all returned to Thorburn Hall, both the Rainsby ladies retired to their private quarters. That left Mrs. Pike as their makeshift hostess, but she was out of her depth given the solemnity of the day, as if a Pekinese had been pressed into service to lead a funeral procession. Without letting anyone take notice, Madeline saw that lunch and then teatime went smoothly, and Drew never had more cause to appreciate her graceful ability to set people at ease even in the most difficult circumstances.

They had just finished the raspberry cranachan when a grave and disapproving Twining took Drew discreetly to one side. "I beg your pardon, sir, but there is a *person* who wishes to speak to you." He handed Drew a card.

Mindful that he was in a house of mourning, Drew did not laugh, yet he couldn't help grinning as he passed the card to Madeline. "Shall we have him in here?" Drew asked, undeterred by the butler's look of alarm.

"Who's this, then?" Mr. Pike asked in his usual bass growl. "A friend of yours?"

"Then he ought to come in," Mrs. Pike said cheerily. "If he's come to pay his respects, we certainly can't leave him standing in the hallway."

"Madam," Twining sputtered.

"No, it's all right," she said. "If he's a friend of Mr. Farthering, he ought to come in."

"Who is it?" Nick asked. "I didn't think you knew anyone up here other than the Rainsbys."

"I told you," Drew said. "We bumped into him at Muirfield. First round."

"Oh." Nick chuckled. "You should certainly have him in."

Carrie pursed her lips. "You only want to devil him like you always do."

"Just who is this mystery man?" MacArthur asked.

Drew took back the card he had given Madeline and held it up. "Chief Inspector Birdsong of the Hampshire Police."

Kuznetsov, who had been lounging artistically against the drawing room mantelpiece, stood up straight, and Mr. Pike glanced at his wife, puzzled.

MacArthur frowned. "Is he here about the accident?"

"I can't imagine it's anything like that," Drew said. "He came for the Open. On holiday. Gullane is well out of his jurisdiction. Well, I'll just have a quick word with him and won't trouble him with a vat of introductions and all the other social niceties. If you'll all pardon me, I won't be but a moment."

He followed a very relieved Twining into the small morning room, where Birdsong stood waiting, his hat clutched in his fist.

"Chief Inspector." Drew shook the man's hand. "It's a surprise seeing you here. What can I do for you?"

"I do apologize for having interrupted. I was on my way back to Winchester, but I thought I ought to stop by. I understand you're a relation of Lord Rainsby. I heard what happened, and I'd like to offer my condolences."

"Very good of you," Drew said with a slight inclination of his head. "His lordship and I were not well acquainted, but this has still come as quite a shock to all of us."

"I took the liberty of speaking to Inspector Ranald here in Gullane, just by way of professional interest, mind you. He seems satisfied the death was no more than an unfortunate accident."

"So it would seem."

"Still," Birdsong added, "knowing you tend to be of an inquisitive nature, you and young Dennison and Mrs. Farthering as well, if you'll pardon me, I thought I'd better tell you something."

"Advice from an expert with your credentials is always welcome," Drew said, his smile guileless.

The chief inspector fixed him with a baleful eye. "I don't know Ranald except by reputation, but I know his type. He won't appreciate your trying to do his job for him, even when the death's accidental."

Drew shrugged. "I haven't done anything but tell him what I saw that day. There doesn't seem to be anything sinister about it in the least."

"I know how it is, Detective Farthering. You puzzle out a few murders and you begin to see them everywhere, even where there isn't one. You think about how someone might have made it look like an accident. You wonder why the police haven't considered this or that or something else. I know. But unless you have more to go on than you do, I wouldn't advise your trying to get round Ranald the way you do me. You've been a help a time or two, I won't deny it."

"Very good of you, Chief Inspector," Drew said.

"That is when you weren't blundering into some kind of trap."

Drew blinked at him.

"But Ranald isn't the sort who'll stand for meddling, no matter who your friends are, so best steer clear. Just a bit of friendly advice."

"I appreciate it, but you needn't worry. I told Lord Rainsby's daughter I would look into things, just to make sure there's nothing amiss. But I don't know of anything that would indicate such a thing. I expect we won't be long behind you on the road to Hampshire. Tomorrow or the next day, provided Lady Rainsby and her daughter seem to be doing well, we'll be back at Farthering Place."

"Very good. Then I suppose, as you usually do, you may completely disregard what I've said."

Drew put a hand over his heart. "You wound me, Chief Inspector. Indeed you do."

"I've a feeling you'll get over it sooner than later. Still, if you do happen to find anything untoward . . ." Birdsong took a card from his waistcoat pocket, identical to the one he'd sent in with Twining, scrawled a name across the back, and gave it to Drew.

"Ellar Shaw," Drew read aloud. "Should I know who this is?"

"He was one of my lads back in Winchester four or five years ago. Good lad. He's here in Gullane now. One of Ranald's. I understand he was here at the Hall when the inquiry was being made."

Drew thought for a moment, then smiled as he remembered a man of perhaps thirty with a high forehead, large eyes that drooped at the corners, and a soft mouth. All he needed was a lace cravat and a powdered wig.

"Soft-spoken chap? Looks a bit like William Pitt the Younger if you squint?"

Birdsong's heavy mustache twitched. "That's the one. I had a chat with him when I was at the station a bit ago. In fact, we talked about you. Much as he wanted to, he said he didn't dare ask you about that business in Yorkshire last year, not in front of Ranald at any rate. I told him most of it was probably made up anyway."

Drew chuckled.

"Anyhow, I thought if you were to insist on poking about in this Rainsby business, you could do worse than have a chat with him. Just don't let on to Ranald, eh?"

"Not a word," Drew promised.

Birdsong glanced at his wristwatch. "Well, I can't afford to stand gossiping while my cab's sitting idle outside. But as Thorburn Hall was on my way, I thought I'd stop by. Just to pay my respects."

"It was good of you. With all that's happened, I didn't quite catch the results of the final round."

"No?"

Drew steeled himself. "Cotton held on for the win?"

"Came in eighth," Birdsong said with a grin. "Alf Perry's the man. Had a stunner of a last day and finished at 283."

Drew sighed. "Poor Cotton, eh?"

"Can't win everything."

Drew escorted the chief inspector to the door and went down the front steps with him to the cab. "Safe trip and give my best to Mrs. Birdsong."

"And to your missus," the chief inspector said. He gave a curt wave as the cab pulled away from the house and onto the road.

"What was that about?" Nick asked when Drew went back into the drawing room.

"The chief inspector just came by to offer his sympathies to the family." Drew smiled and tucked Birdsong's card into his waistcoat pocket. "Quite thoughtful of him."

The next day was Sunday, and Nick and Carrie and the Pikes accompanied Drew and Madeline back to the church. Although Joan did come down to breakfast, neither she nor her mother attended the service. Count Kuznetsov, too fatigued from the activities of the day before, also stayed behind.

Built not fifty years before, the church was solid and simple, hardly more than a rectangle of light-colored stone with a pitched roof. Inside, however, there was that same expectant tranquility Drew knew from his own church in Farthering St. John. He had felt it at the funeral service the day before, and today, as then, he couldn't help but smile at the little dog carved near the base of the pulpit, a reminder of the words in St. Matthew about the woman who came to Christ asking for healing for her little daughter, knowing she was unworthy but still holding to the belief that even the lowliest of people could come to Him for grace.

When the service ended, Mr. and Mrs. Pike returned to Thorburn Hall, leaving the two young couples to take a stroll to the ruins of the twelfth-century church, St. Andrews, on the west side of the village, flanked by the brilliant summer green and pale stone of the old churchyard.

The rest of that day was quiet and contemplative. The ladies of the house both came to tea with everyone else. The secluded morning seemed to have done of Lady Rainsby a world of good. The oppressive, brittle silence from earlier in the day softened into a more companionable quiet that had more to do with reflection than mourning, and she spoke of her husband with smiles and tears.

Joan rarely spoke, and then only when spoken to. She seemed more troubled than grieved, and as soon as the evening meal ended she excused herself, pleading a headache. Drew stopped her before she could go up the stairs.

"I know you must be dead vexed with me," he said with a touch of a rueful smile.

"I don't know what you mean. What have you done?"

"It's more what I haven't done. I saw you looking reproachfully at me all through dinner."

She blushed, smiling a little. "I was not."

"Now, now, I know reproach when I see it. And you're jolly well right, of course, but I haven't been as idle as it might seem."

"You haven't?" she asked, and her blush deepened. "I mean . . . it just seems as though nothing's being done in the least. Not by the police and not by you."

"I told you I'd look into it, and I am. I've had a look at the saddle, but I don't see anything wrong with it except what we already know—that it's old and worn. I've spoken with your stable master, Clarridge, and one of the boys who looks after the horses, and they don't see anything out of the ordinary. And it being the weekend, I couldn't very well go visit the saddlers until tomorrow. But first thing in the morning I'll take the saddle to be looked at. How would that be?"

She breathed out, her lips trembling. "If you would, I'd feel so much better."

"I may not find anything," he reminded her. "Odds are there won't be anything to find."

"I know, and if it were anyone but Dad . . ."

"Sometimes one has only a little catch inside, something that says everything isn't as it should be. I've had less to go on and regretted it when I've tried to pretend it wasn't there." He gave her shoulder a brotherly pat. "You have a good night's sleep and try not to worry."

An almost desperate gratitude flashed in her eyes, and then she merely looked exhausted. With a nod, she started up the stairs, her low-heeled shoes making hardly a sound on the metal steps. She stopped and turned back to him. "I hope you don't find anything."

Without another word, she pattered up the stairs and down the corridor.

The next day, Drew had Phillips drive him and Lord Rainsby's battered saddle over to the premises of Spender and Martin, Saddlers. Mr. Martin was a beefy, red-faced man of hearty middle age. His thick-fingered hands swallowed up Drew's in a vigorous handshake once he'd introduced himself and stated the reason for his visit.

"That was a bad business, Lord Rainsby was, sir. I'm hard-pressed to think of him being throwed from his horse, but they say it can happen to anyone. A pity it is, though."

Drew turned the saddle over on the worktable, the better to display where the girth had come loose. Martin's heavy brows bunched together.

"Are you telling me this girth came loose while Lord Rainsby was riding? And that's what killed him?"

"I'm afraid so."

"No, sir." Martin thumped his heavy hand flat down on the table. "I stitched this one myself. Replaced the girth and made the stitches extra strong. Only . . . last autumn it was. Yes, last October, right before he rode Atalanta for the Thorburn hunt. There's no chance this girth came loose on its own, not even if that horse bolted straight down to Chelsea. No, sir."

"But you see it did," Drew said, pointing at the girth.

The saddler gave it a tug where it was still attached on one side. It didn't budge. Then he looked at the other side. "That never pulled loose there, sir. Look at this." He indicated the holes in the leather where the stitching had gone through. "Do you see any pulling here? Any breakage? No, sir."

Drew narrowed his eyes, studying every detail. "But the stitching could have broken, couldn't it?"

"Not my stitching, sir. No, I won't have it said." Martin leaned closer to the saddle till it was within a few inches of his face, his practiced fingers examining the place where the girth had once been fastened. "His lordship was particular about his saddle. If there was a whisper of a problem, he'd have brought it back to me. Bad stitching, though I'll let my reputation speak for me on that account, would have come to light long before now. If you were to ask me, sir . . . hold on now."

Looking puzzled, he poked a forefinger between two pieces of leather, then picked up an awl and stuck it there. He pulled out a couple of pieces of thread and showed them to Drew, his face grave. "That doesn't belong in the making of a saddle, sir. It's no wonder the girth came loose."

"This isn't what you usually use," Drew asked, touching one of the threads.

"No, sir, it's not. You might think so just to look at it. It has the same sort of color and all. But no, this is nothing more than cotton thread put a few times through to thicken it up, and I shouldn't think it would last long. Not with that girth pulled taut around a horse."

"It couldn't have been used by mistake, I take it."

Martin's eyes flashed. "It could not. Not by me, sir."

"Then how would you imagine that particular thread got there?" Drew asked, not wanting to put words in the man's mouth.

"Surely not from here—you can be certain of that much. Otherwise, if you were to ask me, whoever put that there meant for the girth to come loose. Maybe not that day, nor the next, but in time, sir. In time."

Drew was silent for a moment. He picked up the two bits of thread Martin had found, folded them inside his handkerchief, and tucked them into his waistcoat pocket. "I think you ought to come round to the police station and tell them what you just told me."

Inspector Boyd Ranald of the East Lothian Police was clearly not in the mood to be trifled with. He peered through small, close-set eyes at Drew and the saddler as if he begrudged them not only his time but also the use of the decidedly uncomfortable chairs they sat in.

"Yes, Mr. Farthering, I remember you from the day of the accident. As I told you back at the Hall, we'll be contacting you should we have any questions regarding your statement."

"I understand that, Inspector, but Mr. Martin has some vital information about the accident, and we thought you ought to know about it right away."

As Drew explained their business in his office, his harried expression changed into one of curiosity.

"And when was it you last tended to his lordship's saddle. Mr. Martin?"

The saddler told him what he had told Drew. The saddle, though old, had been well-maintained. Lord Rainsby was always careful to inspect it before he rode. Someone had tampered with the stitching, expecting his lordship to fall and be injured or killed. He did not know who that someone might be. By the time Martin had finished, the inspector's curiosity had faded.

"This stitching, Mr. Martin, you're certain it's not from your own shop?" he asked, running his hand over the thinning fair hair at the back of his head.

"I am, sir. It's nothing near the sort we use for saddles. It's more like something you might mend a blanket with."

"But it's kept in your shop?"

The saddler shrugged. "I expect we have a bit handy. In case we should need it. But for a saddle—"

"And you can swear no one in your shop, not an apprentice or someone you've newly taken on, might not have used this? Not by mistake?"

Martin shot a look at Drew, clearly unsure what he was

supposed to do. "We-ell, I suppose things of that sort can happen, but it seems terrible unlikely. I always tended to his lordship's things myself, and I'd never have done it."

"And you dealt with Lord Rainsby directly?" Ranald asked, looking through the contents of the case file spread out on his desk. "He never sent one of his people into your shop with a saddle that needed looking after?"

The saddler seemed put out. "Well, certainly he did. I'm sure his lordship had much more important things to do than to tend to petty errands, though he did consult me in person from time to time, especially when he wanted new tack for his wife or daughter. But I tell you, it was always his way to check his equipment personally before he rode. He always—"

"And it wouldn't have been even remotely possible that he sent someone in to have a repair done one day when you were out, and someone else at your shop saw to it?"

"I haven't heard any of my people mention such a thing. If Lord Rainsby—"

"But you can't swear it mightn't have happened."

Martin huffed. "I'm sure someone would have mentioned it."

Ranald looked at him, his pale eyes hard, until the saddler wilted.

"No, I can't swear to it."

The inspector nodded in satisfaction and then turned to Drew. "And what part do you play in all this, Mr. Farthering? Apart from having discovered the body after the incident."

"The victim's daughter, Miss Joan Rainsby, asked me to see what I could find out about her father's death. The investigation was so quickly concluded, she feels there could be more to be discovered, and she isn't satisfied with the ruling of accidental death."

"Isn't she now?" Ranald's Scottish accent was suddenly heavier. "Then perhaps she might've come round to speak to us here at the station rather than setting someone with no authority and no experience to muddy the waters."

"I'm sure you're perfectly right, Inspector," Drew said. "I'm doing no more than coming round to speak to you here at the station, in her stead of course, since she and her mother are in mourning."

Ranald pursed his lips. "I see. That's all to the good, then. Certainly if there is new evidence, we'll look into it. Just whom does she suspect of having done the mysterious stitching?"

"She doesn't actually know about the stitching, Inspector. She just told me, as Mr. Martin here has said, that her father was very careful about his riding equipment. She doesn't think Lord Rainsby would have missed normal wear and tear. Not wear in such an advanced state that that piece would have come away like that. I merely told her I would see what I could find out about it. Nothing more."

"No disrespect meant, sir, but let an amateur detective read too many of these penny dreadfuls and he thinks he's equipped to solve real-life murders. It's all nonsense, of course. Just makes our jobs all that much harder."

"Scandalous, I'm sure," Drew commiserated. "But no doubt you and your lads know best how to handle this case. I just thought you'd like to know what I found."

"Very good." Ranald closed the file. "Is the saddle at Mr. Martin's place of business at the moment?"

"In the boot of the Rainsbys' Triumph, actually," Drew said. "Shall we bring it inside for you?"

"I'll see to it, sir," Martin said.

"Very well." The inspector nodded toward the hallway. "Tell

Teague at the front desk to mark that 'Rainsby' and not let it get mislaid."

"Right away."

"Assure Miss Rainsby and Lady Rainsby we'll be looking into it," the inspector told Drew once the saddler was gone.

"Excellent." Drew stood. "I'll tell them you'll be in touch."

"We'll be looking into it," the inspector said severely. "No use upsetting them with a lot of unfounded theories when the simplest answer is most likely the correct one. It's quite possible we will not find anything inconsistent with our original conclusions."

"Naturally that is a possibility," Drew said, "but the saddle—"

"We'll be looking into it," Ranald said more firmly.

"Just as you say, Inspector."

Drew bade the inspector farewell. He was still smiling as he dropped Mr. Martin at his saddlery shop and then ordered Phillips to drive him back to Thorburn Hall. He'd done his duty in reporting his findings to the authorities. If they weren't interested in pursuing the matter, that left him free to follow his own line of investigation. He didn't at all believe Rainsby's death was an accident. Not at all.

— Six —

ady Louisa was sitting in her chaise longue with a neglected book lying open in her lap and a cigarette dan-
gling from her fingers, her black satin dressing gown a
striking contrast to the otherwise white room. Her feet, propped
up before her, were ensconced in little black slippers with a
ruffle of black feathers across the arch. The ashtray sitting on
the small mirrored table beside her was full to overflowing. It
was hard to tell whether she had been crying.

"Mr. Farthering would like a word with you, madam," the
maid said, her voice low and appropriately grave.

Lady Louisa looked up and managed something of a smile.
"Oh, do come in, Drew dear. Forgive me, I was miles away. Is
something wrong?"

He put both hands on the back of a straight-backed chair
with a white fur cushion. "May I?"

"Oh, yes." Her hand fluttered toward the chair. "Please."
She didn't say anything more, and when he also was silent, she
knit her brow. "Is this about Gerald?"

"I'm afraid it is. But if you'll be patient just another moment,

I'll tell you about it when your daughter gets here. I sent your maid for her."

"I'm here."

Wearing mourning far more severe than her mother's, Joan came into the room and shut the door behind her. Drew gave her his chair.

"I won't mince words," he told them. "I took the liberty of inspecting Lord Rainsby's saddle a bit more closely than before, and I had his saddler look at it, as well. It seems part of it was stitched together in a way that was meant to come apart under the pressure of riding."

Lady Louisa caught an audible breath.

Joan's slender hands clenched into fists. "Dad would never have ridden with a saddle in that sort of condition. I knew it. Oh, I knew it."

"But who would have done such a thing?" Lady Louisa asked. "Who could have wanted to kill Gerald?"

"I'm not quite certain they're actually willing to reopen the investigation," Drew said, "but I told the police about it."

There was a flash of temper in Joan's eyes. "You mean that's all? You told the police and you're leaving it at that?"

"Miss Rainsby, I assure you—"

"You assured me that you would find out what happened. You haven't found out anything."

Her mother took hold of her hand. "Please, Joanie, remember yourself."

"Someone *murdered* my father!" Joan cried, springing up from the chair and pulling away from her. "*That* is what I remember."

"Please," Drew said, "hear me out. If it isn't too much of an imposition, I'd like to stay here at the Hall for a while and see what I can uncover. As I told you before, I'm not the police, but if they're reluctant to continue on—"

"Then you will?" Joan took a deep breath and was once more cool and calm. "I'm sorry. I didn't mean to throw a tantrum."

Drew sat her back down. "It's all right. Perfectly understandable." He leaned down to have his eyes level with hers. "And yes, I will do everything I can to find out exactly what happened to your father and who's responsible for it."

Lady Louisa shoved the smoldering remains of her cigarette into the ashtray. "Drew, are you certain? I can't see how it could be—well, be what you say. Gerald didn't have any enemies. No one could have possibly wanted to kill him."

"There's always the possibility," Drew said, straightening. "An old grudge. Financial gain. Some other benefit. We'll just have to find out who it might have been."

"Are you certain it couldn't have been an accident?" she pressed, looking bewildered. "It had to have been."

Drew shook his head. "I'm afraid there seems very little chance of that."

"But who would have had the opportunity to tamper with that saddle? Only our people. Are you saying Clarridge would have done it? But why? What benefit would it give him? Do you think he may have been paid off?"

"How hard would it be to get into the tack room?" Drew asked.

Lady Louisa blinked. "I . . . I don't know."

"It's kept locked," Joan said. "My father was insistent about that, and the door lock is very strong. I don't think it could be forced open without Mr. Clarridge hearing something."

Her mother frowned. "It's open during the day, isn't it? I'm sure I've been down there when there's no one about and I've seen the tack room open."

Joan looked at her as if she were momentarily confused. "It's not like Mr. Clarridge to be so careless."

"Well, perhaps I'm remembering wrong. I don't know. It just seems incredibly bizarre to think someone might have wanted Gerald dead. Why would they?"

"It always seems only other people have such things happen to them," Drew said. "But sometimes it hits close to home."

"Then what do we do?" Lady Louisa clasped Drew's hand. "It couldn't possibly be someone we know, could it?"

"Neither of you know anyone who'd want to kill him?" Drew asked, looking from Lady Louisa to her daughter.

"Of course not," Louisa said. "I'm not saying Gerald was a saint by any means, but he was a good, honest man who always tried to do right by people. Ask anyone."

Joan looked away from her mother, far out over the water. "Maybe he was too honest."

"What do you mean?" Drew asked.

She shrugged. "Maybe he saw something or knew about something that someone had done . . . something wrong. Something someone didn't want getting out."

"Such as?"

She exhaled audibly. "I don't know. I can't think of anything, but what else could it be? Nobody stands to gain from his death but us. Mother has a life estate in the property. I understand I'm to be given a sum in trust, but I won't get the principal until I'm twenty-five."

Lady Louisa nodded.

"Until Mother's gone," Joan said, "I don't really come into much of anything."

Drew was silent for a moment, thinking. "Forgive my prying, Lady Louisa, but might I ask if there's anything more you'll inherit now that Lord Rainsby is gone?"

Louisa lifted her head, startled and looking rather hurt. "As my daughter told you, I have a life estate in Gerald's property, and then the rest goes to Joan upon my death. I understand he left me a certain amount to maintain the Hall and other holdings, as well as to provide for my needs, but it really wasn't necessary. I was left quite comfortable by my father, your great-uncle. If you would like to speak to his solicitors, you certainly have my leave to do so. They will tell you precisely what is in the will."

"No offense meant," Drew said. "Please understand, these things must be asked."

"I suppose they do," she said, softening. "And I was in earnest just now. Twining will give you our solicitor's name and address. It's a firm in London. Can't remember the name at the moment. But I'll be happy to write them, requesting that they show you whatever you'd like to see."

"Thank you. I suppose the police have already asked these things."

Lady Louisa closed her eyes. "I don't know. They seemed satisfied that it was an accident. I don't really remember what all they asked, but they're welcome to look into the will, too. It's quite straightforward."

Joan drew her dark brows together. "I thought your solicitor was Mr. Barnaby in the high street."

"Well, yes," Louisa said. "But just for some minor things. Some of your father's business matters. He'd had the London firm well before then. All his life really. They were your grand-father's solicitors when we all still lived in Cornwall."

"I don't suppose I've ever heard why you're living up here in Scotland when his estate is in Cornwall," Drew said, looking from mother to daughter.

"Oh, didn't you know? Thorburn Hall was my grandfather's estate and eventually passed down to me. When Gerald and I married, his brother Samuel was Lord Rainsby. Gerald never dreamed he'd come into the title, so we made our life up here. Even after he became Lord Rainsby, we spent most of the year in Scotland, though we always went to Cornwall in the winter where it's not so bitterly cold." Lady Louisa smiled and patted her daughter's arm. "Of course, Joan always went to English schools, so you'd hardly believe she's our little Scotswoman."

Joan's desire to roll her eyes was palpable, but she said nothing.

Her mother patted her again. "All that to say you'll have to go to London if you want to see how Gerald's estate is to be settled."

"I can't see that's entirely necessary," Drew said. "Most likely the police will look into it, if they haven't already, but it all seems very straightforward. Nothing out of the ordinary."

"Still, you will stay and see what you can find out?" Joan's hands were clenched into pale fists. "You've simply got to. Especially if the police aren't going to look into it."

"Your mother hasn't said if she wants to be bothered with all of us staying on."

"Of course you're all welcome."

Lady Louisa's words were perfectly cordial, but he could see the reluctance in her expression.

"I know this is a difficult time for you. If you'd prefer, we can all take rooms at the inn in the village. I presume there is one."

"There is, but I won't hear of your doing that." Louisa managed a wan smile. "I won't promise to be a very entertaining hostess for the rest of your stay, but I do hope you'll stay here all the same." Her lips trembled. "If someone murdered poor Gerald, I want to know who it was and why."

Drew leaned over and kissed her cheek. "I'll do my best to find out. Now, if you'll both pardon me, I'd better go tell the others we're staying on a bit."

Drew found Madeline, Nick, and Carrie in the garden. Madeline sat on the chaise with a book in her lap, but the only thing she was reading was the looks between Nick and Carrie as they walked through the roses and out to the folly some yards away.

"Drew." She made a rapid motion with one hand, urging him to come to her without making himself obvious.

With a silent chuckle, he went to her and sat at the end of the chaise. "Are we making progress?"

"I think so," she said, studying the two lovebirds for a moment. "They've been walking and talking and, oh, you know, just being together. Do you suppose he'll ask her soon?"

"I really don't know."

Her hopeful expression darkened. "What's wrong?"

"Everything. I have some news, and I'm afraid it's going to pitch a spanner into the works as far as the grand romance is concerned."

"No." Madeline darted a look toward the other couple. "What's happened?"

"I'll tell all of you at once." He stood. "I say, Nick, would you two mind coming over for a bit of a chat?"

"You've chosen better moments," Nick protested, peering out from behind an ivy-covered marble column.

Carrie laughed and came down the folly's crumbling steps, pulling him with her to where Drew and Madeline sat. "It's all right. What's your incredible news?" The light in her eyes suddenly dimmed into wariness. "What?"

"All right," he said, "here it is. There's new evidence about Lord Rainsby's death. It seems quite unlikely it was an accident."

Carrie's face lost its color. "He was murdered?"

"I expect so," Drew said, glancing at Madeline. Maybe he shouldn't have said anything yet, not until he knew more for certain. "It looks as if someone arranged for the saddle's girth to give way, causing Rainsby to fall to his death. I don't know much more than that yet."

Nick squeezed Carrie's hand and then tucked it into the crook of his arm. "Have you told the police, Drew?"

"They don't seem that interested in the case. I suppose they think I want to be a trumpery detective again and am imagining criminal activity where there is none."

"But you don't have any doubt?" Madeline asked with a glance toward her friend.

"I'm sorry, darling, but I don't. Inspector Ranald thinks it was merely a mistake by the saddlers. I'm not sure when he'll bother to look into it, or if he will at all. I can't leave the ladies of the house wondering what's happened. It's got to be worrisome to think that if Lord Rainsby was indeed murdered, one of them might also be a target."

"He was murdered." For a moment Carrie stood perfectly still, her face blank, her grip on Nick's arm tightening. "I . . . I can't stay here anymore. I'm very sorry. Please excuse me."

Nick's eyes widened as she pulled free of him and hurried away. "Carrie, sweetheart, wait! Don't—"

Drew put a hand on Nick's arm, stopping him from rushing

after her. She didn't look back. She didn't stop or even slow. They could only watch as she disappeared into the house through the French doors.

Nick stood staring at the house for the longest while. Finally he turned back to Drew and Madeline. "I've got to talk to her. I know that look."

"Better not," Drew cautioned. "Give her a bit of time."

There was grim resignation on Nick's face. "I know that look. Whatever she's decided to do, there's no shifting it now."

"Let me talk to her," Madeline said, giving Nick's hand a squeeze. "It'll be all right."

"She can't . . ." He looked toward the house once more. "She can't go. Not now."

"Come on, Nick, old man." Drew put an arm around his friend's shoulders. "Let's have a look at that tack room. The saddle's been put into evidence with the police, but now I'm wondering who might have been able to get at it over the past week or two."

Nick looked over at Madeline, but she was already in the house and gone. He turned to Drew. "I can't let her go. It's been three years, and I'm not letting her make it three more."

Madeline tapped on Carrie's door and then pushed it open. "Carrie?"

Carrie looked up from her seat at the dressing table, her nose and lips red and swollen, her blue eyes shining with tears. "I can't do this again. I can't stand by while everyone around me is murdered."

"I'm so sorry." Madeline squeezed onto the chair beside her and wrapped her in her arms.

"After what happened to Billy . . ." The tears spilled onto Carrie's pink cheeks, and she blotted them away with a lace handkerchief, leaving a dark smudge of mascara beneath each eye and on the lace. "I can't stand it."

"I know," Madeline murmured. "I know. But maybe Drew's wrong this time. Maybe it was just an accident."

Carrie shrugged away from her. "You don't believe that any more than I do. Someone murdered Lord Rainsby, and it's probably someone staying in the house. Or someone who comes visiting regularly."

"Carrie—"

"How do you stand it?" Carrie sobbed. "How do you stand being around this all the time?"

"It's not *all* the time," Madeline said weakly.

Carrie only glared at her.

"Drew doesn't set out looking for this sort of thing, but when he can help, when he can try to see that justice is done and no one else gets hurt, how can he turn his back and do nothing? How can any of us?"

"But you," Carrie pressed. "How can *you* stand it, knowing he's in danger all the time? Knowing *you're* in danger all the time?" Her lips trembled. "We were all nearly killed the last time I was in England. How am I supposed to stay here in this house knowing it might happen all over again? How do you stand it?"

"It does scare me sometimes." Madeline swallowed hard. "I sometimes wonder if Drew might not come home from one of his investigations. And when we're both involved, I sometimes wonder if we're in over our heads."

Carrie nodded. "And you are, aren't you?"

"Sometimes, I suppose."

Madeline didn't say anything else. She couldn't think of anything that might make Carrie reconsider. Nick would be heartbroken. Nick . . . She smiled just slightly.

Carrie frowned. "What?"

"I was just thinking about something Nick told me the other day," Madeline said, "about sheep."

Carrie's forehead puckered. "Sheep?"

"People generally think sheep are stupid, you know, but he says they're not." Madeline squeezed Carrie's hand. "It's only when they're afraid that they make bad decisions."

Carrie blotted her face with her handkerchief again, wiping away the streaks of mascara. She patted her bright hair, all the while looking at Madeline in the mirror.

Finally Carrie turned to face her, her hands in her lap. "I'm going home."

Madeline covered one of Carrie's hands with her own. "Please don't. You've just gotten here, and it's taken forever to get you to come in the first place."

Carrie drew a breath that was almost a sob. "I can't stay here and just wait for someone else to die." She covered her face with her hands and began crying in earnest.

Once more Madeline put her arms around her. "Shh, it's all right. Of course you don't have to stay if you don't want to. But please don't go all the way back home."

Carrie sniffled into her handkerchief again. "But where would I go?"

"Well, there must be a hotel of some sort in Gullane, don't you think? How would it be if you stayed there? Then whatever happens here at the house, you'd be away from it."

"But what about you? And . . ." She glanced toward the closed door. "And everybody?"

"I'd come with you. We wouldn't want to give the nice ladies of the village anything to gossip about, would we?"

Carrie glanced at the door again.

"Nick will understand," Madeline assured her.

Carrie sighed. "He won't like it."

"He'll like it better than having you go back to America."

The tiniest hint of a grin tugged at Carrie's lips. "Drew certainly won't like it."

"He's a big boy and can manage on his own for a day or two. He'll probably be glad to have us out of harm's way." Madeline stood and held out her hand. "Come on. The sooner we tell them, the more time they'll have to get used to the idea."

Once he'd got Madeline and Carrie adjoining rooms with a sitting room at The Swan in Gullane, Drew went to speak to Lady Louisa. It was early, but she was already retiring for the evening. He stopped her at the foot of the stairway.

"I know you must be very tired, but I was wondering if I might have a word with you before you go up. In private, if I may."

"I hope there's nothing wrong," she said, looking dismayed. "I realize this hasn't been the charming holiday everyone expected. Still, I want you all to at least be comfortable."

"No, no, it's nothing like that. Everything's perfectly fine. I just hoped to speak with you about . . . well, recent events."

Louisa smiled wearily. "I may not be able to carry on a rational conversation at this point, but I'll be happy to oblige if you'd like."

They went into her sitting room, more gleaming white on white with silver and mirrored trim, and sat down, she behind the little desk where she no doubt wrote her letters, and he across from her.

"First off, I regret to tell you that, for the present, Madeline and Miss Holland have gone to stay at The Swan in Gullane. Please don't be offended," he said when she began to protest.

"Everything here has been lovely. It's just that Miss Holland had a rather awful time of it when we were all in Beaulieu a while back, and with everything that's happened here, she prefers to be away from it all. She is terribly sorry, needless to say, and hopes you'll understand."

Lady Louisa didn't at all look as if she understood, but she was gracious enough not to say so. "Oh, of course. I'm sorry she's been upset."

"I'm sorry you've been upset with all this," Drew replied. "Naturally, Madeline went along to Gullane to keep her company, though if it's quite all right, Mr. Dennison and I will stay on here for a bit longer. Just to make sure you and Miss Rainsby are looked after."

"I hate to impose on either of you."

"It's no imposition in the least. Twining tells me the police have come back to speak to the servants and to you again. I expect they've given you a bad time of it." He didn't want to make things more difficult for her than they already were. There was always something gentle and easily hurt in her large dark eyes, now more so than ever. "They mean well, no doubt, but they can be rather tiresome."

"I suppose it had to be done." She took a cigarette from the crystal box on the desk and rummaged in the drawer for a match. "I couldn't tell them much. I don't know much." Her eyes brimmed with sudden tears as she struck a light and held it trembling to the cigarette's end. "Gerald and I were just going along as we always had done, and then . . . then we weren't."

"I know. I'm sorry."

She blew out a long plume of smoke and then waved it away. "I should have asked if you minded. It's such a habit, I scarcely know I'm doing it anymore."

"Please, don't worry yourself over it. I know it's been a very trying day for you. I hope you don't mind if I ask you what you told the police."

She blinked at him. "I'm not sure I understand why you're asking."

"Forgive me. I suppose it isn't entirely my place, but now that it's fairly certain his lordship's death wasn't accidental, I feel I owe it to him to look into matters. I just thought I'd see what the inspector's line of questioning was and what you told him." He put his hand over the one she had resting before her on the desk. "It wouldn't be too painful for you, would it?"

"It's all painful," she said with a quivering smile. "But if you can somehow figure out who killed Gerald and why, perhaps that will make it a bit easier to bear."

He patted her hand and released it. "Now, tell me what you told the police."

She was silent for a long moment, smoking and considering. "They really didn't ask me much that they hadn't asked before," she said at last. "They wanted to know if I knew who'd killed Gerald. They wanted to know if *I* had killed Gerald. They wanted to know when Joanie had gone to Cannes and when she had come back. And if she and her father had quarreled. And if I and her father had quarreled." She sighed and then spoke more rapidly. "Did I know of anyone who had any reason to have killed him? Did he have a reason to want to kill anyone? How were we doing financially? Were we very happy in our married life? Was Joan happy at home? Did any of the servants feel they had been treated unfairly? Was Clarridge happy being our stable master? Did I know anything about the saddle?" She breathed out an exasperated cloud of smoke. "I can't remember it all. I couldn't tell them anything anyway. Gerald and I got on well. We always have. Not to say we haven't had the odd spat now and again, but who hasn't? I can tell you and Madeline are just mad about each other, but I expect even you two don't always agree."

"We have our little tiffs, to be sure. Forgive me for asking, but I understand you and his lordship had your own disagreement the Wednesday before his death."

Her pale cheeks reddened. "That—that was nothing. Less than nothing."

"I would very much like to know."

Lady Louisa pressed her lips together, and Drew wondered if she would speak at all. Then she threw up her hands. "It was about Elspeth's protégé, Count Kuznetsov. Gerald said he thought the man was taking things, little things, from the house. I told him not to be absurd. He said he was going to have to ask the count and the Pikes to leave. Well, I couldn't insult Elspeth like that. She would have been mortified. I told Gerald that if he made the Pikes leave, I was going with them. He grumbled about it a bit and said he would tell Twining to keep a close eye on the silverware, and that was that. He put some of my jewelry in the safe in his study. It's still there."

Drew frowned. "And that was all there was to it?"

"I told you it was less than nothing."

"And neither of you said anything to Mrs. Pike?" he asked. "Or Mr. Pike?"

"Good heavens, no."

"Mightn't he have spoken to the count himself?"

Louisa looked as if she were about to protest, but then she checked herself. "I thought the matter was settled between us, but he was always one to give the other fellow a friendly word of advice. You know, just to let him know whatever he was doing wasn't going to be tolerated. I don't know for certain."

Drew gave her a look that encouraged her to continue.

"I'm sorry," she told him, "but I just don't know anything more to say."

"It's all right. And you didn't tell the police about any of this?"

She shook her head. "I didn't see any reason to. It wasn't a proper quarrel at all, and it can't have anything to do with Gerald's death."

"I can't guarantee that part," Drew told her. "What do you suppose would have happened if you hadn't objected to the count being put out of the house?"

"I don't know. I know Elspeth would have been humiliated. Mr. Pike might have sent the count away entirely, and she probably would have never spoken to me again after that."

"I suppose Kuznetsov himself wouldn't have enjoyed that aspect of it, losing his comfy little nest and all."

Lady Louisa's eyes widened as realization dawned on her. "You're not saying he might have killed Gerald. Don't be ridiculous. He's perfectly harmless."

"I'm not saying anything. Just trying to hunt up any possibilities."

She put her cigarette into the ashtray and rubbed her eyes with both hands. "It seems so farfetched for him or anyone we know to be a murderer. It just doesn't happen to ordinary people like us."

"I'm afraid it often does. But if you'll allow me, I'll do my best to shed a bit of light on this particular one, for Lord Rainsby's sake."

She shook her head. "I can't possibly ask you to stay up here and investigate. You've got your wife and Miss Holland and Dennison . . . it would be the most awful imposition."

"Not at all," he assured her, smiling as he stood. "Not at all. Now, I want you to try not to worry. I'm just going to snoop about a bit, nothing indiscreet."

"I suppose you are the expert in these matters."

"Not really, but I'll do what I'm able. If you happen to think of anything that might help, or anything that just seems odd or out of place, do let me know."

"I will. Certainly. But I'm sure the poor count has nothing to do with it."

"Perhaps."

"I suppose Mr. Dennison and Miss Holland were expecting something a bit more cheerful when they came to the Open."

"They'll be all right. So long as they're together."

She got up and came to his side of the desk, one hand outstretched to take his. "It's very good of you." She smiled and briefly touched his cheek. "You're so like your father."

His face turned warm. "I'll take that as a great compliment. Thank you."

"He used to blush, too," she said with the lightest of laughs. "When we were children." She exhaled, still smiling. "It *is* good to have you here, Drew."

— Seven —

When he came back downstairs, Drew found the drawing room dark and empty. Twining informed him that Mr. Dennison had walked down to The Brassie and Cleek, the village pub. He hadn't said when he meant to return. Drew took a walk of his own and found Nick sitting alone in a dim corner of the pub, an untouched mug of cider sitting before him on the table.

"What's this?" Drew thumped himself into a chair, earning a scowl from his friend.

"Go away."

"That's not very pleasant of you."

Nick's scowl deepened. "You've spoilt everything. You and your investigating. Why couldn't you have let well enough alone?"

"Not exactly the reunion you had pictured, eh?" Drew spied a grimy pack of cards on the sill of the shuttered window and snatched it up.

Nick propped his chin up with one hand. "Not half."

"Sorry." Drew started shuffling the cards. "At least she's here and not four thousand miles away."

"For all I've seen of her, she might as well be."

"Now, now," Drew said. "Faint heart and all that. Are you going to let Bunny beat you to the altar?"

Nick huffed. "Bunny. I can't imagine the sort of ninnies he and Daphne will produce."

"Be kind."

"I thought 'ninnies' was kinder than 'imbeciles.'"

"Let's deal with the matter at hand," Drew said severely. "You and Carrie had three very nice days together before all this happened. Are you saying you've made no progress in all that time?"

"All that time? We've been apart two years and I'm supposed to convince her to marry me in three days?"

"You've had letters, haven't you?" Drew rifled through the deck until he found and removed the queen of clubs, then shuffled once more and dealt them each a hand. "It's not as if you hadn't kept in touch with her."

"I know." Nick frowned as he picked up his cards. "What's this?"

"Old Maid."

Nick snorted but made no further protest.

"And be honest," Drew said, taking up his cards and sorting through them, "don't you think she's come here not just to visit but to decide whether or not she'll stay?"

"I hope she has," Nick said, putting down the red jacks, the black twos and the black tens, "but I can't say for certain that's what she has in mind. Especially now."

"Why don't you just ask her?"

Drew discarded five pairs, two black and three red, and selected

a card from the ones Nick held. Not finding a match, he offered
up his own hand.

"I've tried." Nick selected a card and put down the red kings.
"Every time I gather up my courage, something seems to interrupt us." He repeated the process three times more with black
aces, black nines, and red threes.

"Then don't let it." Drew chose a card from Nick's hand,
then let him draw again. "Who's master here? You or those
infernal interruptions?"

"Well, there has been a murder, you know. I couldn't very
well make an impassioned declaration in the face of that."

"I'll grant you, but you had three days before to do your woo-
ing. Why didn't you punch anyone who disrupted your plans?"

Nick looked at the card he'd drawn and scowled. "The main
one was you."

"Me?" Drew smirked, glad to be rid of the queen of spades,
the Old Maid herself. "I never."

"You did. It was when Carrie and I had gone to get a choc
ice. I'd just worked up my courage to really and truly say something, and you came galloping over and dragged us back to the
first hole."

"But Henry Cotton was about to tee off."

"That's as may be," Nick said, letting Drew choose another
card from his hand. "Carrie and I never had a moment to ourselves all the rest of the day and precious little of the time since."

"Dash it all, man, then take the time. She doesn't want anything to do with . . . Hullo."

"What is it?" Nick asked.

"No, don't look round. Just keep talking. But don't make
yourself noticeable. He hasn't seen us, and I'd rather he didn't."

"Who hasn't seen us?" Nick demanded. "What's he doing?"

"Keep it down," Drew hissed. "It's MacArthur. He's going to the telephone."

MacArthur leaned against the wall, his back to them, and picked up the receiver. When he spoke, Drew heard only a low murmur, words here and there.

". . . since the death . . . staying on . . . won't leave it to them . . . could be awkward . . ." Then Mac's voice grew more urgent. "No, no, it's too late now. We must go on with it. Tomorrow, yes. Thought you'd want Schmidt to know." Once again his words became less distinguishable. ". . . as usual . . . yes, here. They know . . ." He was silent for several seconds, his expression intent. "I'll talk to him. I'll—" He broke off.

"He's seen us," Drew murmured, and then he smiled and raised his mug.

Mac gaped at him and gave a little wave. "Right," he said, his voice clear and hearty now. "That's fine then. Tomorrow afternoon. Should be a fine day to play. Cheerio." He rang off and came to Drew's table. "Didn't see you young fellows there. Usually quiet in here this early on. Thought I'd have a round of golf with some old school chums of mine. Either of you played Muirfield? It's a fine course. Old Tom Morris's, you know."

"It's been a bit awkward to bring up that sort of thing at the Hall," Drew said. "Lord Rainsby's death, as you can imagine."

"Oh, of course. Of course. But Rainsby would have wanted us to carry on."

"I daresay."

"Not the sort to sour anyone's enjoyment," Mac said, "especially when it came to a round of golf." His smile was unsteady. "Well, I suppose I'll be on my way. Now that poor Gerald's gone, the company always seems to have one loose end or another that wants tying up."

Not waiting for a response, he hurried across the room and out the door.

"Joan said he's been rather odd lately," Drew said.

"He certainly was just then." Nick leaned back in his chair so he could get a better look at the telephone. "I wouldn't half like to know who was on the other end of that line."

The next morning, in the lull between breakfast and lunch, Drew went up to Lady Louisa's sitting room and peeked in through the open door. Her ladyship was seated at her desk, pen in hand as she read over what she had written.

"'It is very good of Your Eminence to remember us in prayer. We take great comfort—'" She broke off, seeing Drew there.

"I'm sorry to disturb you," he said. "Perhaps I should come back another time."

She sat up straighter and stretched her shoulders. "No, no. I think I need to stop anyway, at least for the present. I don't know how many of these condolences I've answered and how many more there are to do, and it's not something one leaves to a secretary."

"I don't doubt his lordship was greatly admired and is even more greatly missed."

A look of pain and pride crossed her face, and she held out her hand to him. "Come sit down and tell me what you've all been doing. I've been an abominable hostess, I know."

"Not at all," he assured her, sitting across the desk from her. "We couldn't very well abandon you in a time of crisis, could we?"

She looked down at the paper she'd been writing on. Drew remembered the invitation she had sent, asking them to come up for the Open. He remembered Madeline remarking on the loveliness of Lady Louisa's copperplate script. This now was a rather unsteady imitation.

"I suppose it's easier to do the little mundane things than think too much of what's happened." She ruffled a stack of letters in the tray beside her. "Or of all the important things that will have to be seen to. Death duties and a million other legal matters I know nothing about. Gerald always saw to everything."

"Your solicitor should be able to guide you through it," Drew said. "He'd be the most familiar with the details. But if there's any way I can be of help, do let me know."

"But that's not what you came to see me about."

"No," he admitted. "I was just wondering about something Lord Rainsby said to me."

Her dark brows lifted. "About what?"

"You were kind enough to invite me and my wife to stay for the Open, and even more kind not to object to us bringing along our friends."

She laughed softly, and some of the tiredness in her eyes eased. "I told you I love having company."

He nodded. "But I want you to think very carefully now. Whose idea was it to invite us?"

"Whose idea was it? I . . . I suppose it was both of ours. I was looking at the *Times* about Lord Hurstlyn's wedding, and Gerald pointed out that photograph of you and Madeline. She looked so lovely. The description said she wore rose satin. Anyway, he said we ought to have some young people come up to the Hall. For Joanie, you know. And we talked about getting reacquainted with your branch of the family and that we'd both seen your photograph in the papers when you were in some of the charity tournaments, and it just seemed a brilliant idea to have you come for the Open."

"He told me he suggested it."

Louisa shrugged. "It could have been."

"He also said he suggested it for a particular reason."

"You mean because of Joan."

"He didn't mention that to me, no."

"Then why?"

Drew pondered what to say next. Lord Rainsby hadn't wanted to trouble his wife, especially with unfounded gossip. But now he was dead, and there was obviously more going on at Thorburn Hall than first met the eye. The master of the house was no longer available for questioning, but the mistress was. "Did your husband ever mention being concerned about Mr. MacArthur?"

"About Mac? No, of course not. Concerned about what?"

"That's just the problem," Drew admitted. "He didn't actually say. He told me he didn't want to stir up trouble if there wasn't any, and that he didn't want to worry you for no reason. And he didn't want to put ideas in my head about what might be going on."

"I suppose that makes sense." She tapped her lips with one finger. "I don't know of anything, but then Gerald was always keeping things from me." She smiled. "Nothing scandalous, so don't get that look on your face. You told me yourself he said he didn't want to worry me. That's why I know next to nothing about his business affairs or the estate. Now I wish he'd taught me how to look after it all."

"So he never mentioned MacArthur? They didn't have a falling-out?"

"Of course not. They'd been the best of friends since before the war."

"And his lordship never got cross with him? They didn't have words, even something that's been patched up since?"

She waved one hand negligently. "Even the best of friends have their fallings-out, don't they?"

"Tell me what you remember your husband complaining of about him."

"Oh, little things mostly. Mac wanted to expand the business and sell to some foreign companies, but Gerald didn't think the trouble of dealing with all the regulations would be worth it. They quarreled about politics sometimes, but men always do."

"What about politics?" Drew prompted.

"I really don't know," she said, exasperated. "That sort of thing bores me to distraction, and the minute they'd start bickering over it, I'd stop listening."

Drew thought back on what MacArthur had said about politics the morning Lord Rainsby died. "What was his lordship's opinion of Mr. Hitler in Berlin?"

"Not a good one. I thought he'd order Mac out of the house over it the last time."

"Was it that bad?"

"They didn't come to blows," she said. "Only just nearly. Mac said he thought maybe Mr. Hitler was strong enough to stabilize Germany and keep the Bolsheviks at bay. Gerald told him Hitler was a bully who ought not to be humored."

"And then . . . ?"

"Then we didn't have him to dinner for some time. But it blew over, at least for the most part. Gerald liked him. Always had. But, really, who wouldn't? I never had a disagreement with him. Well, except once. He always tells me I spoil Joan, and I suppose he's right, but what's a little girl for but to be pet and spoilt?"

"To be sure," Drew said with an indulgent smile. "Has she quarreled with MacArthur?"

Lady Louisa shook her head. "Not quarreled. Not really."

"But she doesn't care for him."

"Oh, he was always telling Gerald and me that she was too grown up now to always be given her way. It wasn't good for her. Now you give me the name of just one young girl who appreciates anyone who tries to spoil her fun."

Drew chuckled. "I'm afraid you have the better of me there."

"I tell her all the time she won't appreciate us until we're gone." The spark of humor in Louisa's eyes died, and she looked down, absently stroking the black velvet trim on her sleeve. "Poor child."

Drew was silent until she looked up again. "And you don't know of anything else his lordship could have been concerned about with MacArthur? They didn't quarrel again?"

She shook her head. "No. I'm sorry. There isn't anything. Mac seemed busier than usual, not coming to visit as much as he had, but I thought that was because the business was picking up and he didn't have the time."

"That seems the most likely case," Drew said, and then he stood. "I trust you'll be joining us at lunch?"

"Yes. I've been up here alone long enough. Gerald wouldn't have wanted that. Not because of him."

"No, of course not." He gave her a wink. "I've had a peep into the kitchen. Welsh rarebit and strawberries with clotted cream."

"Strawberries for you, I'm afraid, but not me. I'm terribly allergic. But Gerald loved them and so does Joanie, so we have them often, especially when we have guests. But Cook usually makes cinnamon apples for an alternative, so I don't have to miss out on a sweet entirely."

"Apples or strawberries, we can't do without you."

That made her smile again. "We can't have that, can we? Will Madeline and Miss Holland be joining us?"

"I'm afraid Mr. Dennison has taken Miss Holland into Edinburgh for lunch and perhaps a look at the sights. But I'm going to fetch Madeline at precisely eleven-thirty and escort her back here."

"Lovely," Lady Louisa said.

"Oh." Drew turned at the door. "Do you know if Mr. MacArthur has a particular lady friend just now? I understand he and his wife parted ways not too long ago."

Louisa's smile faded. "Yes, poor man, though he never speaks of it. But I don't know that he's seeing anyone at the moment. Of course, he wouldn't say anything about women to me. I suppose he and Gerald talked about that sort of thing. Men always do."

"We're notorious gossips," Drew admitted. "It's a terrible scandal."

"You know, now that you ask, I think there is someone. Gerald saw them together a time or two."

"He didn't know her name by chance?"

"Not that he ever told me." Lady Louisa thought for a moment. "All he said was that she was an attractive blond girl. Far too young, but never tell Mac I said so."

He put one finger to his lips. "Mum's the word."

Drew took the short walk into Gullane with nothing more in mind than collecting Madeline from The Swan and escorting her back to the Hall for luncheon. As he passed a little tearoom called Juster's, he noticed a motor car parked in the street. It was a drab color, small, cheaply made, not the kind that would generally attract his attention, except he was almost certain he'd seen it before.

He slowed as he walked alongside it, peeping into the front seat to see if anything looked familiar. There wasn't much, but he certainly recognized it. A leather bag, three or four notebooks with little scraps of paper sticking out from between the pages, a scruffy-looking wool scarf in a hideous shade of mustard that looked as if it had been stuffed under the seat at least since the previous autumn and left out in all weather, a newspaper . . .

He frowned. It was today's edition of *The Rosyth Register*, a local newspaper from about thirty miles west of Gullane. Most of it was covered up by the notebooks, but he could see it all the same. Rosyth. Coincidence?

He took a quick look round. The street was still empty, so he took a pencil from his coat pocket and used it to open one of the notebooks. Figures, sketches, notes that made little sense to him except he was certain they had to do with mapmaking. Still careful not to touch anything, he used the pencil to prod the leather bag, but it didn't budge even slightly. Something heavy inside, no doubt. Tools perhaps? They had to be.

He made a slow circle around the car. Nothing unusual. The rear seat was empty. He didn't dare try to open the boot. Still, that newspaper . . . it was such a little thing, but then Lord Rainsby had given him precious little to go on.

Seeing nothing else of note, he strolled again in the direction of The Swan. He had just passed the tearoom door when it opened behind him.

"Farthering."

He was not surprised to turn and see MacArthur.

"Hullo." Drew offered the man his hand. "Stopped in for a

bite of lunch? You should have come over to the Hall. I'm sure Lady Louisa would have enjoyed seeing you."

MacArthur shrugged and fiddled with the hat he still carried. "Thought I'd better make myself scarce a bit for now, don't you know. Joan and all."

"Yes, well, perhaps that's best. So where are you bound? Off to work?"

"Done for the day, I think," MacArthur said. "At least the outdoor bit of it. Now I must take my notes back home and make them into something useful."

He glanced toward the notebooks in the front seat, and his eyes widened almost imperceptibly. He tossed his hat into the car, and it just happened to land so it blocked Drew's view of the newspaper.

Drew smiled. "I see. I hope you didn't have to travel too far this morning. That can be rather tiring day in, day out, I suppose."

"Not this morning, I'm happy to say. I did some work down on the beach about a mile east of here. Almost a holiday, it was such light work."

"Jolly nice for you, I'd say, though I wonder you didn't leave your car at home and walk, it being such a pleasant day."

MacArthur gaped at him for a moment. "No. Heh, uh, no, wouldn't do at all. Too much to carry, and more in the boot, don't you know. Wouldn't do at all."

"Right," Drew said. "I suppose that's why you're the expert. Well, if I can't convince you to come back to Thorburn with me, I suppose I'd better go collect Madeline before she thinks I've forgotten her."

"She's far too charming for that," MacArthur said with blustering gallantry, and Drew tipped his hat.

"I'll tell her you said so. Good afternoon."

It seemed rather obvious now that MacArthur had been to Rosyth that morning and didn't want anyone to know it. Rosyth was where the navy dockyard was located, not far from the naval base at Port Edgar. Drew would have a lot to discuss with Madeline during their walk back to the Hall.

Luncheon at Thorburn Hall was interrupted by Twining's announcement of the arrival of Inspector Ranald. Sergeant Shaw, looking more than ever like Pitt the Younger, was at his side. Drew was determined to make an ally of the man.

"I understand, Sergeant, that we have a mutual acquaintance in Chief Inspector Birdsong of the Hampshire Police," Drew said once the inspector had bid Lady Louisa good afternoon.

The sergeant beamed at him. "Yes, sir. I was in Winchester my first two years with the police."

"More to the matter at hand, Shaw," Ranald snapped.

"Yes, sir," the sergeant said, his face suddenly stone. "Sorry, sir."

Ranald glared at him and then turned to Lady Louisa. "Do forgive me, my lady, but I have business with Count Kuznetsov."

The count dabbed his mouth with his napkin. "With me, Inspector?"

Ranald gave him a curt nod. "I should like to make an inspection of your things, if you please."

"My things? Most certainly not. It is an impertinence, sir, and I won't have it." Kuznetsov stood and put his hands on his hips, his chin thrust defiantly forward. "This is a civilized country, and I am not required to have my personal effects rifled through without a proper warrant."

Ranald took a folded page from his coat pocket and handed it to the count. With a sneer, Kuznetsov opened it and glanced over it. Then his mouth tightened. "This is an outrage." Lady Louisa stood, her napkin clutched in her hand. "What do you mean by this?"

"It's ridiculous," Joan muttered under her breath. Pike took the paper from the count. Mrs. Pike tugged his arm lower, and they both looked over the document.

Pike returned it to the inspector. "Looks legal to me."

"It is all perfectly in order, sir," the inspector said, sounding as if he was already bored with the entire matter. "Now, if you will accompany us to your quarters, Count Kuznetsov, we will make this as brief as possible."

Drew stood to go with them, but Ranald held up his hand. "Just the count, if you please, Mr. Farthering. If anyone else is required, I will send the sergeant down."

Drew sat again, unable to do more than shrug when Madeline looked questioningly at him. Everyone stayed at the table, speaking in low voices, drinking what was left of their morning tea or coffee, until Ranald and Shaw escorted Kuznetsov back into the dining room. The sergeant carried Kuznetsov's small traveling bag. The count turned his eyes martyr-like toward heaven.

"I beg your pardon, Lady Rainsby," the inspector said, "but I would like to know if you recognize this." He held out his hand, displaying a gold ring set with two emerald chips.

Lady Louisa took it from him, looking from it to Kuznetsov to Mrs. Pike. "It's one of mine. Not very valuable. Why have you brought it down here?"

"When was the last time you remember seeing it, my lady?" Ranald said, bypassing her question.

"I'm sure I don't know, Inspector. I wear it now and again

just for sentimental reasons. An old school friend gave it to me. Why?"

"We found it and a number of other valuables in Count Kuznetsov's luggage."

Ranald took the case from his sergeant, set it on the table, and opened it. Inside were several small items. Lady Louisa pressed her lips together.

Mrs. Pike wrung her podgy little hands. "Oh, Louisa, there must be a mistake. I'm sure he can explain everything. Misha, tell her. Alfred, you have to get the inspector to understand."

"I understand perfectly," Ranald said, and he put one hand on Kuznetsov's shoulder. "Mikhail Kuznetsov, I arrest you for the murder of Lord Gerald Rainsby on or about the morning of June twenty-seventh. Sergeant Shaw, if you please."

There was a general and startled intake of breath as Shaw took firm hold of the count's arm.

Kuznetsov's already pale face went white. "Murder? I . . . Madam. Mr. Farthering."

"I must warn you," Ranald said, "that anything you say will be taken down and might be given in evidence."

"This is ridiculous," Mrs. Pike yipped, her stout little body quivering with indignation. "Murder? I've never heard anything so rude. Alfred—"

"Be quiet, Elspeth," her husband told her. He stood between her and Ranald. "Now, what is this about, Inspector? My wife—"

"Your wife, sir, should do a better job of choosing her friends."

Pike's heavy jaw quivered, but he said nothing.

"Yes, Inspector, what is this about?" Drew asked. "You may have grounds to charge him with theft, but murder?"

"I'll have to ask you not to interfere, Mr. Farthering. Finding these items in the count's possession was the last bit of confirmation we needed in order to bring charges."

"Mr. Farthering," Kuznetsov pled, "surely you can convince these Cossacks that I am entirely innocent."

"Patience one moment," Drew told him. "Now, Inspector, precisely what evidence do you have against this man?"

Ranald smirked. "Besides all the stolen articles?"

"They're hardly worth bothering over," Lady Louisa said, her tone severe. "I can't see how they prove anything."

"Mr. Farthering," the Russian protested, "dear sir, you must tell them that all of that was a misunderstanding of the most innocent variety. Surely Lady Rainsby would not want such scandalous doings here in her own home." He looked desperately at Lady Louisa, but she responded with only a shake of her head.

"Please, Inspector, it's very true," Drew said. "To be sure, there are these little items and there was the matter of some spoons, but that's been sorted out already. Lady Rainsby—"

"Her ladyship already told us about that, sir," the inspector said implacably, taking charge of the prisoner. "If you will just step aside now, thank you, we'll just be going."

"But Inspector—"

Ranald stopped short where he was, still with Kuznetsov by the arm. "Mr. Farthering, I have had quite a chat with your Chief Inspector Birdsong. I don't know how they do it down in Hampshire—rather curiously, if you ask me—but here in Scotland we have our own ways. And when one man has good reason to kill another and that second man ends up in the kirkyard, well then, we look upon that first man with a rather disapproving eye."

"You don't think he could have killed Lord Rainsby over a few demitasse spoons, do you? That's absurd."

"It may seem so to you, but that is a motive. Perhaps not just the spoons, but all these valuables. And, actually, not over these items themselves, which we understand amount to less than a hundred pounds, but for fear his lordship was going to speak to his patroness, Mrs. Pike, over what he'd done and cause her to withdraw her support."

"It's a travesty," Kuznetsov said. "Madam would never believe such a tale. She would—"

"Inspector, you must stop this nonsense at once." Mrs. Pike pushed away her husband's restraining hand, looking more like a breathless Pekinese than ever. "Misha, now you must tell him you did no such thing as killing his lordship or anyone. Louisa, you simply cannot believe such tales."

"I will have to ask you to compose yourself, madam," the inspector said. "This gentleman is under arrest, and if you attempt to interfere with duly sworn officers in the performance of their duties, you could be charged with a criminal offense yourself."

She blinked, horrified, then clutched Drew's arm. "Please, Mr. Farthering, surely there's something you can do. Lady Rainsby—"

"Lady Rainsby won't be able to do anything just at the moment," Drew said as soothingly as possible. "I'm afraid these gentlemen have to carry on doing their job until we can get everything sorted."

Kuznetsov made a squeak of protest.

"But I'll see what I can find out," Drew assured them both. "In an unofficial capacity, of course," he told Ranald. "Surely the accused has the right to counsel and to visits from friends and family."

"We will do everything possible to put everything right," Lady Louisa said, a touch of urgency in her voice, and then she took her friend's arm. "Don't worry, Elspeth dear."

"Everything will all be seen to," the inspector said. "In time." He put on his hat and tugged at the brim. "Good afternoon, Lady Rainsby. Ladies. Gentlemen."

Ignoring Mrs. Pike's continued objections, he propelled his prisoner out of the dining room. A moment later there was the sound of his car sputtering to life out on the front drive, and soon it faded into the distance.

It took a few minutes and promises of immediate action to calm Mrs. Pike. Joan moved as far away from her as possible, obviously nettled by the little woman's lack of restraint.

"Ridiculous," she muttered again, lighting one of her ever-present cigarettes. "The worst they could charge the buffoon with is being insufferably annoying."

"Well," Mrs. Pike huffed.

Lady Louisa patted her hand, glaring at her daughter. "I'm so sorry this has happened, Elspeth. It has to be a dreadful mistake."

"Sounds to me," Drew observed, "as though they had to make an arrest, no matter how little they have to go on. Just so the public would see something was being done about the case. Now I expect they'll assign some poor blighter fresh out of school for his defense and he'll be hanged by Friday."

"No, he will not," Mrs. Pike insisted. "We'll have our Mr. Devlin from London come up. I'm sure he can be here by this evening."

"Elspeth," Mr. Pike rumbled warily, "Devlin is involved in a very important case just now. He can't—"

"Now, yes, Alfred. Yes, he can. You can arrange everything, I know. You'd like Mr. Devlin," she told Drew, waving her plump hands and brightening again. "He's a terribly clever man for a solicitor and dances beautifully."

"I'm sure that makes all the difference," Lady Louisa soothed.

"Let's go into the library and have some tea to settle us down. What do you think?"

"Yes," Mrs. Pike said thoughtfully. "Tea would be just the thing. Oh, it's just too irritating. You don't think Misha could have killed his lordship, Louisa. You can't think so."

"No, no. Of course not."

By then she had the other woman through the dining room door and halfway down the corridor.

"I'd better go telephone down to London," Pike said with a sigh. "Devlin won't come, but he ought to know someone up here who can take the case."

Joan watched him trundle away. "I don't know which of the two is more absurd, she for buying the so-called count's clap-trap or he for humoring her." She gave a humorless huff of a laugh. "Ridiculous."

"It does seem a bit ridiculous, Ranald actually arresting the man," Drew said. "But, again, I suppose once it got out that that saddle was tampered with, he felt he ought to be seen doing something about it."

Joan looked up at him, the sneer gone from her lips, leaving a vulnerable softness in her expression. "Are you making any progress yet? Anything at all?"

"No," Drew admitted. "I'm sorry." He studied her piquant face, trying to judge whether she was up to answering his questions just now. He decided to forge ahead. "Do you know anything about Mr. MacArthur? About his personal life, I mean. Your mother thinks he's seeing someone. Do you know anything about that?"

She shrugged, her expression turning hard again. "I couldn't say. He was always so chummy with Mother and Dad, I don't know how he'd have time for anything else. And Dad, he was too busy most times, which left Mother and Mac chatting away as if they had been the ones in the war together. But a girl?" She smirked. "I don't know. Why do you ask?"

"Just trying to find out who's who and what's what." Drew smiled. "I think you and I agree that Kuznetsov is a very unlikely murderer. But I'm rather stumped over who's a better candidate."

"Can't say I've paid much attention to the older set lately." She wandered off, still smoking, thoughtful lines in her forehead.

Drew took Madeline's arm, and they walked out into the garden.

"I hadn't anticipated this particular turn of events," he told her.

"Me either." Madeline plucked one of the abundant pink roses and brought it briefly to her nose. "I wish she'd been paying attention."

"It would have helped." He looked out over the water, listening to the endless rush against the rocks and sand. Port Edgar and Rosyth Dockyard weren't so far up the coast.

"What are you thinking?" she asked.

"Just wondering about Mac and who might make up that foursome he was arranging."

"What do you mean?"

"What was Lord Rainsby thinking when he asked me to investigate? I suppose a mapmaker sees a lot of places and knows many things . . . or might find them out anyway. Pass them along perhaps. At the right price."

"Why else would Mr. MacArthur lie about being in Rosyth?" She pressed a little closer to him. "It's a scary thought."

He nodded, leaned over and kissed her forehead. "I suppose I'll go round to see the count tomorrow. If Ranald will let me."

— Eight —

The police station in Gullane was fairly much like any Drew had seen, small and drab with a wall of cubbyholes behind the front desk and two small holding cells. The officer on duty, a Scotsman with blazing red hair and absolutely no sense of humor, finally agreed to let Drew have five minutes with the prisoner only, as he said, to spare himself the bother of looking to see whether there was a local ordinance prohibiting infernal nuisances.

Drew found Kuznetsov seated on the edge of the cot that was pushed against the back wall of his cell, head in hands and shoulders drooping. Drew had to speak to him twice before he deigned to look up. Even then that lasted only a moment before he looked back down again.

"There is nothing that can be done," he said, his voice low and mournful. "You may as well go now."

"I thought you might answer a few questions for me before I leave you to your own devices," Drew replied, lounging against the wall to his left.

"Questions? I was questioned for three days without rest by

the Bolsheviki before I escaped and was smuggled out of Russia. I am no stranger to interrogation."

"I promise it won't take that much of your time." Drew gestured to the unoccupied end of the cot. "May I?"

Kuznetsov inclined his head in almost-regal acceptance. Drew sat down and looked directly into the other man's dark eyes. "Who are you, really?"

"What do you mean, sir?" Kuznetsov drew himself up, chin defiant. "I am Count Mikhail Yevgeni Kazimir Sevastyan Kuznetsov, second son of Kazimir Artemiy Savely Kuznetsov, and one time of the court of His Imperial Majesty, Tsar Nicholas the Second of blessed memory."

"Mikhail Kuznetsov and his father and elder brother were killed in August of 1917," Drew said, "when the tsar and his family were taken to Tobolsk 'for protection.'"

Kuznetsov slumped back against the brick wall. "Yes, Gregor and Papa were slaughtered by the Bolsheviki, but they took me prisoner."

"I've had my solicitors look into this for me," Drew said, unimpressed with the look of deep grief on the man's face. "All three were killed that same day and buried in a mass grave."

Kuznetsov covered his eyes with one languid hand. "It was horrible. I was thrown in with the dead, shot through the shoulder and arm and side, and grazed along the temple. I was driven nearly mad, returning to consciousness only to find myself wrapped in some sort of coarse cloth and smothered with earth. I could not even scream."

Drew nodded patiently. "And yet here you are."

"It was my great good fortune that three passing peasants heard me and managed to free me before I perished of pure fright."

"They heard you not screaming?"

Kuznetsov pursed his lips. "I did the best I could to make it known I was yet alive. Fortunately, the Bolsheviki were as incompetent at burial details as they were at most everything else, and there was no more than a foot of earth covering me. The peasants quickly dug me out and put me in their cart, covered over the grave again, and smuggled me away to freedom."

Drew nodded. "You weren't pursued?"

"No. I spent months in the most hideous of peasant dwellings, recovering somehow despite the dearth of proper food or sanitation. When I was well again, I was smuggled into Poland and eventually made my way into Germany and then France. It was nearly a year between the time I left Russia and found my way to your England."

"And the Bolsheviks never caught you again?"

Kuznetsov looked piously to the heavens. "I thank God."

"That's quite a tale," Drew said, a slight smile touching his lips. "But I must know something. If it isn't too painful for you to discuss, of course."

Kuznetsov made an airy gesture with one hand.

"I'd like to know," Drew said, leaning confidentially closer, "how they managed to interrogate you for three days if you and your father and brother were shot the day they took the royal family to Tobolsk and you were buried with them."

"That was another time I was taken prisoner," Kuznetsov said, clearly unfazed. "I was in Minsk in service of His Imperial Majesty, and the Bolsheviki—"

"No." Drew held up one hand. "While I am certain the story of your interrogation and subsequent escape is a fascinating one, perhaps it's best saved for another time."

"If one of the sisters from St. Elisabeth's hadn't been willing to sacrifice her second-best habit—"

In spite of his best efforts, Drew couldn't keep from chuckling, and Kuznetsov drew himself up again.

"No offense meant," Drew said. "I was just picturing you disguised as a nun, wimple and all."

"If you knew what I'd risked even then for the tsar and his family—"

"Have you ever even been to Russia?"

Kuznetsov sighed. "Ah, well, believe what you will. I am indeed a man without a country."

"You are a man without shame, I will grant you that much," Drew said. "No, don't bother looking tragic. Mrs. Pike isn't here at the moment."

"It grieves me to think you hold such an opinion of me, sir."

"You'll feel a trifle more grieved if you're hanged, I promise you." Drew glanced toward the front desk, where the officer who had admitted him was watching with keen, suspicious eyes, and lowered his voice. "Let's drop this Russian count nonsense, shall we? If I'm going to help you get out of this tangle, I need to know the truth."

Kuznetsov stared at him, eyes narrowed. "Why should you help me?"

"You're a despicable thief, an outrageous liar, and the most abominable sponge I believe I've ever met," Drew told him, "but I don't think you're a murderer. At least I haven't seen any evidence of it."

"That's something," Kuznetsov said, brightening.

"Now, why don't you tell me who you really are?"

Kuznetsov shrugged lazily. "Thief, liar, and sponge fairly much covers it, I think. But I rather like to think of myself as a Robin Hood, stealing from the rich what they can well afford to lose, and giving to the poor."

"The poor being yourself, I take it."

"Call it an entertainment expense if you like," Kuznetsov said. "As you can tell, Monsieur Pike is not deceived about me in the least. But it pleases madam, his wife, to think she is a great patroness to receive such little flatteries as I am in a position to give, sparing him the need to give them himself. For that he is willing to pay, despite his grumbling. And when we go to visit, I also pay court to our hostesses, such innocent attentions as their husbands have long neglected and cannot be troubled to remember."

"That would explain your attentions to Lady Louisa."

"But of course. And if in such a place I help myself to a little remembrance here or there, is that not the smallest of remunerations for my excellent services?"

"I can't say I recommend your methods, but at least you seem to have reasoned it out to your own satisfaction. Now tell me about you and Lord Rainsby."

"I suppose he didn't care for my . . . borrowing his cuff links."

"Stealing them, you mean."

Kuznetsov shrugged indifferently. "He left them on the sideboard. I thought he didn't want them anymore."

"Naturally. And what else?"

"A pearl bracelet that was carelessly left locked in a bureau upstairs."

Drew pursed his lips. "And?"

"The silver letter tray. Four seafood forks. Half a dozen of those gold-plated—"

"In other words, whatever you could smuggle out without its being missed. Too bad you didn't get away with those demitasse spoons."

Again Kuznetsov shrugged.

"And is this your usual practice when you go visiting?"

"Certainly not!" The count's dark eyes turned stormy. "Only when I am in particular need of cash, and only where I think there is a good chance of not being caught."

Drew couldn't help a low laugh from escaping, not at the man's petty crimes but at his brazenness. "And when you *are* caught?"

He made a dismissive gesture. "It is the merest of accidents. A foolish mistake when packing the bags. A teaspoon fallen unnoticed into the cuff of a trouser or a jacket pocket. A watch so similar to my own, combined with a bit too much port after dinner the night before. Every item, I assure you, I was just about to return with apologies. Surely these things could happen to anyone."

"And no one has ever accused you of theft?"

"Sometimes a small payment is required to smooth down the less agreeable of our hosts, especially when we stay in hotels. From time to time, monsieur scolds and then is scolded by madam for disturbing my rather delicate sensibilities. And then he is made to become more generous with my spending money so I will have no need to create such a scandal when next we go to visit. Such things one must bear, she will tell you readily, when in the presence of great genius."

"Lord Rainsby had had enough of this, is that right?"

"He said nothing to me," Kuznetsov said, "but I understand he and Lady Rainsby quarreled over whether or not I should be put out of the house. It seems that before they could reach an agreement on the matter, his lordship had his accident. Tragic. Quite tragic."

"Is that all the police have against you?" Drew asked. "This quarrel of the Rainsbys?"

"To my knowledge, yes. And that anyone in or out of the house could have tampered with his saddle." There was a wounded look in the Russian's expression. "Also because I am not British."

"And you didn't kill him? Just so you didn't lose your nice cozy berth with the Pikes?"

"I did not."

Drew studied his face for a long moment. For once, he felt as if the man was telling the truth. "Very well," he said, standing. "I'll do what I can to find out what really happened to Lord Rainsby. I owe the family that much."

"Ah, yes." There was something sly, something like amusement in the Russian's eyes now. "A fine family, no matter how one might be attached to it."

To Drew's surprise, it was Sergeant Shaw who unlocked the cell and walked with Drew out of the station.

"I thought escorting visitors would be left to the lowly constables," Drew said, looking about to see if Ranald was within hearing distance.

"I heard you'd come to see Kuznetsov." Shaw also peered down the hallway. "Just between two private citizens, I can't say I agreed with the inspector on his arrest. Not much of a motive, if you ask me. But once it got about that the accident was no accident, most likely, I suppose he felt he had to show that those in his department weren't sitting about doing nothing."

"Seems a poor reason for depriving a man of his liberty," Drew said. "Not that this particular man might not deserve to be deprived of his liberty for a certain period, but that doesn't make him a murderer."

"No." They were at the street door now, and once more Shaw looked about. "Look here, Mr. Farthering, unless and until there is further evidence that proves otherwise, the inspector is satisfied he has his man and has assigned me to work other cases. Me, I'm not so satisfied."

"So, what do you have in mind?" Drew asked. "Perhaps an informal exchange of ideas?"

"Two private citizens, say, simply discussing the day's news?" Shaw looked indifferent. "Might be done. In strictest confidence, mind you."

"Naturally."

"Are you familiar with Gullane, sir?" the sergeant asked.

"Not really. I've walked about a bit with my wife and our friends, been out to Muirfield."

"There's a pub not far from the course, The Brassie and Cleek. Many of our visitors pass it by. Now that's a great shame, sir, because it's as fine a place to have a nice chat with a friend as ever I've seen."

Drew suppressed a smile. "I was there quite recently, in point of fact. Is there any particular time you'd recommend?"

"Hard to say. It's quiet most evenings. Now and again there's a Friday or Saturday worth a chance visit. At least that's when I go, if I go at all. But I think tonight or tomorrow night might be the ideal time. I've always found that about seven o'clock things start to get interesting."

"Well then, I'll have to give it a try this evening. I don't think I'd be able to wait till tomorrow."

The sergeant nodded. "I wager you won't be disappointed, sir. Don't forget, The Brassie and Cleek, just off the main road."

Madeline peeped into the dress-shop window, admiring a shell-pink dress with puffed sleeves and a sweetheart neckline. She tugged Carrie's arm.

"Isn't that darling? It's just a little day dress, probably cotton, but it's so sweet. Nick would love you in that."

Carrie put a hand to her red-gold curls. "You know I can't wear pink. Too bad it's not white."

"What about those?" Madeline pointed out a pair of cream-colored pumps sprinkled with a rainbow of polka dots. "You should get those."

Carrie's somber expression didn't change. "Don't be silly."

"I'm not. No one could possibly be unhappy wearing shoes like that."

One corner of Carrie's mouth twitched. "I'm not so sure that's true. Besides, what would I wear them with?"

"Anything you want. Whatever you choose, there's got to be a dot on them that matches it."

"Now you *are* being silly."

"All right," Madeline admitted, "you couldn't wear them to a formal occasion, but they'd be lovely for afternoon tea or shopping or nearly anything. They'd be perfect for a summery cream-colored linen dress."

"I can tell you already they would be too big for me. I can never find shoes that fit."

"Maybe they have another pair inside." Madeline gave her friend her most appealing look. "Please. Just try them on."

"They won't fit, I promise you."

"All right. If they don't fit, I won't say anything else about it. If they do, you have to get them."

She led Carrie into the shop. The freckle-faced girl who waited on them was no more than fifteen, and she had such a thick Scottish accent it was hard to understand her most of the time. But once she had sat them down and made much of Carrie's "wee darlin' foot" and lamented she herself had feet "like a great dray horse," she disappeared into the shop's back room to see what was in inventory.

"She's not going to have any that fit," Carrie said, getting up so she could look around.

Madeline joined her. "Then we'll have some made for you. My treat."

Carrie scoffed. "That would take forever."

"Good. Then you'll have to stay with us a while longer." Carrie made a great show of looking at a pair of long black gloves.

"You don't really want to leave, do you?" Madeline asked.

"Not really."

Carrie only shrugged, not meeting her eyes.

"I know you love Nick. Don't say you don't."

Carrie didn't answer.

"He's crazy about you. You do know that, don't you?"

Carrie still said nothing, unfastening and refastening a tiny jet button on one of the gloves as she stared out the shop window. Then her fine brows knit. "Isn't that Mr. MacArthur?"

Madeline looked out the window and saw the man walking on the other side of the street. "Turn this way a little," she urged. "Pretend we're looking at this dress."

As she spoke, a woman turned from where she had been looking through magazines at the newsstand across the way. Young and fair-haired, dressed in a tailored dark skirt and jacket that did not quite conceal her curvaceous figure. It was the girl they had seen twice at Muirfield, once with MacArthur and once with the man they had assumed was a caddie.

There was something purposeful, even grim, about her expression when she walked to MacArthur's side and spoke to him. Something in his reply must have pleased her, because the sunniest of smiles bloomed on her face as she leaned up and kissed him. Then she took his arm, looking up at him in almost-worshipful bliss. A moment later they had reached the corner and were gone from sight.

Madeline nodded. "I see."

"Can I turn around now?" Carrie asked. "Not that I didn't see everything anyway. What was that about?"

"I'm not sure," Madeline said. "Drew thinks that just might be why Mr. MacArthur is no longer married to Mrs. MacArthur."

Carrie put a gloved hand on her hip. "I can tell when someone's after a sugar daddy."

"That was not a fatherly kiss," Madeline agreed, and she tugged at Carrie's sleeve. "Hurry. We might still be able to see where they went."

"Wait," Carrie protested. "The girl's bringing back my—"

"I'm sorry, miss!" Madeline called as she pulled Carrie toward the door. "We'll come back!"

They reached the corner where the couple had disappeared, but that part of the street was deserted. Madeline looked up and down the street once more, scanning the names of the different shops. None of them seemed any more likely than the others to be the destination of MacArthur and his young companion.

"We shouldn't be following him," Carrie said, her drawl more pronounced in her agitation. "What if he saw us? What in the world would we say?"

"We'd say we got turned around going back to the inn and we don't know which way to go and couldn't he direct us."

Carrie pointed back the way they had come. "But it's just—"

"I know it's just over there. I know any six-year-old could find his way back, but it doesn't matter if you look helpless enough. Someone like our Mr. MacArthur wouldn't expect us to worry our pretty heads over directions."

Carrie giggled and then caught a sudden breath. "There he is."

Madeline tugged Carrie back into the doorway of a jewelry shop and pretended to look in the window. She could see MacArthur's reflection in the glass. He came out of the bookstore, took a quick look around, and then headed back toward the high street, passing behind but not noticing them. A moment later, he turned another corner and was gone again.

"Come on."

Madeline strode over to the bookstore, a place called Dunst's, very tiny, even for a place like Gullane. But judging from the window display, it was well stocked. There was a whole stack of copies of a book called *Enter a Murderer* by an author Madeline had never heard of and whose name she wasn't sure she could pronounce. Whatever else happened, she was determined to get herself a copy before she left.

"What are you doing?" Carrie protested, scurrying after her. "We can't go in there. They'll know we've been following him."

"Don't be silly. How can they possibly know that?" Madeline reached for the doorknob. "We're just in town for the Open, and you're visiting from America. We're looking for some books on local history and, for my golf-loving husband, something about Muirfield. Right? And I want that new mystery."

Carrie nodded, despite not looking entirely convinced, as Madeline pushed open the door. There was a jangle of bells, the kind that was a combination of several small bells, clashing together in merry discord. The gray-haired woman behind the counter was placid and plump, her smile slightly shy.

"Good afternoon, young ladies. May I help you?"

Madeline forced herself not to look at Carrie and hoped

Carrie was wise enough not to look startled. Judging by her accent, the woman was German. That didn't automatically add up to something sinister, of course, but it seemed rather a coincidence that Mac would have come in here. Maybe he had just wanted a book. But where had the girl gone? Certainly not out the front door.

"We're just looking really," Madeline said. "I hope you don't mind if we browse."

"We wanted some golfing books," Carrie said, her voice a little higher pitched than usual.

Golfing books? Madeline struggled not to cringe. *Please don't say anything else, Carrie. Please.*

"Some books about golf? They are very popular during the Open." The older woman came from behind the counter and led them over to a table where a variety of books on the game were on display. "Did you want something about golf history or how to play? Or perhaps something about our course? Muirfield is nearly two hundred years old, you know."

She sold them a book on the Open and one about the Firth of Forth and the Naigo Marsh mystery Madeline had seen in the window. Madeline managed to discourage Carrie's whispered questions until they had made their escape back into the high street.

"What good did that do?" Carrie demanded, walking as fast as her short legs would allow. "It's just a bookstore."

"Maybe. Maybe not."

Madeline looked right and then left, preparing to cross the street to The Swan. When she looked right again, the blonde was standing directly opposite them, smoking a cigarette. Seeing Madeline had noticed her, she gave a brash little wave and hurried over to them.

"You're Mrs. Farthering, aren't you? Isn't it funny our meeting at last? My friend Mr. MacArthur pointed out you and Mr. Farthering to me last week at the tournament. I have to tell you, your husband is perfectly charming. He ought to be in the cinema, don't you think?" She dropped her cigarette to the street and extinguished it with a brusque turn of her shoe and then smiled at Carrie. "Hello. I'm Lisa Shearer. I work at Dunst's. It's not much of a shop, is it? But I guess I should be glad for the work. Anyway, I saw you both and thought I'd better introduce myself."

"I beg your pardon," Madeline said, a bit taken aback. "Yes, I'm Mrs. Farthering. This is my friend, Miss Carrie Holland, who's visiting from America."

Carrie managed a polite nod. "Hello."

"Yes," Lisa said, "I remember you at the Open, as well. Isn't it just too bad about Lord Rainsby? I understand it was a very exciting third round, and Mac and I were disappointed to have to miss it, but he and Lord Rainsby were great friends. It just wouldn't have looked the thing if we'd gone."

"You didn't go anyway?" Madeline asked.

The girl lifted one shoulder. "Not without Mackie. It's just not as much fun alone."

"No, I suppose not."

"I can tell you'd be terribly put out if you had to go about without Mr. Farthering," Lisa said pleasantly. She put a gloved hand on Madeline's arm. "He's the one I've read about in the newspapers, isn't he? Not just in the society pages but for solving crimes and things?"

"A few times," Madeline said reluctantly.

Lisa released Madeline's arm and put her hand over her heart. "Good gracious me, I think I'd be terribly worried if

Mac did that sort of thing. I mean, anything could happen to him."

Madeline smiled coolly. "My husband is well able to take care of himself."

"Well, of course he is. I can tell by what I've read, he's more than a pretty face. And he's got that mate of his, Dennismoore or something, to give him a hand."

"Dennison," Carrie corrected, her mouth taut.

"Yes, that's the name." Lisa stopped for a moment, thinking, and then smiled again. "And you're Carrie Holland. Now I know where I've heard of you. You were in that business at Winteroak House, down in Beaulieu. That must have been terrifying." Her mouth dropped open at the stricken look on Carrie's face. "Oh, do forgive me, Miss Holland, that was so thoughtless of me. Please accept my apologies. That must have been so terrible for you."

Carrie merely nodded her head, but now there was a tinge of anger in her usually sweet expression.

"And think," Lisa said, looking with concern at Madeline, "how awful it would be to lose not a brother or a beau but a husband that way." She shook her head. "I'm so glad my Mackie isn't the sort to put himself in danger like that. If we were married and he wanted to investigate Lord Rainsby's death, I'd have to put my foot down. I really would." She laid her hand on Madeline's arm once more. "But you know how men are, always wanting to play the hero. They never get over being boys, do they? Even Mac, and he's hardly a lad anymore." She giggled. "Don't tell him I said that. Of course, I'm mad about him, just as he is. He pretends it doesn't bother him, the difference between our ages, but I think sometimes it does. He tries to make himself look as young as possible, and I say who wants to look old anyway?"

"We haven't seen much of Mr. MacArthur since the funeral," Madeline said, her voice intentionally grave. "Do tell him Carrie and I said hello."

"I will. And you tell that ducky husband of yours to watch out for himself. His sort don't come along every day."

She brought her hand up to her black felt hat before the wind could carry it off and, laughing, hurried down the street toward the bookstore.

Carrie's lips tightened into a fierce pucker. "I don't know when I've ever heard such rudeness."

"I don't know if I'd call it rudeness," Madeline said. "If that wasn't meant to warn us off, I don't know what it was."

"Just who does she think she is?"

Madeline looked down the now-empty street. "That's what I'd like to know."

— Nine —

Drew made sure to be at the pub just before seven that evening. About a quarter past the hour, Sergeant Ellar Shaw came in and walked past his table.

"Sergeant Shaw," Drew said, lifting his half-full glass of cider.

"Mr. Farthering." Shaw's pale eyebrows inched up his forehead. "What a surprise."

"Come sit down and discuss the day's news with me."

"I'd be most obliged, sir. Simply as a private citizen, mind you, and not in any official capacity."

"That doesn't mean you can't give a fellow a bit of advice, does it?" Drew flashed his most guileless smile. "After all, if I'm not to get myself killed by my meddling as Chief Inspector Birdsong so often recommends, wouldn't you be willing to do what little you're able to see that doesn't happen?"

Shaw sat across the table from him.

"Excellent." Drew beamed at him. "Now, seeing as we both have grave misgivings about the likelihood that your current detainee is in fact guilty of more than petty theft, I was wondering if we might have a brief discussion about one Mr. Reginald MacArthur."

Shaw's affable expression darkened. "Mr. MacArthur, sir?"

"I'd like to know what you know about him."

"Nothing out of the ordinary. Makes maps and such. Friend of Lord and Lady Rainsby. Is there a reason you ask?"

Drew told him briefly about Lord Rainsby's concerns.

"The devil of it is that he was so deuced vague about it all, I didn't think much of it. Now that he's been murdered, I wish I'd pressed him for more specific information."

Shaw considered for a moment. "But you have your own suspicions, is that it, sir?"

Drew frowned. "*Suspicion* may be too strong a word. *Wondering* is a bit more precise. For example, why would MacArthur claim to have been in Gullane all morning when he'd clearly been at least over to Rosyth and back? And I've been wondering since the first day of the Open who that blond girl is."

"Blond girl?"

"I'd say she stands about up to my chin, fair hair, young but not ingénueish. I don't know a great deal more about her than that. I've seen her with MacArthur a few times. My wife saw her going in and out of the bookshop when she was in the village, though she wasn't sure if the girl actually has any connection with it or was just passing by."

"You mean Dunst's. I think I know the girl you're talking about. About twenty-five? Easy on the eyes?"

Drew nodded.

"You must mean Miss Shearer." Shaw grinned. "A real pip, isn't she?"

"She is that. I'm just wondering what's behind those obvious attractions."

"Anything in particular?" the sergeant asked.

"Tell me about her," Drew said rather than answering him.

"Don't know much. She hasn't had any dealings with us at the station. Works at the shop helping out the old lady. Delivers orders when need be. Helps out behind the counter. Lives over the shop, I believe." Shaw shrugged. "Been here in Gullane eight or ten months, I'd reckon. Maybe a year, but I don't think it's been that long."

"And the other lady? Mrs. Dunst, I presume?"

"Yes, Mrs. Clara Dunst. She came here, oh, sixteen or seventeen years ago. War refugee, I'm told, and glad to have got out. Harmless old soul."

"Hmmm."

If MacArthur was selling information to the Germans and this Lisa Shearer was his contact, where better might she find cover than with an unsuspecting old lady from her own country? It was an enormous assumption to make based on the infinitesimal bit of information he had so far, but it was certainly something he could look into.

"You don't know someone called Schmidt by any chance?" Drew asked.

Shaw shook his head slowly. "Not here, no. There *was* a fellow in Winchester who sang in the choir. Little chap but with a booming bass voice. That was ten, fifteen years ago now."

Drew chuckled. "Any reason Miss Shearer would be in touch with him?"

"Can't imagine why," Shaw said. "Don't know of him or any other Schmidt being in Gullane. Does she have an interest in someone by that name?"

"I don't know." Drew exhaled. "Just a thought. Do you know if she keeps company with one of the caddies over at Muirfield?"

Shaw frowned. "Any one you'd especially like to know about?"

"I couldn't tell you his name," Drew admitted. "In point of fact, I never saw him myself. But my wife saw him and Miss Shearer together in the clubhouse on the first day of the tournament. Tall fellow, quite handsome she says, very blond but with dark eyes."

"Sounds like Jamie Tyler to me. Still this side of thirty?"

"I expect. Who's he?"

"Lord Rainsby asked the inspector to have him checked over a few months ago. Wanted to find a reason to have the man brought in."

"Why's that?"

"From what I've heard, he was seeing his lordship's daughter, and that didn't quite meet with approval. We never found anything, of course, except the man's a bit of a bounder when it comes to the ladies. But there's not actually a law against that."

"Well, well," Drew said, "it's a small world entirely."

"And you think he has some connection to Miss Shearer, do you?"

Drew looked thoughtfully into his cider. "I'm not quite sure. She just doesn't seem to be what she presents herself to be. I wish . . . Look here, Shaw, you don't happen to know any Germans, do you?"

"Germans, sir?"

"I need to borrow someone who speaks fluent German. Someone who can tell a convincing tale and not give the game away. Any ideas? Obviously, Frau Dunst will not suit the purpose."

"Have you tried the German embassy?"

"Let no one tell you you're not a droll man."

Shaw frowned. "What do you want a German for?"

"I'd like to carry out a little experiment if I can. I might not really prove anything, but it could be quite interesting."

The sergeant considered for a moment. "It's not anything too hard to do, is it? I mean, you don't need a sprinter or a weight lifter, right?"

"A child could do it," Drew assured him. "The right child, mind you. Do you have someone in mind?"

"Might have. If it doesn't take too long."

"Not more than a minute. If that."

"All right," Shaw said. "I might have someone who'd suit."

"Excellent. I thought you would perhaps have some connections in the area."

"As you might expect, most of my connections are related to the force somehow, and you know the inspector isn't exactly receptive to your methods of investigation."

Drew nodded. "And he has persisted in making the most ill-conceived arrests I have ever seen, even—if you'll pardon the observation and not repeat it to Chief Inspector Birdsong—in Hampshire."

Shaw pursed his lips. "You know, sir, I can't help being a bit sad I left before you started helping out down there. The chief inspector must be a treat to listen to when he goes on about meddling amateurs."

Drew laughed. "You have no idea."

"Sadly," the sergeant added, "my inspector doesn't keep an open mind on the question of civilians participating in investigations, so the usual resources won't be available. But I think I know someone, just as a private citizen, mind you, who might be just what you're looking for. What's the plan?"

Remembering the bit of telephone conversation he had over-heard in the pub, Drew leaned closer and lowered his voice. "I think I know when and where Mr. MacArthur is going to be meeting Lisa."

Shaw made a telephone call from the pub and, between him and Drew, the necessary arrangements were made. After it was done, Drew bid the sergeant good-night and made his way to The Swan to have supper with Madeline.

"She was trying to scare us," she said, once she'd told him about her meeting with Lisa Shearer. "I think she expects me to ask you to drop the case. And she was abominable to Carrie. I wanted to hit the girl over the head with my handbag."

"From what you told me, that was a definite threat. I hope we haven't landed in a nest of spies like that couple in *The 39 Steps* the other day. They ended up in Scotland, too."

"Ugh, don't remind me. It was very good, but maybe a little too close to home. I hope Nick took Carrie to something fun. She doesn't need to be thinking of spies and murder just now."

"True," he said, "but I do. Oh, and remember that caddie you saw Lisa talking to on the first day of the Open? His name's Jamie Tyler, and he just happens to be the man Lord Rainsby warned away from Joan before she went to Cannes."

"Not really."

"Yes, really, and don't ask me how he fits in with Lisa yet, because I haven't a clue. Tell me, darling, why would a jolly nice English girl who clerks in a bookshop want to threaten anyone? Especially a fine fellow like me?"

Madeline reached across the table and took his hand. "You will be careful, won't you?"

"Me?" He laughed and brought her hand to his lips. "Of course I'll be careful. When was I ever not careful?"

"Do you want me to write you a list?"

"Darling." Again he kissed her hand, first the back and then, more tenderly, the palm. "Do you want me to abandon the case? I will, if you truly want me to."

Her anxious expression softened. "No, I suppose not. Not yet. The poor count can't be left to languish in prison when a child of two could tell he's not guilty. We can't leave the Rainsbys not knowing what happened, either." She tightened her grasp on his hand and then let him go, a faintly self-conscious smile on her full lips. "So how do you think Lisa fits into all of this?"

"It's early days yet, but I can't help but go back to what Lord Rainsby said about Mac and about what Mac himself said to me the morning Rainsby died. He'd changed, according to his lordship, in the past little while, and I found out our Miss Shearer hasn't lived in Gullane even a year yet. Let's just suppose that in the execution of her duties delivering books for old Mrs. Dunst, she finds herself in excellent position to find out who in this area might be willing—at the proper price, needless to say—to give to Mr. Hitler and his people bits of choice information that might give them a particular advantage should a conflict arise between our two nations. Besides Rosyth and Port Edgar, who knows what other locations they may have targeted?"

There was a touch of anger in Madeline's expression now. "Why does it always have to be the nice ones? I like him. He seems just so . . . decent."

"That's what bothered Lord Rainsby. He knew the man, and then again he didn't." Drew took a deep drink of his after-dinner coffee, not as soothed by its rich warmth as he had expected to be. "But we don't really know yet. Maybe he's just making his maps for the local town councils. Maybe Lisa just wants him left alone after the tragic and accidental death of his dear friend. Maybe this Tyler fellow's just a caddie. And maybe Birdsong was right and I imagine sinister plots where there aren't any."

She eyed him narrowly. "You don't really believe that."

"No," he admitted. "There is definitely something untoward going on here, yet I don't want to rush off to tell MI5 when I've so little to go on. And don't suggest Inspector Ranald, darling. He'd want more proof than MI5 would ask for."

"I suppose you're right." With a huff, she leaned her chin on one hand. "How are we going to prove anything, one way or the other? It's not as though Mr. MacArthur and Miss Shearer are going to tell you the truth if you ask them what they're up to."

"Ah, but that's where my little experiment comes in. It may not prove anything. In fact, it's more likely to be a bust than not, but it may be very telling. All we can do is try."

Before she could reply, Nick and Carrie came into the dining room of The Swan, still talking over the film they had just seen, a jolly romantic comedy with Fred MacMurray and Claudette Colbert. Carrie looked so happy just to have spent a pleasant evening with Nick, Drew thought it wise to comply with Madeline's silent plea to say nothing about his plans for the next day. Instead, he ordered more coffee and some of Mrs. Drummond's excellent trifle for everyone.

Drew watched from the window of the greengrocer's as MacArthur stood across and little ways down the street in front of the butcher shop. Every so often the older man glanced at his watch. But it was not quite time, and if Lisa Shearer was who Drew suspected she was, she wouldn't be late.

She was one minute early.

Mac looked more wary than eager when he saw her walking toward him, but she showed no emotion at all. She merely came to his side and said something close to his ear. Then she smiled and took his arm, and they walked out of the shade of the shop's awning and down the street.

Drew waited until they were almost to the corner and then went barreling out of the grocer's.

"Pardon me," MacArthur said, his eyes wide. "Farthering. Where'd you come from?"

"Sorry about that." Smiling, Drew caught hold of the man's hand, pumping it up and down. "I thought you were going to be on the links today."

"That . . . well, er, one of the chaps had a headache," Mac blustered, "so we made it for next week instead."

"That *is* a pity. Oh, I beg your pardon." He swept off his hat and made a little bow toward the blonde. "Good afternoon, miss." Drew looked expectantly at MacArthur.

"Oh, ah, yes, forgive me. Lisa, allow me to introduce Mr. Drew Farthering. He and his wife are staying at Thorburn Hall. Farthering, this is Miss Lisa Shearer, a, uh, friend of mine."

"Pleased to meet you, Miss Shearer. I believe you met my wife and her friend yesterday. And we saw you out at Muirfield last week during the Open."

She smiled, displaying perfect teeth. "I'm sorry Mac didn't introduce us then. I always enjoy meeting his friends. And, yes, I did meet Mrs. Farthering and Miss Holland yesterday. We had a nice little chat, though surely your wife didn't bore you with our girl talk."

"In point of fact, she did, Miss Shearer. Not that I was bored, to be sure. It's very kind of you to be concerned about us, and I hope if you wish to send me any other messages, you'll address them to me directly. I'd hate for my wife to be bothered with my petty affairs."

Before she could reply, one of the passersby, an elderly gentleman leaning heavily on his cane, stopped next to her and offered whatever was wadded into his gnarled hand. "*Entschuldigen Sie bitte, das ist aus ihrer Tasche gefallen.*"

The girl's hand twitched toward the bag over her shoulder, and then she stopped herself and turned to the old man with a puzzled expression. "I'm sorry?"

Drew forced himself not to look smug. She was a cool one, after all, but not quite cool enough.

The old man blinked at her and cleared his throat. "Do pardon me, miss. I thought you were one of the young German ladies who lives in the flat next to mine."

Lisa smiled, coolly polite. "No. Sorry."

"I hope I have not annoyed you." He made a courtly bow and opened his fist, displaying a lady's lace handkerchief. "I thought perhaps this was yours."

"I'm very sorry, but no, it isn't."

"I beg your pardon." The man lifted his dark Homburg hat in a brief display of snow-white curls under a dark, brimless cap. "Gentlemen. Good afternoon." Using his cane, he turned and made his way slowly past the grocer's and around the corner.

Lisa watched him until he was out of sight. "Mine indeed," she said. "As if I'd carry such a pitiful-looking scrap of a handkerchief. I expect he thought I'd pay him for it."

"He was just being polite," MacArthur told her with a glance at Drew. "There was no harm done."

She merely shrugged, and then smiled once more and clung to his arm. "Now, Mackie, don't let's quarrel over something so silly on my afternoon out. I thought you were going to take me to Edinburgh to that tea shop I've been just perishing to try."

"Well, naturally. I'm sure Mr. Farthering will excuse us."

Drew raised an eyebrow. "You must have quite a generous employer, Miss Shearer, to have a holiday on a Thursday afternoon."

"Mrs. Dunst is a dear," Lisa said. "I've had to work late several nights this week, bringing in new inventory, and she gave me this afternoon to make it up to me. Poor thing, she struggles as it is to keep me and herself on what the shop makes, but she tries to show her appreciation how she can."

"I suppose she has no family."

"I'm afraid not."

"Ah. Then you're the one who looks after her." Drew gave her the mildest of smiles. "That's good. I'd hate for anyone to take advantage of her kindness and trust."

"You needn't worry, Mr. Farthering. I'll see to her."

"Excellent. Please tell her that if she needs anything while I'm here in Gullane, she need only call on me. We can't have too many bookshops, if I'm any judge, and I'm only too happy to give her any assistance I'm able."

"I'll tell her," Lisa said, a knowing glint of humor in her blue eyes. "Though, really, Mr. Farthering, perhaps we both should carry our own messages."

"Very true, Miss Shearer. Very true." Drew bowed again and tipped his hat. "Well, don't let me keep you two. I'm glad we've met at last. I suppose I'll see you about the Hall now and again, Mac. Enjoy your tea."

Drew waited until they were gone and then strolled into the grocer's once more. The old man with the cane was watching from the window Drew had been at when Lisa first arrived.

"Not only does the young lady not speak German," he said, "she doesn't care to hear it spoken."

Drew took back the handkerchief, exchanging it for a five-pound note. "You've done wonderfully. Thank you."

The old man looked a trifle bewildered. "This seems much too generous for such a small bit of work, young man. I'm not even certain what I have done."

"Worth every penny, sir, I promise you. Now mum's the word, eh?"

There was something delightfully old-fashioned about the old man's bow. "You have my assurance. And God make your way a successful one."

"And yours, sir."

"Oh," Drew added before the other man could leave, "give my best to Sergeant Shaw."

The man's rheumy eyes lit. "Next time I see him going into his flat, I will tell him. We nearly always meet each other on the stairs. But I fear he will tell me no more of this affair than you have."

"Some things are best kept in the dark," Drew said. "Perhaps someday the good sergeant will explain it all to you."

"Perhaps he will."

They shook hands and parted.

"I'm back," Drew announced once he had returned to The Swan later that afternoon, setting down the package he carried under one arm. "Anything new to report?"

Madeline put her arms around him, pressing close. "Only that Nick and Carrie have been out all day, and I've missed you terribly."

149

He laid his cheek against the top of her head, breathing in the lilac scent of her hair. "I can't say I much care for this living apart, but I suppose it can't be helped for now."

He felt her giggle against his chest. "We'll have some lovely catching up to do when this is all over, won't we?"

She looked up at him, and he smiled. "We most certainly shall. For now, though, would you like me to tell you what I uncovered during my travels?"

"Yes, please. But first let me see what you've brought me."

He laughed, watching her tugging at the strings on the package. "You're an acquisitive little creature and a presumptuous one. Those are mine."

She was undeterred, and he finally cut the knot with his pocketknife. She pulled the paper and strings away.

"Oooh." She beamed at him, opening the first of the two books, a heavily illustrated volume of patterns for crewel embroidery. "Isn't it delicious? Look how pretty that one is."

He didn't much care one way or another for embroidery, but the look on her face when she showed him a photograph of thread-painted birds and flowers made the book worth every penny.

"I told you, that's mine." He tried taking the book from her, but that only earned him a swat on the hand.

"What's this one?" She picked up the novel, which had on its dust jacket a portrait of a girl in a powdered wig and Georgian dress. "*The Convenient Marriage.*"

"It's a romance, according to Mrs. Dunst at the bookshop. She says it's a delight and I ought to have it." He held out his hand. "Come along now. Don't keep me waiting."

"I ought to make you read it, just for telling such outrageous lies."

He kissed her cheek. "All right. I got them both for you, because you got nothing for yourself when you were there yesterday."

"Nonsense. I got that new mystery by that woman whose name I can't pronounce. Actually, I got it for us. But thank you, darling." She grinned. "How like my ducky husband to bring me these. I'd forgotten how much I enjoy Mrs. Heyer's novels, and I haven't had a new one in ages. But I thought you went out to track down Mac and Lisa, not go shopping for more books."

"I did, but then I was a bit worried about old Mrs. Dunst. If Lisa's got something going on, the poor woman is right in harm's way."

"What did you think of her?"

He shrugged. "She's just as you described her: shy and silver-haired, perhaps a bit too fond of her own cooking, looks more at home in the last century than the present one. Lisa says she's got no family, so I made sure she knew we'd be keeping an eye on the lady, at least from a distance."

Madeline drew him down beside her on the floral sofa, eyes eager. "What about Lisa? Do you really think she's a Nazi spy?"

"I can't say that for certain quite yet," he admitted, "but she does speak German, or at least understands it, no matter how much she pretends she doesn't."

He told Madeline about the little experiment he had conducted, repeating the German phrase the old man had been told to say.

"What does it mean?" Madeline asked.

"Just that something had fallen out of her handbag. He had a handkerchief in his hand, but he was careful not to let her see what it was. If she didn't speak German, there was no reason for her to reach for her bag."

"So she did reach for it?"

"Just the slightest bit, yes. She nearly carried off not knowing what he'd said. If I hadn't been watching for it, I would never have noticed. It was only a tiny slip, but it was a slip nonetheless. She knew exactly what he was saying. So, if she is not involved in something at least somewhat dodgy, why would she pretend otherwise?"

"That makes it look bad for Mac," Madeline said. "Unless we're to believe she's no more than a romantic interest."

"That's seeming less and less likely all the time, though we still don't know enough to be certain yet." He thought for a moment. "Tell me again about the time you saw her in the clubhouse at Muirfield. When she was talking to that caddie, Tyler."

Madeline's forehead puckered. "There wasn't all that much to it. He went over to her, they exchanged a few words, and then they went their separate ways. I don't have a clue what they talked about, though she seemed a little brusque. Do you think it means something?"

"I don't know. Did he give her anything? Or take anything from her?"

"I don't think so. At least I didn't see anything."

"Did he touch her at all? Her hand or her sleeve? Or maybe he picked up something from the floor?"

Madeline shook her head, and then she stopped. "He did. He took her hand. It was just for an instant, but I remember it now. She pulled away from him, but he definitely held her hand. Do you think she gave him a note or something?"

"Could well be. Now I'm wondering if Lord Rainsby suspected him and Mac both. He may have had more than one reason for wanting Joan to steer clear of him. If he had, I wish he'd told me about it before it was too late."

He sighed and then saw that had brought a look of concern

to her face. Without warning, he pulled her into his arms. "Very well, Mrs. Farthering, tell me your deepest, darkest secrets or I'll never let you go."

She pressed her lips together and turned her face dramatically away.

"Oh, it's that way, is it?" He narrowed his eyes at her. "Very well, me proud beauty, tell me your deepest, darkest secrets or I *will* let you go."

"No, no!" she pled, turning to him with the back of one hand pressed to her forehead. "Not that! Anything but that. I'll tell you anything." Then she gave him a pert kiss on the nose. "But over dinner. I'm famished."

Drew and Madeline went into Edinburgh to the little French restaurant the Pikes had recommended. He tried his best to leave the investigation behind him for the evening, and for the most part he did. Still, he couldn't help but think about it now and again. But once he'd left Madeline at her room back at The Swan with no more than a longing good-night kiss, he decided he'd see if Lady Louisa was still up.

If Mac was involved with Lisa, and Lisa had connections to Tyler, that brought everything round to Lord Rainsby's unspoken suspicions. The only thing Drew knew to do was to see if Louisa knew more about it than she had already told him. He found her reading in the library.

"Good evening," he said, coming only partway into the room. "I didn't know whether you would have already retired."

"Oh, Drew, do come in. What time is it?" She glanced up at the crystal clock on the mantel. "I was so engrossed in my book, I didn't realize it had grown so late."

"Has everyone else gone to bed?"

"Yes. It's been very quiet. Poor Elspeth is distraught about Count Kuznetsov, of course, and Mr. Pike doesn't quite know what to do with her. And Joanie is so unhappy. She tries to pretend she isn't, but I don't think she always can. It's been an awful time for everyone."

"Forgive my bringing this up," he said after a moment's silence, "but I understand Lord Rainsby and your daughter had a quarrel before his death."

Lady Louisa's mouth tightened. "What has that to do with anything?"

"I was told they had words before she went to Cannes."

"I don't know what you call 'words.' Girls her age always squabble with their parents, don't they?"

"I was just wondering if you knew what they had discussed."

Looking faintly annoyed, Lady Louisa thought for a minute. "It was hardly anything, really. Joan hasn't been much out in the world yet. We've tried to make it plain to her that there are men who might . . . show interest in her because of her money and position rather than out of any genuine feeling. She claims she would know if someone like that was pursuing her, but she's such a child yet. An attractive man, a man of experience, a man of the world, well, he could turn the head of a girl who didn't know any better. We merely wanted her not to be deceived."

"So there was someone like that?"

Louisa sighed. "One of the caddies from Muirfield. Taylor or Tyler or something of that sort."

"Tyler, I believe."

"Tyler, then. Gerald told me he has a most disreputable character. More than one girl's father has had to pay him off to stave off a scandal. Do you believe it? Joan wanted to bring him here. Naturally, we told her she would do no such thing. I'm afraid Mac is right. We've indulged her far too much, and I won't say there weren't words exchanged, but it all blew over. She went to Cannes to cool off a bit, and that was all there was to it."

"I see." Drew paused for a moment. "I hate to be indelicate about anything so personal, but I must ask. Was there . . . any sort of payment made?"

"No. Well, perhaps a very small one. Gerald played at Muirfield one afternoon a few weeks ago, and he had the man brought to him at the clubhouse afterwards. He made it clear that if he continued to annoy our daughter, he would come to regret it. The caddie was a bit sullen about it according to my husband, but he seemed to understand where he stood. Joan was furious, of course, although I think she understood . . . in time."

"Naturally."

Lady Louisa's expression was cool. "I'm sorry, but there's not much more I can tell you about it. I wasn't there. Actually, I never met the man. My husband said he'd be considered quite attractive, in a low sort of way, but I'm afraid that was about all."

"Did he mention anything else Tyler said?"

Louisa shook her head.

"Was there any sort of political objection to him?"

"Political?" Lady Louisa frowned. "You mean he was Labour? Of course, I expect he would be, a man like that, but that wouldn't have come as a surprise to my husband. He'd object to it, naturally, but that was all part of why we didn't want him seeing Joan."

"No, I mean more than that. I understand his lordship objected to some of the things Mr. MacArthur has said about the current political situation in Germany. Is it possible this Jamie Tyler shared his sympathies toward Mr. Hitler?"

Lady Louisa laughed. "That's just as silly as your asking about Mac earlier on. What difference does it make what that man in Germany does? It's all just so much talk. If his people like it that way, that's their business, isn't it?"

"Yes, I suppose. Except for the ones who've got the short end of the stick over there."

Her forehead wrinkled. "You don't think it's really as bad as that, do you?"

"It doesn't sound very hopeful. But maybe our PM and Mr. Roosevelt and some of the other chaps in charge can convince Hitler to behave himself. Someone has to stand up for the defenseless."

"Yes," she said, her eyes troubled now. "Of course they will."

"Anyhow, did Lord Rainsby say anything about that when he told you about Tyler? Anything political at all?"

"No. Nothing. He said they talked about Joan and nothing else."

Drew smiled at her, and she seemed to relax again.

"But you will see they release Elspeth's count, won't you? The poor dear, she's terribly upset."

He promised to do what he could and bade her good-night.

— Ten —

The next morning, Drew went to the clubhouse at Muirfield, looking for the caddie with light hair and dark
eyes. There was no sign of him inside, so Drew strolled
out to the first hole, watching as several parties teed off. There
were a number of boys and young men caddying for the players,
but none of them fit the description of Jamie Tyler.

"Carry your bag, sir?" A fresh-faced boy with a thick Scottish accent and a sprinkle of freckles over his upturned nose
touched the bill of his cap. "I'm Jem. I know the course like our
back garden. Happy to give you advice or keep shut, however
you like it."

"That would be capital," Drew told him, "but a chap called
Jamie Tyler was recommended to me. Do you know him?"

Jem made a sour face. "He's out with a party. Did you want
to wait?"

"How long ago did he go? Perhaps we could catch him up
on the inward half." Drew watched a quartet of portly busi-
nessmen and their caddies come off eighteen and head toward
the clubhouse.

"Don't know if I could say exactly." Jem followed Drew's gaze. "Though he went out right after Bobby Lang, if I'm not mistaken, and there's Bobby coming in just now."

"Ah, excellent," Drew said. "I'd count it a great favor if you'd point out Tyler when you see him."

"You're not a husband, are you?" Jem asked speculatively.

"A husband? I am married, yes, but I have a feeling that's not really what you're asking."

"Well, no. I mean, sometimes Jamie, er, caddies for ladies," Jem said, "and then their husbands come later, asking after him."

"I see. And are all of them husbands? No fathers perhaps?"

"Aye," Jem said thoughtfully, "but I thought you a wee bit young for that. Might be a brother. Either way, you'll pardon me if I can't hang about talking when I've got my living to get. If you don't care to play . . ."

"Not to worry." Drew fished in his pocket. "Wouldn't want you to miss out when you've already been so helpful." He gave Jem what he would have paid for carrying his bag and a little over.

"Very good of you, sir," Jem said, touching his cap.

"So this Tyler fellow has been involved in some . . . disputes?" Drew ventured.

"Wouldn't say disputes," Jem said. "Just talk mostly. Jamie knows he'd be banned the course if he didn't keep such things under his hat, so to speak." He paused, shading his eyes against the afternoon sun. "There he is. The tall, blond chap. Dark cap and jacket."

The man Jem pointed out was a striking mixture of light and dark. Hair so blond it was almost white, eyes and eyebrows a dark contrast to his fair skin, there was an artist's perfection in the classic, almost pretty features, square jaw, and lithe, muscular frame. Little wonder a girl like Joan Rainsby would be drawn to him.

"I see him," Drew said, "thank you. You've been very helpful."

Jem paused for a moment. "Excuse me, sir, I don't mind if you say it was me pointed you in his direction, but the rest of what I said, well—"

"Not a word," Drew assured him.

Jem touched his cap once more and hurried away. Drew made his way toward the clubhouse, reaching the door at the same time as Tyler.

"I do beg your pardon," Drew said. "Jamie Tyler?"

"I'm Tyler," he said affably enough, his accent indicating he was more likely from Manchester than Edinburgh. "But I was hoping to get a bit of something to eat before I go back out. You might want to try one of the other fellows if you're starting out now."

"I didn't come to play, actually." Drew made a quick introduction. "If you wouldn't mind the company, I would be happy to see to lunch for both of us."

Tyler lifted a dark brow. "Very kind of you, sir, but the dining room is only for members and their guests."

"Yes, of course, but there's a pub just down the road that probably isn't as particular. What do you say?"

The caddie looked faintly wary. "Look here, what's this about? Is there something you want from me?"

"Just a few words is all. It would be much less awkward to discuss things over lunch rather than standing here blocking the doorway, eh?"

After a moment's consideration, Tyler shrugged. "I'm never

one to turn down a fair offer. Can't take all afternoon, though. Not on a Saturday."

"Half an hour," Drew promised. "Not a moment more, unless you're slow about eating your greens."

They entered The Brassie and Cleek and quickly found themselves a table.

"All right, we're here," Tyler said once the girl had thumped a pint of beer and a mug of cider on the table and hurried off to fetch their orders of chicken-and-leek pie. "What's this about?"

"I take it you've heard about what happened to Lord Rainsby last week," Drew said, watching his expression.

Tyler shrugged. "I heard he was killed when he was thrown from his horse."

"He may have had a bit of help there."

The caddie looked faintly surprised. "Really? That's too bad, but what's it got to do with me?"

"I understand you and Miss Rainsby are acquainted." Drew took a sip of his cider. "I'd be very interested in knowing more about that."

"Wait a minute. Are you with the police?" Tyler shoved his chair back and sprang to his feet. "You have no right—"

"No need to get your back up," Drew said, and with one foot he pushed the chair under the man, making him drop back into his seat. "I'm nothing so official as that. I'd just like to know about you and Joan Rainsby."

"Joan? Why?"

"Well, I suppose I rather more mean you and her father. I understand he warned you off."

"I pick up a few bob here and there teaching people how to play golf," Tyler said, his handsome face sullen. "She wanted me to teach her, and then, well . . ."

"You became friends," Drew supplied.

A slow, smug smile touched his mouth. "We had a bit of fun. You know how it is."

"Fun the young lady paid for."

The caddie shrugged. "As I told you, I'm never one to turn down a fair offer."

He took a silver case from his coat pocket, removed a cigarette from it, and offered it to Drew, making sure he saw the engraving on it: *Always, J.*

Drew took it from him. A man would have to carry a good many golf bags to be able to afford something as fine as this. "From her, I daresay."

"She was always a freehanded girl," Tyler said, lighting up and then blowing out a stream of smoke from the corner of his mouth.

Drew slid the case back across the little table to him. "Very nice. Too bad Rainsby put a stop to it, eh?"

Tyler shrugged one elegant shoulder. "Not much I could do, if you want to know the truth of it. She was packed off to Cannes, and I went back to Muirfield."

"It's a nice club. I take it you do all right for yourself, tips and all."

"It's enough to keep me in last year's shoes and a room over the greengrocer's," Tyler said, only the slightest bit of acid in his tone.

"Nothing like Thorburn Hall, I suppose."

"A grand place, that," the caddie admitted. "I don't think I'd have much trouble getting used to living there."

"You've been in the Hall, then."

Tyler snorted. "Seen it from the road. His lordship wouldn't have wanted the likes of me coming inside, even through the tradesmen's entrance."

"Pity. So you and he met just the one time, is that right?"

"That was all." There was a glint of hardness now in the caddie's eyes. "He had me brought before him in one of the private rooms in the clubhouse. Told me if I didn't stop annoying his daughter with my attentions, he'd see I was banned the course and every other course in Scotland, England, Ireland, and Wales. Then he tossed a hundred-pound note onto the table, as much as daring me to take it."

"You did, of course."

Again that touch of smugness was in his expression. "No reason not to. It might be he saw it as an insult. To me it was a hundred pounds."

"Seems he got off rather easily," Drew said. "I've heard of men paying a great deal more than that to end an . . . awkward entanglement."

"That's how it was." The caddie met Drew's gaze without flinching, tapping ash into the blackened brass bowl that served as an ashtray, and then crushing out the cigarette entirely when the girl appeared with their lunch.

She set down two plates of well-browned pie and still-hot dark bread, and left them to busy themselves with napkins and cutlery and the first silent bites of their meal.

"I'm curious about you and Miss Rainsby now," Drew asked after a few minutes. "Do you hear from her?"

Tyler swallowed a deep drink of his beer to wash down the chicken and pastry. "I hear she's been in Cannes since. Not much chance of her staying in touch."

Drew glanced at the silver cigarette case that still lay on the table. "'Always' didn't last too very long."

"At least *J* can stand for Jamie as well as Joan." Tyler grinned, slipping the case back into his pocket. "In case anyone should ask later on."

Drew watched him as he swallowed down generous bites of pie, followed by deep draughts of ale. He was certainly not suffering from a guilty conscience.

"You don't happen to know anyone called Schmidt, do you?" Drew asked.

Tyler shook his head and shoveled in more pie. "Should I?"

"Perhaps not."

They finished their lunch in silence, and Drew left him at the Muirfield clubhouse precisely one half hour after they had left it.

When he returned to Thorburn Hall, Drew found a message waiting for him. According to Twining, it had been left by Hugh Barnaby, the Rainsbys' solicitor, who had called before lunchtime but did not care to wait.

Dear Mr. Farthering,

I should be very glad to have you call on me at your earliest convenience this afternoon regarding the death of Lord Rainsby. My office is in the high street directly opposite the news agent's. I shall be in until six o'clock. If you cannot come until later, please ring me and I will wait.

He had signed his name and written his telephone number beneath it.

"Did he say what he wanted?" Drew asked.

"No, sir."

"Was this about Kuznetsov?"

The slightest bit of disdain crept into the butler's stoic expression. "I couldn't say, sir."

"I couldn't help but notice that from the moment he came to the Hall, you haven't shown much of a liking toward him."

Twining's thin lips tightened. "I beg your pardon, sir. It was improper of me to give such an impression of any of Lady Rainsby's guests. It's hardly my place—"

"Certainly it's not," Drew assured him, "but that doesn't mean your observations might not prove valuable in this investigation."

There was a flicker of interest in Twining's usually impassive face. "I don't know that I can be of any real help, sir. He hasn't said or done anything in my presence that would cause him to be suspected of anything untoward. I'd never have pegged him a murderer, whatever else he might be."

"Still, there must be some reason for your disliking him." Drew leaned conspiratorially closer. "Just between the two of us, eh? Absolutely outside your professional capacity."

"Not quality, sir." There wasn't a bit of uncertainty in the thoughtful pronouncement. "I've served the Rainsbys since I started out blacking boots when I was a lad. I know quality—whether or not it comes along with money or a title—and Count Kuznetsov's got none of it."

Drew chuckled quietly. "I'm glad I'm not the only one to realize it."

"He knows the act right enough, and he's very good at it, but it's an act for all that. Now, you take Mr. and Mrs. Pike," Twining said, his tone becoming more conversational. "Salt of the earth. Can't say a word against them. But quality? Pardon me, sir, but no. More at home at the local pub, if you ask me, and Mrs. P. so eager to appear well-bred, she'd fall for a charlatan such as the count. And needless to say, there are those with all the advantages of blood and breeding who manage to be as common as small beer."

"A daresay you've seen your share of that, as well."

"True enough, sir. True enough."

Drew lifted one eyebrow, inviting the butler to continue. "Any specifics you'd care to mention?"

Twining opened his mouth and then shut it again, looking startled before his face fell into its habitual impassive lines. "I do beg your pardon, sir."

So there was someone in the household, or someone close to one of them, who also wasn't quality. "Just between ourselves, Twining," Drew said as if it were of no moment whatsoever.

The butler's voice was as correct and impersonal as always. "It is truly not my place to carry tales, sir. I apologize for having overstepped myself as regards our guests."

If Drew pressed now, the man would shut up like Barclays on a bank holiday. Best let it alone for now. "No need to apologize, Twining, and no offense meant. It's just that old Denny, that's Mr. Dennison's father who runs my old place in Hampshire, he knows more than anyone about everyone, and I thought who better to ask about the goings-on here than the chap who keeps things going, eh?"

The butler raised one severe eyebrow. Denny could have taken lessons from him. "And I trust, sir, he knows how to keep such information to himself."

"But in the event of a police investigation . . . ?"

"He would, no doubt, supply such information as pertained to the investigation." Twining gave a nod that was somehow smug and deferential all at once. "Will there be anything more, sir?"

Clearly Drew was dismissed.

Drew didn't bother to have Phillips bring out the car again. He merely walked the short way into the village. He found Barnaby's office with no trouble and went inside. Almost at once, the solicitor hurried out to greet him, one hand outstretched. Fortyish, Drew assumed, and dressed a good ten or fifteen years younger than he ought.

"Thank you for coming on such short notice, Mr. Farthering."

Drew shook his hand. "Not at all. I'm sorry I wasn't in when you called earlier."

"One always takes that chance," the solicitor said, smiling as he ushered Drew away from the girl at the front desk, past the bespectacled middle-aged woman in his own outer office, and into his cluttered sanctum sanctorum.

"Do make yourself comfortable." Barnaby shut the door and gestured toward the leather chair before his desk. "I'll keep this as brief as I'm able."

Drew sat. "I understand this is concerning the Rainsby matter."

"Precisely. I've, er, heard that you're looking into the circumstances of Lord Rainsby's death, and I thought you might be interested in his last consultation with me."

"Oh, yes?" Drew leaned forward in his chair. "This wouldn't be a violation of any privileged communication between you and your client, would it?"

Barnaby perched on the corner of the desk, hesitating but not for more than a moment. "To be honest, Mr. Farthering, I'm not quite sure what I ought to do. I can't say for certain whether it has anything to do with the murder. The police took down the information, but they seem convinced they have their man, a petty thief who has nothing to do with Lord Rainsby's estate."

"I get the impression that this Inspector Ranald would rather have things wrapped up neatly without any bother to his lordship's family."

"He's not one to let himself be swayed by anything that doesn't fit his theories," Barnaby said. "Or take others' advice."

"I suspected as much."

This time the solicitor's hesitation was palpable.

"If you don't think this is something you ought to tell me," Drew said when it seemed the man would never speak, "I would certainly understand."

"No." Barnaby walked around the desk and clutched the high back of his chair. "Lord Rainsby's dead. If what I have to say will help us find the reason why, then I will gladly say it." He pulled the chair out and sat. "On Tuesday of last week, the eighteenth, Lord Rainsby came to consult with me. He said he was rather in a hurry and wanted to get straight to what he'd come to do."

"What had he come to do?"

"He wanted me to draw up a new will for him."

Drew's eyebrows went up. "And the police didn't find that to be significant?"

The solicitor's expression turned decidedly cold. "They did not. As I told them, his lordship called last week to discuss the particulars, and I told him I'd have it prepared and let him know when he could come back to sign it. Sadly I never saw him again."

"But you did have the thing prepared?"

"I did."

Drew hesitated. This is where it got dodgy. Lawyer-client privilege and all that. Still, he had to give it a go. "Might I see it? The new will, I mean."

Barnaby narrowed his eyes. "I shouldn't, you know . . . but seeing as you're helping with the investigation . . ." He pressed a button on the intercom on his desk. There was a corresponding buzz from the outer office, followed by the crackling voice of his secretary.

"Yes, Mr. Barnaby?"

"Bring me Lord Rainsby's current file, if you would, please, Miss Grahame."

"Certainly, sir."

A moment later, the middle-aged woman brought in a thick folder full of papers and a number of official-looking envelopes. "Will there be anything else, sir?"

"Not at the moment, thank you," Barnaby said, opening the folder and taking out the unsigned will.

"I beg your pardon, Miss Grahame," Drew said before she could leave the room, and then he turned to Barnaby. "May I?"

"Certainly." Barnaby handed him the will. "It's not valid, of course, but it does contain his last expressed wishes."

Drew glanced at it, then showed it to the secretary. "You have no doubt seen this will before now."

"Yes, sir. I prepared it."

Drew nodded. "So you took down the information as Lord Rainsby was telling it to Mr. Barnaby?"

"Oh, no, sir. Mr. Barnaby and his lordship talked it all over in here that last day he came to call. Then after he'd gone, Mr. Barnaby gave me his notes on how Lord Rainsby wanted his will, and I prepared it for him."

"And that's the usual way it's done?" Drew asked.

"Yes, sir. The client states how he'd like his property disposed of upon his death, and Mr. Barnaby sets it down all nice and legal for him. And afterwards I type it up."

"Then he comes back later to sign it?"

Miss Grahame nodded. "That's the usual way of it, that is. Poor Lord Rainsby, and after . . ." She looked regretfully at the paper Drew held. "Well, it's not my place to say, of course, but it seems things couldn't have been very happy for him at home."

"That will do, Miss Grahame," Barnaby said, and the woman ducked her head.

"I beg your pardon, sir. Thank you, sir." She scurried out of the office, closing the door behind her.

Barnaby gave Drew some time to read the pristine document.

"As you can see," he said after a moment, "he wanted everything left to his daughter and to exclude his wife entirely."

"'For reasons of which she is well aware,'" Drew read, and then he looked at the solicitor. "Did he discuss those reasons with you?"

Barnaby scoffed. "Certainly not. I could tell he was fairly well nettled over them, whatever they were, but he didn't say anything more about it to me."

"Did she know he came here that day?"

"I have no idea. I got the impression at the time that she did not. He said he told everyone he was going somewhere else, his club or some such. I really can't remember the particulars."

Drew scanned the paper once more. "Any other significant changes from his previous will?"

"I couldn't say," Barnaby admitted. "I didn't handle his previous will. He only ever consulted with me about business matters here in Scotland. His will and other personal matters were handled by his London firm. All I can suppose is that he was so angry about whatever had happened between himself and Lady Rainsby, he didn't want to wait to exclude her until he was in London again."

"Maybe so," Drew murmured, still thinking. "Maybe so. Besides his daughter, I see there are others he provided for."

"Yes, a few pet charities, pensions for servants, his foundation, something for a nephew who lives abroad, I believe. I suspect that's the same as in his current will." Barnaby smiled thinly. "He hadn't rowed with any of them, eh?"

"No, I suppose not." Drew sighed. "Is there anything else of note that you remember from that day?"

"I'm sorry. No."

"You say he was nettled. Was he in a state as if whatever had happened had taken place that very day?"

Barnaby frowned. "No, I would say it was more of a cold sort of fury, too raw to be old but well contained all the same. He'd thought out what he wanted to do."

"He didn't have any other business he wished to discuss with you? No other concerns?"

The solicitor shook his head. "I'm just sorry he was unable to sign this new will so his last wishes would be carried out. Of course, if I had known what was to be, I would have had it prepared for him to sign that day. I feel as if I've been horribly negligent."

"It's a tragedy," Drew said, "but none of us is guaranteed his next breath. You couldn't have known." He stood. "You've been most helpful, sir. I do appreciate your time and trouble."

"I'm pleased to offer my assistance." Barnaby gave Drew's hand a firm shake. "It's a bad business, this. I hate to make any assumptions based on a will that was never executed, but it's hard to overlook the part Lord Rainsby's considerable fortune could have played in everything that has happened."

"Financial interests are always the first consideration," Drew said. "I suppose you've been over all this with the police already."

"Naturally. But if you have any other questions, please don't hesitate to call."

Drew awoke that night stiff-limbed and cotton-mouthed, more weary than before he'd gone to sleep. At first he was alarmed not to see Madeline curled up on the other side of the bed, but then he remembered where she was and why. He resisted the urge to telephone The Swan just to make sure she was there, safe and sound. She was. He knew she was. No need to rouse the whole village just because this case was getting to him.

He didn't want to rouse the house, either. If he turned on the faucet in the bathroom just enough to get a mouthful of water, it shouldn't make too much noise. Then maybe he'd be able to get to sleep again. It was half past two.

He slipped out of bed and went to the sink, glad the water made only the softest hiss as it came out of the pipe. He drank a handful of it and then splashed his face. The coolness helped, but the room still felt too warm. Too close. He couldn't remember his dream, only that he had been searching for something, something lost in a desert of hot sand. Or was it one of the hazards on the course at Muirfield?

He went to the open window, hoping to feel more of the breeze. All was quiet outside, everything as it should be. He noticed the vague outline of a motor car someone had left parked under the trees near the road. The grounds keeper wouldn't care for that, but otherwise . . .

He froze. Something had moved near the car. First he thought it was the swaying of the tree limbs in the pale light of the moon, but then he saw something else. Some*one* was moving in the shadows, making for the back of the house.

Drew shoved his feet into his slippers and threw on his dressing gown. Another glance out the window showed him that the figure was nearly at the kitchen door. He snatched up the poker that leaned against the hearth and then slipped out the door, closing it behind him with the tiniest metallic snick.

He padded soundlessly down the hall to the back stairs and down to the kitchen. Soon he was standing by the door, listening for the soft click of the lock. Finally it came. Whoever it was had a key. The figure moved inside and latched the back door closed again. There was a moment of silence, a slight rustling sound, and then silence again. Then the door next to Drew began to swing slowly open. Whoever it was had crept across the stone floor without shoes on.

Drew pressed himself back against the wall near the hinged side of the kitchen door and held his breath, hoping whoever it was didn't open the door wide enough to hit him. He needn't have worried. The door opened just enough for a slight figure in black to step into the dark corridor. Drew put down the poker he had held at the ready and stepped from behind the door.

"Joan."

She gasped, and he immediately shushed her. "Don't wake the house."

Her shoes clutched in one hand, she put the other over her mouth, her breath coming in little hitches until she was steady again.

She grabbed his sleeve and pulled him into the kitchen with her. "What do you think you're doing?" she hissed, dark eyes blazing in the dim light of the low-banked hearth fire. "I nearly came out of my skin!"

"Sorry. I thought you might be an intruder. With everything that's gone on, one can't be too careful. What were you doing creeping about out there at all hours?"

"I . . ." Her lips trembled into a taut little smile. "I was feeling all shut in up in my room. I had to get a little air, that's all." The smile turned defiant. "I could ask you the same thing. What were you doing up to even be able to see me?"

"You have me there," he admitted. "It *is* a little close upstairs." He didn't tell her about the nightmare.

"I'm glad you're keeping watch, though." There was something vaguely troubled in her expression. "I shouldn't like anything else to happen. I just wish all of this would go away, you know?"

She looked as if she desperately wanted a cigarette, even though he could smell the last one still on her clothes. His eyes were adjusting to the darkness now, and he picked a little bit of hay off her sleeve.

"Visited the stables, did you?"

Her eyes widened, and she brushed her hand over one shoulder and then the other and finally down the back of her head. Two more fragments of hay drifted to the floor, and her once-pale face turned suddenly crimson.

"I just wanted to see my horse. Sometimes I—" there was a tiny catch in her voice—"I just need to feel I'm not alone, to hold on to something warm, something breathing." She swiped a hand over her eyes and gave a derisive huff. "Don't listen to me. I don't know what I'm saying."

"It's a natural thing to want to be comforted," he said softly. "To be admired. Loved." There was another piece of hay sticking out from under the collar of her blouse. He pulled it out and handed it to her. "But there are those who take advantage of that need, who play on it for their own ends, not caring who they hurt."

She lifted her chin and tossed the bit of hay to the floor.

"Believe me," he said, "I know how it is. The infatuation. The utter obsession with one person. The willingness to do anything and everything just to hold on to that perfection. The profound need to believe everything you've been told is true, that you are loved and desired and, by some miracle, at least to that one person, as fascinating a creature as the one who fascinates you. I know, too, what it's like to find out it's all a lie and that you'd been played for a fool all along. It's not pleasant, and I'm sure that when he tried to keep Tyler away from you, your father was only trying to protect you."

"Dad didn't know him." Her whisper was fierce, but the firelight caught the sparkle of a tear in her eye. "He didn't understand how we feel about each other. I know Jamie has done some things he's not proud of. I know he has a past. I don't care. I love him. I want him."

She wiped her eyes and stood there glaring at him. He hadn't expected such a depth of passion from her.

"I know you think I'm a bad girl. Well, I am a bad girl, and I don't care."

Rather than wicked, he thought she merely looked young and a trifle foolish. "I'm curious," he said. "Whose car is that out there? Your fellow's?"

"Jamie doesn't have a car. I'm not sure whose that is, but it's hard to see much of anything out there at the moment." She looked toward the pantry. "I'm a bit hungry. How about something to eat? Just to tide us over till breakfast."

He shook his head, still watching out the window. "You stay here. I'm going down there to see what I can find out."

"Are you sure you should? Maybe you ought to wait till you can see a bit better. In the morning—"

There was the sputter of an engine, and then the motor car eased out of the shadows and onto the road. Before Drew had a chance to do any more than wonder about the identity of the driver, the car was gone.

He frowned as he turned back to Joan. "Might have been nothing, anyway."

— Eleven —

Madeline looked out of her sitting room window at The Swan and down into the street. Where were they?

"Nothing?" Carrie stood on tiptoes in an attempt to see, too.

"Nothing. It would be only fair if we went to dinner without them."

"In that case," Carrie said, "we can just have Mrs. Drummond bring us up some sandwiches, and I'll get out of these shoes."

Her dainty pumps were white, as were her dress, her gloves, and the pearl-trimmed Juliet cap that sat on the arm of the sofa. White was the perfect color for her, a pristine canvas to set off her brilliant hair.

"I suppose it's not quite the same without them." Madeline gave her arm a squeeze. "But don't worry. Nick will be here, and he'll be smitten as always. That is, if Drew hasn't dragged him into some kind of escapade."

Carrie looked stricken. "You don't think—"

"No, I don't think they're up to anything too outlandish. It's more likely they're poking their noses where they don't belong and forgot what time it is."

There was a tap on the door.

"See?"

Madeline flung open the door to find Drew and Nick standing there and looking like two very naughty, grubby schoolboys. "You're late." Madeline narrowed her eyes. "What in the world have you been doing? You're filthy, both of you."

"Now, now, darling, don't scold." Drew gave her a careful peck on the cheek. "We're not as bad as all that, are we?"

"You're not fit to go out," she said. "Denny would be ashamed of you both, and I hope you didn't let Plumfield see you. Why do you look as if you've just swallowed a canary?"

Drew walked into the sitting room with Nick right behind him. "I daresay you'll be happy to see us, filth and all, once we show you what we've brought."

"What I have brought, thank you very much," Nick corrected. "And I've brought it for Carrie."

"Oh, dear. What have you been doing now?" Carrie was still at the window, looking afraid to come closer in her all-white ensemble. "Nick, you can't really expect to go to dinner looking like—"

"We may have a slight delay," he said, "until everything can be arranged. I trust you won't mind too much."

He and Drew had such a look of eager delight, Madeline wasn't able to keep the sternness in her expression.

"What is it?" Carrie asked with a little smile.

"Close your eyes and hold out your hands," Nick replied as he reached into his coat pocket. "You too," he said to Madeline.

They both did as they were told, and after a bit of rustling, there was a piercing, plaintive cry.

"Oh, Nick!" Carrie squealed. "A kitten!"

Madeline's eyes flew open. Nick held a squirming little bundle of orange fur that must have been dozing in his pocket all this time.

"We found him out in the stable at Thorburn Hall."

"The little darling," Madeline cooed, reaching for it, but Nick was already setting it in Carrie's gloved hands.

"For me?" she said, her eyes as blue and bright as the kitten's.

"Wait, Carrie." Madeline snatched up a towel and took the kitten from her. "Poor baby, he may be the only thing in Scotland more in need of a bath than those two."

"We decided that because he is Scottish, he ought to have a right royal name," Drew said, following her into the bathroom. "He's been Bonnie Prince Charlie ever since."

Charlie gave a yowling mew and tried to wriggle out of Madeline's hands, but Drew took him from her again. "As you say, I'm already filthy. I'll hold him for the time being."

"Is he really for me?" Carrie asked once more.

"If you want him," Nick said, searching her face. "You do, don't you?"

"Of course I do." She started to take the kitten from Drew but then looked at her immaculate white outfit. "But maybe not right this minute. Do you think he'll mind a bath very much?"

"He seems too young to be away from his mother," Madeline said.

Drew stroked the still-squalling kitten with his finger. "He's probably five or six weeks old, so I daresay he's old enough to be weaned but young enough not to be happy about it. We asked about and it seems the stableman's sister took the mother and her two other little ones back to her house in the next village, only they seem to have missed this one. Somehow he got himself stuck up in the loft, and we had a devil of a time getting him down."

Madeline brushed off his coat and then sneezed at the dust and chaff she had stirred up. "Excuse me," she said with a sniff. "No wonder you're such a mess. What exactly were you doing in the stable when you were supposed to be taking us to dinner?"

"Give us a minute to tidy up and then we'll take the kitten to Mrs. Drummond. Perhaps she can look after him while we're at dinner. Then we'll tell you all about it."

Just minutes later, they left Charlie with the innkeeper and made their way to an Italian place down the street. It was small and hardly elegant, but it smelled deliciously of freshly baked bread, roasted garlic, steaming pasta, and savory chicken and beef.

They had barely placed their orders when Madeline demanded to know what Drew and Nick had been up to. "Don't come to take us to dinner filthy and smelling of horses and not tell us what happened."

"We don't still smell of horses, do we?" Drew asked, looking positively alarmed.

She laughed. "No, thank goodness."

"It's not all that exciting," Drew assured her, "except for finding Charlie."

"But what were you doing? Why were you in the stable in the first place?"

"I chanced to see Miss Rainsby coming in very late last night. She had some bits of straw on her jumper. On the back mostly."

Madeline raised an eyebrow.

"I thought," Drew continued, "since Nick and I were heading into the village and no one at the house would miss us, we might have a look about out there. Not just to have a look at

the number of cigarette ends left behind—some of them Joan's
brand, others not—but to see how difficult it might be to get in
without a key. Despite what Joan said, we didn't find it hard at
all. We also went down to the cottage out in the woods beyond
the stables. I doubt anyone is living there, though the place
hasn't been abandoned altogether."

"A cottage?" Carrie looked at Nick. "How do you know
someone's been there?"

"Cigarette ends again," he told her. "Joan's again, it seems.
Fresh footmarks too—boots far too large for her little feet."

Madeline's eyes widened. "You can't mean she was meeting
someone there, too?"

"Could be," Drew said. "We don't know quite yet. It could
be just a coincidence. About the cigarettes, I mean. There was
also a strange motor car parked near the road. Under those
trees just where it makes the bend. When I talked to Joan last
night, she seemed rather determined for me not to notice it."

"Whose car?"

"Couldn't say, but it drove away not long after she came in.
And I'm given to understand that Muirfield caddies are generally without the means to afford motor cars."

Their meals arrived, and the saltimbocca alla Romana, followed by tiramisu with the most excellent coffee Drew had had
since his arrival in Scotland made him content to let the case
rest for a while. For the evening, a lovely wife and good friends
were more than enough.

They stopped to see Mrs. Drummond after dinner. Much
to Carrie's delight, the kitten was clean and fluffy and sleeping
soundly in a basket near the stove.

"There's Charlie," she said, scooping it up and cuddling it,
even as the kitten protested having its sleep disturbed.

Mrs. Drummond chuckled. "That's noo a Charlie, miss. More a Charlene."

"What?"

Carrie looked at Nick, Nick gaped at Drew, and Madeline laughed at all of them.

"Bonnie *Princess* Charlie, is she?"

"I thought . . ." Nick began.

"No need to look smug, Mrs. Farthering," Drew said. "Most ginger cats are male, as you well know. We merely assumed—"

"I don't care." Carrie pressed her lips to the kitten's fluffy head. "Charlie or not, she's a bonnie thing and Bonnie she shall be."

"I like it," Nick said, touching its red-gold fur and then Carrie's red-gold curls. "Nothing prettier."

She blushed and, bidding Mrs. Drummond good-night, hurried to the stairs. Nick followed her, and they spent a moment with their heads together, their voices low and intimate.

Drew smiled as he took Madeline's arm. "I suppose we'd be wise to walk very slowly toward them."

"That would be thoughtful," she said, pressing close to his side. "I'll be glad when we don't have to be apart anymore."

"No more so than I will. I hope we'll have this all sorted out soon."

"Have you talked to Joan?"

He shook his head. "We chatted just a bit when she crept into the kitchen last night. I'm fairly sure she was meeting that caddie out in the stable. But who might have been at the cottage, I couldn't say. I hadn't looked out there until Nick and I did this evening."

"Maybe you'd better ask her about it," Madeline said, and then her forehead wrinkled. "I just can't imagine her seeing two of them on the same night. I hardly believe she's seeing one. As much as she tries to hide it, I don't think she's the hard-edged sophisticate she makes herself out to be."

"I don't know what to make of her. She claims she and Tyler are passionately in love. It may be so."

"If that's the case, who's the other man?"

"I'll talk to her about it," Drew said, "but I think you'd better be with me when I do. She seems a fairly straightforward and level-headed girl, I know, but she's still rather young."

Madeline put her arms around his neck and stood on tiptoes to touch her lips to his. "And you don't want to tramp all over her delicate sensibilities."

"More or less."

There was a decided twinkle in her eyes. "You're such a brute."

"You know what I mean. As much as I hate to admit it, Nick's right. I can be a bit ham-fisted at times, especially with the ladies."

She kissed him again. "Only when you have a lead and you're trying to get right to the point."

"I suppose I do get overeager, but that, darling, is why I need you." This time he kissed her. "We're so much better together than apart, don't you think? How would I ever get out of all these scrapes if I didn't have you?"

"And without you, how would I ever get into them?"

"You'd find a way," he said, giving her a squeeze and releasing her. "Now, shall we say good-night? If we wait much longer, I'm afraid Nick will have to be dragged out bodily."

Nick and Carrie were standing closer than before, their gazes locked. He had his arms around her waist. She cradled her sleeping kitten in one hand and cupped his face with the other. Drew cleared his throat, and they stepped reluctantly apart.

"Come along, Nick, old man. It's just a few hours till Sunday services. You needn't look as if you're about to spend a year at sea."

He and Nick escorted the girls up to their sitting room and said their farewells, promising to return in the morning. Then the two of them walked back to Thorburn Hall.

Joan and Lady Louisa did not attend church the next morning, though the Pikes did. Afterward, once Nick and Carrie had turned in at The Swan to have lunch and Mrs. Pike and Madeline walked on ahead toward the Hall, Drew slowed his pace to match Mr. Pike's lumbering gait.

"How is Mrs. Pike holding up?"

"Right enough, I suppose," Pike rumbled. "I have a business dinner to attend on Wednesday, courting the financier Camden Emerson to invest in my company. That ought to take Elspeth's mind off things here for a bit."

"She seemed her usual chipper self at the service. I had no idea she was such an enthusiastic singer."

Pike gave a rueful chuckle. "I suppose you could say that."

"I was afraid this business with the count would have upset her."

The big man shook his head. "In a way, I think she rather likes it. After all, if Kuznetsov was appealing as a tragic refugee and misunderstood artiste, he's even better as a man wrongly accused and persecuted for his nationality."

Drew smiled. "I think you must be terribly fond of Mrs. Pike to have put up with all this for so long."

"One day I'll toss our so-called count out a window," Pike said matter-of-factly. "See if I don't. But a murderer? I don't know."

"No," Drew said. "I don't suppose you have any theories about what actually happened to Rainsby."

Looking away, Pike said, "No. I just wish I hadn't let Kuznetsov talk us into coming for the tournament. We'd all have been better off had I declined."

Drew stopped short. "It was his idea?"

"Insisted on it."

"That's odd. I got the impression he wasn't the least interested in the tournament."

"Still."

"I suppose he thought he'd pick up at few worthwhile trinkets at the Hall that would never be missed by anyone." *The scoundrel.*

"I don't think so," Pike said. "Elspeth was planning to accept an invitation to Lady Edrret's, and I'm sure he always returns home with a bit of her plate, no matter how much Elspeth denies it. Much more profitable than anything Thorburn Hall has to offer. Nevertheless, he convinced my wife the Open was the event of the season and we simply must make the trip to Scotland."

Drew could see her just up ahead, fluttering her plump hands and chattering away. There was no use questioning her about what Kuznetsov had said. She probably hadn't thought twice about it. Even so, he promised himself he'd take it up with the count at his earliest opportunity.

They arrived back at the Hall just in time for lunch.

"No, you haven't missed it, sir," Twining told Drew. "Cook tells me it will be ready at half past. I was just going to inform Miss Joan. Sometimes when she's reading, the time gets away from her."

"Shall we fetch her in for you?"

The butler made a slight bow. "I would be most gratified, sir."

Joan was sitting out in the rose-covered folly, clearly not reading the book in her lap. She started when Madeline called to her.

184

"May we join you?"

"Certainly." She marked her place with one finger and slid to the end of the marble bench. "Do sit down."

"*Anna Karenina*," Madeline said, nodding toward the book. "How are you liking it?"

Joan sighed. "Wretched. Real life is depressing enough at the moment. I don't know why I picked this one up."

Drew remembered the story. Adultery, alienation, misery, suicide . . . "I'd much rather read Wodehouse myself. A bit of Jeeves and Wooster most always puts one right."

Joan merely looked annoyed. "That twaddle. I'm not saying it isn't amusing in its way, but it's hardly full of deep meaning."

Drew took the book from her, marked the place with the ribbon bound into it, and shut it firmly. "Well, there's only so much 'deep meaning' we mortals can take in one sitting." He glanced at Madeline and then plunged ahead. "I know this must be a very upsetting time for you, and I'm sorry to have to address it at all, but I did promise your father I'd look into things for him. I can hardly drop the matter now, can I?"

There was a slight quivering of her lower lip. "Maybe it's best not to know. After all, it won't bring him back."

Madeline gave her hand a soothing pat. "But at least we'd be able to stop whoever it was from hurting anyone else."

Joan blinked. "Anyone else? What do you mean?"

"The killer wouldn't be able to kill again," Drew said. "I shouldn't like that to happen if we could have stopped him in the first place."

"No," Joan murmured. "No, of course not. Do . . . do you think this killer really would? Kill someone else, I mean."

"They often do."

"But why? If someone wanted my father dead, then it's over and done with. Why kill anyone else?"

"Sometimes it's more convenient to do away with a confederate than to trust he will remain silent."

Joan looked down at her book and didn't reply.

"Tell me something," Drew said. "About that car that was parked under the tree the night I saw you coming into the house late."

Joan's eyes grew wide, and she pursed her lips. "What about it? I told you it wasn't one of ours, I'm certain of that much. Does it matter?"

"Still, did you recognize it? Do you know whose it might be?"

"I don't know. I couldn't see."

"And you're sure your Mr. Tyler doesn't have a motor car?" Madeline asked.

Joan snorted. "Very sure."

"Tell me about that cottage in the woods," Drew said, watching her face. "Do the two of you ever meet there?"

There was a flash of something in her eyes. Temper? Fear? "No."

"I noticed a number of your cigarette ends near the stoop and along the path there."

"Mine?" She gaped at him, obviously surprised, and then gave him a tremulous smile. "Oh, yes, the cigarette ends. I sometimes go there to think, to get away from everyone. That's all."

"I see." He didn't see. Not quite yet. But he was beginning to wonder. "But you were alone."

"Naturally."

No one said anything for a while, and the only sound was the squabbling of a pair of starlings overhead.

"I've been meaning to ask you," Drew said after a moment.

"That will your father never signed, I know the police have asked you about it already. Have you come to any conclusions about it yet? Anything come to mind about why he would change his will and exclude your mother?"

Joan looked at Drew with fierce eyes and a set mouth. "I think it's all a mistake. Mr. Barnaby must have misunderstood what my father wanted. Dad would have gone back to sign it and seen what rubbish it was and made Barnaby start again."

"A fairly egregious mistake, don't you think?" Drew asked.

"Does any of this really matter?" she said, ignoring the question. "My father is dead. Nothing's going to change that. Maybe . . ." She hesitated a moment and then became defiant. "Maybe you should leave well enough alone and go back to Hampshire. It was probably Kuznetsov, anyway."

Drew studied her for a moment. She was as eager for him to stop investigating as she had been for him to begin. What was she afraid of? It seemed ludicrous, even if she were seeing two men at the same time, that she would meet them in such short succession. Judging from the bits of hay still on her clothing, she had come directly from her tryst in the stable when Drew met her creeping into the Hall. But if she'd met someone at the cottage first, why hadn't he driven away earlier? Something about it didn't add up. Why had she so desperately wanted him to find her father's murderer and now suddenly did not? And what did she really think about her father's unsigned will?

Madeline gave Drew a subtle look that told him she had the same misgivings. He squeezed her hand in acknowledgment.

"Don't you worry," he told Joan. "I don't mean to abandon you quite yet. You've given me some things to consider, and I hope I won't have to trouble you any more on a Sunday. By the way," he said before she could object, "Twining sent us to fetch you in for lunch." He offered her his arm. "Shall we?"

Madeline took his other arm, and they made their way into the house.

❖

As they walked to Gullane early Monday morning, Drew told Nick about his conversation with Joan.

"Two things," Nick said after he'd had a few minutes to digest everything. "Either she's behind the thing herself or she's protecting someone."

"If she were behind her father's death from the beginning, why would she practically beg us to look into it all?"

"No, I suppose she wouldn't." Nick paused to add a handful of pink thrift to the bouquet of wildflowers he planned to give Carrie when they met for lunch later on. "First off, she doesn't seem the type, and before she insisted that saddle be looked at, no one thought Lord Rainsby's death was anything but an accident."

"Precisely. Which means she's protecting someone. The caddie's the most logical choice, but if that's the case, why would she admit he was in the stable with her but deny he was the one driving the motor car?"

"I suppose another talk with Mr. Tyler is in order." Drew sighed. "I don't seem to be figuring out much of anything about this case yet. Still, a nice chat with Mr. Barnaby might shed some light on this will business."

"Are you sure he'll see you without an appointment?" Nick asked.

"That's why I wanted to start out bright and early, old man. The office opens at nine. If he's like old Whyland in London, he doesn't start taking appointments until at least ten. We'll have a few words with him and then have plenty of time to spend with the girls before lunch. Can't say fairer than that, eh?"

"Very nice, I'm sure," Nick said, but then he came to an abrupt stop in the middle of the road. "Look here, Drew, I know you're eager to hash this all out again, and I'm keen enough to do it, but when we get to the inn I hope you'll leave all the murder talk for later. Carrie and I had a lovely lunch and a splendid afternoon and evening together yesterday. We didn't talk about Lord Rainsby or Lady Rainsby or Joan or MacArthur or anyone. She was happy, and I very nearly popped the question right then. She may very well have said yes, too."

"To be sure," Drew murmured.

"Anyhow, I don't want you spoiling it all. Let's just have a pleasant meal, all right?"

Drew put a hand over his heart. "I solemnly pledge that I will not bring up anything about the case or about murder or any aspect of death. We'll have a jolly nice lunch, and Miss Holland shall not be worried in any form or fashion. How's that?"

"All right then." Nick gave him a grudging nod, and then there was a sudden hint of mischief in his eyes. "But until we get there, let's see if we can figure out what little Joan is hiding and what more Mr. Barnaby can tell us."

The remainder of their walk was occupied with a number of theories, from the mundane to the absurd, about who could have killed Lord Rainsby, and it wasn't long before they reached the solicitor's office.

"I hope Barnaby won't be all day about seeing us," Nick grumbled as Drew reached for the door. "I don't want to keep Carrie waiting, and you know how solicitors are, always rambling on about—"

A piercing shriek came from inside, followed by a low wail and the sound of running footsteps. Drew turned the doorknob, but it was pulled violently out of his hand as the door flew open and Barnaby's secretary practically fell into his arms.

"Sir!" she gasped. "Oh, sir. Mr. Barnaby, he's—he's—oh, sir . . ." She clung to him, flooding his shirtfront with tears. He pried her away from him, trying his best to see her face. It was dead white, and her horn-rimmed glasses hung wildly from one ear.

He settled her glasses properly on her face, trying to soothe her. "What is it, Miss Grahame? Tell me. What's wrong with Mr. Barnaby?"

Somehow he knew the answer before she managed to speak.

"He's d-dead . . . in his office there. Dead!" She began wailing again, and he put his arms around her, calming her as best he could.

"It's all right. Shh, it's all right now." He looked at Nick over her head. "Better take charge here, old man, while I see what's what. There now, Miss Grahame, Mr. Dennison here will look after you while I go see if there's anything I can do for Mr. Barnaby."

Nick tucked the flowers under one arm and managed to pry her away from Drew. "Look, there's a lovely bench just over there," he said, his voice low and gentle. "Why don't we sit for a moment and let you collect yourself?"

Drew looked through the open doorway into Barnaby's front office. Everything looked quite normal. The girl who had been at the desk when he'd been here before wasn't in yet. He stepped inside and immediately noticed the odor. There was no mistaking the smell of death.

The smell intensified as he walked through Miss Grahame's immaculate office and into Barnaby's. The inner office looked much like Drew remembered it. The only difference now was the body slumped over the flurry of papers on the desk, a wine bottle and glass spilled over them, and the pervasive smell of decay. From the indications left on the floor, in the chair and on the papers, it seemed the man had spilled the wine when he slumped over. Or perhaps he'd spilled the wine and then slumped over. But that was after at least some of those papers had been scattered. Perhaps the murderer hadn't wanted to wait until Barnaby was dead before searching for what he—or she—wanted.

Drew swallowed hard, trying not to think too much about the smell. Careful not to touch anything but Barnaby's lifeless wrist, he assured himself that the man was in fact quite dead. He breathed a brief prayer for mercy over him and then inspected the desk drawer that stood open. A file drawer but without any files. Had the jumble on the desk once been stored there? Or had the missing files left the office along with the murderer?

Drew craned his neck to peer into the half-open drawer in the middle of the desk. It was a shallow one, the kind intended to hold pencils and other sundry items, but there was nothing of note inside it. Judging by the pair of tickets tucked away there, Barnaby had intended to go to the theater the coming Friday evening. Pity.

That left the bottom drawer, directly under the open one. Too bad it was closed. Drew leaned down to get a better look. There were a number of fresh marks on the wood and on the brass lock itself, marks made with an edged tool of some kind. He glanced toward the door and, not seeing Inspector Ranald storming through it threatening him with incarceration, attempted to nudge it open with the toe of his shoe. It wouldn't budge.

There was nothing else in the office of note, and eager to breathe more wholesome air, he hurried back out to the street.

— Twelve —

When Drew stepped outside, he saw that Nick was gone and two elderly ladies had taken his place on the bench with the distraught secretary.

"He said to tell you he's gone for the police," one of them said as she supplied Miss Grahame with a fresh handkerchief and nodded toward the milliner's shop next door. "We wanted to take the poor dear into our place and give her some tea, but he thought we'd better not, at least until you came back."

"Yes, better to wait," Drew said, seeing Ranald and Shaw and a pair of constables following Nick back down the high street. "The inspector will want to talk to her."

"Why am I not surprised to find you mixed up in this, Mr. Farthering?" the inspector growled when he reached Barnaby's office.

"I suppose Mr. Dennison told you why we happened to be here," Drew said, "and I have to say I'm glad we were. For Miss Grahame's sake, I mean."

Ranald turned to the woman huddled on the bench. "I'll

have to ask you a few questions, Miss Grahame, if you'll be so kind as to come into the office here."

Miss Grahame looked at Drew, terror on her tear-blotched face.

"Mightn't she go with the ladies into their shop until she's a bit calmer?" Drew asked. "There's no need for her to go back inside at all, is there?"

Shaw nodded. "We'll get much more of use from her, sir, when she's had a chance to settle down."

Ranald gave the sergeant a curt nod, and Shaw helped Miss Grahame into the shop. The two older ladies stood to follow her, and Ranald looked at them narrowly. "I'll have to ask what you have seen, as well."

The women looked at each other, wide-eyed.

"Nothing, Inspector," the one with the handkerchief said. "We heard the poor dear scream and came out to see what the matter was."

"It was horrible just to hear her tell it," said the other. "I shan't sleep, I tell you."

"All right then, Mrs. Dundee," the inspector said, his mouth taut with impatience. "I want you both and Miss Grahame to stay in your shop till I can come speak to you."

"Oh, yes. Certainly, certainly."

"We'll send Dr. Portland over to see to Miss Grahame," Shaw told them, "as soon as he's had a look here."

The two women hurried off, whispering and looking back, and Ranald gestured toward the still-open door to the office.

"I suppose you have no objections, Mr. Farthering?"

"None," Drew said, "though I can't tell you more than you can see for yourself."

Ranald posted his two constables outside the door just as

Shaw emerged from the milliner's, and Drew and Nick followed the inspector and his sergeant inside.

Drew and Nick were late for lunch. Mrs. Drummond's close-set little eyes were round with a peculiar mix of fear and excitement as she served the meal and listened in on Drew's description of the morning's events.

"Poor Miss Grahame found him there? And after almost two days? Mercy."

She thumped a plate of minced collops and tatties down in front of Madeline, who looked at it warily. It was just ground beef, onion, and oats with a side of potatoes, but no doubt it looked rather suspect to the uninitiated.

"Yes, I'm sorry to say," Drew said. "She's been quite upset."

"I can well imagine, sir." Mrs. Drummond's Scottish burr thickened with her excitement. "Mrs. Dunn says he'd been dead since Saturday night, slumped over his desk and already starting to spoil."

Nick set his fork down and drank a bit of water.

Carrie pushed her plate away untouched and contemplated her bouquet of wildflowers instead. "There can never be just one."

"Dr. Portland's had his hands full," Mrs. Drummond agreed, setting down the finnan haddie chowder and a potato-cabbage-cheese dish she called rumbledethumps. "He hasn't had so much coroner work since I can't say when. Now, what else can I get for you? More of the collops?"

Once they had assured her they didn't want anything more, she hurried back to the kitchen.

Madeline picked at her food, and then seeing Drew watching her, she coolly took a large bite of the chowder.

195

"I never thought I'd be pining for our Chief Inspector Birdsong," Drew said, starting on his own plate. "He might grumble and grouse, but he would at least tell us a bit more about what happened."

"They can't blame this one on Kuznetsov," Nick said. "Someone must have had that wine bottle ready for him, don't you think?"

Carrie pressed her lips together. "I don't suppose you could just leave this one alone? Either of you?" Drew and Nick both looked at her, and she sighed. "No, I don't suppose you could."

"Carrie," Madeline began, but her friend stopped her.

"I'm going upstairs now," she said, laying her napkin aside. "I'm sure you'll all want to go find out every lurid detail. When you're through, let me know."

She stood, the bouquet in one hand, and Drew and Nick immediately got to their feet.

"Carrie." Nick grabbed her hand. "Please don't go."

She freed herself and made it to the dining room door before he caught her again.

"Carrie."

She tried to pull away again, but this time he wouldn't let her. He leaned down a little, his whispers urgent, and gradually her expression softened. She said something in reply, and he pressed a fervent kiss to her hand. Then he let her go, and she disappeared into the corridor.

He returned to the table. "I'm going to leave the sleuthing to you for a bit, old man," he told Drew. "Carrie and I will be spending the rest of the day taking in the sights. If nothing else, there's a great lot of water to look at."

"Good," Madeline said, giving his arm a squeeze. "That's a wonderful idea."

"I don't expect there's much we'll be able to find out about the investigation right off, anyway," Drew said. "Ranald will probably be playing it close as usual. Madeline and I will see what we can dig up on our own and report back later. Meanwhile, you'd better see to your young lady. You're not likely to find another who'll put up with your foolishness."

"I'm quite sure of that," Nick said, and with a grin he sprinted off.

"I hope it's not too late," Drew said once he had gone. "I feel bad for them both, especially with this new incident."

"It certainly hasn't helped." Madeline took another bite of the rumbledethumps. "I can't imagine Inspector Ranald won't be interested in that will now. And in Lady Rainsby."

"I suppose they will want to talk to her about it," Drew said. "I don't know why, but for some reason the poison surprises me."

"Why should it? Though it does show premeditation, and it's almost sure he must have known whoever brought him the wine. Count Kuznetsov isn't in a position to have given it to him."

"Seems logical."

They ate in silence for a few minutes more. Madeline was right. Unless he had a confederate, Kuznetsov couldn't have been involved in Barnaby's murder.

"I suppose," Drew said, "the wine could have been in Barnaby's possession some time before he actually drank any of it."

"You mean like Lord Rainsby's saddle. Someone planned it ahead of time."

"Perhaps." Drew ate more of the chowder. It was actually rather good. "We need a great deal more information before we can start to theorize about it, and Ranald isn't likely to tell us a thing."

Madeline smiled over her glass. "Maybe I could ask him."

"As charming as he would no doubt find that, I really haven't time to be detained for assaulting a police officer."

"Then what *can* we do?"

"Well, to begin with, I'm hoping Sergeant Shaw can tell us more about Mr. Barnaby himself."

Once they'd finished their lunch and settled the bill, Drew and Madeline walked back to Hugh Barnaby's office. Drew tipped his hat to the weary-looking officer standing guard at the door. "Good afternoon, Constable."

"Afternoon, sir. I beg your pardon, but there's a police investigation on these premises, and I'll have to ask you and the lady to stay clear."

"Yes," Drew said, "I was here when the body was found. Might I ask if Inspector Ranald is still present?"

"Not just now, sir. I believe the inspector's gone back to the station, if you'd care to call for him there."

"No, no. It's not as urgent as all that. Perhaps Sergeant Shaw is still here."

"He is, sir, but I'm not sure—"

"Never mind, Rodgers," Shaw said as he came down the front steps. "I'll see to this gentleman. You go inside and help Yellin with those files."

"Right you are, Sergeant."

The sergeant waited until Rodgers had gone into the building before he said anything. "I suppose the gossip's already got round the village."

"There's nothing swifter," Drew said, and turned to Madeline. "You remember the highly recommended Sergeant Shaw, darling. Sergeant, I trust you haven't forgotten my wife."

"That would be very difficult, sir." Shaw gave her a nod. "Mrs. Farthering, ma'am."

"I understand the inspector has returned to the police station," Drew said. "Does that mean you might be willing to tell us a bit more about the case? I don't doubt you've turned up some important evidence while I was away."

Shaw took a quick glance down the street and then up the other way. "I could tell you a few things," he said, lowering his voice, "but only because Chief Inspector Birdsong says you might have a thought or two worth hearing, and because he says you're all right."

Madeline gave him a most charming smile. "He's a nice man, isn't he? Even if he pretends not to be."

"Yes, ma'am. And he was always fair to us men, even if the pay wasn't enough to keep a cat on."

"Pity," Drew said. "I'd still like to hear what you've found out."

Shaw shrugged. "There's not all that much more since you were here, sir. The doctor says the victim died on Saturday night or very early Sunday morning as a result of taking poison. He wasn't sure about the exact type of poison yet, but he suspects arsenic. As you saw yourself, some papers and perhaps other things were taken."

"Rather an odd sort of robbery," Drew observed. "Seems more like there were documents the murderer wanted, things not valuable to anyone but the murderer himself perhaps?"

"That could be the way of it, sir. A solicitor isn't usually in possession of items that have intrinsic value, but he does have information regarding wills and estates and other things that might be worth a great deal to other parties not normally privileged to see them."

Drew peered into the doorway, not actually stepping into the building. "I take it the poison was in the wine bottle."

"We haven't done extensive testing as yet, but the coroner did say the man was poisoned and certainly there's poison in the bottle."

Drew moved closer to the door, but Shaw stood his ground.

"I'm sorry, sir, but I can't let anyone in unless he's officially connected with the investigation. Inspector Ranald's orders."

Drew winced. "He didn't happen to name any parties specifically, did he?"

"I'm afraid the inspector doesn't care for amateur sleuths, sir. Not even in books."

Madeline's lips twitched, though she managed not to laugh.

"Perhaps my wife and I can help you puzzle this case out, along with the Rainsby matter," Drew said, giving her a reproving look, "and get you a nice promotion in the bargain. How would that be?"

One side of Shaw's mouth turned up. "Can't say I'd complain, sir, but it'd be you who'd get the accolades, not me."

"Our names need not appear," Drew assured him. "I never did much care for those newspaper accounts, anyway. They almost always get everything wrong." He gave the officer a hopeful look and nodded toward the doorway once more.

Shaw shook his head. "Chief Inspector Birdsong tells me you can both be trusted to keep confidential information confidential, so I'll tell you what I can about the case. But I won't be able to let you inside, not as long as there are orders to the contrary."

"I'll concede defeat," Drew said with a sigh. "But aren't you ordered not to speak to me about the case, as well? In your official capacity, of course."

"That, sir, was not mentioned. Now, if Inspector Ranald were to see you and me standing here chatting, it might be mentioned, so we'd ought to take care he doesn't, eh?"

"That seems to be advised in this instance." Drew took another look up and down the street. "Before any of your mates come down to see what you're up to, what else can you tell me about Barnaby?"

"Not much, I'm afraid. As you saw, someone tried to break open a drawer in Mr. Barnaby's desk. The locksmith is up there now opening it for us."

Madeline tilted her head to one side. "Why do you suppose there was only one glass?"

"There was another found broken in the alleyway behind the office," Shaw told her. "Both are being checked for fingerprints, though it seems quite likely there will be either none or Mr. Barnaby's only."

Drew nodded. "More than likely. What else?"

"Not much more of note. Not yet. But, uh . . ." Shaw glanced back into the building, hearing footsteps. "If there is, there's always The Brassie and Cleek. Fair enough?"

Drew shook his head. "I think that will do nicely."

He and Madeline slipped away just as Shaw was called back inside.

"Perhaps," Drew said, taking his wife's arm, "there's more we can find out on our own. Mrs. Drummond was kind enough to give me the late Mr. Barnaby's home address."

Mr. Barnaby lived in a stylish Georgian home not half a mile from his office. Drew knocked on the front door, and after a silent moment, he and Madeline were admitted into the house by a young maid. The girl looked positively unsettled when Drew handed in his card and asked for Mr. Brogan.

"Mr. Brogan, sir? I don't know—"

"We need to speak to him about Mr. Barnaby," Drew prompted, "if you'll be good enough to fetch him. May we speak to him in here?" He gestured toward the small parlor just off the front hallway. Finally, the perplexed girl showed them in.

No more than a minute later, a wizened little man came to the parlor door. "I'm told you wished to speak to me, sir."

"Are you Brogan?" Drew asked. "Mr. Barnaby's valet?"

The man inclined his balding head. "I am, sir. Well, valet and butler and whatever else is required. Of course, now there's only the house to be closed up and Mr. Barnaby's things to pack away. Is there something you wish to know?"

Drew motioned for him to come into the room and shut the door after him. "We'd like to know about Mr. Barnaby, if it's not too much trouble."

He sat on the striped divan across from the window overlooking the street, and Madeline sat next to him.

"I beg your pardon, sir, but are you with the police?" Brogan asked.

"No, but I was there when poor Miss Grahame discovered the body. I'm a relation of Lady Rainsby and looking into the matter of his lordship's death for her. It's a possibility that the two incidents are related."

"I don't know what I can tell you, sir. Mrs. Brogan, my wife, does the cooking, and she and Ella, the girl who let you in, do the cleaning and such. It's not a large house, and Mr. Barnaby wasn't one to entertain much, not more than once or twice in the year, so it was a rare occasion for him to have friends in. He was never one to take staff into his confidence."

"He didn't have a young lady he was seeing?" Drew asked.

The valet colored faintly. "Naturally, Mr. Barnaby had several lady friends he escorted to various functions. He was by no means a solitary gentleman, and he received many invitations."

"Was there one in particular?" Madeline asked. "Perhaps one he was serious about?"

"I think there must have been someone he saw regularly in the past few weeks," Brogan admitted. "Mr. Barnaby was a very private gentleman, of course, and he never brought his young ladies here, but I could tell all the same."

"How did you know?" Drew asked.

"His wardrobe, sir. And his daily routine."

Drew glanced at Madeline. "How do you mean?"

"He began dressing . . . differently," Brogan said. "And he became quite particular about wearing scent, especially when he'd go into the office for the half day on Saturdays."

Drew nodded. "What else was different?"

"I don't precisely know how to describe it except to say he seemed to wish to appear as stylish as possible. As prosperous and fit as he was able. He began wearing lifts in his shoes, sir, and even, though I advised strongly against it, went to be fitted for a toupee. Of course, a gentleman of forty-seven will never be what he was at twenty-five, will he? And a woman—I mean, the right sort of woman—would understand that."

Madeline shook her head in sympathy.

"Normally, it hadn't been his habit to stay out late on Friday and Saturday nights," Brogan continued. "He had his club in Edinburgh, if he wasn't invited somewhere else, but even then he rarely stayed late. But for the last little while, he mightn't come in at all. Even on a weeknight."

"And he never mentioned the lady's name?" Drew asked. "It wasn't Schmidt by any chance?"

"Schmidt, sir?"

"Mr. Barnaby never mentioned anyone called Schmidt?"

"I have never heard him use that name," the valet said. "But if it was a lady friend of his, he wouldn't have. Still, I thought there might be an announcement of some kind forthcoming. He seemed quite enchanted with this one in particular."

"How could you tell?"

The valet looked deeply troubled. "Upon at least three occasions, sir, he wore a corset."

"Ah," Drew said, determined to keep his expression as grave as the other man's, "that *is* quite telling."

"Yes, sir, it is. And now to know that this woman has gone and killed him, right there in his own office if you please, well, it's not right. It's just not right."

Madeline's eyebrows went up.

"Is that what you think happened?" Drew asked. "We hadn't actually got that far along yet."

"I don't know for certain, sir," Brogan said, looking faintly abashed. "But who else could it be? Poison like that? It must have been his young lady. A lovers' quarrel, my missus says, and I can't disagree."

"I can't disagree, either," Drew told Madeline as they walked back to Thorburn Hall. "It does seem odd, though, that this mystery woman would kill him just after he gave important evidence about the will of a man who'd just been murdered, don't you think?"

"True," Madeline said, "and it seems, in the proverbial fit

of jealous rage, the woman would be more likely to conk him over the head with the wine bottle rather than poison it ahead of time."

"Precisely." Drew frowned. "And if she does exist, what was this woman looking for in that locked drawer?"

"And what did she take from the office?" Madeline added.

Drew tapped one finger against his chin, thinking. "No, darling, it won't do. There must have been a woman of some variety. Barnaby's vain attempts to make himself look grand definitely point that way. The question is whether she was the same woman who poisoned that wine. Or if the one who poisoned the wine was a woman at all."

Dinner at the Hall that night was a quiet affair, just Lady Louisa and Joan, the Pikes, and Drew and Madeline. Afterward the two couples played bridge, but Mrs. Pike could never remember what trumps were or that her husband was her partner and not her opponent, so it wasn't a very entertaining match. Louisa was charming, if subdued, as she looked on, trying to help Mrs. Pike concentrate on the play, while Joan merely stood at the library window, smoking cigarette after cigarette as she stared at the darkness. It wasn't until the game broke up and everyone was retiring for the night that Joan finally spoke.

"I'm out of cigarettes."

Lady Louisa gave her a look of indulgent reproof as she rummaged in her handbag. "You smoke too much, dear. It's not good for you."

She fished out an unopened pack, and Joan took it without comment, immediately tearing it open and lighting up again.

Drew watched her for a moment, and then caught a startled breath.

Everyone looked at him.

"I do beg your pardon," he said, patting his chest with a look of discomfort. "Perhaps a bit too much dinner."

"I'm so sorry." Lady Louisa looked grieved. "If something didn't agree with you, I'll certainly speak to Cook about it in the morning."

"No need. Truly, it's nothing. Everything was divine, but I do think it's time I escorted my wife back to The Swan and then retired. A good night's sleep ought to put me right again."

"Poor dear." Madeline took his arm, patting it. "Good night, everyone. Dinner was lovely, Lady Louisa. Thank you."

She walked him swiftly out of the library. "What is it?" she asked when they reached the front door, her voice low. "And don't tell me it was too much dinner."

He answered with a slight shake of his head and hurried her outside, saying nothing until she shut the door behind them.

"Tell me. I know that look."

"The cigarettes," he said with a glance back at the house. "I hadn't noticed it before, but Lady Louisa smokes the same brand as Joan."

Madeline's eyes widened. "Then she could have been the one coming from the cottage."

"Or at least Joan might think she was, or question if she was. Little wonder she changed her mind about our investigating any further."

"True," Madeline murmured. "She's already lost her father. I can hardly blame her for not wanting to lose her mother, too."

He thought of his own mother, his natural mother, someone

he knew nothing about. He'd been so involved in the case that he hadn't really had time to consider again what he ought to do about her. If he told Mr. Whyland to keep looking for her, suppose his people actually found her. Suppose she was nothing like he imagined her to be. Suppose she had done something heinous, then what? He couldn't blame Joan for not wanting to know something awful about her mother or even for trying to deny what she did know.

"Maybe it's Tyler and not her mother she's trying to protect," he said. "Either way, it's a bit twisted, but love is a funny thing."

They walked along in the moonlight, the quiet broken only by the rush of water to the shore.

"So, would you?" he asked when they had almost reached the village.

"Would I what?"

"Would you still love me if you knew I had murdered someone? Someone you loved?"

"That's a horrible question." She tightened her hold on his arm. "I don't even want to think about it."

"But suppose I had. Would you?"

For a long moment, she studied his face. Then she looked away. "I don't know. I suppose I'd wonder if you were ever the man I thought you were." She smoothed his hair back at the temple, her eyes meeting his again. "The man I love."

Perhaps no one ever knew such things until faced with them. She was right. It was a horrible question.

"I'm sorry, darling." He pressed a kiss to her cheek and then her lips. "It was beastly of me to even ask. I promise never to put you in an awkward situation by murdering someone and then asking if you still love me."

"Silly." She pressed closer to him. "I wish you would just figure out who the murderer is so we can go home and get Carrie and Nick married."

He chuckled and wrapped her in a tight hug. "You realize we have absolutely no say in the matter, don't you?"

She nodded against his chest. "But it's what I wish all the same."

"Come along." He tugged her hand, quickening his stride as they came into Gullane. The Swan was just down the street. "The two lovebirds have had all day to moon over each other. It's up to us to bring them to their senses, at least until they reconvene tomorrow."

They found Nick and Carrie in the inn's otherwise-empty dining room, Mrs. Drummond doing her account books in one corner as they lingered over their hours-old supper. Reluctant to be parted themselves, Drew and Madeline sat a while, drinking coffee and sampling some of the landlady's very excellent apple scones.

Finally, Drew and Nick escorted their ladies upstairs, made their farewells, and headed back toward Thorburn Hall. There were a lot of things Nick needed catching up on.

Drew had just come downstairs for breakfast the next morning when he heard Inspector Ranald and Sergeant Shaw at the door, asking to be announced to Lady Louisa. From behind the inspector, Shaw gave Drew a warning look.

"Good morning, Inspector," Drew said, going over to shake the man's hand. "I didn't expect to see you so soon."

"Mr. Farthering. No, I didn't expect to be here as soon as this, either. In fact, I didn't expect to be here at all."

Drew glanced over his shoulder at Shaw, who was looking

rather grim. "I take it you found out more about the Barnaby matter."

Ranald gave a curt nod. "We did."

"Well, come in, Inspector. I know Lady Rainsby wouldn't want you standing on ceremony at this late date. She *is* the one you've come to see, isn't she?"

"She is."

"Is Lady Rainsby at breakfast, Twining?" Drew asked.

Although his demeanor was flawless, Twining's tone as he surveyed the inspector was frigid. "I will see if she is receiving visitors."

"And Miss Rainsby?"

"Miss Joan has gone out for the day."

"Just as well," Ranald said, and he fixed one glum eye on Drew. "The less I have to bother with people not actually involved in the case, the better."

"As you say, sir."

Once Twining had gone to speak to Lady Louisa, Drew turned to Inspector Ranald. "I realize you don't want any interference from amateurs, Inspector, but Lady Rainsby is my cousin. I'd like to be of whatever help to her I'm able, if she'll allow me."

"Suit yourself."

Ranald said no more until Twining returned.

"Her ladyship will receive you here, Inspector Ranald." He led the three of them across to the drawing room.

Lady Louisa appeared a few minutes later, perfectly dressed and coiffed as always. "Good morning, Inspector. Sergeant." She looked from one to the other, weary lines around her dark eyes. "Is there something I can do for you?"

"I presume your ladyship is aware of the murder of Mr. Hugh Barnaby."

She nodded.

"We've thoroughly examined Mr. Barnaby's office, and there are a few questions we would like to ask you."

"Certainly."

Drew came to stand behind her. "Would you like me to stay, or would you prefer to talk to Inspector Ranald alone?"

"Please stay, Drew dear." She patted his hand. "Yes. Please." She smiled distractedly. "Forgive me, all of you. Do sit down. Now, what is it, Inspector?"

"Has Mr. Barnaby been to your home at any time in the past few weeks, Lady Rainsby?"

She thought for a moment and then shook her head. "I don't believe so. It's possible my husband may have had him here, but if he had, he never told me about it."

Ranald nodded. "Do you by chance own a sapphire-and-pearl bracelet? Earbobs and a cocktail ring to match?" He looked at his notebook. "A carved jade bracelet with gold fittings? A platinum-and-diamond necklace, hair clasp, and bracelets? Diamond-and-ruby marchioness necklace with matching earbobs?"

Lady Louisa's forehead puckered. "Why, yes, Inspector. I do."

"I'd like to see them, if you please, your ladyship."

"If you like."

She rang for her maid, and soon the girl came back, fidgeting as she stood there under everyone's expectant eye.

"They're not there, my lady,"

"What? That can't be right, girl. Did you look in the jewelry case in the cupboard?"

"I did, my lady. They aren't there."

"Oh." Lady Louisa got to her feet. "Lord Rainsby must have

put them in the safe with the other jewelry. As you know, he was worried about things being taken. I'll be just a moment."

"We'll go along, if we may," the inspector said, his expression grim.

"If you like. It's this way."

She led them all into Lord Rainsby's study where she removed from the wall a painting of an eighteenth-century hunt, revealing the door of a safe behind it. With a practiced hand, she turned the dial and then the handle, and the door swung open. She stood there a moment, unmoving, and then turned back to the others, her face perfectly white.

"They're not here." She pushed aside some of the other items in the safe, papers and a packet of ten-pound notes, a small wooden case that appeared to hold old coins. "They're just not here."

She took out a few pieces of jewelry, quality but not particularly impressive, but none of them could possibly be the items Ranald had described.

The inspector pursed his lips. "And how, my lady, would you account for their disappearance?"

"I—I don't know." She looked at Drew, tears filling her eyes. "I suppose they must have been stolen. I don't know what else could have happened to them if they're not in the cupboard with my other jewelry. Oh . . ." She held on to his arm as she sank into a nearby chair. "After everything else that's happened, I don't know what to do or think."

He stood next to her, one hand on her shoulder. "I suppose you have a particular reason for asking, Inspector?"

Ranald kept his attention on Lady Louisa. "I would like to know where you were on Saturday night, my lady."

The night Barnaby was killed. Drew didn't like the covert look on the inspector's face.

"Saturday night?" Louisa thought for a moment. "I—I was here, of course. I had dinner with Mr. and Mrs. Pike and my daughter, and then I went to my room."

"And what time was that, my lady?"

"About eight-thirty, I believe. Before nine anyway."

Ranald glanced at his sergeant with an almost imperceptible nod. "A bit early, wasn't it, your ladyship?"

Lady Louisa's hold on Drew's arm tightened. "I had a monstrous headache and wanted to lie down."

"I see." Ranald noted her answer. "I suppose Mr. and Mrs. Pike can corroborate your story? And Miss Rainsby?"

"And the servants, if you like," she said, the quaver in her voice taking the intended bite out of the words. "I went up to my room and took a headache powder and went to sleep. I didn't wake up until the next morning. That was all."

"I see," Ranald repeated. "And where were you, Mr. Farthering?"

"I'm afraid Mr. Dennison and I were out at the time. We had dinner with my wife and her friend, Miss Holland, then spent a bit of time walking the beach. It was . . . after ten, I believe, when Nick and I got back to the Hall. Everyone was already in bed."

"Right." Ranald focused on Lady Louisa again. "Was it your maid who gave you the headache powder?"

"My daughter, actually," she said, her voice cooler than before. "We both take them from time to time, but I had run out, so she got me one of hers."

"And you didn't wake during the night?"

She shook her head. "I'm usually quite a light sleeper, but I don't think I even stirred until morning. I suppose I was very tired after everything that's gone on lately."

"That may be." Ranald made more notes. "Where is Miss Rainsby? I'd like to speak to her as well, if I may."

"She went into Edinburgh to have lunch with a school friend of hers and do some shopping. I don't expect her home until this evening."

"Very well, we'll speak to her another time."

"What is this all about?" Lady Louisa demanded. "Why are you asking all these things? Why did you ask about my jewelry? If someone has stolen it, does that mean you've caught him?"

"No, my lady," Ranald said. "Those particular pieces of jewelry were found in a locked drawer in Mr. Hugh Barnaby's office desk, along with a list of dates and places we'd like to ask you about."

"Dates and places?" Drew asked. "What dates and places?"

"That's what we'd like to find out."

"Mr. Barnaby?" Lady Louisa said. "Mr. Barnaby had my jewelry? How could he have got it? *Why* did he have it?"

Drew watched the inspector's face, knowing from his utter lack of expression what would come next.

"Was Mr. Barnaby blackmailing you, Lady Rainsby?" Ranald asked at last. "Those jewels would make a handsome payment, I should think."

Louisa's hold on Drew's arm was growing painful. "Black-mail . . . ?"

"But they always seem to get greedy, don't they?" Ranald continued. "Asking for more and more until there's just nothing to do but end the matter."

"No," she breathed.

"Had he found out you'd murdered your husband in order to keep him from signing that new will?"

213

"Don't be ridiculous."

"The new will that excluded you for reasons of which you are well aware?"

Her lip quivered. "No."

"What were those reasons, Lady Rainsby?"

She looked pleadingly at Drew. "I don't know. I don't know of any reasons. He never said such a thing to me."

"And then," Ranald insisted, "you decided if you'd done one murder, no reason not to carry on with another?"

Drew glared at the inspector. "Look here, Ranald—"

"No!" Lady Louisa cried. "No, no, no! I never did anything of the sort. Drew, tell him—"

"This seems nothing but conjecture," Drew said. "What proof do you have?"

"The jewelry."

"Stolen."

Ranald shrugged. "The list."

"Rubbish."

"The will."

"Unsigned," Drew said. "Besides, Lady Rainsby was home the night of the murder. You could ask a number of witnesses to corroborate that. All of them would swear to seeing her go up to bed directly after dinner."

"They could swear as to her going up," Ranald conceded. "But could they swear as to her not coming down again?"

Drew pressed his lips together. He had no answer for that. Not yet.

"Forgive me, your ladyship," Ranald said, looking almost smug, "and no disrespect meant, but I'll have to ask you to come down to the station for more questioning regarding the murders of your husband and of Mr. Hugh Barnaby."

He took her by the arm, but she pulled away from him, all ice and self-control now.

"You'd be wise to engage a solicitor to be present during questioning," he added mildly.

"Her solicitor has just been murdered," Drew reminded him, "and hadn't you ought to caution her about her statements being used against her in court?"

"Yes, well, it's not an arrest," Ranald said. "Not quite yet. Merely questioning. But if you would like to telephone a solicitor's office, your ladyship, you may do so now."

Again she looked at Drew with pleading eyes. "I don't know of anyone. Mr. Barnaby always saw to everything for us here in Gullane."

"I'll see to it, Lady Louisa." Drew helped her to her feet. "I don't suppose I might—"

"You will be informed when her ladyship is allowed visitors," Ranald said, sounding as if Lady Louisa was indeed under arrest. "For now, you'd do as well to stay put."

"But my daughter," she said. "Someone must tell her—"

"Now that would be an excellent job for our amateur sleuth." The inspector took firm hold of Lady Louisa's arm, not allowing her to pull away this time. "Do let Miss Rainsby know that we have made progress in the case," he told Drew. "We will be keeping her informed. Sergeant Shaw."

Shaw glanced at Drew and then opened the study door to show the inspector and his prisoner out.

— Thirteen —

Nick came downstairs just as the inspector's car pulled away from the house with Lady Louisa in custody.

"I seem to have missed all the best bits," he said. "Not exactly a shocker, though, after what you told me last night. What do you think?"

"I'm not convinced about Lady Louisa's guilt, but now Joan makes much more sense."

"I would have thought the indomitable Mrs. Pike would have been in the middle of everything, threatening to chain herself to the inspector's rear axle rather than see Lady Louisa taken away."

"I'm given to understand Mrs. Pike finally convinced Mr. Pike to take her to visit Count Kuznetsov in his time of need."

Nick nodded sympathetically. "I see."

"And to buy a new hat."

"Naturally."

Drew considered for a moment. "I suppose this means the

count will be released. They really didn't have much of a case against him. I'd very much like to have a talk with him about why he so badly wanted to come to the Open. I can't help but think there's much more to all this than just a pleasant little family killing."

Joan came back from Edinburgh about teatime with a stack of parcels and a much more serene expression on her face. Drew gave her a moment to hand her parcels to one of the maids, and then he took her into the drawing room and asked her to sit down. He hated to upset her, but she had to be told that her mother had been charged with her father's murder and Hugh Barnaby's as well.

"Why?" Joan fumbled in her handbag. Hands shaking, she removed a cigarette from her case and lit it. "What—what did they say? Why would she have killed Mr. Barnaby anyway?"

"Before I give you the theory the police seem to have concocted, I'd like to know your thoughts on it. Can you think of any reason she'd do such a thing?"

Joan shook her head. "She hardly knew him. My father was the one who dealt with him, and that wasn't very often, at least that I'd heard of. I suppose there's the will my father asked Mr. Barnaby to draw up. I don't understand that part at all, but he'd already told the police about it. It's not like Mother was trying to make sure nobody knew about it. Why should she kill him over it now?"

"I've wondered the same thing," Drew said. "It hardly makes sense."

She took a deep, slow drag of her cigarette. "It's not at all like her. What do the police say?"

"They think he was blackmailing her."

"Then why would he tell the police and you about the new will?"

"The more I think about all of this, the more I'm convinced this bit about your mother is all wrong. And Kuznetsov is wrong, too. I'm thinking your father's and Barnaby's deaths are part of something much bigger."

Her eyes widened. "You don't think Mr. Barnaby had anything to do with my father's death, do you?"

"I don't know for certain," he admitted, "but I have wondered."

"But it doesn't make sense. Why would he want to help someone kill my father?"

"Perhaps because your father knew more than he should? Or was a threat to the killer? And then perhaps Barnaby himself became a threat, because he knew what the killer had done."

She looked away, gnawing her lower lip, her brows pulled together.

"The police claim he was blackmailing your mother," Drew said. "Do you think he was the sort who'd do that?"

"I didn't know him really, so I don't know what he might have done. Dad never talked to me about his personal affairs. He just said Mother and I would be taken care of should anything happen to him and that we needn't worry. I just want you to find whoever's behind all this. Mother's been through enough as it is." She took a few more puffs on her cigarette. "I have to go see her. I can't just leave her there in jail."

"Better to wait a bit," Drew advised. "They probably won't let anyone see her just yet. Tomorrow we'll telephone and see what we're allowed to do." He gave her hand a comforting squeeze. "I don't believe she's guilty, and I haven't given up trying to find out who is."

She nodded, her lips trembling into a smile. "I'm so very grateful, Drew."

"But you must understand, I might uncover things you won't like."

"As part of this something bigger you were talking about?" There was a tinge of fear in her dark eyes. "What is it?"

"I know you've heard Mr. MacArthur talk about Germany and Italy and other events taking place in the world just now."

The fear turned to annoyance. "I always wished Dad would biff him one on the nose. They got into some rows over that, I can tell you, but surely you don't think Mac would have killed him over a political tiff, do you? It's ridiculous."

"No, but I've wondered if Mac might have gone beyond just talk."

"You mean spies, state secrets, and all that? Don't be silly. Mac? No. I never liked him, but no."

It wasn't just Mac, of course. There was the blonde, Lisa Shearer. Perhaps Barnaby had been part of it, too. Drew remembered some of the things he'd said when they'd met in Barnaby's office. And, worst for Joan, there was Jamie Tyler. Were they all in it together?

"I don't have anything but speculation just yet, so I'm telling you this only because I don't want you to worry about your mother, no matter how bad it seems at the moment."

"Thank you, Drew. I mean that. I just couldn't take any more bad news just now."

"I know it's been rough. Hold tight and we'll get it all sorted, right?"

She nodded, blinking hard. "I trust you, Drew."

He couldn't disappoint her.

Drew made his way to the clubhouse at Muirfield and requested a private room. He thought he might have some difficulty because he wasn't a member, but when he told the pro-
prietor he was working on behalf of the late Lord Rainsby, the
man was eager to cooperate, saying he would send Jamie Tyler
to Drew the moment he came in from the course.

Drew settled into one of the clubhouse's overstuffed chairs.
A few minutes later he heard two sharp knocks on the door
and then it swung open.

"Mr. Tyler," Drew said.

The caddie's professionally pleasant expression turned cool.
"Oh. You again." He shut the door and, arms crossed over his
chest, came to where Drew sat. "Well?"

Drew nodded toward the chair opposite his own. "A few
words, if you don't mind."

"No bother for me. I'm done for the day." Tyler wadded up
his cap and stuck it in his back pocket. Slicking back his hair
with one hand, he sat down.

"All right, here it is, and I want the truth."

Tyler lifted his dark brows, an incredulous half smile on his
face. "You do, do you? Or what?"

"Or I'll let Inspector Ranald handle the questioning in future."

Tyler's eyes narrowed. "What do you want to know?"

"Do you happen to know where Joan Rainsby was Friday
night?"

The caddie was silent for a moment. Then he shrugged.
"Where does she say she was?"

"I really haven't the patience for games. If you happen to know where she was that night, then say so."

"There are certain things a gentleman doesn't discuss."

"A gentleman does," Drew told him evenly, "if it has to do with a murder investigation."

"What do you mean? What has that night to do with the murder investigation? Her father was killed nearly two weeks ago."

"Look here, either answer the question or tell me you're not going to. Either way, tell the truth."

"If you like. Makes me no odds. I'm only trying to be discreet about a lady. Anyhow, she was with me."

"What time was that?"

The caddie shrugged. "Maybe one or so, until about quarter past two. More or less anyhow."

"Where?"

"In the stables, out there at Thorburn Hall."

Drew exhaled, nodding. That lined up with when he found her coming back into the house that night. "All right. How did you leave?"

Tyler smirked. "In very good spirits."

"Were you in a motor car?" Drew asked, unamused.

"No."

"Do you own a motor car?"

Tyler snorted. "On what I make?"

"You didn't drive one that night?"

"No, I walked from the village. It was a fine night and it isn't far. Why do you ask?"

"What about Saturday night?" Drew pressed.

"I stayed in. I walked the course four times that day and I was tired."

"I suppose someone can vouch for that," Drew said, watching his eyes.

"Maybe. Why?" Tyler asked. "What's this about?"

"Do you know a man called Barnaby? A solicitor by trade."

"No. Why do you ask?"

"He was murdered Saturday night. In his office. On the high street. Have you heard about it?"

Tyler pressed his lips together. "I'd heard there was a murder. Not much more than that."

"You never met him? Never heard of him?"

"Why should I?"

"He was the Rainsbys' solicitor. Took care of all of Lord Rainsby's legal matters here in Scotland." That only earned Drew another shrug. "Miss Rainsby never mentioned him?"

"Not that I can remember. Discussing solicitors was rather far down on the agenda whenever we met."

"I can well imagine." Drew was silent for a moment, considering how to proceed. "And what about the lady herself? Now that her father can no longer object, do you intend to marry her?"

For only an instant, there was an odd look on the caddie's face, but it was immediately replaced with his usual slow, knowing grin. "Make an honest woman of her, eh?"

"It's been known to be done."

Tyler snorted. "I'm not much of the marrying kind. Not that I wasn't tempted once she threw herself at me. Thorburn Hall wouldn't half be a nice change from carrying bags all day."

Drew pressed his lips together. The chap really was a first-class swine.

"But I can't see myself being tied to anyone the rest of my life." Tyler leaned back in his chair and put his hands behind his head. "There are too many girls I've yet to meet to be leg-shackled to just one."

"Girls like Lisa Shearer?"

Tyler lifted one dark brow. "Who's that?"

"You don't know her?"

"Can't say I do."

Drew kept his expression blandly neutral. "My mistake, then. I'd heard she was seeing one of the caddies at Muirfield. Must be someone else."

"Understandable." Again Tyler looked smug. "I know a lot of girls."

"I imagine you do, a man of the world such as yourself. I suppose you get about quite a bit. So, what's your take on world events?"

Tyler looked baffled. "Not really my game."

"Surely you have an opinion about what's going on in Germany and Italy."

The caddie snorted again. "What should I care? None of that puts a ha'penny in my pocket or beer in my mug."

"And if it did?"

Tyler's jaw tightened. "What do you mean?"

"If you could turn a profit? Perhaps sell a bit of information here or there that might be of use to someone with such leanings?"

The caddie's eyes flashed, his mouth twisting into a sneer. "Why, I'd sell, man. Anything for a few pence, eh? Britain? Germany? You know my type. I can see it in your face. Well, you have the right of it, as no doubt you always do. Jamie Tyler's my country. The only one I'm loyal to, anyway." He crossed his arms and slumped back into his chair, jaw set hard. Clearly he was done.

Drew pushed a pound note across the table to him. "Thank you for your time."

Tyler didn't move. "I'm dismissed? Sir?"

"Do as you please."

Drew left the room, not knowing whether or not the caddie had taken the money.

Drew walked out of the clubhouse and, thanks to information provided to him very unofficially by Sergeant Shaw, made his way to the home of Miss Ethyl Grahame. She had a room at Mrs. Kensington's just round the corner from Barnaby's office. It was a stolid but respectable two-storied house with abundant red roses in the front. Soon he and Miss Grahame were seated in the small parlor. As was proper, the door was not quite pulled to.

The woman sat on the sofa peering at him through her spectacles with red-rimmed eyes. "I don't know that I can tell you anything, sir. You were there."

Somehow she looked older than she had the last time he saw her. Perhaps it was the dowdy cotton dress and shapeless cardigan she had on. Perhaps it was the bedroom slippers that must have been at least a decade old.

"What did you tell the police about that day?"

"There wasn't much to tell. I'd just got into the office when I noticed that smell . . ."

She was tearing up, so he gave her an understanding smile. "I suppose you liked working for Mr. Barnaby."

"Well enough," she said, settling again. "I'd been employed by him for the past thirty-two years. Well, I say Mr. Barnaby. I started as private secretary for Mr. Ingram, who was head of the firm at the time. Then he went to keep bees in Sussex, and we always thought it was quite amusing, you know? Just like Sherlock Holmes."

That seemed to cheer her a bit, and Drew nodded, encouraging her to go on.

"Anyway, I worked for Mr. Barnaby after that, eight years now. Never a grumble about my work, I can tell you, and I thought I'd stay working for him until it was my time to put my feet up for good." She dabbed at her eyes with her cotton handkerchief. "Now I don't know what I'll do. The men these days, they want smart young things doing their typewriting and dictation. I'm fifty-six, Mr. Farthering."

"I'm sure it must have come as a great shock," he soothed, making a mental note to have someone from his company look into vacancies where her skills and experience might be appreciated. "I think the only thing that can be done for Mr. Barnaby now is to see if we can find out who murdered him."

She sniffled again and then nodded. "You're quite right. I don't really know, sir, that I *can* be of help. Mr. Barnaby, well, you saw him in the office. He wasn't so much younger than I am, but he always was that careful the way he dressed, the way he did his hair, and how he never would wear his eyeglasses when there was a young lady about the office. Not Masie, mind you. She wasn't his type. He liked women with some style and sophistication to them. With the London look, if you know what I mean."

Drew nodded.

"Liked the young ones, did Mr. Barnaby, not to speak ill of the dead. Old enough to be their father, most of them, but I suppose that's as may be."

"And you think he was meeting one of them at the office the night he was killed?"

"I can't think it was anything else."

"Did he usually meet women up at the office?" Drew asked.

"No. Not until the past few weeks. I mean, if that was what he was doing."

"But that's what you believe he was doing."

"It seems so, by the state of the office on those Monday mornings after." She colored and then cleared her throat. "I don't mean anything untoward, sir, but there were often empty wine bottles in the bin. Sometimes the odd box of sweets, empty or nearly so. That sort of thing. And cigarette ends. More than Mr. Barnaby could have smoked on his own for the whole week sometimes."

"Was Mr. Barnaby the political sort, Miss Grahame?"

"How do you mean, sir?"

"Was he the type to talk about world affairs at all? Or how things should be managed here at home?"

"Well, he sometimes did. Mostly when he read the newspapers and saw there were strikes or that sort of thing. Or waste in government. He thought things could be better run, more orderly and efficient. Like they do in Germany, or so he said."

He frowned, thinking. Then, realizing she was afraid she had said something that displeased him, he softened his expression. "Is there anything else you can tell me, Miss Grahame? Anything at all?"

"I'm sorry, sir, no. I just don't know what else I could tell you." She dabbed at her eyes again and gave him a hopeful smile. "Would you care for something before you leave? Mrs. Kensington made some lovely custard tarts just this morning. Won't take her a moment to bring some up with tea."

"Very kind of you," he said, standing and reclaiming his hat from the little table at the end of the sofa, "but I'm meeting my wife and some friends for dinner at The Swan. You can reach me at Thorburn Hall if you think of anything more I should know."

"I will. Thank you."

He went to the door and turned back to her. "Is it possible someone else in the firm will keep you on now? Surely you're far too valuable to lose, especially now that Mr. Barnaby's gone. You'd be just the one to help whoever takes on his old cases. Tell the fellow what's what, eh?"

She brightened measurably. "Do you think so? They've been very kind, letting me have a day or two to collect myself."

"I'm certain of it. And if they don't happen to remember, you make sure and tell them."

He tipped his hat and walked out to the street, thinking about what she had said. Lady Louisa was a smoker, to be sure, and stylishly attractive for her age, but no one, not even the most smitten suitor, would mistake her for a girl half as old. And Lisa Shearer smoked, he was certain of it. There would be a good many things to discuss over dinner.

Madeline rose the next morning to find Carrie curled up at the window of their sitting room, her cheeks and nose pink and a cup of coffee in her hands.

"What are you doing up so early?" Madeline pulled the tie of her robe a little more snugly around her waist and went to sit beside her. "Are you all right?"

Carrie shook her head.

"Anything I can do?"

Again, Carrie shook her head. "I had an awful night. I can't stand being cooped up here like this, but I can't stand the idea of leaving, either. Not as long as . . . everybody is staying."

"So long as Nick is staying, you mean." Madeline smiled sympathetically. "Where did you get that coffee? I could use some just about now."

"You can have this. I haven't touched it."

Carrie handed Madeline the cup, and Madeline immediately set it down. "It's cold. How long have you been sitting here?"

"I don't know." Carrie ran one hand through her tousled red-gold hair and drew a hard breath. "What am I going to do? I can't stand thinking something awful is going to happen any minute. I don't know how you do it."

"I had to make a decision." Madeline smiled more to herself, remembering. "Drew and I almost didn't get married, you know."

Carrie blinked at her. "What?"

"Oh, I was so confused and afraid I was making a mistake, I almost left him and went back home to Chicago. And that would have been the worst mistake of my life." Madeline clasped her friend's hand. "And all because I didn't trust God with my future."

Carrie looked away but didn't let go of Madeline's hand. "I just wish I could be sure."

"It wouldn't be faith if we could see everything ahead of time."

Carrie's mouth twitched at one corner. "It'd be nice all the same."

"I suppose it would." Madeline patted her hand and released it. "You never did tell me what time you perched yourself out here."

"I don't know. Maybe around six?"

"It's after seven now. You can't just sit here moping all day. Come on." Madeline stood and hauled Carrie up with her. "Go get dressed, something pretty now, and we'll have a nice walk along the beach. Getting out into the fresh air will make things look a lot better, I promise."

"I don't know." Carrie looked out the window to the street below. "I think I'll just stay here."

"Now, don't be that way. The beach is very pretty in the early morning, and the tide probably brought in all kinds of interesting shells and things."

Carrie shrugged listlessly.

"Maybe," Madeline added, "if we walk toward the Hall, the boys will see us and ask us to breakfast."

That brought a hint of a smile to Carrie's face. "I suppose it would be nice to get out in the fresh air for a little while."

Madeline grinned. "I'll race you."

— Fourteen —

adeline and Carrie walked along the shoreline toward Thorburn Hall. The sea air was fresh and crisp, and they stopped to watch a flock of sandwich terns fishing among the rocks, their grating *kear-ik kear-ik* loud in the early morning quiet.

"Better?" Madeline asked as Carrie stood watching one of the males present his mate with a courtship offering of fish.

"Aren't they sweet?" Carrie's eyes were bright now, her cheeks rosy with sun and briny air rather than tears.

"Just like you and Nick."

"Go on." Carrie huffed and started off down the beach again, only to stumble and nearly fall.

"I told you not to wear those shoes."

Carrie darted a glance at Madeline's feet and made a face. "I couldn't very well let Nick see me in something like what you've got on."

Madeline took her arm, her expression warm. "You could wear army boots, honey, and he'd think they were glass slippers."

Carrie smiled faintly, but the smile was more sad than happy. "I know he would. Oh, Madeline, what *am* I going to do?"

"You know I can't decide that for you."

Scowling, Carrie quickened her pace as they approached the boulder-strewn beach below Thorburn Hall. Then she stopped abruptly and shaded her eyes. "What's that down there?"

A police car had pulled off the road, and two officers were standing over something that looked like a bundle of rags that had washed up with the tide. A little knot of people—an elderly couple, several children, a middle-aged woman with binoculars and a hiking stick—stood looking at the bundle and murmuring among themselves.

"All right," one of the officers was telling them as Madeline and Carrie drew nearer. "There's nothing to see here. Everything's being looked after." He looked over at the girls and raised his voice. "I beg your pardon, ladies, but I must ask that you carry on with your walking." He turned again to the others. "Ladies and gentlemen, please. This is an official investigation. I must ask you to go on about your business."

"Are we not to know anything, young Phelps?" the old woman asked. "Not even a wee bit of it?"

The officer shook his head. "I'm sorry, Mrs. Ellis, but you've got to go now. No doubt there'll be something in the papers in time. Now come along."

She took her husband's arm, tugging him along with her, muttering darkly, though he didn't look as if he quite knew where he was or what was happening.

The children, being warned again, scattered across the beach while the woman with the binoculars clutched her hiking stick and headed down the road behind Madeline and Carrie.

With a glance at Carrie, Madeline slowed to let her catch up. "What was that about?"

The woman lifted one heavy eyebrow. "It's a body. I saw

before they covered him up, poor man. Must have been rather a fine-looking man too, from what I saw, although it's hard to tell so much when they're dead."

Carrie kept her eyes on the road ahead and said nothing, but her lips were pressed into a hard, taut line.

"Was it an accident?" Madeline asked. *Please, don't let it be another murder.*

"They won't say, of course," the woman said thoughtfully. "But his front was all over with blood, and I heard one of the constables talking about the sort of gun it must have been. Can you imagine? Oh, I beg your pardon. I suppose they're ever so much more common where you're from, I daresay. Pistols, I mean, not a proper hunting rifle or that sort of thing. Those we have, of course, but that's different, isn't it? Still, it seems a shame. A young man like that. I suppose he had got in with the wrong sort." She glanced back toward the scene of the crime, but there was little to see from this distance. "You are American, I take it?"

Madeline nodded. Carrie merely walked straight ahead.

The other woman looked grimly pleased. "I thought as much. Well, I suppose we'll have to wait till the next edition of the news. Here's my turn. Good morning."

She scurried off along a little track that veered away from the water and was gone.

"Carrie," Madeline began. But Carrie didn't turn, didn't slow. Madeline hurried after her. "Carrie."

Carrie stumbled and then bent down to rub her ankle. Madeline stopped beside her.

"Are you all right?"

"No, I'm not all right. I'm not all right at all." She sniffed and then fished her handkerchief out of her handbag and dabbed her nose with it. "I'm sorry. I promised myself I wouldn't let all this get to me again. People die, right? They do. That doesn't mean we're in danger, right? Or Nick—" She looked up and put on a stiff smile. "Nick."

The boys were scrambling down the steep path that led from the house to the beach.

"Hullo, sweet." Nick went straight to Carrie, and she huddled against him.

"We didn't expect to see you down here, but we saw the police and thought we'd see what's what." Drew kissed Madeline's cheek. "What's happening over there?"

Carrie glanced at Madeline. "I—I don't know. The police won't let anyone near. They told us to keep walking."

"Did you see anything?" Drew asked Madeline.

"I'm fairly sure there's a body on the rocks over there, but as Carrie said, they wouldn't let us stop and look."

"Probably not something either of you want to see, darling. I believe that's Sergeant Shaw over there now. Let me just see what he'll tell me. Won't be half a moment."

Drew loped over to where the body was. There was a second police car pulled up there now and another officer, Sergeant Shaw. Drew spoke to him for a moment. Then he knelt beside the body and lifted up the blanket that covered the face. He pushed the blanket to about halfway down and motioned for Shaw to come closer. He pointed at something on the body and then put the blanket back into place and stood.

For another minute or so, he walked carefully around the area, bending down now and then before going back to speak to Shaw. The sergeant shook his head decisively, frowned and then pulled a handkerchief from his pocket. Drew looked at the contents and then jogged back to where the other three were waiting for him.

"Definitely a body," Drew said. "Not quite what I expected."

"Drowning?" Nick asked.

"No. Shot through the heart. Dead before he hit the rocks."

"There was a woman there when we first came up," Madeline said. "She mentioned something about a pistol. But who is it?"

"The caddie. Jamie Tyler."

"Oh," Carrie breathed. "Poor Joan."

"We'd better go on back to the house," Drew said, looking back toward the crime scene once more. "I know the inspector will be by any minute now, and doubtless he'll be in no mood for my antics. The good sergeant will keep us informed if there are any developments." He took Madeline's arm. "I think we'd better go and talk to Joan, darling. I don't want her to hear about this from one of the servants or from the next edition of the paper."

"Are you all right, Carrie?" Nick asked as they climbed the path back up to the Hall.

She lifted her chin. "Of course I am. I know I've been a ninny about all this, but I'm not going to be anymore." She clasped his arm, struggling for a moment with a step that was higher than the others. "You'll figure this out, and that'll be the end of it, right?"

"Of course." He put his hands around her slim waist and lifted her up to the next step. "Not to worry."

Madeline watched them for a moment and then hurried after.

When they reached the Hall, Drew immediately sent for Twining. "Has Miss Rainsby rung for her tea this morning?"

"I don't believe so, sir. Is something the matter?"

Drew glanced up the stairway. "Is she usually up at this time of the morning?"

"No, not generally, sir. Like many young persons, Miss Joan has always been rather a late sleeper." The butler looked at the crystal clock on the mantel. "She should be rising soon. May I send up a message with her breakfast?"

"Does she generally request a newspaper with her tea?" Drew asked. "Or would she have had occasion to see one this morning?"

"I don't believe so, sir. I could ask Agnes, but based on my own observations, I don't believe Miss Joan ever looks at the papers until the afternoon."

"All the same, could you see that whoever brings up her tray makes sure not to include the morning papers? Thank you, Twining."

"Just as you say, sir."

Drew looked out the window down toward the sea. He couldn't see anything of the spot where Tyler's body lay, but it was possible that from some parts of the house, perhaps from the roof, it would be visible. "Oh, I say, Twining?"

"Yes, sir?"

"Do you know if there's been any gossip among the servants this morning?"

"There is always gossip, sir."

Drew smiled faintly. "Quite. But something alarming. Just this morning."

"I understand the Russian gentleman is to return to us sometime today." In spite of Twining's always correct demeanor, Drew could still tell the butler found this news decidedly alarming. "Mr. and Mrs. Pike have gone round to fetch him."

"Besides that."

"All the staff were churning amongst themselves, trying to see what was amiss down on the beach," Twining said. "But I let them know in no uncertain terms that their duties lay inside the Hall and not outside of it. They know no more than I do about the matter."

"Good. Please see that no one says anything upsetting to Miss Rainsby until I've had a chance to speak to her. It's very important."

"Certainly, sir." Twining gave a half bow. "I will see to it personally."

"And yes, please send up a note with her breakfast asking if I might come speak to her as soon as is convenient."

"It's not likely to be in the papers, is it?" Madeline said once the butler had gone. "I mean, they only just found the body."

"Not likely, no," Drew admitted. "But I don't know how long they've been out there or if some reporter mightn't have happened on it before dawn and hurried off to write a lurid account for the early edition. No sense having Joan seeing that instead of us breaking it to her gently."

"Breaking what to me?"

All four of them looked up to see the daughter of the house standing in the drawing room doorway, her face pale, her eyes puffy as if she hadn't slept well. Nick and Drew both stood.

"Good morning," Drew said, going to her. "I hope my message hasn't disturbed you. I most distinctly told Twining to say I'd wait until you had a convenient moment. You can't have eaten yet."

He led her to an overstuffed chair, and she sat down.

"I'm not hungry. I couldn't stand even the smell of whatever was on my tray this morning. When Agnes brought your message, I was already dressed anyway, so I thought I may as well come down." She smoothed back her dark hair on one side. Evidently she had done no more than run a comb through it before coming downstairs. "So what is it you have to break to me? Is it more about my mother? It is, isn't it? Have they found something else against her?" She ran her hands through her hair, disarranging it again. "Oh, I can't stand this. I could hardly sleep, thinking about everything that's happened. It *is* Mother, isn't it?"

Madeline went to her, sat on the arm of the chair, and put an arm around her shoulders. "No, no. It's not that at all."

"Actually, in its way, this might help your mother's case," Nick said. "Don't you think so, Drew?"

"Possibly, though we can't know that quite yet."

Joan looked from one to the other of them, clearly bewildered. "I don't understand. If it might help Mother, then—"

"It's about Mr. Tyler," Madeline said gently.

"No." There were sudden, fierce tears in Joan's eyes. "I don't believe it. They've been trying to blame Jamie for everything, from Father's murder to the devaluation of the British pound. Whatever they say he's done, it's not true. I know it's not true."

"I wish it were just that," Drew said, "but I'm afraid Tyler is dead."

Joan blinked and her forehead wrinkled. "Wh—what? No. No, he can't be dead. I saw him just last night. We went to Edinburgh, where nobody would know who I am and gossip about me. We had dinner at a little pub. We parked in a grove of trees just off the road on the way back." She looked pleadingly at Madeline. "We were going to be married. As soon as everything with my mother was settled, we were going to be married."

Carrie glanced at Nick, wrapping herself in her arms and saying nothing.

"I'm so sorry," Madeline murmured, pulling Joan closer.

Joan clung to her for a moment, perfectly silent but trembling visibly. Then she pushed herself away and blotted her face with the handkerchief from her skirt pocket.

"Is there someone you'd like us to call?" Drew asked. "A friend? An aunt perhaps?"

Joan shook her head, her face blank now. "Just tell me. Tell me what happened."

"Someone shot him," Drew told her. "Last night or early this morning."

"Shot him? Where is he? I have to go to him."

"There's no use doing that. The police won't let you down there. Believe me, he's dead. I saw for myself."

"Down where?" she demanded. "What's happened to him?"

"He was found on the rocks by the water, not far from the house."

"But . . ." She looked bewildered. "Why would he be down there?"

"Wouldn't he have been going back to Gullane after he'd seen you home?"

She shook her head. "He didn't see me home. I dropped him at the end of the high street, just round that corner where the road bends. People in the village can't really see much of that part of it. I thought it was best. Why would he have come back this way?" She caught a trembling breath. "Oh, Jamie, why didn't you just go home?"

"What time did you let him out?" Drew asked after she'd had a moment to collect herself.

"I—I don't know. We didn't leave the pub until after midnight, I remember, but I can't be sure about anything else. I got home maybe an hour later, maybe two."

Drew frowned. "Did you speak to anybody in the house,

someone who might remember the exact time? It would help us in narrowing down when he was killed."

"I didn't speak to anyone, no. Agnes was up. I saw her in the hallway. I don't know if she'd remember the time, but we could ask her if it would help."

"What was she doing that time of night?" Madeline asked.

"I don't know. I hardly noticed her. One doesn't, you know."

Shortly after she was summoned, Agnes peeked into the drawing room. "You wished to see me, Miss Joan?"

Her face told the story as plainly as if it were written there. She'd heard about Tyler.

"Come in, please," Drew said, and he brought over a straight-backed chair, one of those stark modern things that populated the house.

Looking as though she were on trial, Agnes sat down. "Is there a problem, sir?"

"No need to worry. I take it you've heard about the incident down by the water."

She ducked her head, not looking at her mistress. "Yes, sir. I'm so very sorry, Miss Joan."

Joan nodded just the slightest bit but said nothing.

"We'd just like to know," Drew said, "if you heard anything last night. Something out of the ordinary, perhaps?"

"I canna be certain, sir. I was asleep, and I thought I heard something and went to look, but it was just Miss Joan coming in. There wasn't anything else."

"Fine. And did you happen to notice the time?"

"That I did, sir," the maid replied. "It was twenty minutes past one. I looked because I was that turned around and thought I might've overslept myself. But it wasn't nearly time to get up, so I took myself back to bed."

"I see. Was there anything else you noticed, either then or later, anything at all? Perhaps you heard something? A motor car backfiring? The slam of a door?"

Agnes shook her head. "No, sir. I went to sleep again, got up at my usual time, and started work. It was then I heard about . . . well, about what had happened down there. I mean, after the master and then madam being taken away and now—"

Joan made a half-strangled little sound, and Madeline gave Drew an urgent look over the girl's head.

"Yes, thank you, Agnes," Drew said smoothly. "It has been a difficult time. That will be all for now. If you happen to think of anything else we ought to know about, don't hesitate to come to me."

Agnes stood and made a small curtsy. "Thank you, sir." She turned anxiously to Joan. "Is there anything I can do for you, miss? I'm so very sorry."

Joan shook her head, and with another bob, Agnes scurried out of the room.

Drew dropped to one knee beside Joan's chair. "Would you like to stop for now?" He looked at Madeline. "Perhaps you could help her upstairs."

"No," Joan said, a determined set to her mouth. "I'm all right. It's not going to get any easier, and I want to know what's happening. I can't stand to think—" She drew a hard breath. "Just ask me whatever you want to know."

"All right." Drew stood again. "Did Tyler say anything unusual to you? Was he having trouble with anyone at Muirfield, or at the place where he took lodgings?"

"Nothing."

"I was down there just now," Drew said gently. "I saw what

had been in Mr. Tyler's pockets. It can be quite helpful sometimes, seeing that."

She merely looked at him, bewildered.

"Mostly it was the usual thing," Drew told her. "A few coins, some tees, a ball marker, not much more. But there was also a 1914 Star. Do you recall seeing that before?"

"I think so, yes. He dropped it once when he took his latchkey out of his pocket. One night when I let him out in the village. He said it was his father's. From the war."

"I see. I expect he must have been quite proud."

She glared at him, blinking back tears. "Of course he was. Do you think just because he hadn't any money, he had no finer feelings? You didn't know him. Nobody knew what he was really like." She gulped down an unsteady breath and then another. Then she quieted and folded her hands in her lap. "I'm sorry."

"It's all right," Madeline said.

"We just spent the evening together," Joan said, her voice flat and emotionless now. "He told me that when all this was over, he was going to tell Mother we would be getting married whether or not she liked it. We quarreled a bit because I didn't think now was the time. He said we couldn't wait forever, that we had our lives to live, too. You don't think—? Oh, I don't know. I can't believe any of this is true." She held her clasped hands to her mouth, taking slow, shaky breaths.

Drew pulled her hands gently away from her face. "What is it you're thinking?"

"Nothing. It doesn't even make sense."

"What?"

She looked pleadingly at Madeline. "Did you ever wonder if someone you knew, someone you loved and trusted wasn't who he said he was? And it was so awful, you didn't even want to think it, but you couldn't help it because all the evidence made it look that way?"

Drew could feel Madeline's eyes on him, though he never looked away from Joan. Yes, he knew that feeling, a horrible, terrible feeling where the world seemed to be spinning backward and there was nothing to grab hold of.

"What is it you're thinking?" he asked again.

"It's just who'd want to kill him, and why?"

"I understand there might be several husbands who might be interested," Nick offered.

Joan scowled at him. "That's old news. If any of them wanted to kill him, he'd have tried ages ago. I mean now. Who'd want to kill him now?" She swallowed hard, steadying herself. "My father said he was going to. If Jamie didn't clear off. Of course, he's gone now, too. But he and Mother both didn't want me seeing him."

"You're not saying your mother could have been responsible for his death, are you?"

"No. I told you it didn't make any sense. I told you it's too awful. But the police think she killed Father and then Mr. Barnaby. If she would do that, or if she and an accomplice would do that, then why wouldn't she have Jamie seen to, as well?" She bit her lip. "I—I haven't been honest with you."

"No? What do you mean?"

"That night you saw me coming in from the stable. You knew I'd been with Jamie, but I didn't tell you what else happened."

"As I recall," Drew said, "you were quite adamant that there was nothing out of the ordinary going on."

"I was in the stable with Jamie." Her face turned pink, but she lifted her chin and forced herself to go on. "I walked with him to the road, watching him until he had gone over the rise. Then I saw that car parked there under the trees. You remember?"

Drew nodded.

"It was Mr. MacArthur's car. I recognized it. But I couldn't understand why he'd left it there. The only thing out that way is the cottage, so I thought I'd see if he was down there for some reason. I was going to see him off if he was. I know he was great friends with Mother and Dad, but I didn't like how he acted as if he lived here."

"Go on."

She took a deep breath. "I was only about halfway down the path when I heard voices, so I stayed close to the trees, in the shadows, until I could see who was coming." She shook her head. "Oh, Drew, it was Mother. She was laughing, coming from the direction of the cottage with a bottle of wine in one hand and her clothes all rumpled. And he was back there. He'd been in the cottage with her. I could hear him telling her to hurry home before anyone knew she was gone. And she said they wouldn't wait so long next time."

"You didn't see him come out, too?"

"Oh, no. I had to get back home before they knew I'd been there."

"Neither of them saw you?" Drew asked. "And you didn't say anything to your mother later?"

Joan looked down, shaking her head. "It was too awful. I couldn't say anything."

"That doesn't mean she killed anyone," Madeline said.

"But that's not all," Joan said. "The night Mr. Barnaby was killed, that Saturday night, Mother said she had a headache after dinner and went up to her room."

"That's what she told the police," Drew said.

"Well, I was a little worried about her so I went up with her. She said she was out of her headache powders, so I went and got one of mine. She took it from me and said she was going straight to bed. I went to my room and got ready for bed myself. I read for a while, and when Agnes brought up my chocolate at ten, I told her Mother wasn't feeling well and that I was going to go check on her. Agnes said she would do it if I liked, and I told her I would appreciate it very much." She licked her dry lips. "It was just a minute or two before Agnes came back. She said Mother was in her bathroom with the door locked and wouldn't answer her knock. I thought maybe she was really ill and couldn't answer, so I went to see what was the matter. I didn't get any answer either, so I rummaged in her bureau and found the key to the bathroom and opened the door. The bathroom was empty."

"Where had she gone?"

"That's the terrible thing about it. I don't know. I told Agnes to search the house quietly, and I'd do the same. Neither of us could find her. I was looking in my father's room when Agnes came and got me. She said Mother was in her bed, fast asleep."

"What? Where had she been?"

"I don't know. I started to wake her, but she was very soundly asleep, and I really didn't want to disturb her. She hadn't slept well since my father died. I thought maybe she'd been restless and had gone for a walk in the garden or something and then had come back and gone back to sleep. I didn't think much of it until we heard Mr. Barnaby was murdered. Once we heard about that, I asked where she'd been."

Drew raised his eyebrows expectantly.

Joan shook her head. "She told me she'd been asleep. From the time she lay down until her maid brought her tea the next morning, she hadn't moved. I didn't ask her about it after that. I . . . oh, I didn't want to think about it. I didn't want to say anything because she just couldn't have done something so horrible." She squeezed her eyes shut. "But then I looked in the medicine cabinet there in her bathroom. She had almost half a box of those powders left."

Drew glanced at Madeline, who looked at him round-eyed.

"The same sort she borrowed from you?" he asked. "The ones she said she was out of?"

Joan nodded fiercely.

"And what did you do next?"

"God forgive me, I took them and put them down my toilet. I didn't want the police finding them. I didn't think it could be what it looked like. I didn't want to think it. But now that Jamie's gone, I can't go on lying. I can't go on making excuses for her. If she lied about being in bed all night that night, what reason could she possibly have, that night of all nights, except that she did kill Mr. Barnaby? And why would she kill Mr. Barnaby unless he knew something she had to keep quiet. He'd already told about Dad's new will, so it had to be something else. Something very serious."

There was pain and pleading in her dark eyes, but Drew could offer her little comfort.

"Something like murder."

— Fifteen —

id you say anything to Agnes after your mother was taken away for questioning?" Drew asked quietly.

Madeline gave Joan a handkerchief, and she blotted her face and blew her nose.

"Actually, Agnes came to me. She said she knew my mother couldn't have anything to do with what happened to Mr. Barnaby and she wasn't going to say anything about her not being in her room the night he was killed, so I didn't need to worry."

Drew nodded. "I was just wondering if we might have her back in here for a moment."

"Oh. Yes. Yes, of course."

She rang for Twining, and a few minutes later the maid crept into the room, her pale blue eyes wide. "You wished to see me, Miss Joan?"

"I asked her to send for you, Agnes," Drew said. "I'd like you to tell us about Saturday night."

"What do you want to know, sir?"

"Just tell us what happened when you brought up Miss Joan's chocolate."

Agnes shrugged, a very poor attempt at nonchalance. "I brought it up about ten, sir, and then I went to help Molly with the last of the scrubbing. Saturday nights, Cook wants the whole kitchen cleaned top to bottom, and sometimes I help."

"Where was Lady Rainsby at that time?"

"She said after dinner that she had a headache, and Miss Joan took her upstairs to lie down."

"And when was the next time you saw her?" Drew asked.

"Well, I never saw her go out or come in after that, sir. I brought her breakfast the next morning, and she looked like she hadn't slept well."

Drew glanced at Joan. "Why do you say that?"

Agnes squirmed a little. "She just looked sort of groggy-like and unsteady."

"I see. Now, think very carefully, Agnes. Between the time you took Miss Joan her chocolate and the time you brought Lady Rainsby her breakfast Sunday morning, did you see Lady Rainsby?"

Agnes lifted her determined chin. "Miss Joan said she was worried about her mother, and I looked into her ladyship's bedroom and saw she was sound asleep in her bed. That was the only time I saw her, sir."

"Thank you, Agnes," Drew said gently. "I believe you."

The maid exhaled, her eyes immediately going to her young mistress, like a puppy's looking for approval. Joan merely pressed her lips into a grim line.

"I want you to tell me one more thing, Agnes," Drew said, "and I want you to tell me the truth. Still considering the time between when you brought Miss Joan her chocolate and when you brought up Lady Rainsby's breakfast, was there a time when you looked into her ladyship's bedroom and did *not* see her there?"

The maid licked her lips, deliberately looking away from Joan. "As I said, sir, I didn't see her go out or come in after she went upstairs after dinner."

"That wasn't my question," Drew said gravely. "Was there a time you looked in and saw that Lady Rainsby was not in her room?"

"I did look in once, as I think about it now, sir, and she wasn't in her bed. But her bathroom door was closed, so it's natural to assume she was in there."

"And, since you and Miss Joan were concerned about her, did you knock to see if she needed anything?"

"Well, yes, sir, I did."

"What answer did you get?"

The girl wrung her hands. "I—well, I—oh, Miss Joan, what shall I say?"

"Tell him the truth, Agnes," Joan said tautly. "It's too late for anything else now."

"She wasn't there, sir," Agnes gasped, tears springing to her eyes. "I went to get Miss Joan, and she unlocked the door, but no one was there. Then we both looked all over the house. And then I went back to her ladyship's room, and there she was, sleeping like a baby. Oh, sir, I don't know where she was or what it means. She's been a kind mistress ever since I come to the Hall to work and all the girls say the same, and I wouldn't want to bring her to harm. I just can't think it of her, not anything bad like they're saying now, but that's what happened Saturday night." She pulled up her crisp white apron and buried her wet face in it, sobbing until Madeline went to her and put a comforting arm around her shaking shoulders.

"That's all right," Drew said. "Thank you, Agnes."

Agnes looked at Joan with anguished eyes. "I'm so sorry, Miss Joan. I didn't know how else to answer."

Joan nodded and wiped her own eyes. "It's all right, Agnes. That will be all."

"Yes, miss, thank you." The maid curtsied and left the room, shutting the door behind herself.

"All the staff are very devoted to Mother," Joan said. "Poor Agnes. Now I'm thinking if she had said something earlier, if we both had said something, Jamie might not be dead."

"That's possible," Drew said, "but there's something else we should take into consideration. It just might be that none of this has anything to do with Lady Louisa at all."

"But why would she have lied about the headache powders and about being in bed all night?"

"I haven't figured it all out yet, but I'm still wondering if this is something much darker than a domestic murder. Something your mother doesn't know anything about."

Joan dabbed her eyes, brightening faintly. "What you mentioned before, could it possibly . . . ?"

Drew gave her a comforting pat. "I can't make you any promises just yet, and I might be turned the wrong way round."

Nick snickered, which made both Madeline and Carrie smile.

Drew gave them a stern look. "Anyway, Joan, don't despair. I know this has been awful for you, but hold tight until I've done a bit more nosing about. I can't promise you, of course, but I don't think your mother is responsible for any of this."

She clasped his hand as if it were her only lifeline. "Thank you, Drew. I hope you can somehow make sense of it. I don't—" twin tears spilled from her closed eyes—"I don't know why anyone would want to kill Jamie. And if it's because he was in love with me, I don't know if I could bear it."

Wadding the handkerchief in both hands, she buried her face in it and wept. Madeline wrapped both arms around her, and the other three quietly left the room.

"What are you thinking?" Nick urged once Drew had shut the door behind them.

"Nick," Carrie breathed, tugging his arm.

She had been quiet all this while, but every emotion, every fear, every worry, every trace of anger had been plain in her expression as she listened to Joan and then Agnes. She wanted no part of any of this, even if she wasn't saying as much.

"I don't want to jump to concussions, as Mrs. D. always says," Drew told them, "but I can't help but think this all has to be part of what happened to Lord Rainsby and Mr. Barnaby."

"Exactly." Nick laughed humorlessly. "Quiet little Gullane? Even during Open week, I doubt they've had three murders, much less three unrelated ones all at once."

"I agree," Drew said. "But it's how they're related that we might be looking at the wrong way round."

Nick frowned. "What do you mean?"

"Well, even if she doesn't want to say it right out, it's obvious Joan is worried that her mother is back of all this. Killed her husband so she could have her lover. Killed her solicitor because he was blackmailing her over it. Killed the gigolo, or had her lover see to it, so he wouldn't ruin her daughter. But what if that's not the connection at all?"

"You mean Mac and his fascist sympathies?" Nick shrugged. "I can't say I quite see it. Even if he is selling information, that doesn't mean Barnaby was in on it with him, does it?"

"I don't know," Drew admitted. "Miss Grahame said Mr.

Barnaby did have some rather admiring things to say about that fellow in Berlin when I spoke to her about his murder. Suppose all that about the will itself was rubbish? Yes, Rainsby was there and met with Barnaby when Barnaby claims he did, but we have only his word for it that Rainsby wanted to change his will. The secretary never heard Rainsby say anything about the will. What if the entire tale about its being changed was simply nonsense?"

"Why would he want to do that?"

"Because, my dear shortsighted fellow, then he and MacArthur could do away with Rainsby without anyone looking any further than the widow for someone to blame."

"Then why kill Barnaby?"

"Because he knew about Rainsby, of course," Drew said. At least it was a possibility.

"And Tyler?"

"That one's a bit more difficult to explain. There's likely more to Barnaby's death, as well. All I'm saying is what if this has nothing to do with Lady Louisa and everything to do with MacArthur selling secrets to the Germans? After all, we know Tyler met Lisa that day out at Muirfield, but later on he denied it. Why? What could possibly be the connection between them if not something of that sort? And if it were simply what it seemed at the time, Tyler was rather one to brag on his conquests than deny them, don't you think?"

Nick snorted. "That's true enough. But then there's the medal."

"I haven't sorted out *how* it's all connected quite yet, just that perhaps it's something we ought to look into."

"If that's the case," Nick said, glancing at Carrie, "you don't think we might be in over our heads, do you? Those Nazi coves won't stick at anything."

"True," Drew mused. "Very true. Look here, I know you two have been apart just ages, and looking into murder and mayhem isn't exactly how you envisioned your time together now." He looked at Carrie with such exaggerated concern that it coaxed a smile from her. "I don't mean to make light of this," he added, smiling himself. "So if you two would rather go back to Farthering Place until this is all seen to, I'd certainly understand. In fact, I'd feel better if Madeline went along with you. You'd need a chaperone, anyway."

"Madeline isn't going anywhere just yet."

Drew turned to see his wife standing not three feet behind him, hands on hips and the light of battle in her eyes.

"Oh, hullo, darling." He leaned over and kissed her cheek. "How's Joan bearing up?"

"I got her to lie down upstairs for a while. Twining is bringing her some tea."

"Splendid. Now, as I was saying—"

"As *I* was saying, I'm not leaving just yet. Not as long as you're here. I don't mind staying in Gullane if that helps, Carrie, but I'm not going back to Hampshire and leaving that girl with no one but the servants to look after her. Good heavens, her father's been killed and the man she loved too, and her mother is the prime suspect. Somebody has to be here for her."

Carrie bit her lip. "I know." She looked up at Nick. "You don't want to go either, do you?"

"Carrie, sweet—"

"No, now, be honest, you don't."

He took her hand. "This wasn't at all what I expected when I finally got to see you again, but I don't know how we can just pack up and leave the poor kid on her own."

"But the police—"

252

"I know that's what the police are for, but they don't seem to be faring any better than we are at the moment in solving these crimes. I just . . ." He wilted at the look of hurt in her eyes. "Carrie."

Drew glanced at Madeline and then turned to Nick. "Perhaps the two of you ought to go back to Farthering Place. Mrs. Devon would look after Carrie, I'm sure. In fact, I could wire her to have Rose Cottage ready by the time you get there. Carrie could stay there until Madeline and I get everything sorted out up here. How would that be?"

"Would you like that, sweetheart?" Nick asked Carrie. "I daresay that's much more the sort of holiday you had in mind."

Carrie bit her lip. "I suppose it isn't right to just leave Miss Rainsby hanging. I oughtn't to be so selfish when she's got so much to trouble her just now." She blinked, her blue eyes bright with tears. "I know how it is when someone you love is suddenly gone. I don't know how I would have stood it if you all hadn't been there with me. If you hadn't found out what really happened. It doesn't seem fair to expect her to go through it all alone."

Nick pulled her close and pressed a kiss into her hair. "You don't have to—"

"No, it's all right. Really. I may not be as brave as the rest of you." She managed a tiny smile. "Or maybe I should say as foolhardy. What if we just carried on as we were? You don't mind coming back to The Swan, do you, Madeline?"

"Not at all," Madeline said. "If you're sure you don't mind."

"No. Not as long as your husband gets this figured out before too much longer." Carrie looked at Nick over Madeline's shoulder. "And makes sure to look after Nicky."

Drew smirked at the sudden color in Nick's face. "Don't

you worry. I'll make sure darling Nicky is safe and sound every moment of the day."

"I mean it." Carrie took Nick's hand. "You both have to look after each other."

"We will, sweetheart," Nick said. "We've been doing it since we were in our cradles."

"Except for that time you hit me in the head with a metal train engine," Drew said, rubbing his scalp.

"We were barely two," Nick protested.

"Still, it was hardly neighborly."

"It's a wonder either of you survived childhood," Madeline said, tucking her arm into Drew's. "Now, if we're to get this case solved, then we'd better figure out what we're going to do next. All of us."

Kuznetsov and the Pikes returned to the Hall late that afternoon, Mrs. Pike beaming at her protégé and the count looking convincingly martyr-like.

"My months of hiding from the Bolsheviki were not so harrowing," he moaned, arranging himself artistically on the divan in the library, "but I was younger then and able to bear so much more." Mrs. Pike patted his arm, and he seized her hand, kissing it fervently. "You have saved me, madam, indeed you have. One of my delicate temperament was never made to be locked away."

"I suppose I have," she said, looking extremely pleased with herself. "Did you hear, Alfred? Poor Misha would have died if I hadn't come for him."

"He looks healthy enough," Pike grumbled.

"Death of the soul," Kuznetsov said, covering his eyes with

one aristocratic hand, "is far more bitter than death of the body. I am quite certain I shall never recover."

Twining announced tea, and the count was the first one in the dining room. Drew sat next to him as he made quick work of a mound of scones and cucumber sandwiches. And while Mrs. Pike told the others how she had braved all danger and escorted the count out of durance vile, Drew managed a quiet conversation of his own.

"I'm curious," he said, keeping his voice low. "Mr. Pike said coming here was your idea. Says you insisted on it, even at the expense of another invitation he claims would have been far more . . . entertaining for you. Why is that?"

Kuznetsov's mouth turned up at one corner. "A trifle, to tell the truth. Looking for something that once belonged to my sister."

Drew smirked. The man was the most outrageous liar. "Your sister? I hadn't heard you mention her before."

"No? Well, one doesn't like to be tedious about one's family matters."

"I haven't heard the Rainsbys mention her, either. Has she been to the Hall?"

Kuznetsov gave a careless shrug. "I don't believe so. I can't imagine her ladyship ever met her."

"But she lost this item here at the Hall."

"Oh, no. But I happen to know it's here all the same. It's a very long story, and I won't bore you with it just now."

"Very thoughtful of you, I'm sure," Drew said. "And your sister's name?"

"Her name?" Kuznetsov blinked at him. "Mary Smith. Charming, isn't it?"

"Lovely. Not very creative, to be sure, but lovely."

Kuznetsov clicked his tongue reprovingly. "It is most ungracious of you, sir, I must tell you. I share with you the intimate secrets of my family, and you scoff. Most ungracious."

Before Drew could ask him anything more, Mrs. Pike demanded his attention.

"Misha, how are you feeling now? That horrible prison food hasn't upset your digestion, I hope."

"I can hardly swallow anything, madam," he said mournfully. "As you see." He gestured to the mound of delicacies on his plate, but it was there only because he had scarfed down his first plateful and then replenished it.

"Oh, dear." Mrs. Pike turned to her husband. "I told you, Alfred. I really cannot go tonight. I can't leave Misha in such a state, especially when he's only just returned to us. Now, you just ring up that nice Mr. Emerson and tell him we'll see him another time."

Pike glared at Kuznetsov. "You know I can't do that, Elspeth. It took me weeks to get that invitation, and I've wanted to make his acquaintance for three or four years now. I have a number of projects that need investors with his means, and if he's interested, he's likely to want to bring in his friends, too. I'm not going to miss this opportunity. Misha will be perfectly fine here at the Hall. Any of the servants will be happy to call in emergency medical aid if it's required in our absence."

She turned her face away from him with a huff. "That's a horrid thing to say. Besides, I understand the servants have this evening off."

Madeline patted her arm. "I'm sure he'll be fine. Drew and Nick will look after him until you get back."

Drew glanced at Nick, sure the startled look of dismay on his face was a mirror of his own. "We will?"

"Will you?" Mrs. Pike's pout turned into a smile. "Oh, I would feel ever so much better. I told Misha already that it would be good for him to have some young people to spend time with. He's too much involved in his art. I tell you, it's not good for him."

"It's just what he needs," Mr. Pike said, and he looked at his pocket watch. "You'd better come and dress now, Elspeth. It's a long drive out to Emerson's and we don't want to be late. You'll all excuse us, won't you?" He hurried his wife out of the dining room, not waiting for a reply.

For the next little while, Nick tried to convince Carrie to stay and have dinner with them at the Hall. It seemed for a while she was wavering, but when the Pikes came down to leave for their engagement, Carrie convinced them to drop her at The Swan on their way through the village. Madeline had no choice but to go along with her.

"Then we'll all go," Drew suggested. "No reason we can't have another of Mrs. Drummond's fine suppers, is there?"

"Oh, but you mustn't," Mrs. Pike protested, the veil on her pillbox hat quivering. "You boys must look after Misha. I'm counting on you."

Drew sighed. "Would it do if just one of us stayed on?"

"Well . . ."

"One nanny is enough, isn't it, Elspeth?" her husband grumbled.

"I suppose so," she agreed reluctantly. "He may be so exhausted from his ordeal that you won't hear a sound from him until morning. Poor, dear Misha, his body is too frail to contain so large a soul." She put both hands over her heart with a wistful smile.

Mr. Pike took out his watch once more. "The car will be waiting. You girls come along if you're going."

Nick looked anxiously at Drew, and Drew turned him toward the door. "Go along. I'll look after poor, dear Misha."

"Stout fellow." Nick swatted him on the back and then hurried out after the Pikes with Carrie on his arm.

"I want to stay with you," Madeline said, twining her arms around Drew's neck.

"Better go, darling. You don't want Carrie to be at the inn alone once Nick has to come back to the Hall."

"I suppose not." She looked dejectedly at the floor and then surprised him with a scorching kiss. Afterward she looked coyly up at him. "I'd better go before I make the Pikes late. Good night." She gave him a pert little wave and then was gone.

Drew stood there for a moment, breathless. Then he flung himself into an overstuffed armchair and picked up his discarded copy of *War and Peace*.

It was going to be a long night.

⬱

Two hours later, not having heard a peep from Kuznetsov or Joan upstairs, Drew found that he had read little more than forty pages of his book. There was too much yet that didn't make sense, Tyler's death least of all. The man had been to the pub late last night, Drew had heard that much.

The moment Nick returned to the Hall, Drew was out of his chair and picked up his hat. "I can't say I expected to see you so early, but I'm glad of it."

"Carrie was practically nodding off in her soup," Nick said, "and Madeline and I convinced her to get some sleep. Where are you off to?"

"I've been thinking about where Tyler was directly before he went out to the beach. It seems to me it would be most instructive to find out what anyone at The Brassie and Cleek had to say about his final visit there."

Nick shrugged good-naturedly. "I suppose another walk up to the village won't do me any harm."

"Better not, old man," Drew said with a glance toward the stairs. "Someone's got to look after the artiste."

"Oh, not really. Really?"

"We did agree to do it. Now be a good lad and stay here till I get back. I don't like Joan being here alone as it is. Somebody ought to look after *her*, don't you think?"

"All right. I'll stay. But mind you don't get yourself into any trouble. I promised your wife I'd at least encourage you to behave."

"I always behave," Drew assured him. "In some way or other."

Drew wasn't surprised to find The Brassie and Cleek nearly empty on a Wednesday night. A pair of old duffers sat quarreling over their checker game in one corner while half a dozen young rowdies played darts in the back. Other than that, the place was subdued.

Drew went to the bar and ordered a mug of cider. "Not much trade tonight."

"Early yet, sir," the barman said, taking his money. "In an hour or so, we'll fill up a bit."

Drew nodded and turned, half facing the room, leaning one elbow on the bar. "So, did you know him?"

"Know who, sir?"

"The man who was murdered last night. Jamie Tyler."

"Aye, I did that, sir. He was a regular here, you know," the barman said. "And he was here last night. Right before he was killed."

"Yes, I'd heard. Did he say anything in particular?"

The barman drew his heavy eyebrows together. "Not that I heard. As I told the police, I served him a mug of beer and then another. Then someone rang up for him. After that, he was off. That was the last of it. He wasn't one to say more to a barkeep than 'Give me a pint' and 'Let me have another.'"

"A telephone call?" Drew leaned closer. "Do you know who it was?"

The barman shook his head. "A woman is all I know. Sounded young, but not too young, if you know what I mean. Not too young for the likes of Jamie Tyler."

"And he didn't say anything about her?"

"Not to me. You might ask Jem over there. He and Tyler had a pint now and again. He was in last night, as well."

He pointed to the dart players gathered there, and Drew recognized the fresh-faced young man who had pointed Tyler out to him at Muirfield. Drew thanked the barman and went over to the group.

"Jem?"

The young caddie turned, then broke into a smile. "Yes, sir. Good evening, sir."

"You remember me from the course?"

"I do, sir. I never forget a gent who tips well, though I'm sorry I don't believe I ever got your name."

"Drew Farthering." Drew shook his hand. "I understand you were in here with Jamie Tyler last night."

The boy's jovial expression clouded. "Not with him, no, but we had a drink. Professional courtesy and that, right? Bad business what happened to him. Not that we were mates, mind you, but it was a bad business all the same."

"True enough. Look here, I'm trying to find out what happened to him. It would be quite helpful if you'd tell me what he said last night."

"It wasn't much," the caddie admitted. "But I'll tell you what I told the constable. I saw him come in and looking black as thunder. He ordered a pint and sat at a table by himself. Now me, I don't like to leave one of the lads without someone to tell his troubles to, so I went over and sat down. He said that was all right, but he didn't want to talk. I didn't much care either way, so we just drank and didn't say anything. After a bit, he shoved back his mug. I don't know what the look was on his face. Maybe anger. Maybe a little bit of fear."

"Fear?"

Jem shrugged. "Anyway, he told me he'd quarreled with his girl. I said I was sorry, but he didn't say anything more. Then Mr. Bathgate over there came to tell him he was wanted on the telephone."

"Did you hear any of what he said?" Drew asked.

"Nah. Harry and Will McGinty were rowing at the bar, and you'd never hear cannon fire over them."

"I suppose he didn't tell you anything about it."

"No, sir, not a word."

"Was he on very long?"

"Not more than a minute. Maybe half that. Afterwards he came back to the table and, not bothering to sit again, threw back the rest of his beer. I asked him if he was going, and he said he had to."

"That was all?" Drew asked, disappointed.

Jem's freckled face turned grim. "No, sir, though it didn't seem much at the time. He said, 'Did you ever think you'd hit straight for the green and end up in the middle of a hazard? Devil of a time getting out.' Then he left eightpence for Bathgate and went."

"He didn't say anything else?"

"Not a word," Jem said.

"What do you think he meant?"

"I suppose he meant his girl. She was well off, I understand, and they'd had a row. Maybe he decided she wasn't worth the trouble. Anyhow, she must have been the one who telephoned."

"Could be," Drew said, and he couldn't help but remember his conversation with Tyler just yesterday. *Anything for a few pence, eh?* Had he truly sold out his country to those who would destroy her?

He'd denied knowing Lisa Shearer, and yet Madeline and Carrie had seen them together at Muirfield. Yes, he and Joan had quarreled, but they were going to be married. Whether Tyler's intentions were honorable or just mercenary, he had been planning to marry Joan no matter what her mother thought. Or at least he'd told her as much. So what was this "hazard" he'd gotten himself into? And who was it on the other end of that telephone line?

— Sixteen —

rew thanked Jem with half a crown and swiftly made his way back through the village. It was getting rather late for a walk, but he needed to clear his head and think. He had to sort out all the half-formed suspicions that needled him but wouldn't sit still long enough to be examined. He considered going back to the Hall to chat things over with Nick, but then he decided it would be a more attractive prospect to stroll over to see Madeline at the inn. She was always able to help him see a case from a different angle, past his own experiences and preconceptions. Truth be told, he missed having her with him.

And then there was that kiss . . .

He turned down the high street. She could have led him a merry chase, as mad about her as he was, if she had been the sort of woman to treat a man that way. But then again, if she'd been that sort, it was likely he wouldn't be so mad about her, so it seemed to be sorted quite nicely just as it was.

He was soon at The Swan, standing beneath Madeline's open window. He'd once seen Douglas Fairbanks as d'Artagnan climbing up to his lady's window and clinging to the sill for a stolen kiss. Why not?

It took him only a minute to shinny up the ivy-covered trellis. He lifted his hand to tap on the window frame and then checked himself and made a swift count of the windows from the east corner of the building. It wouldn't do to have reached Miss Holland's window by mistake or, heaven forfend, the window of some elderly spinster who kept a cosh handy in the event Nazi spies should creep into her room. Assured that this was the fifth one along, he gave a discreet knock.

He waited for a moment and, getting no response, knocked again. There was a rustling inside the dark room. Then, without warning, something cracked down on his knuckles, almost sending him crashing back onto the street.

"Hey!"

Madeline peered out, a raised umbrella in one hand. "You," she breathed, and she laid the erstwhile weapon on the writing desk she was leaning over. "What in the world are you doing here?"

"That's no way to behave," he said, swinging himself up onto the sill. "Here I've come all this way to compare your light to the east and you to the sun, and you don't even have the consideration to have a lamp burning." He rubbed his stinging knuckles. "We won't mention your unconscionable behavior."

She looked at him for a moment, a little pucker between her fine brows. "What's going on? Why are you here?"

"No good trying to fool you, is there? All right then. I was thinking about what happened to Jamie Tyler last night and wondering about Mac and Lisa. You haven't seen either of them about tonight, have you? In the inn or anything?"

"No. Why?"

"You and Carrie saw Tyler and Lisa talking that first day at Muirfield, right?"

Madeline nodded.

"But he denied knowing her. Why do you think that would be?"

"I don't know."

"I talked to one of the caddies over at the pub just now," Drew went on. "Tyler had a telephone call last night, after he had quarreled with Joan. The barman says it was a woman. They're assuming it was Joan. Maybe apologizing. Maybe asking him to come back. Who knows?"

"Sounds reasonable," Madeline said. "But you don't agree."

"No, I don't. The barman didn't know and Tyler never said who it was, but what he did say, right before he left the pub, was that he'd hit into a hazard and it was deuced hard getting back out. Does that sound like a man talking about a girl? Especially this man? I could see him breaking off with a girl with never a look back, even if she were in trouble. No, this is something deeper, I'm certain of it."

Madeline's eyes widened. "You think he was in with Mac and Lisa, selling information or helping them some other way?"

"Could be. He told me it was all one to him, British or German." Drew frowned. "Still, the way he said it, I don't know. And the caddie I talked to recently, the one Tyler was drinking with last night, he said Tyler looked afraid. Why should he look afraid?"

Madeline thought for a moment. "Unless he was helping Mac and Lisa, maybe just a little bit, until he realized the seriousness of what he was doing. Joan said he always carried that medal of his father's. It must have meant something to him. England must have meant something to him. Maybe he hadn't really meant to betray his country. Whatever he'd done was so inconsequential and they paid so well, he didn't see any harm in it. And then later he realized how dangerous it would be to try to get out."

"And when Lisa called him, he went to tell her he wasn't going to help them anymore, so she or one of her people—I'm assuming she has people somewhere—one of them shot him."

"That's terrible," Madeline said. "I don't suppose there's any way to prove that."

"Not yet, no." Drew smiled at the anxiousness in her eyes and tapped the tip of her nose. "But we'll figure it all out in time. For now, I want to know why you'd already gone to bed. That's not much like you."

"Carrie was tired, and you weren't here." She perched herself on the desk so they were facing each other and gave him a coy smile. "So I didn't see any reason to stay awake, either."

"And I've been finding it deuced hard to sleep without you beside me."

She touched his cheek with the backs of her fingers. "I've missed you, too. I don't like being apart like this."

"Nor I." He brought her hand to his lips and, holding it against his heart, leaned back against the window frame. "I'd chuck the whole thing if I hadn't promised Joan. But I've just got to prove her mother isn't guilty. And if there's something with international consequence going on, I can't just stand by and let it happen, can I?"

"No," she said, and her eyes warmed. "Of course not."

"You always understand." He kissed her hand again, smiling despite the sudden tightness in his throat. "And that, my darling, is why I had to come see you. And why, should you ever decide to leave me again, I shall throw myself into the sea."

"Silly boy, I didn't leave you. I just had to keep Carrie from going home until Nick figures out what to say to her."

"Yes, and he absolutely refuses to heave her over his shoulder and carry her off to the registrar as I advised him."

She laughed softly. "You did not."

"Well, it would certainly make it easier on us if he would."

"And I'm sure that's their first concern."

"I suppose not, though it's terribly selfish of them."

"Terribly," she agreed. "I don't suppose Nick has actually come up with anything persuasive to say to her."

He shook his head. "Has she shown any sign of wavering?"

"Not that I can tell."

"Will she at least agree to come back to Hampshire for a visit?"

"She hasn't said so yet," Madeline told him, "but she hasn't refused, either."

"I suppose that's a good sign. If we can get this business worked out without something else upsetting happening, maybe she'll stop thinking the whole of Britain is overrun with homicidal maniacs."

She sighed. "When are we going to be able to return home? I really do miss you."

"Soon, darling." He put his arms around her waist and pulled her closer, close enough to rest his forehead against hers, to feel the soft warmth of her breath. "We'll figure out who's being so nasty here and then soon we'll be back at Farthering Place. In our own home. In our own room." He touched his lips to hers. "In our own bed."

She put her hands behind his head, bringing his mouth to hers again in a tender kiss. Then she pulled away and brought her lips close to his ear. "Are you coming in?"

"Why, Mrs. Farthering," he murmured, "what would the neighbors say?"

"They'd say— What's that?"

He huffed. "Well, that's a fine way to talk."

"Shh." She squeezed his hand, her expression suddenly urgent, her voice hardly a whisper. "There's someone in the street. He hasn't seen us."

They sat very still in the unlit window, watching as a tall, athletic-looking man came toward them, looking ahead and behind himself and into every close and alleyway.

"It's Mac," Drew murmured against Madeline's ear. "What's he doing out here at this hour?"

Madeline shrugged, shaking her head.

Then Mac was gone. He'd turned onto the street where the German lady had her bookshop.

Drew looked at Madeline, but before he could do more than open his mouth, her eyes narrowed. "You are not going after him."

"Can't just let him get away. I might actually find out who this Schmidt is this time." He swung his legs out over the street. "I'll be back as soon as I figure out what he's doing."

"At least tell me you have your gun with you."

"Not on this outing. Sorry."

"Fine," she said, snatching up her robe. "I'm coming, too."

"Oh, no. Not this time. If I get into trouble, I need someone back here to call for help."

"Drew—"

"I've got to go, darling, otherwise I'll lose him." He lowered himself back to the trellis but still hung from the windowsill. "Kiss me goodbye?"

"Drew—"

"If I'm gone more than twenty minutes, send Shaw after me. He's just a few doors down."

She leaned down and kissed him fiercely. Then he dropped silently to the street and followed Mac toward Dunst's. Drew could see him just up ahead, moving slowly, warily, obviously up to something he didn't want known. Loyal Englishman, indeed. Drew wanted to kick him all the way to Berlin along with his Nazi friends. Well, time enough for that once he had the goods on him.

When Mac reached the bookshop, he looked furtively around and then disappeared into the narrow opening that ran between it and the shop next door. There were no lights on in the front, but when Drew crept along behind him and round to the back, he saw there was one in the rear, dim behind the drawn shades, but there all the same.

Drew pressed himself back into a shadowed doorway as Mac took one last look behind him and then gave a series of knocks, one long, two short. An instant later, the door was opened. Drew caught a fleeting glimpse of the old woman who ran the shop, and then all was darkness again.

He crept up to the window and was surprised to find that, despite the lowered shade, it was partly open. It was a pleasant night, but it was also June, and an unventilated room could grow close very quickly. An electric fan hummed just beyond the window, probably on a nearby table, jumbling the conversation inside. He could hear MacArthur and then someone else—not the old woman but a man. If he wasn't English, he certainly spoke the language without a trace of accent.

"This has everything?" he was saying. "Installations, roads, everything?"

Mac murmured something about elevations and other map-making terms. The other man asked several questions, his words sometimes unintelligible but his satisfied tone unmistakable.

Well, he wouldn't be satisfied for long, not if Drew had his own way. Once Inspector Ranald knew what he had overheard and—

"Shh."

Drew started and then was perfectly still. He didn't want to in any way inconvenience the owner of the little revolver that was currently pressed against his cheek.

"Don't make a sound. Don't move."

He blinked, recognizing the voice even as soft as it was.

Lisa.

He waited for her to order him inside. Waited, worse, for the click of the trigger being pulled back. But neither of those things happened. Perhaps something would distract her. It would take only an instant to wrest the gun out of her hand. Why hadn't he told Madeline just now how much he loved her?

"Anything else you want?" Mac asked. "For the present, anyway."

"No," said the other man. "This is good. Very good."

There was the sound of a drawer sliding open and then closed.

"I wouldn't take this if I weren't in such a bind," Mac told him. "Still, I think you chaps have it right. If we're to keep England strong, we'd do well to follow the example of Mr. Hitler."

He said something more, but the whir of the fan made all but the word *soon* unintelligible. The other man laughed and said something to the woman, and then there was the clinking of crystal. Clearly the bargain had been made, and to the satisfaction of both parties.

"Get down on your knees," Lisa breathed into Drew's ear, and she motioned with a handkerchief, white against the surrounding darkness. "Up against the wall, under the window."

She shoved him down with her free hand, still with the revolver against his head. It was now or never. He tensed, ready to spring, and then froze when several men swarmed out of the shadows. Two of them, pistols at the ready, positioned themselves on either side of the window. Two at the back door. The rest went to the sides and, Drew presumed, to the front of the shop.

One of the men at the window looked at Drew and then scowled at Lisa. She returned him a somewhat disgusted shrug and then pressed herself flatter against the wall when there was a sharp knock at the front door.

"All right, Schmidt, or whatever you're calling yourself, open up," said an authoritative English voice. "This is MI5."

At that, there was a scramble inside the room, the slamming of cupboards and drawers and the unmistakable sound of weapons being snatched up. Next came the sound of the front and back doors splintering, followed by shouting and swearing in both German and English, a brief but violent struggle, and then silence. The only shot fired had shattered the window above Drew's head.

"All right, Mr. Farthering," Lisa said, returning her pistol to the small bag slung over her shoulder as lights popped on in the upper floors of some of the surrounding shops. "You can get up now."

He scrambled to his feet and glanced in the window. The shade had been torn down in the struggle and he could see Mac inside. He was smiling broadly and having his hand shaken by the man who seemed to be in charge of the whole operation.

Drew turned back to Lisa. "I, er, seem to have stumbled into a rather delicate situation. Sorry about that. Though you might have told me what you were up to."

"I didn't have time, and you wouldn't have believed me, anyway. It was all I could do to make sure you didn't give us away or get shot before we had everything secured." She dug in her purse and pulled out a cigarette. Drew lit it for her. "We've been working months on this operation," she said after she had taken a few puffs, "and we didn't need amateurs spoiling it all at the last minute."

"Sorry."

"If Schmidt had got away, I think I would have gone ahead and put a bullet in your head myself."

Drew grinned. "Who is he? Someone from here?"

"He's a London man. That's why he needed Mac and me to do the groundwork for him up here. He pulls the strings and comes in at the end to pay off and collect his information."

Drew wrinkled his forehead. "Not German?"

"No. Just a first-class traitor. This wasn't his first job, but I promise it will be his last."

"I would have been happy to help you catch him if you had asked."

"You've been a great help, actually," she said with a bit of laugh. "The more you poked your nose into things, the worse Mac looked and the more Schmidt believed him a traitor. Mac even used you as an excuse to move this meeting up a week."

"I don't know if I should be pleased or insulted."

She dropped the cigarette to the ground and crushed it with her shoe. "You'd better come in and meet my chief."

Drew glanced into the room once more. The old woman, clearly Schmidt's confederate, and the man himself were being led away, both handcuffed and glowering.

"Your chief seems rather occupied at the moment. Could we postpone introductions for now?" He took his watch from his waistcoat pocket and held it up to the window, the sixpence that hung from the chain glimmering silver in the faint light. "If

I'm not back at The Swan in less than four and a half minutes, my wife is going to telephone Sergeant Shaw and tell him I'm being done to death by Nazi spies and need rescuing."

"We can't have that," Lisa said. "Consider the introductions postponed."

Drew nodded. "Before I go, might I ask you if you happen to know what Mr. MacArthur was doing on the evening of the fifth?"

"What day was that?"

"Friday a week ago. The night he left his car parked under the trees near the stables at Thorburn Hall."

"Oh. I believe that's when the chief met him at a little cottage we use sometimes, about a quarter mile from the Rainsby property. Not really a road a car can get down. I understand they were going over the details about how we'd handle tonight."

"And you were at the bookshop here doing what? Making sure Schmidt and Frau Dunst were occupied while this meeting was taking place?"

Her eyes narrowed. "Yes, Mr. Farthering. How did you know that?"

"Seems logical."

"No, I mean how did you know I was here?" Before he could answer, she held up one hand. "No. I know. Mrs. Farthering, right?"

"I could never get along without her. Still, forgive my bluntness, but I really must ask. You and MacArthur there, you two never—"

Her eyes flashed. "Never."

"His wife didn't divorce him over you, I take it."

"Of course not," Lisa said. "But it's not my place to say anything else about that. Still . . ." She took a deep drag of her forgotten cigarette and then blew the smoke straight up. "I'd have let her fry."

So Mac was the stout fellow Lord Rainsby had originally thought him to be. Not a traitor or a murderer or, it would seem, even an adulterer. Madeline was going to be disappointed.

"What about Hugh Barnaby? The man who was murdered this past weekend. Does he have any connection to any of this?"

"No. Why should he?"

"I don't know. He said a few things that made me think he might have sympathies in that direction," Drew said. "But surely Jamie Tyler was in it."

"Who?"

"Jamie Tyler, the caddie."

Lisa shrugged and shook her head.

"My wife saw you talking to him at Muirfield the first day of the Open. Good-looking fellow, tall, dark eyes, very blond hair."

"Oh, that one. I remember him. The hound wanted me to meet him at the pub that night for drinks and, no doubt, more. I sent him off with a flea in his ear, I can tell you. As if I didn't have more important things to do than waste my time with his sort." She drew a quick breath. "Wait a minute. You said Jamie Tyler. He wasn't the one they found on the beach this morning, was he?"

"He was."

She winced. "I shouldn't speak ill of the dead. I hadn't realized."

"You're saying you didn't know anything about him? He wasn't involved in any of this with Schmidt?"

Again she shook her head. "Sorry. That time at Muirfield was the first and last time I ever saw him. I never even got his name."

That made this whole thing all the more puzzling. So much

for his brilliant theory about Mac, Barnaby, and Tyler being part of a ring of Nazi spies. He'd have to start all over again.

"Well, as I said, I'd best get back to Mrs. Farthering before she raises the watch."

Lisa lifted one blond eyebrow. "I don't actually have to tell you to keep all this to yourself, do I?"

"You may rely on me," he told her, and then he hurried back to The Swan.

As Drew expected, by the time he jogged back to the hotel, Madeline was fully dressed and leaning out her window, watching the street he'd followed Mac into. The worried lines in her face smoothed into relief and then a smile and then a scowl.

"I was just about to go over to the police station to get Sergeant Shaw," she said when he climbed the trellis back up to her window. "Was that a shot I heard?"

"Only a little one."

"I suppose he got away and I'm lucky not to be a widow right now."

"He did not get away." Drew kissed her pursed lips. "But, yes, you are decidedly lucky I've returned to your eager arms." He scrambled over the writing desk and into the dark room. "Don't put on the light, darling. No need to scandalize Mrs. Drummond. I'll tell you all about it, but I'm afraid what I've found out only makes the investigation that much more confusing."

"What do you mean?"

He sat down with her on the settee, one arm around her waist. "Now, if you'll just let me tell it straight through and hold your questions till the end of the presentation—"

"Just tell me you're not hurt." She stroked the hair back

from his forehead, her anxious eyes all that were visible in the dimness.

"Darling." He pulled her closer. "I am perfectly fine. What is it you told me your grandfather used to say, the one from Georgia?"

He felt her giggle.

"'Fine as frog's fur split four ways.'"

"There," he said with a chuckle, "and what could be finer than that?"

"All right. Now tell me what happened with Mr. MacArthur. You didn't do anything silly like tie him up somewhere, did you?"

He told her what had happened at the bookshop, tactfully omitting the bit about the gun that had been pressed against his head.

"Then Mac couldn't have been the one Joan heard with her mother that night," Madeline said when he'd finished. "But she was so sure."

"I know. But remember, she saw her mother coming down the path, but she never actually saw Mac. Maybe she just assumed he was the one Lady Louisa was meeting because of his car."

Madeline frowned. "She seemed awfully sure."

"She did, but she's never liked Mac. Maybe she let that convince her he was the one when she didn't see or hear enough to be certain."

"I suppose," Madeline said, not sounding at all convinced. "But who could Lady Louisa have met if not Mac?"

"The puzzler is that Mac *was* at the cottage that night. That was his car I saw parked under the trees near the road. So the question is where would she have been coming from and with whom? Now that I can't blame the murders on Nazi spies and

British traitors, I'm right back where I started—a simple domestic murder for the sake of the dead man's estate. But if my cousin is the murderer, I'm deuced to know how she did it. She had to have had help, and that brings us back to our mystery man." He turned the great jumble of conflicting facts over in his mind. "I think there's only one thing for it tonight."

"Get a good night's sleep and talk it over again in the morning?"

"Nonsense. It's hardly eleven. I think we should go back to Thorburn Hall and talk this all over with Nick. Now that we know more about what Mac *wasn't* doing, maybe we sort out what's left and make something of it."

"I was afraid you were going to say that." Madeline laughed softly. "I suppose we may as well see what the three of us can come up with."

"The four of us," Carrie said.

— Seventeen —

Drew and Madeline both started and then turned to see Carrie, just a slim white silhouette standing in the darkened doorway into the hall. She had Bonnie cradled in one arm.

"I want to know what's going on," she said, hurrying to them so she wouldn't have to raise her voice to be heard. "I couldn't sleep and my room was too warm, so I went to open the window and I saw you climb up. I heard that shot, too. I'm sorry. I know I shouldn't listen in, but I heard you talking and I had to know what happened. Nick wasn't with you, was he?"

"Not to worry," Drew said. "I left him minding Kuznetsov."

"I don't know why you bothered," Madeline said. "All he ever does is eat and sleep. Nick probably won't see him all evening."

"I believe Nick found a book in the Hall library about increasing the yields on forage grasses," Drew said, "and I doubt he's looked up since."

"I want to go with you," Carrie said. "Back there. I want to know what's happening and what you're planning to do about it." She caught a hard little breath. "So I can decide what I ought to do."

Madeline squeezed Drew's hand again, a silent plea, and he squeezed back in acknowledgment.

"If you like," he told Carrie. "But it is rather late. If we're going, we ought to go now. What about Bonnie?"

"I'm going to take her to Mrs. Drummond."

The lights in the corridor and down the stairway were dim but serviceable. There was a brighter light at the large rolltop desk where Mrs. Drummond checked her guests in and out, and the woman was there herself, writing in a well-worn ledger. She looked not at all certain about the wisdom of the young ladies being out at all hours, but she took charge of the kitten and made no complaints.

"Do you have a latchkey?" Drew asked quietly, mindful of the hour.

Carrie and Madeline both nodded, and he led them out the front door and onto the street. It was little more than a mile back to the Hall, and it was good to see its lights there overlooking the sea.

They entered through the side door, the one Drew used when he'd left, and made their way silently up to the library.

"Still awake, old man?" Drew said, pushing open the door.

Sprawled sideways with his legs hanging over the arm of an overstuffed chair, Nick looked up from his book. He'd switched from forage grasses to the latest Agatha Christie, *Three Act Tragedy.*

"Oh, hullo, Drew. Madeline. Back again, are you?" he asked lazily. Then, seeing Carrie, he leapt to his feet, dropping the book and almost upsetting the table lamp beside him. "I didn't expect you here this late. Is something wrong?"

"Sit down, Fred Astaire." Drew shoved him back into the chair. "We've got to regroup."

Madeline and Carrie sat on the sofa next to him, and Nick reached over to take Carrie's hand. "Are you sure everything's all right, sweetheart?"

"Besides the village being overrun with German spies, you mean?" Carrie gave him a tremulous smile. "And Drew nearly being killed?"

"What?"

Drew looked up to see who had spoken. Joan was standing in the library doorway, one hand over her mouth.

"What do you mean?" She glanced back into the corridor and then came into the room, shutting the door behind her. "Excuse my eavesdropping, but I heard someone down here and came to see what was happening." Drew and Nick both stood, but Joan waved them back down and sat in the chair across from Drew. "What did you find out?"

"I know MacArthur couldn't have been the man you heard on the path in the woods Friday night," Drew said.

"But he must have been. His car was parked there."

"True, his car was parked where you saw it, and he was indeed at the cottage, but I happen to know your mother couldn't have been there."

Joan merely stared at him.

"Wait a minute," Nick said, looking as dumbfounded as she did. "You'd better catch us both up."

Drew gave them a brief account of his adventure that night, again omitting the part about his being held at gunpoint.

Nick whistled under his breath. "That does set everything

on its head. No wonder you thought we ought to hammer it all out again with the new information taken into account."

"If Mr. MacArthur wasn't on the path that night, who do you think it could have been?" Madeline asked Joan. "Is there anyone else you could have mistaken him for?"

"I—I don't know." Joan looked at Drew, a touch of fear now mingling with her bewilderment. "Are you saying there's someone else involved? You know I never liked Mr. MacArthur, but I couldn't live with myself if something I said got an innocent person hanged."

Madeline patted her hand. "I don't suppose you have any doubt about seeing your mother there, though."

Joan pressed her lips together. "I wish I could tell you otherwise, but I definitely saw her. I know she says she never left her room on Saturday, but she wasn't there when I looked. Just ask Agnes." She closed her eyes. "Oh, it's just too awful. Father and then Mr. Barnaby and then—then poor Jamie."

"Don't worry," Madeline said. "We'll figure it all out. There must be some explanation for all this."

"But what could it be besides that Mother and whoever she had helping her killed all three of them?"

"Let's go back to the man in the woods," Drew told Joan. "What sort of voice did he have? What exactly did he say?"

"I hardly remember now. It was a normal voice, nothing remarkable."

"Not any sort of accent, then?"

"No, a normal English voice. He just told her to hurry home and not to let anyone see her." Joan got to her feet, both hands pressed to her temples. "Oh, I can't think about this anymore. I can't believe any of it still, but I know what I saw. I know what I heard."

Drew and Nick stood too, and Drew went to her. "I don't want you to worry. As Madeline said, we're going to sort this all out. Is there anything else you remember?"

"I don't know anything else." Joan's voice rose and cracked. "I saw her coming home that night, and I heard someone with her. I heard her arguing with my father over something."

"You said they were arguing about Mac," Drew reminded her. "You were very sure."

She bit her lip. "Maybe I jumped to conclusions there, too," she admitted. "Neither of them named names. I thought they meant Mac, but I see now I could have been wrong. I don't know, I tell you. I just don't know."

Drew couldn't help but feel bad for her. He'd wanted all this while to prove that her mother was innocent, yet now it seemed all other options had been ruled out. It was, all in all, quite a shock.

Madeline put her arm around the girl's shoulders. "It's all right. You don't have to think about it just now."

"And if it's bad news about your mother," Drew said, "we'll see you through it. You won't have to face it alone."

"No," Madeline assured her. "You can count on us for anything."

"Thank you." Joan looked as if she might cry, but then she took a deep, calming breath. "I'm sorry, but I've got a throbbing headache. I'd better go to bed."

Everyone told her good-night, and she hurried out of the room, pulling the door almost closed behind her.

"I don't know what to think," Drew said, almost more to himself than to everyone else. "It just doesn't fit. Why would Lady Louisa kill Barnaby? If he wanted to blackmail her, why would he tell the police about the new will? What good would killing him do her after that?"

He remembered the man telling him about the proposed will and the rest of Lord Rainsby's visit with him. *"It's hard to overlook the part Lord Rainsby's considerable fortune could have played in everything that has happened."* But Lady Louisa had a considerable fortune of her own.

"Maybe he knew more about her," Madeline said. "Things we haven't found out yet. About her seeing someone. I hate that there's no other explanation, but she must be the one. She must be."

"And Tyler?"

"She—I don't know. Maybe she found out Joan was seeing him again."

Nick frowned. "It does seem a bit odd that she would be worried over that while she was sitting in jail waiting to be tried for her husband's murder, especially going so far as to arrange for someone to have him killed."

"Wait." Madeline clutched Drew's arm. "Where is Count Kuznetsov?"

Drew looked at Nick. "Have you seen much of him this evening?"

"I haven't seen him at all," Nick replied. "But he does tend toward vanishing for hours at a time." He smirked. "So long as there isn't a meal to be had."

"That's what I mean." Madeline's grip tightened. "After Lord Rainsby died, Lady Rainsby spent a lot of time in her room. The count was supposedly napping most afternoons, too. What if they were together most of those times? All this while we've been thinking he was just a harmless charlatan, but you've seen how slick he is with the ladies, most especially the older ones. What if he wanted to be more than just someone's protégé? What if he wanted to be master of the house and be set for life?

What if he seduced Lady Louisa and convinced her they should get rid of her husband so they could marry? He was the one who insisted the Pikes come here in the first place, remember?"

"Don't be ridiculous, darling," Drew said. "Kuznetsov?"

"No, listen to me. We know Lord and Lady Rainsby had a quarrel over him. She told you that herself. What if it wasn't about his taking things from the Hall? What if Lord Rainsby suspected something between them? That would explain why he wanted to change his will and why Barnaby was blackmailing Lady Rainsby."

Nick wrinkled his forehead, and then his eyes widened. "Then Kuznetsov must have been the one who killed Tyler. You've heard him do impressions to amuse everyone. I don't doubt he could have made himself sound like a female on the telephone in order to lure Tyler out to the beach. If his Russian accent is put on, why not an English one? Why couldn't he have been the one coming down the path behind Lady Rainsby the night Joan saw her?"

"For the simple reason, my dear imbecile, that he was in Inspector Ranald's jail at the time." Drew huffed and propped his chin on one hand. "The two of you build a fair case, and I couldn't rightly say any of it is beyond what Kuznetsov might do given reason enough. But it won't do. If there is such a thing as an ironclad alibi, he has one for Barnaby's murder and for the night Joan saw her mother in the woods."

"I feel so bad for Miss Rainsby," Carrie said. "All this must be so terrible for her."

Nick went over to sit on the sofa beside Carrie. "Poor girl. But she saw her mother. Lady Rainsby must be lying."

"If anyone but Joan had claimed to have seen her that night, I—" Drew stopped. Anyone but Joan.

Madeline looked at him strangely. "What is it?"

"I'm an idiot."

Nick snorted, and Carrie swatted the back of his hand.

"Anyone but Joan," Drew said aloud, and then he slapped his own forehead. "How could I have been so monumental an idiot?"

"*What is it?*" Madeline demanded.

"What if we've got it all backwards?" Drew laughed, and then glancing at the slightly ajar door, he lowered his voice. "What if it's not Lady Louisa who's lying but her sweet, brokenhearted young daughter, Joan?"

Nick nearly choked. "What?"

"Think about it. Who's the only one who heard Lord and Lady Rainsby arguing and could understand even part of the conversation? Who's the only one who saw Lady Louisa meeting someone out in the woods? Who's been dropping little tidbits here and there about Lady Louisa, not wanting us to check into any other possibilities?"

"But why?" Nick asked.

"The money, old man. The money. Father has a lot. Mother has a lot more. But poor Joanie hasn't any unless they give it to her. They don't want to give it to her, not if she hangs on to her beloved caddie, so what better to do than dispose of Pater and let dear old Mater swing for it, eh?"

"That means she must have killed him," Madeline said. "If she loved Jamie so much, why would she kill him? And why would she kill Barnaby?" Her eyes suddenly lit. "The will!"

Drew nodded. "Exactly. Somehow she coaxed or bribed or coerced him into claiming Rainsby had drawn up a new will. Again, no one heard him actually ask for a new will. The secretary merely typed up what Barnaby told her to. Then, once it was done, of course Joan couldn't leave any loose ends. And if she can make it look as if he were blackmailing her mother and MacArthur, that's just one more knot in the noose. Heavens, it's diabolical."

"But Jamie," Madeline insisted, "why kill him?"

"Maybe he said he was leaving, or maybe she found out he was seeing someone else. It doesn't matter. We've got to get Ranald out here right away."

"But Lady Louisa—"

"Wait."

They all hushed, and there was the distinct sound of footsteps on the stainless-steel stairs.

"Call the police," Drew told Madeline. "Then you and Carrie stay in here and lock the door. Come on, Nick. You go round the back and see she doesn't get out that way."

Carrie grasped Nick's hand, not letting him go, her piquant face lined with anguish. "Let her go," she pled. "Let the police see to her."

"It won't do anyone any good if she's halfway to Reykjavik before they get here." He pulled her up beside him and silenced her with a firm kiss. "Stay here, sweetheart. I'll be back."

"Quick, man," Drew urged. He hugged Madeline close and then released her. "Hold down the fort, darling."

Nick darted through the side door that led through Lord Rainsby's study and eventually to the back of the house. Drew hurried out the front way, into the corridor and then up the stairs. Drat these metal stairs. There was no way to get up them without the whole house hearing it. Still, he padded up as quietly as he could and started down the corridor toward Joan's room. There was no knowing just where she was or if she was armed. If he was right, she'd killed at least three people. No good making it a fourth.

He began by opening each door he passed and peeking inside. So far, nothing. No one.

Once Drew and Nick were gone, Madeline locked the library doors and telephoned Sergeant Shaw. After she'd convinced him that "nice Miss Rainsby" was likely to have committed several murders, he said he was on his way and hung up the phone.

"I don't like this," Carrie said, her blue eyes enormous. "I don't like the boys being out there."

Madeline merely listened, praying all the while that God would keep everyone safe until Joan could be taken into custody and questioned. Oh, how could she? How could anyone so cold-bloodedly destroy her own family? It still didn't make sense. If she'd loved this caddie enough to murder for him, why had she ended up killing him, too? Why had she—?

Madeline's eyes popped open. That sounded like a groan and something heavy falling.

"Nick!" Carrie leapt from her seat and, after a moment's struggle with the lock, threw open the library's side door.

"Carrie, don't! Wait!"

But Carrie was already in Lord Rainsby's study and then out the other side into the hallway.

"Nick! Get away from him!"

At her cry, Madeline rushed into the corridor. Nick was on the floor, the upper half of his body slumped against the door that opened onto the back stairs. Joan was struggling to move him out of the way, her dark eyes fierce and determined, but she couldn't budge him.

"Get away!" Carrie snatched up the fireplace poker Joan had obviously used on Nick and rushed at her. "Get away!"

With a curse, Joan turned back the way she had come, scrambling up to the next floor. She'd have to run into Drew up there. Madeline couldn't let her.

"Is he all right?" she asked Carrie, her breath coming hard.

Carrie nodded, touching her fingers to the long, narrow welt along the side of Nick's head. "I think he's just out cold."

Madeline nodded toward the poker she still held. "Keep that. Use it if you need to."

"Madeline—"

But Madeline was already heading back through the library. She'd go up the front stairs. She couldn't wait. She had to warn Drew.

— Eighteen —

Drew kept moving down the corridor, pushing open doors, peering into rooms, finding them empty. Where could Joan be?

The place was eerily quiet. The Pikes had gone into Edinburgh, the servants had the evening off, and Kuznetsov was likely sound asleep. Or was he somehow involved in this mess after all? Would he be waiting round some dark corner with a gun or a kitchen knife?

"Where have you got to, young Miss Rainsby?" he singsonged half under his breath as he cracked open her door and looked inside. Empty. No Joan.

He frowned. Nick would have hailed him by now if she'd come down the back way. The roof? No, there was no escape from there, unless it was a very final one. Even from where he stood, he could hear the low roar of the sea below. Where could she—?

"Looking for me, Drew?"

He winced, turning slowly around to face Joan and the small pistol she had pointed at him. Doubtless it used the same type of bullet they'd find lodged in Jamie Tyler's heart. "I think it's time we talked."

She shrugged. "I haven't anything to say to you. Let me leave and I won't use this."

"Where will you go?"

"I'll think of something."

He glanced at the pistol. "Yours? The police have been all over the house several times now. You must have quite a fine hiding place for it."

"I do. A little hollowed-out place in my bedpost. You have to know just where to press to make the door pop open. Inspector Ranald clearly did not know. Even my mother doesn't know. It was a secret of the Rainsbys from years gone by. My father showed it me and gave me this to keep there. In case of burglars or something."

"Joan—"

"Really, I have to go. I'm sure one of your stalwart little band has rung up the police, and they're not likely to appreciate my recent activities."

"Where will you go?" he asked again. Where was Shaw? "You know every constable in Scotland, England, and Wales will be looking for you within a few hours. Passport, traveling expenses, identification—all of it will have to be provided for. Do you think you can drive off an island?"

She stared at him, dark eyes cool, the pistol still pointed at his heart. "You're a nice man, Mr. Farthering . . . even if you are a bit of a dope."

"I do apologize for my shortcomings, but I would be remiss if I allowed you to believe that another murder at this juncture would be to your advantage. You could very easily kill me, I know, but you'd never get away with it."

"I don't know about that." A slight smile touched her lips. "Besides, the hangman doesn't much mind whether one commits one murder or a dozen. He gets his fee only once."

"That's a pity for the hangman," someone said from the doorway.

Joan sprang back and then exhaled. "What do you want? Or are you too stupid to see you've stepped into the middle of something?"

Kuznetsov came into the room, dressed in a tweed jacket with a robin's-egg-blue cravat and a Tyrolean hat. Traveling clothes. "I thought, seeing how things were going, you might want a bit of help. Would you care for a lift?" The Russian accent was gone. Now he sounded very English. "You'd better hurry if we're going to get out of this at all."

"You'd help me?" she asked, a glimmer of daring in her dark eyes. "Have you got a car?"

"In the drive. I wired one out of the garage. It may well be your own."

Joan scowled at him.

"Anyhow," he continued, "Mr. and Mrs. Pike won't be back till late. Mr. Pike is about ready to toss me out a window as it is. Now, if you were to make it worth my while, I can get you out of the house and out of the country."

She raised one eyebrow. "How?"

"My dear girl," Kuznetsov said with a sly twinkle in his eye, "if a man is going to make his living by his wits, he had best acquaint himself with all the exits."

"And you can get us out of the country?"

"I can. For half."

"Half?"

"Half of whatever you've got squirreled away. If I'm not

mistaken about a girl like you, whatever it is, it will keep us both rather nicely for some time to come."

Her mouth tightened into a grim smile. "Agreed. I'll just see to him and we'll be off."

Kuznetsov held out his hand. "I'll do it."

She hesitated, and he lunged for the pistol, trying to wrench it away from her. She set her jaw, straining to keep hold of it, hissing curses at him.

Drew sprang toward them. "Kuznetsov, don't—"

There was a deafening crack, and Kuznetsov fell heavily against her, the weight of his body tearing the gun from her hands and sending it skittering under the bureau. She twisted away from him and bolted out of the room. Drew glanced after her, hearing the clatter of her steps on the stairway, and then he knelt by Kuznetsov. A vivid patch of red was spreading across his shirtfront.

"What were you thinking?" Drew demanded, dragging the coverlet from the bed and then wadding up one corner of it to press against the wound. He looked frantically toward the door, hoping someone had heard the shot and would bring help. "What in heaven's name were you thinking?"

A smile ghosted across Kuznetsov's face. "Saving," he panted. "Saving you."

"Me?" Drew pressed harder, trying to keep the blood in the man. The dark eyes were losing focus. "Why? Kuznetsov, why?"

The breath seeped out of the older man's nostrils.

"Come on, man." Drew shook him, still pressing down. He had to keep him from slipping away. "Tell me why."

"Do you know what it means?" Kuznetsov wheezed. "My— my name?"

There was a sudden clamor in the corridor.

"Drew." Madeline flew into the room and dropped to her knees at his side. "What happened? Are you hurt?"

He grabbed her hands, pressing them down on Kuznetsov's chest in place of his own. "Put as much weight on the wound as you can." He fished the pistol out from under the bureau and put it in her lap. "Use that if you need to. I don't know if Joan will come back this way, but don't let her past you if she does."

Madeline's eyes widened. "Drew."

"Did you ring the police?"

She nodded.

"Where's Nick?"

"Hurt. Carrie's looking after him. I don't think it's bad."

"All right. Don't worry. Joan's not armed now." He kissed Madeline's temple. "I'll be back. I've got to stop her before she gets away."

"You ought to hurry," Kuznetsov muttered.

Drew shook one finger at him. "You stay right where you are, understand? No cashing out before you explain yourself."

Kuznetsov merely closed his eyes and made no answer. Perhaps he would never wake again.

Drew sprinted into the corridor. "Joan? Joan!" He could hear her spike heels striking the floor as she hurried on ahead of him. Back to her room, of course. If she had all the valuables packed up, ready to be carried off, she'd want to take them along. It was an expensive business, this disappearing, and she'd need plenty of capital.

"Give it up, Joan! You're only making things worse."

He dashed after her, hearing a door slam just as he reached her quarters. She wasn't there. Kuznetsov's room? Somewhere else? There were nine or ten doors to choose from, all of them maddeningly white and maddeningly alike. Which one?

"Joan! Don't be a fool! Come out!"

It was insanity. Why hadn't she immediately run out of the house? That, too, would be insanity. She'd have been tracked down before morning. But this?

"Joan!"

The door at the far end of the hall, Lady Louisa's door, flew open and the fugitive ran across to another door, flung it open and disappeared inside, slamming the door after her. Drew was right behind her.

The roof.

She had fastened the latch on the hallway door, but it was easily forced. That left only the spiral staircase, which led up to the roof. She was already at the top of the gleaming white metal steps, using the key she'd got from her mother's bedroom to open the door to the outside.

"Joan, wait!" If she got outside and locked the door after herself, he'd never get to her in time. "Wait. Listen to me."

Her eyes wild, she got the door open but fumbled with the key when she pulled it out of the lock. It fell to the bottom of the spiral stairs. He was nearly on her now as she stumbled out onto the roof, her dress stark white against the black velvet of the night sky.

"Joan." He reached toward her. "Please. You don't want to do this."

"Don't I? You know as well as I do I'll never get away now. Kuznetsov, if that's even his real name, was my last hope and he sold me out. May as well make an end of it now."

"You don't know what might happen in a trial. Once you give your side of it—"

"You mean they might put me away for life rather than hang me? That would be jolly, wouldn't it? Well, it doesn't matter.

I haven't any excuses. My father wasn't a brute. My mother never humiliated me in front of my friends. I wasn't starved and beaten and locked up in a garret until I was sixteen. If they were at fault in any of this, it was through indulgence. But I finally found something they wouldn't let me have."

"Jamie Tyler."

Her mouth tightened. "They couldn't keep me from marrying him, but they could keep me from having enough money to hold on to him. I knew what he was. I didn't care. Don't you see? I didn't care that he was a gigolo. I didn't care how many women he'd had or how many fathers and husbands had paid him off, I wanted him. And to get him I needed money. He wouldn't have minded waiting if he'd known I'd get it all eventually, but when Dad told me he'd cut me off if I married Jamie, and Mother backed him up, what else could I do?"

"Some would suggest murder isn't the best alternative," Drew said. "What about Mr. Barnaby?"

"He was the easiest part of all this," she said, and she looked slyly pleased with herself. "It's quite astounding what a bit of flattery, a touch of 'Oh, what a big, strong man you are' will do with these middle-aged, straitlaced types. Get them to believe you're a young innocent helpless to resist their charms and there's nothing you can't make them do for you."

"I see. And I suppose you convinced him it would be worth his while to claim your father had requested a new will, the provisions making your mother a suspect in his death. Then afterwards, having no more use of him, he had to be made away with. So you were the one he had a tête-à-tête with that night, and it was you who brought him that bottle of wine."

She smirked. "Our gardener keeps cyanide for killing wasps. He never missed the bit I borrowed." She glanced behind her, and the crash of the surf on the rocks below all at once seemed very near. "Now, if you'd be so kind as to turn around and go back down the stairs, I won't take up any more of your time."

Again he put up one hand. "Wait. Just wait. I understand why you killed your father and why you killed Barnaby, but why Tyler? If you loved him as much as you claim, why did you kill him?"

She pressed her lips together, saying nothing.

"Tell me," Drew said.

"It was stupid. I went to tell him he didn't have to worry any longer. There was no one to stand between us, and he needn't stay away anymore."

"I take it he didn't welcome the news."

Her eyes flashed fire. "He said it was best that we moved on. That I would need some time to recover from what had happened with my parents and that neither of us should make any rash decisions when everything was in such turmoil. He—" her voice cracked—"he patted my shoulder and said it would be better this way. Better if we let each other go."

"And you weren't going to let him go."

"After all I'd done for him? For us? He couldn't just leave me."

"Did he know?" Drew moved a half step closer to her. "Did you tell him what you'd done for him? Everything you'd done for him?"

"I didn't have to. I could see it in his eyes. He knew what I'd done and it frightened him. *I* frightened him."

The man may have been a cad, but at least he'd drawn the line at murder.

"He told me again that we ought to end it, and I said I'd make him sorry if he went. He didn't believe me. Not until I'd turned the gun on myself and told him I wouldn't go on without him. He told me not to be a fool and tried to take it from me. And . . . and . . ." There was a tight hardness in the lines of her mouth, but her eyes brimmed with tears.

"The gun went off," Drew said at last.

"I wouldn't have done it. He knew I would never have killed myself. He looked so surprised when he was shot. And then he just fell." Her mouth turned down into a pout. "It wasn't fair. It was all taken care of. I'd got all the money and the estate and no one would have been the wiser, and then he had to go and spoil everything by being careless with a gun."

"Thoughtless of him," Drew murmured, studying her face, her petulant, cruel-mouthed face. How had he ever thought her naïve and in need of protection? "Then what did you do? I thought perhaps the killer had tossed the gun into the sea, but you had that little hiding place so you needn't worry about the gun being found. Pity your mother was already in jail. You might have blamed that on her, as well."

Joan thrust out her chin. "If it weren't for her, Jamie wouldn't be dead. He and I wouldn't have quarreled and he wouldn't have been killed. She ought to hang. It's only fair."

"I'm curious," Drew said, moving another step closer. "How did you manage it? Making it look as if your mother had gone out that night when she hadn't? Or should I say when she couldn't?"

Her mouth twisted into a sneer. "You're so smart, you tell me."

"I've no doubt that whatever you gave her for her headache that night was meant to put her out. Did you give her something to make her feel ill in the first place?"

"I mashed up a strawberry in her soup. The broth was strong enough to cover the taste. She's allergic, you know, and it gave her an awful headache. I'd done it before when I wanted her out of the way, so I knew it would do the trick."

"I thought it might be something along those lines," Drew said. "I must admit, though, I'm rather stuck as to what you did with her while she was unconscious. Or was it something as simple as having the maid lie for you?"

"Agnes?" Joan snorted. "I could never trust that ninny with something that important. It was simple enough, though. All I did was roll Mother over against the wall, wedged a bit into the space beside the mattress, and toss the pillows and coverlet over her. That way it appeared, if one didn't look too hard, as if the bed were empty."

"Ah," Drew said, "I should have known."

"Agnes, the ninny, barely gawked at the bed. And when she saw the bathroom was empty, she went searching all over the rest of the house."

"Deftly played, as well as that business about the path down to the cottage. But what if MacArthur had had an alibi he could speak about?"

Her mouth twisted up on one side. "I guess that's where the joke's on me. I thought he didn't want to speak because he'd been with that blond girl."

"But she had been at the bookshop that night, so we knew Mac wasn't telling the truth about it. Worked out nicely for you, I'd say."

He moved a step closer still. Joan stiffened, springing back from him. Closer to the edge of the roof.

"Don't do it," she warned. "I'd sooner end up in the sea than at the end of a rope."

"I thought you said you never meant to kill yourself, that the gun was merely for show."

"That was when Jamie was still alive." Her expression turned hard. "None of my options are very attractive at the moment, are they? I'd rather go out on my own terms."

He moved closer again, and she backed up against the low wall that encircled the rooftop.

"I mean it now. Don't imagine I don't. If you have any other questions, best ask them now. It won't do you much good to ask them later."

He held up both hands, not wanting to goad her into doing anything foolish. "I just want to know about Tyler. Seems to me that as long as you were funneling money into his pockets, there was no need for you to marry him. Neither of you appeared to have a moral objection to carrying on as you were. Why go through all this for just a veneer of respectability?"

"You still don't understand, do you?" She smiled faintly, and for just that instant she seemed the ingénue he had first imagined her to be. "He'd have found someone else before long. Do you think he wanted to live over the grocer's the rest of his life? *This* is what he wanted." She gestured toward the mansion beneath their feet. "If we were married, he would have been able to live here. He would have been able to go wherever he wanted without someone telling him he wasn't allowed or that he'd better use the trade entrance."

Drew remembered the first time he'd spoken to Tyler, there in front of the clubhouse at Muirfield. *"The dining room is only for members and their guests."* How that must have galled the man year after year.

"And for that," Drew said, inching closer, "he needed you."

"I would have given him everything he wanted, and he would have loved me." Again she lifted her chin, eyes fierce as she glared at him. "Don't you dare pity me."

"Very well," he said mildly. "If you won't have pity, perhaps you'd prefer truth. He would have hated you. Perhaps not right away, but in time."

"No," she breathed.

"And you would have despised him for being someone you could buy. But it seems he wasn't quite what any of us thought. He wouldn't take you and your money once he realized how you got it."

"It's not true. He would have. He would have loved me. I fixed everything so he would love me and never leave." She drew a sobbing breath. "He would have loved me."

"I suppose we'll never know for certain now. But it's getting a bit late, don't you think? You've left rather a mess downstairs, and I think the police will want to have a chat with you before bedtime."

He held out his hand to her, and she stepped farther away, against the wall. She glanced back, out over the rushing sea below, and then turned to him again. She was utterly calm now.

"I don't want to talk to them. I don't want to talk to anyone. Not ever again." She smiled only the slightest bit, the smile of a porcelain doll or a shop mannequin, and stepped up onto the wall.

"Joan. Look here, don't be a fool." He looked around, desperate for help from someone, anyone. *Dear God, please.* "You don't want to do that. You don't—"

He leapt at her just as she stepped into the empty air, catching her around the middle and then realizing too late that they were overbalanced. Together they tumbled into the darkness below.

— Nineteen —

Drew landed on his back with Joan still in his arms, not sure if the stars he was seeing were in the sky or swirling out of his head. An instant later, the breath rushed back into his lungs, and he rolled over, pinning her to the floor before she could struggle away from him. By some miracle they'd landed on the balcony that led to her bedroom, the one overlooking the sea, about an eight-foot drop from the rooftop above. He hadn't seen it in the darkness, hadn't remembered it was there, but she had.

"Get off me!" She kicked his legs and pounded his head and shoulders with her fists, burning the air with a string of the foulest epithets he'd ever heard. "Get off!"

"Language," he said, twisting her arms behind her and then getting them both to their feet. She skewered his foot with the one spike heel she still wore, making him gasp. He pushed her arm up higher, eliciting a hiss out of her.

She glared at him, breathing heavily. "I should have killed you when I had the chance."

"My wife would have been quite put out if you had done," he

said, a taut thread of anger under his affable tone. "She rather likes me, don't you know."

"She's a bigger idiot than you are."

"Steady on now." He swallowed hard, still breathless himself. "I won't have that said by you or anyone."

"It's true." She made a sudden attempt to break away and then stopped when she found it only made him tighten his hold. "You probably can't help being a fool, but she chose to marry you anyway."

"That I put down to the mercy of a gracious God." He sobered when he considered what he was taking her to. "One you'll have to face one way or another."

"Don't," she begged. "You know what they'll do to me. You can't let that happen." She began to sob now, and for once the tears were real. "It was for Jamie. All of it was for him."

"No," Drew said, pushing her ahead of him through the open French doors that led into her bedroom. "It was all for you."

The police had arrived by the time Drew escorted Joan down to the drawing room, where they immediately took charge of her. The doctor had come as well, and he and Drew hurried up to Joan's bedroom. Several of the servants had returned to the Hall by then and stood gaping at the sight before them. Madeline was still kneeling at Kuznetsov's side, keeping pressure on the gunshot wound. He hadn't yet come to.

The doctor made a brief examination, replaced the blood-soaked coverlet with proper bandaging and then ordered that Kuznetsov be taken to his own room to be tended to.

"Where's Nick?" Drew asked Madeline once the doctor was gone.

"Still outside Lord Rainsby's study, I think," she said. "Let me clean up a little and then we'd better see how he's doing."

Nick and Carrie were still where Madeline had left them. It was a relief to see Nick sitting up and, apart from the long bruise down the side of his head, looking relatively unscathed. Carrie was sitting on the floor beside him with one arm around his shoulders as she tenderly patted his face with her handkerchief.

"Let a girl get the better of you, did you?" Drew asked with a grin. "Shocking. What is British manhood coming to?"

Nick scowled and then winced. "You don't look quite the thing yourself, old man. Did you let her get away?"

"Miss Rainsby is safely in the custody of Inspector Ranald, thank you very much, though not without leaving a wide path of destruction behind her."

Drew hauled Nick to his feet, steadied him and then helped him to the sofa in the study. Without too much coaxing, he lay down with his head in Carrie's lap, and Drew and Madeline told them everything that had happened. Just as they got to the point where the police arrived, Dr. Portland came in.

"A lot of blood," the doctor said when he had finished with Kuznetsov and come back down to the library, "but I don't think he's in real danger. It looks much worse than it actually is. Could have been very nasty, of course, but the count seems to lead a charmed life."

Drew gave him a wry smile. "And I suppose, even under the circumstances, he couldn't resist as dramatic a performance as he could muster."

"My nurse will stay and look after him as long as is necessary. Now, if you will sit up, young man," he said to Nick, "we'll see what can be done about you."

After cautioning Nick to take it easy for a day or two and to ring up if he didn't feel better soon, and making sure Drew wasn't also in need of his services, the doctor went away. Nick was packed off to his own room with one of the footmen assigned to keep watch over him. It was nearly two o'clock by then, and Carrie was persuaded to spend the rest of the night in the room she had occupied before.

Everyone else seen to, Madeline shooed Drew up to their room and immediately began fussing over him. "You know, Plumfield will not be pleased to see what you've done to those trousers."

Drew grinned and then winced. "Good thing we sent him and Beryl straight to their quarters directly they got back to the Hall. Don't tell him yet, but I think I've torn a hole right through the elbow of my coat and my shirt."

"What in the world did you do?" she demanded, helping him out of both articles of clothing.

By the time he'd bathed and put on clean underthings and let her nurse his cuts and scrapes, she knew the whole story.

"So Joan never meant to kill herself, even at the last," she said, dabbing a wet cloth to the bloodied split in his lower lip.

He flinched slightly, gritting his teeth. "She knew precisely where that balcony was, thank God."

Madeline dabbed at a scrape on his cheek, looking searchingly into his eyes, her own filled with equal parts worry, relief, and annoyance. "Anyhow, she was right about one thing."

He pulled her into his lap, ignoring the strain it placed on the bruised and wrenched muscles of his legs. "What's that, darling?"

"You *are* an idiot."

"Darling!"

She smoothed his still-damp hair back with both hands and then clasped them behind his neck as she leaned close to kiss his forehead. "Well, you are," she murmured against his cheek. "You knew she wasn't going to kill herself. At least you should have known after what happened with the caddie. She wasn't going to kill herself then either."

"That's what I thought at first," he admitted, "but you didn't see the look of her when she stepped up onto that wall. I couldn't just let her do it, could I? After all, she might have got away."

"I'm glad you didn't let her talk you into letting her go."

"No fear." Drew shifted a bit to ease the ache in one hip. "She was rather smug about her ability to manipulate people. I wasn't about to let her carry on. Not knowing the lengths she'd go to get what she wanted."

"I don't understand," Madeline said. "How could anyone do the horrible things she's done? And all for a man who didn't really care a thing for her?"

"I don't know, darling." He held her closer. "I don't understand it myself. As best I can tell, it wasn't about him in the long run. He was just something she wanted and was told she couldn't have."

She curled up against him. "I want to go home. This hasn't been at all the fun time I was hoping it would be."

"No. I think it's time we left. Once Lady Rainsby is seen to, of course. I hate to think of what she must be going through just now."

"I suppose they'll release her right away," Madeline said, "and she'll be left in all this emptiness by herself. Should we ask her if she'd like to come stay with us at Farthering Place for a while?"

He took her face in both hands. "Have I ever told you what a nice person you are, Mrs. Farthering?"

She looked up at him through her dark lashes, coloring prettily. "You've mentioned it a time or two."

"Consider it mentioned again." He kissed the tip of her nose and released her. "And we shall ask Lady Louisa to come and stay, if not now, then once things have quieted down. You know how it is. When there's a tragedy, people are so helpful at first. But after a while they go back to their regular routines, and the bereaved one is left quite alone with nothing to go back to."

There was a touch of wistfulness in Madeline's expression. "Like Carrie."

"No, not like Carrie. Carrie needn't go back at all. She's loved and wanted here. It's up to her if she cares to stay."

"True. But then there's our tragic count. After all that's happened, I'd be surprised if Mr. Pike doesn't toss him out on his ear. Then what will he do?"

"What he's always done, I suppose. Land on his feet somewhere else. I don't suppose he told you anything more while I was after Joan, did he?"

She shook her head. "He passed out right after you left. What do you think he meant? All that about his name. Do you know anyone called Kuznetsov?"

"There was a Tommy Konstantinov at Eton, if I remember right, but his family have been in England since Henry the Fifth's time. No one else even comes close. Why do you think he put himself in harm's way for me?"

She got up and pulled him to his feet. "Tomorrow you can ask him about it. For now, you need to sleep. Doctor's orders."

"The doctor never said anything of the kind," he protested as she led him over to the bed and tucked him in.

"Wife's orders, then," she said, getting under the coverlet beside him. "And that's much more important."

Drew closed his eyes and was asleep before she even had time to switch off the light.

As soon as he'd dressed and breakfasted, Drew went to Kuznetsov's room. As white and modern as the rest of the house, it seemed more like a hospital ward than a bedroom, especially with the stern-looking nurse sitting reading beside the patient's bed. Kuznetsov lay pale and languid under the white sheets, his eyes closed, his breathing deep and regular. But he stirred when the nurse asked, sotto voce, what Drew wanted.

"My valet told me the count requested my presence regarding an important confidential matter."

Kuznetsov opened one eye and then both.

"Let us alone a while," he told the nurse in a surprisingly sturdy voice and in the accent he'd used before, the one that was convincingly English. "I have a feeling a discussion between Mr. Farthering and I is long overdue."

The nurse scolded them both about not overtiring the patient and instructed Drew to call her the instant there was any sort of difficulty, but then she left them alone and shut the door after herself.

"I'll have you know that Mrs. Farthering is not very pleased to be left out of our discussion. She's positively perishing to know what you meant last night."

There was an enigma in the older man's expression. "I will tell it to you and then leave it to your own judgment what you wish to tell her."

"How are you feeling?" Drew asked, taking the nurse's chair.

"Although, even being shot, you look sturdier than you ever did when you were our noble artiste."

Kuznetsov laughed softly and then winced. "It was getting to be a bit tedious being so delicate."

"Kept you out of any actual work, though."

Kuznetsov bit his lip and held up one hand. "I must ask you not to make me laugh, if you please. I'm not quite sure what all has been rearranged and sewn back together inside me, but I'm not allowed to do anything that might pull it all loose again."

"Fair enough," Drew said. "But I think I'm due an explanation at this point. If not for you, I'd be the one who'd just been reassembled, and that only if I were fortunate to survive in the first place. Why ever did you do it?"

"I saw you were in over your head with that spy business and thought I'd better keep an eye on you. And our dear Miss Rainsby struck me all wrong the moment I met her. I thought I'd better keep an eye on her, as well. I suppose she saw me as a kindred spirit. I can't say I didn't try to drop a hint here and there. It wasn't hard to convince her I was willing to help her escape if I were compensated sufficiently."

"That still doesn't explain why."

"Consider it my first step on the path to redemption."

"I'm afraid that's not quite good enough, old man. I want to know why you kept her from shooting me. And what did you mean about your last name?"

Kuznetsov huffed softly and then put one hand over his right shoulder where his stitches must have been. "I don't suppose you're very familiar with the Russian language."

Drew shook his head. "French, a smattering of German and Italian, some Welsh, that's about it for me."

"It's funny, you know, that fellow MI5 took away the other night, his name was Schmidt. At least the name he went by, yes?"

"That's right," Drew said.

"I suppose it's in every language. Schmidt, Smit, Kowalski, Demirci, Fabbro . . . Kuznetsov."

"Smith. No matter what nationality you're pretending to be, it's easy to remember your name is some form of it."

Kuznetsov nodded. "And because it is my real name. In my native language."

"I haven't quite decided what your native language is. You do them all so convincingly."

The artiste gave a gracious nod. "You are too kind. However, I think you should know that I was born a Frenchman, as you were."

Drew frowned. "How did you know that?"

"Oh, it isn't hard to find out. Not when one makes the effort. In France, there are a number of surnames that are tied to the occupation of blacksmith: Lefévre, Faure, Favre, Fabre." He paused for a moment, watching Drew's face. "Fabron."

Drew caught his breath. Mikhail Kuznetsov. Michael Smith in English. In French, Michele Fabron. "You're—"

"Your mother's brother."

Drew opened his mouth and shut it again. It was too insane to be believed. It was—

"Monstrous," Kuznetsov said, his accent and demeanor suddenly Russian again. "Yes, I know. Poor fellow, but we must bear it, must we not?"

Drew laughed, still not knowing what to say. "I— You—"

"I'm afraid there's no escaping it," Kuznetsov, or rather Fabron, told him, reverting to the English accent he'd used before. "I will confess when I heard Mr. and Mrs. Pike mention that you would be at Thorburn Hall for the Open, I was determined to meet you. I wanted to know what you'd be like and, to be brutally honest, I was hoping I could touch you for a bit of a loan. But, to my great surprise, you turned out to be a rather nice fellow. Nothing like the spoilt snob I was expecting to find."

"Thank the Lord for small favors," Drew said. "But good heavens, man, you have to tell me about my mother. Where is she? *How* is she? How did you know who I was?"

There was a touch of rue in the man's smile. "Your mother died this past January. Consumption. All these years, she would never tell anyone who your father was, only that he had taken you away to England when you were born and that you were better off with him. I have a feeling she was afraid I might try to take advantage of the connection." He shrugged, again the charming rogue, though he couldn't quite hide the depth of feeling in his eyes and voice. "At the very end, she took a newspaper clipping from the little box where she kept her treasures, a photograph with your name under it. 'He's very like his father,' she told me, and that was the last she ever said."

"That was all," Drew murmured. "Did—did she have anyone? Any family?"

"She married, but her husband was killed at Verdun during the war. She lost the child she was carrying, his child, and after that she lived alone."

Then that was it. After so long wondering, waiting, searching, that was it. There was nothing more Drew could do. "I wish I'd known. I wish I'd been able to do something for her. I wish—"

"She lived alone. That doesn't mean she was lonely." Kuznetsov, no, Fabron slipped his hand out from under the sheet and patted Drew's arm. "She worked in one of the finest shops in Grenoble, and fashionable ladies everywhere were eager to have their hats made by her. She had many friends and no lack of invitations. True, she died far too young, but she was not unhappy, and she was not in want." There was a twinkle now in the older man's eye. "No doubt she despaired of me ever making anything of myself besides a nuisance, but she seemed to have little else to complain of. I believe you would have liked her. I know she would have liked you."

That made Drew smile in spite of himself. "I'm glad."

He looked at the man lying there in the bed. His uncle. His *uncle*. It seemed impossible, but somehow Drew believed it. He studied the man's face. Handsome. Aquiline. Good-humored. Had she been like him?

Drew cleared his suddenly tight throat. "I don't suppose you have a photograph of her, do you?"

Again the man flashed that enigmatic smile. "Do you like Russian literature?"

Drew hesitated and then glanced at the stack of books on the bedside table. On top lay a copy of *The Brothers Karamazov*.

"She never could abide it for the most part," his uncle said. "She always said she'd rather laugh than cry. Still . . ." He nodded toward the book.

Drew picked it up and opened the front cover. There were not one but two photographs inside. The first was old, sepia-toned, faded. It showed a girl of about twenty and a boy of ten or eleven standing before Notre-Dame Cathedral. The other appeared to be more recent. Judging by the clothing, perhaps only a year or two old. The man in this one was clearly the boy from the other photograph. Kuznetsov. No, Fabron. And the woman—

Drew studied the first picture once more, searching his memory for the right dates. He'd been told she was about twenty when he was born. She was a fetching twenty too, dark and finely featured like her brother, round-limbed and willowy, with something of the same enigma in her smile.

The more recent photograph showed her in front of a little cottage. She was holding a basket of wildflowers and wearing a full-skirted dress, white or light-colored. She must have been in her middle forties then. Though she was lithe and slender still, her lovely face held the unmistakable mark of her illness, the ethereal stamp of death.

"A friend of ours was good enough to send us to the country for a month," his uncle said. "We thought it might cure her. It didn't, of course, but as you can see, she was happy."

Drew nodded, for a moment unable to say anything.

"May I keep these?" he asked at last. "I don't suppose I'm anything like her."

"Not so much. But then she said you were very like your father. I suppose that was for the best."

"Yes, I suppose it was." Drew looked at the photographs again. Not all that much, but at least now he knew. "Perhaps these are all you have of her."

"I brought them for you. I have others."

Drew tucked the pictures gratefully into his waistcoat pocket. Madeline would want to see them. Would it make a difference? Not likely. He'd already told her the story. It seemed ages ago now, sitting on the floor with a batch of newborn kittens, still reeling with the newly revealed truth about himself, he'd told her. They had been little more than strangers at the time, but there had been something about her even then that told Drew he could trust her with his secrets, with his heart. She would want to know what he'd found out, especially since it was the last.

He looked up to find his uncle watching him, reading his face no doubt.

"What will you do now?" Drew asked.

His uncle gave a small shrug. "The doctor says I can't be moved for a few days. With everything that's happened, I don't feel I ought to stay any longer than that."

"You know, Kuznetsov," Drew began, and then he stopped himself. "I don't suppose I should keep calling you that. What ought I to call you?"

"Not Uncle, I implore you," the wounded man said with an air of horror. "It's terribly aging."

Drew raised his eyebrows expectantly.

"Your mother used to call me Renard, but that was only when she was more amused than vexed at me."

"Fox." Drew laughed softly. "Somehow that seems to fit perfectly. But for now, how about just Michel?"

"There are worse things," his uncle said, "and I've been called most of them."

"I'm surprised Mrs. Pike hasn't been in here looking after you."

"Ah, dear madam. She really is a kind and trusting woman, and I've taken abominable advantage of her. But I trust I've amused her, too, in my small way. However, Mr. Pike has informed me most graciously during her tearful visit this morning that they were returning home and I would not be joining them. Therefore, I am cast adrift. Friendless and penniless."

"Always the poor unfortunate," Drew said mildly, picking up the letter on the bedside table. Two one-hundred-pound notes fell out of it.

"I said penniless," Michel said quickly, "not poundless. And truly, what can I do with only that? I shall no doubt starve in the streets."

Drew put the letter and the money back on the table. "Most men don't make that in half a year, you know."

Michel blinked. "Don't they?"

"The doctor's surgery is at his house. He often has patients to stay if they need observation or have no one to look after them."

"Ah, excellent. I will need a place to recuperate."

"You will," Drew said. "And I believe his fee is two hundred pounds."

Michel started and then wilted back against his pillows.

Drew chuckled. "Not to worry. I told him I'd pay it and any other expenses."

Michel brightened.

"Legitimate expenses," Drew added.

Michel sighed. "And after?"

There was a tap at the door and then it opened.

"I hope I'm not interrupting," Madeline said, looking in, the rose-and-green floral print of her dress a welcome splash of color in the otherwise colorless room. "Only the nurse said the count ought to have his rest." She smiled warmly at the patient. "How are you feeling this morning?"

Michel heaved a doleful sigh. "Ah, madam . . ." He broke off at Drew's dubious look and smiled instead. "I am progressing nicely, thanks to the good doctor and his frightful nurse."

"My wife and I spoke at length about you last night," Drew told him as he got up to give Madeline his chair. "We're both awfully grateful to you. Keeping me alive and everything."

Michel waved one artistic hand. "Nothing at all, I'm sure."

"It meant a great deal to us," Madeline said.

"Anyhow," Drew continued, "we thought, once you're feeling up to it, you might find the sunny Riviera a pleasant place to spend a few weeks. Our treat, of course."

"It's too kind," Michel said. "Really, too kind."

"We'd better let him have his rest." Madeline stood. "If you've finished your important conversation."

"Just done," Drew told her, patting his waistcoat pocket. "And I think you'll be very interested in knowing what we talked about."

She gave the wounded man a coy little glance. "You won't mind if he tells me, will you?"

"I expected he would before I told him," Michel said.

"Oh, good." She squeezed his hand. "Then I won't tire you with my questions."

"She saves that for me," Drew admitted.

"I'm so glad you're going to be all right," she told Michel, making a great show of ignoring Drew's comment. "I don't suppose we'll be seeing you after this, though."

He clasped the hand that still rested on his and brought it gallantly to his lips. "One cannot tell the future, madam. That must be left to heaven."

"Then I'll pray that God will bless you and send you His very best."

He said nothing for a moment, but for once it seemed as if there were no façade between him and them, no part he was playing. And then a cavalier smile touched his lips. "I can see no use He might have for, what did you label me, dear boy? A thief, liar, and sponge?"

"You may well be surprised," Drew said, "if you give Him half a chance."

With a laugh, Michel let Madeline go and put his hands lazily behind his head. "You mustn't expect too much, you know, and I make you no guarantees. The sun on the Riviera is hot and makes it difficult to think of anything more weighty than where one shall be dining that evening and in whose charming company."

He smiled and closed his eyes, looking despite his pallor as if he were already lounging on the beach. A moment later, the nurse returned. She said nothing, but the stern clearing of her throat let Drew and Madeline know that visiting hours were over.

— Twenty —

Twining was waiting for Drew when he came out of the patient's room.

"I beg your pardon, sir, but we've received a telephone call from Inspector Ranald. Lady Rainsby has been released and will be returning home. She's asked for Agnes to bring her some fresh clothing and whatever else she may need and to attend her there. I thought perhaps—"

"I'd be happy to escort Lady Rainsby home," Drew said, "and to see to whatever details might be required by the police. Madeline, darling, would you like to come along? It might be a comfort to her to have you there."

"Of course. I'll just get my gloves and handbag."

Phillips drove them into Edinburgh, with Agnes perched, silent and pensive, on the seat next to him, Lady Louisa's monogrammed traveling case clutched in her arms. Beside Drew in the rear seat, Madeline, too, was silent. The drive seemed much longer than it actually was.

Lady Louisa looked thinner than when Drew had last seen her. Definitely paler. There was nothing stylish about the gray, sack-like prison uniform she was wearing. Later, in her own somber but well-fitted garments, with her hair and makeup done, she still looked thin and pale. She looked older now than the woman who had greeted him and Madeline in the drawing room at Thorburn Hall at the beginning of the Open, the woman who'd told them all how much she enjoyed having people come to stay.

Still, she stood with her back ramrod straight and her head held high as she asked to see her daughter. After some discussion with his superior, the officer on duty said he would make inquiries. It wasn't long before he returned.

"She's refused to see you, my lady."

Tears sprang into Lady Louisa's eyes, but she responded with only a gracious nod of her head.

Drew thanked the officer and then took Lady Louisa's arm. "I'm very sorry. Perhaps later on."

"Yes," she said, her mouth a taut little smile. "Yes, later would be better. We both—we both have a great deal to think over."

"Naturally. I understand it will be a while before the case is brought to trial. Do you have someone . . . ?" He trailed off, not quite knowing how to make the question any less awkward. Of course, there was no one now. Even so, she always seemed to handle dire circumstances with grace.

"My sister and her husband have an estate over in Stirling. I'm sure she'll let me come stay for a while. It's far enough away from all this, yet close enough for me to help the police with whatever they need and perhaps even come see Joanie when she's ready."

"Madeline and I will have to come back up for the trial," Drew said. "Until then, if there's any way either of us might be of service, please don't hesitate to ask."

Madeline took Lady Louisa's hand. "Drew and I thought

you might want to spend some time down at Farthering Place after this is all over."

Lady Louisa immediately shook her head. "Thank you, but no. I have to be here for Joanie. She'll need me once she realizes what she's done. She's hardly more than a baby, they have to see that. She couldn't have meant for all this to happen. It must have been that terrible caddie, leading her on, telling her what to do. Terrible."

Drew and Madeline exchanged a look, but neither of them said anything.

"Perhaps later on, then," Madeline said. "You know you're always welcome. Any time at all."

They escorted her back to Thorburn Hall and left her in the company of her maid. It didn't seem appropriate to bother her with their own plans, so Drew and Madeline went to inform Twining that they, as well as Mr. Dennison and Miss Holland, would be leaving the next morning.

"Here's my address in Hampshire," Drew told the man. "There's really no one but you to look after Lady Louisa now. If she's in any sort of difficulty, I want you to promise me you'll let me know."

Twining bowed gravely. "I know it is hardly my place to say so, sir, but it's very good of you. Lady Louisa's family have stood by my people for nearly three hundred years. I shall certainly stand by the last of theirs."

"Good man," Drew said. "I'll rely upon that."

Before the butler could do more than repeat his grave bow, the pert little maid popped into the drawing room and announced Mr. MacArthur to see Mr. Farthering.

"Shall I bring tea, ma'am?" Twining asked Madeline, "or will Mr. MacArthur be staying to luncheon?"

"No, no," MacArthur said, blustering into the room in his usual way. "Not staying but a moment. I just heard about poor Louisa and what happened with Joan. Terrible business. Terrible. I wanted to see if I could be of any assistance." He shook Drew's hand, then bent politely over Madeline's. "To be honest, I never felt right about the girl, but there was nothing I could ever actually nail down. Never expected anything more than a fit of temper, though. Nothing quite so shocking as this."

"Her parents can't make excuses for her now," Drew said. "I suppose there's nothing left for her to do but face the consequences."

They were all silent for a moment, and then Mac exhaled heavily. "At least you don't have to deal with a traitor, as well. My only regret in my part of the business was that Rainsby died suspecting I'd betrayed my country. I know it worried him every time I mentioned how much I admired something Hitler had done. There was a while there I thought I'd pushed it too far and he'd have no more to do with me. I even thought he might have me charged with treason."

"Thinking back on what he told me before he died," Drew said, "I can see that's what he was hinting at. I suppose he didn't want to report you to anyone official without some kind of proof, and that was why he called me in."

"I'm sorry I couldn't have taken you both into my confidence from the beginning, but when a secret is not one's own to share, well, I'm certain you understand."

"Of course we do." Madeline gave him a pretty smile. "Though I can't say I liked it very much watching my husband creep into the darkness after you, thinking you might be lying in wait for him around the next corner."

"Turns out it was the young lady you should have been worried about," Drew said with a look of comic regret. "Where is she now, by the way? You both certainly had us fooled."

"I'm not quite certain," MacArthur admitted, "but it sounded as though she might be going to Berlin to do a bit of reconnaissance for our side. Such a little slip of a girl, isn't she, to be doing that sort of job, eh? But I suppose that's why she's so good at it."

"Very brave of her, too," Drew added. "Can't help but admire her spirit. She *is* German, isn't she?"

"She is. Devoted to the place, I can assure you, which is why she'd like to see someone other than this Hitler fellow in charge of it, and before there's the kind of trouble we had back in my day."

"Or worse."

Mac nodded at him. "Precisely. There are already rather grim signs of what might be coming, especially for her people."

Drew wrinkled his forehead. "Her people?"

"She's Jewish," Mac said. "Though I suppose you might not suspect that just from looking at her."

"No," Drew admitted, "not right off. I expect that's what makes her so valuable an agent."

Madeline looked at the older man, just a touch of mischief in her expression. "Then there was never anything between you and her. I mean, anything of an . . . unprofessional nature."

Mac chuckled. "You flatter me, ma'am. Miss Shearer is a deuced attractive woman, well beyond my reach even when I was a young blade your husband's age. But she is also an accomplished actress, and if she wanted to make everyone think we were involved romantically, by George, that was what everyone would think."

"Not to be indelicate," Drew said, "but your wife . . ."

Mac sobered. "Ah, yes. Amanda." He stroked his mustache

and cleared his throat. "Amanda found someone whose company she preferred to mine."

"And you divorced her."

"Actually, I agreed to let her divorce me. It was the gentlemanly thing to do, sir. Even if she no longer wished to be, she was still my wife. It was my part to shield her from scandal, even a scandal of her own making, so I allowed her to file suit."

Drew nodded. "Afterwards, then, all of that fell in nicely with your little charade. Lord Rainsby was right when he told me at the very start what an admirable fellow you were. With enough chaps like you, and one or two more girls like Lisa, we might somehow stave off the storm that's brewing in Berlin."

"We can try, young man. We can certainly try. So long as you young folk keep your eyes open here at home."

Drew shook his hand. "God with us, sir, we'll do just that."

MacArthur made his farewells, and Drew and Madeline were left to themselves.

"Where do you suppose Carrie and Nick are?" Madeline asked. "She's going home. I'm sure she is, and I don't want her to. He can't let her."

Drew sighed. "I know. I know. It'd be a deuced shame if he did. Confound the man, he's got to stand up for himself. She doesn't give a hang whether his father's our butler or the Archbishop of Canterbury. Why they should both be miserable the rest of their lives is something I'll never understand." He caught her hand in his. "I believe they're out in the garden. At least Nick said he was going to look for her there. Surely even he can manage something that simple."

"Maybe we should go find them. We can pretend we've come to tell them lunch is ready."

They were nearly out of the garden and on to the meadow

when they finally spotted Nick and Carrie walking slowly along the path that led eventually to the road. There was something solemn and earnest in their faces as they talked. Something almost desperate.

The two of them were at the stone wall now. No doubt they'd be turning back toward the house in a moment. Drew lifted his hand, meaning to call to them, when Madeline swiftly pulled him into the folly and out of sight.

"They're coming this way. Maybe we shouldn't interrupt."

They sat in silence, unable to see the couple now, but it wasn't long before they heard the rustling of grass and then Nick's low voice.

"Carrie, sweetheart, I know I haven't any right to even speak to a girl like you. I'm not anyone, and you're—you're—"

"Don't say that," Carrie replied. "You know I don't care about that. I just—"

"Won't you hear me out?"

Drew glanced at Madeline. They really should make their presence known. Madeline put one finger to her lips and breathed into his ear, "It's taken him forever to say anything. Don't spoil it now."

She was right about that much. Drew stayed where he was, his arm still around Madeline in the cool stillness of the folly, and looked through a small opening in the flowering vines.

"Please don't go," Nick said, his voice soft and pleading. "Sweetheart, you can't."

Carrie lifted her chin. "Do you think I ought to stay here and have you always involved in his murders? Do you want me to stand by and watch you be killed?"

My murders? Drew caught an indignant breath, but Madeline squeezed his arm to silence him.

"What do you want me to do?" Nick asked. "Leave Farthering Place? Leave England? I'll do it for you."

She bit her lip. "Would you? Would you really?"

"I would," he said, and then he looked grieved. "Yet I still couldn't promise you nothing would ever happen to me. Even if I were a very dreary chartered accountant who lived in a flat only a quarter mile from my office and never went anywhere but there and to the greengrocer's round the corner and the church across the road, I couldn't promise you I'd never be hit by a bus or come down with double pneumonia or have a piano dropped on my head from an upper floor. But suppose that's not for another year? Or ten? Or fifty?"

"Nick . . ."

"At some point we have to trust God with our lives, don't we? Otherwise we spend our days huddled in a corner afraid to take a step outside. But what a waste that is when there's so much we're meant to do with the time He's given us."

She looked away from him, eyes brimming with tears, and then she blinked hard and put on a tight smile. "Madeline told me what you said about the sheep."

Nick gaped at her, and she nodded.

"About how they're only stupid when they're afraid."

He swallowed hard. "They can be taught and remember what they've learned, like—like which kind of pail has their food in it and that sort of thing. It's only . . ." His voice cracked, and he brought her gloved hands to his heart. "Oh, Carrie, don't do something stupid just because you're afraid."

"I don't want to go. I don't want to leave you." Her breath came in a little hitching gulp and she broke into sobs. "I don't want to go back home when there's nobody there anymore. I don't want to go when home is wherever you are."

"Then stay." He gathered her in his arms and pressed his cheek to her red-gold hair. "I'd rather have one day, one hour, with you and nothing more rather than never having even that. Please, Carrie, sweetheart. I can't promise you a set number of days or years, only that I'll spend every moment I'm given loving you. That much—" his voice broke again—"that much I can swear to."

Madeline's grip on Drew's arm tightened, and he looked down at her. There were tears standing in her eyes.

"Darling," he breathed, but she only shook her head and again put a finger to her lips.

He kissed her temple and then looked back through the folly's flowering vines. Nick was still holding Carrie in his arms, waiting, desperate. *Don't let her go, old man. Make her see what she'd be throwing away.*

Carrie gazed up at him, fear and distress and something else less definable in her eyes, and then she looked away. "Nick, I can't—"

He snatched her up against him, her toes barely touching the ground as he silenced her with a kiss.

"Well, that's one way," Drew murmured, and Madeline ducked her head against his shoulder to cover a giggle.

Carrie clung to Nick, one hand gripping his lapel, the other sliding up to caress his bruised face.

"Tell me you don't love me." His voice was low, urgent. "Tell me you don't love me and I'll let you go."

"Nick—"

"Just that and I won't say another word."

"Nicky," she said softly, smiling despite the tears that sparkled in her eyes. "I was going to say I can't—I can't let you go. I can't tell you I don't love you, because I do. More than anything in the world. And if that means staying here while you and Drew and Madeline track down thieves and murderers and con men and international spies, then I guess it does. It doesn't mean I won't be afraid for you, for all of you, every time you get mixed up in something like this, but I guess if I had to go back to South Carolina and end up married to Kip Moran my whole life, well, I'd just kick myself for the next fifty years."

She brought his mouth down to hers, and with Nick's expression equal parts astonishment and delight, they kissed again.

"Satisfied?" Drew whispered to Madeline.

"I think that will do very nicely," she whispered back, beaming.

"They're not likely to notice much of anything at this point," Drew said. "Shall we make our escape?"

She took the arm he offered, and they scurried toward the meadow into the cover of the trees.

Nick and Carrie were married by special license the next day in a small, cluttered, and abominably stuffy registrar's office in Edinburgh. Afterward, following a lavish wedding supper at the grandest hotel in town with just Drew and Madeline in attendance, they retired to the bridal suite. Drew and Madeline, with Bonnie in their charge, settled into their own just slightly less grand accommodations on the next floor but one.

"I suppose Carrie will one day regret not having a huge bash in a real church," Drew observed once Beryl and Plumfield had finished their duties and vanished into their own quarters.

"They're not everything." Madeline stood at the dressing table, an alluring picture in her peignoir of ivory silk and antique lace, and touched her fingers to the flowers that lay in a bowl of water before the mirror. She had worn the violets and tea roses as matron of honor. "I wouldn't be surprised if Bunny and Daphne's big wedding lasts longer than their marriage. Besides, if Carrie had wanted all that, she could have come to stay with us at home until the arrangements were made. And that would have taken considerably longer than waiting three Sundays just so the banns could be read."

He tossed his dressing gown across a chair, careful to avoid the sleeping kitten, and stretched out on the deep, downy bed. "I thought all you ladies wanted the trappings and pomp of your special day."

Her eyes turned soft and warm. "I think all she wanted was him."

"Hmmm, and you made me wait six months."

That made her laugh, a sweet, silvery sound he never tired of. "We'd known each other only six months by then. I think the ladies in Farthering St. John are still scandalized. Carrie and Nick have known each other for three years now. I can understand why they didn't want to wait for all the fancy things. Besides, their wedding was lovely just the same." She sighed happily. "I'm so glad you were able to arrange everything so they didn't have to wait at all."

He pulled her down onto the bed beside him. "It never hurts to know an archbishop or two."

"They've had to wait long enough as it is without adding another three Sundays to it."

"True. Well, Mrs. Farthering, are you ready to go home at last? We'll have a good deal of explaining to do when we come back without Nick, you know. Denny will think he's been mislaid somewhere between Edinburgh and Hampshire."

Madeline giggled. "Nick sent him a telegram saying he and

Carrie were married and they'd be going straight on to Paris for two weeks. Denny wired back just two words: *High time.*"

"Ah, well, that's been seen to then. All we'll have to face is Minerva, Eddie, and Mr. Chambers. They will no doubt adopt decided and unfavorable opinions about Bonnie. You know how cats are."

"They'll get used to her," Madeline said. "They got used to each other, didn't they? And before long the honeymooners will take her with them to Rose Cottage." She sighed again. "Oh, weren't they a lovely bride and groom? I hope they'll be as happy as we are."

He was silent for a time, studying her as she lay drowsing against him in her silk and lace, with her hair falling in dark rills over his shoulder. "You look rather a bride yourself in that, you know."

She turned and put her arms around his neck, the languor in her eyes becoming something a bit warmer. "A bride who's ready to go home and stay there for a while."

"I'm ready to go home, too. Our own home. Our own room." He touched his lips to hers. "Our own bed."

Drew pulled his wife closer and then closer still, thinking as he kissed her that he, too, hoped Nick and Carrie would be as happy as they were. But somehow he couldn't imagine any mere mortal could possibly be.

Not even close.

ACKNOWLEDGMENTS

To David Long, Luke Hinrichs, and all the incredible people at Bethany House who make Drew's adventures possible. Has it been six books already?

To all my writer friends, who understand what this life is like.

And as always, to my dad, who valiantly tried to teach me to play golf. Even if I could never hit the ball, I still learned to appreciate the game.

Thank you and bless you.

Julianna Deering, author of the acclaimed *Murder on the Moor* and *Dressed for Death* in the DREW FARTHERING MYSTERY series, is the pen name of novelist DeAnna Julie Dodson. DeAnna has always been an avid reader and a lover of storytelling, whether on the page, the screen, or the stage. This, together with her keen interest in history and her Christian faith, shows in her tales of love, forgiveness, and triumph over adversity. A fifth-generation Texan, she makes her home north of Dallas along with three spoiled cats. When not writing, DeAnna spends her free time quilting, cross-stitching, and watching NHL hockey. Learn more at JuliannaDeering.com.

Sign Up for Julianna's Newsletter!

Keep up to date with Julianna's news on book releases and events by signing up for her email list at juliannadeering.com.

More from Julianna Deering

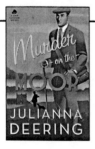

When mysterious incidents begin occurring on a moor in Yorkshire, an old friend begs Drew for help. At first it seems to be simply bad luck—fires started, livestock scattered—but then the vicar is murdered. As danger closes in, Drew and Madeline must determine what's really going on and find the killer before it's too late.

Murder on the Moor
A Drew Farthering Mystery

CPSIA information can be obtained
at www.ICGtesting.com
Printed in the USA
LVOW11*1737131117

556109LV00013B/161/P